GASP!

A novel of revenge.

Frank Freudberg

BARRICADE BOOKS • NEW YORK

Published by Barricade Books, Inc.
150 Fifth Avenue
New York, NY 10011

Printed in the United States of America.

Interior design by Ling Lu
Typesetting and compositiom by CompuDesign

Library of Congress Cataloging-in-Publication Data

Freudberg, Frank, 1953–
    Gasp! : a novel of revenge / by Frank Freudberg.
        p. cm.
    ISBN 1-56980-071-5 (cloth)
    1. Terminally 1ll—United States—Psychology—Fiction.
    2. Tobacco industry—United States—Fiction.
    3. Terrorism—United States—Fiction.
    4. Revenge—Fiction.
    PS3556. R446G37   1996
    813'.54—dc20   95-51077
                                                                    CIP

First printing

To my mother and father

"Revenge! That feral justice,
Suited more to beast than man.
Yet it furies through the human heart,
And knows no other clan."

——Poet unknown

✦　✦　✦

Author's Note

At one time, I believed writers write by sitting quietly at desks letting their imaginations go to work. For me, every step of the way, my raggedy manuscript and I needed extensive help from family, friends, and a great editor. Writing *Gasp!* was far from a one-man show. Those who helped me know how grateful I am.

——Frank Freudberg

PART

1

1

Friday, October 1
Martin Muntor's row house
Philadelphia

It had taken Martin Muntor two weeks to get everything ready, a full week longer than he had planned. For a man with less than a year to live, a week had been too much time to lose.

All that was behind him now. Despite the sharp, relentless pains in his chest and back, he felt good. He felt great. He realized he hadn't felt this good in months. Maybe years. Maybe *ever*.

In a matter of days, three or four at the most, Muntor would be assuming a permanent place in the history of the world. And then no one would ignore him. No one would ever again succeed in pretending he didn't exist.

But Muntor couldn't rest quite yet, and so he rose wearily from the worktable in his living room and stretched. He paced around. He opened dusty blinds and leaned against a window to see the sky.

A perfect day, he thought when he saw the slate-gray clouds. *Dark and ominous. God is the best set designer you could want.*

Muntor sat down once more, anxious to complete his task. He needed to seal another twenty or thirty envelopes, and then that would be it. All 700 packages would be finished.

He lit a Camel cigarette and began working.

Twenty minutes later he was done. He got up from his chair and caught a glimpse of himself in the mirror that hung on the wall over the living room sofa. Drawn, nearly emaciated. Older than his fifty-six years. Not a handsome sight.

One thing was missing from the reflected image, he realized. There was no evidence of absolute evil. *I don't think I look like the monster they're going to say I am.*

Each morning for nearly two weeks, the dying man had been getting up before dawn to seat himself at the worktable. Nothing was more important to him than this project. The early hours had proven the best; he was strongest then. He'd make coffee and have high hopes of how many packages he'd be able to finish that day.

But most mornings, after only a couple of hours of effort, he'd lose steam. The dexterity left his fingers. The muscles in his back stabbed at him. And then his eyes quit focusing on the close, exacting work despite the assistance of the illuminated magnifying glass mounted on a swivel arm and clamped to the edge of the table.

On those few mornings Muntor felt he was able to work through the pain and discomfort, his body resisted him with another barrage of difficulties. Catching his breath required more and more effort, the dull pain in his chest tightened its grip, and the coughing fits became increasingly violent. Some days, Muntor would find the strength to work three or four hours, but that was his maximum. Then he'd have to quit. Getting to the sofa a few feet from the worktable seemed like crossing the Serengeti Plain, but he'd get there, ease himself down, pull up a blanket, and sleep for hours.

Now that Muntor had finally finished the most taxing part of the project, the assembly work, he felt better. The physical troubles had less impact on him. The tedium was over, and there, on the floor next to the worktable, was the fruit of his labor—six large cardboard boxes holding 700 FedEx envelopes. Each one stuffed and sealed with a form attached that would direct the envelopes to addresses all over the United States.

Once more, Muntor did the mental calculation he'd done many times before. Thirteen dollars to ship each package. Times 700. Nine thousand, one hundred dollars. That was going to be the most money he'd ever spent at one time. In his pocket, in the wallet with the fake identification, he had a cashier's check for the exact amount of the shipping charges. He had called FedEx. No, he had been told, he wouldn't need to set up an account. No, the seven hundred envelopes all at once weren't a problem. Sure, they'd accept a cashier's check from a local bank.

I am going to go through with this, he kept telling himself. Nothing was going to stop him, although he had good reason to give up. He'd been in pain, extreme pain, but he had a way around that. Muntor knew he could give himself an injection—a homemade combination of prescription painkiller and amphetamine crushed together by mortar and pestle in his kitchen and injected into his arm. But somehow, he felt that was cheating. And if he started giving himself shots now, what would he do when he really needed them?

For the first time in his life, he found himself committed to something. In grade school, they had called him *quitter,* and they had been right. But this time was different. This was payback time, and this was his last chance to make his mark, to accomplish something of note.

Where were those second thoughts, the doubts, the lack of confidence that he'd known all his life? *They keep their distance now.* He smiled and the skin around his eyes crinkled. *They don't want to go up against me on this one. They don't like to lose.*

Muntor slipped the last pack into the last envelope and struggled with each heavy box, carrying them one by one, piling them by the front door. He wanted nothing more than to get to that sofa, sleep, rest his burning eyes, if even for only a few minutes.

But he couldn't.

Not now.

Not today.

Not quite yet.

Martin Muntor had one more thing to do.

2

Saturday, October 2
The Executive Suite
TobacCo, Inc., World Headquarters
Asheville, North Carolina

A telephone rang on an immense mahogany desk in the Executive Suite of TobacCo, Inc., the world's largest cigarette company. Without looking up from the quarterly financial reports he was studying, W. Nicholas Pratt, president and CEO, switched on his speakerphone.

"Yes?"

"Mr. Pratt?"

Recognizing the voice, Pratt grimaced, cut off the speaker, and picked up the telephone.

"Why aren't you calling on my scrambled line." It wasn't a

question. Pratt's voice was icy. Valzmann should know better.

"I'm at a pay phone up in Pennsylvania, sir, in the mountains, looking for a site, and my cellular phone won't work up here. Your private number is on the cell phone's autodial, and so I had to call . . ."

Pratt silenced him with a derisive laugh. "You commit that number to memory."

"Yes, sir."

"Now what do you want?"

"It's about Tom Rhoads. I've just gotten a report from one of my men. He's gone three days without a drink. Been to two AA meetings."

Pratt pursed his lips, exhaled, and thought. He leaned back and ran a finger between the tight shirt collar and his neck. Even on Saturdays, Pratt wore a suit.

"That won't do," Pratt said. "I need him out of control, acting wild. We need a ready-made chump. Eventually someone's going to come up short one research scientist. If Rhoads straightens up and flies right, we won't be able to use him." Pratt paused, fishing for an idea. A moment later, he found one. He sat up straight and snapped his fingers. "I know what. I want you to start in on him, wear him down. Aggravate him. Drive him to distraction. Chase him back into the bottle. It won't be difficult. What's that piss he drinks?"

"One-hundred and fifty-one proof Bacardi rum," Valzmann said. "*Straight.* It's like drinking rubbing alcohol, just not as flavorful."

"Put the Pennsylvania project on hold and come back. I want you to see to it that Rhoads's life here in Asheville becomes one big unbearable cesspool of frustration. Think about how you're going to do it and call me back. *On my secure line, Valzmann.* And I do *not* want Rhoads to know someone's fucking with him. Everything you do has to be subtle, plausible. Things that could happen to anybody on any day. Understand?"

Valzmann enjoyed the occasional dirty-tricks assignments. They provided a break from the other illicit things Pratt had him do. The dirty tricks brought back memories of his days as a CIA man in Brazil when he served as liaison with the military regime that came into power there in 1964. He'd think of something good to do to Rhoads, something to help justify the two or three hundred thousand in cash he managed to get out of what Pratt called his "special projects" slush fund every year.

"I'll call you back," he said to his boss.

Later that day, a different telephone rang in the Executive Suite. This one sat inside a locked drawer in Pratt's desk.

Pratt put a gold Mont Blanc fountain pen down on top of a stack of proposed magazine ads. At Pratt's request, TobacCo, Inc.'s ad agency had prepared a campaign to attract first-time smokers. The telephone rang again, and he unlocked the drawer, pulled it open, and picked up the receiver. "Yeah?"

"I've got it," Valzmann said.

"I'm listening."

Valzmann heard no hint of forgiveness in the CEO's voice for the earlier error of calling in on the wrong line. The demerit would remain on the books Pratt kept in his head. No one ever liked to cross the CEO.

Pratt had been an army officer in Vietnam. He had been captured and kept in a river, hunched over in a partially submerged bamboo tiger cage, for fifteen months. About once a month, he had told Valzmann, the VC commanders would come around and announce he was to be executed the next day. Sometimes, to amuse themselves, they'd bring in an interpreter and have him dictate a farewell letter to his family. Then early the following day, they'd drag him screaming out of the cage, put a pistol to his head, and pull the trigger, or tie a grenade around his neck and pull the pin. Then they'd laugh and spit and urinate on him.

Occasionally they'd put the cadaver of another American in the cage with him and leave it there for weeks. The only visible scar Vietnam left on Pratt was an upper lip tic that, when active, bared his canines like a dog about to attack. Valzmann was sure Pratt lived in dread of the next execution scenario.

"Next time Rhoads eats in a restaurant," Valzmann began, "which is just about every meal, we'll slip something into his food. Puking, violent diarrhea, the whole mess. That'll lay him up for a few days. When he finally feels that he can get more than ten feet away from a toilet, he'll want to go somewhere. But then his car won't start."

Pratt thought about this. "No flat tire. Too obvious."

"Right. Something electrical."

"Okay. What else?"

"The gastrointestinal thing will have kept him up nights. He'll be exhausted. He'll need sleep. A little trash fire on his floor around three in the morning to set off the fire alarm. Wake him up. Maybe even cause a building evacuation."

"Good. He'll be inching closer to a drink by then."

"That's not all. Eventually he'll get his car fixed, and when he's ready to return to work, on his way to World Headquarters, what if an old lady rear-ends him?"

Pratt laughed.

"Cockroach infestation in his kitchen," Valzmann continued. "We know he's scared of them, so where will he go to hang out while waiting for the exterminator? A bar, probably. And to add to his misery, we'll also be loading up a bunch of unauthorized charges on all his credit cards, Visa, MasterCard, American Express, Texaco, the department stores, his long distance company."

"He might not see the statements for a month."

"No. We'll put enough charges on them so that he'll be over his limit all the way around. Then, when he keeps getting declined, he'll call the credit card companies, screaming. When he denies that he's made the purchases or that he's lost his wallet, they'll cancel all his cards. What a migraine."

"Good."

"There's still more."

"Don't take all the anticipation out of it, Valzmann. Tell me any more and I'll start to feel sorry for the sap and call off the assignment."

Pratt and Valzmann roared.

Pratt hung up, slid the drawer closed, and took out his calculator to perform his once-a-day ritual. He looked at a computer screen that displayed yesterday's New York Stock Exchange closing price of TobacCo, Inc.'s common stock. Two hundred and fourteen dollars per share, up $7/8$ of a point. He multiplied the share price by 825,000—the number of shares he owned.

"One hundred and seventy-six million and change," he said out loud in the empty suite. "That'll keep me in Biltmore Forest at least until payday. Not too shabby for the dumb skinny kid they beat up every day at St. Raymond's orphanage. Not too shabby at all."

Pratt took a deep breath, exhaled jauntily, and went back to the proposed ads. He decided to reject them. They weren't bad, but the subliminal message they were supposed to convey, *You're twenty-one now, you can smoke if you want to,* just didn't come across loudly and clearly enough.

3

Monday, October 4, 10:26 A.M.
Bay View Mall, Boston

Raising two small children by herself made Millie Charlesdon's job at Tunn's Tobacco Shop in the mall seem like a leave of absence. She enjoyed every moment of it. At nine-thirty each morning, she arrived at the shop. At nine-fifty-nine, she unlocked the glass doors, plucked the occasional dead fly or moth out of the display in the store window, and opened for business.

A little before ten-thirty Monday morning, the FedEx delivery man stepped into the shop and rapped his knuckles on the glass case that displayed a variety of imported pipes and lighters.

"Millie."

She looked up. "Hey Greg."

"Something for you today." She wrinkled her brow in puzzlement. He handed her the FedEx Letter envelope and a clipboard. "Sign right here."

Then she smiled. "Wow, for me?"

She signed the form.

"Alrighty then," the driver said. "See you." He retrieved the clipboard and returned to his dolly stacked with other packages.

"Hope so," she said, jauntily carrying the envelope back into the stockroom. No customers were present. She poured the tepid coffee out of her mug and refilled it with fresh. Millie found a chair and sat down. She tore open the envelope and shook the contents onto a desk.

Out tumbled a pack of Easy Lights rubber-banded to a disposable lighter, a regular envelope marked "Survey Enclosed," a cheap pen, and a letter addressed to her, personally, on the stationery of TobacCo, Inc. Millie knew the company's regional sales manager. That was probably why the package was sent to her. She pulled the personalized letter from under the cigarettes and lighter and smoothed it out on the desk.

October 1

Ms. Millie Charleston, Assistant Mgr.
TUNN'S TOBACCO & GIFTS, INC.
Bay View Mall
Boston MA 02109

Dear Ms. Charleston:

Thank you for taking the time to read this. We are conducting a consumer survey because we've changed the taste of Easy Lights and want to know what consumers think about the difference.

Complete the enclosed survey form now, and you'll be $100 wealthier in just a few minutes! TobacCo, Inc. will mail you a check within five business days.

We need your feedback right now, so our offer of $100 applies only to the first 250 respondents. We sent surveys to 500 tobacco retailers via overnight mail, and so by midday Monday, all participants will have received them. May I suggest you complete the form right now? It's simple. Here's all you do:

- Open the enclosed pack of Easy Lights and enjoy one cigarette just as you would any other.
- Complete the survey. We've even enclosed a pen for your convenience!
- Immediately dial the enclosed 800 number listed below. One of our opinion researchers will ask you to read your responses.
- Provide our researcher with your name and address—work or home, whichever you prefer—and we'll process your $100 payment today.

Thanks and please keep enjoying Easy Lights , Primos , and other fine TobacCo, Inc. products!

Jack D. Keller

Vice-president, Product Development

P.S. *If you are not over 18, if you are not employed by a tobacco retailer, or if you do not regularly smoke cigarettes, please discard this survey.*

Millie checked her watch.

Ten twenty-six. *I'm getting me that hundred bucks, honey. The good Lord knows I can use it.*

An occasional smoker who had never tried Easys before, Millie knew her survey responses would be of little value to TobacCo, Inc., but she didn't plan to mention that when she called to get the one hundred dollars.

She removed the cellophane from the pack, took out a cigarette, and put it to her mouth. She flicked the lighter and brought a bead of flame to the cigarette.

Millie inhaled. A vicious cough burst out of her throat.

The smoke had blistered her mouth, throat, and lungs. Her eyes opened wide, and the burning cigarette dropped into her lap. The room spun so fast she saw nothing but a whirl of muted color. She coughed again, and a choking sound came from deep within her chest. Still on the chair, she doubled over, gasping. Her diaphragm convulsed, forcing air into her lungs. The current burned the back of her throat like a blowtorch.

She panicked, as if submerged in water without warning. She tried to scream but couldn't. *What's happening to me?* Her respiration became a staccato series of violent grunts and snorts. Furious coughing hammered her chest. She swallowed air spasmodically. Millie, no longer able to breathe, could only choke. Eight or ten seconds after lighting the cigarette, the poisoned smoke had annihilated her respiratory system. Her lungs had been rendered incapable of harvesting oxygen from air.

Millie's jaw locked open, and she fell thrashing, wild-eyed, onto the floor. Her body jackknifed, every muscle contracting then relaxing, contracting then relaxing, in pantomime of the gasping mouth of a caught fish fighting for air. Her fingers spread wide and rigid. Her hands jerked up in front of her as if to stop an oncoming truck. Bladder and bowels convulsed and emptied. At the moment of death, an agonizing spasm wrenched Millie Charlesdon's back into a shape it had never known in life.

For another half-minute, the corpse continued to jerk, writhing sideways on the unswept stockroom floor, crashing into steel filing cabinets, smashing into boxes, the overturned chair, and finally, a cinder-block wall.

4

Monday morning, October 4.
Tommy "T.R." Rhoads's apartment
Asheville, North Carolina

At forty-two, on a good day, preferably one slightly overcast, Tommy Rhoads could be mistaken for a handsome man.

He was tall and wiry, his hair curly and brown, his gait agile. Rhoads's face was angular and awkward. He had the habit of leaving his mouth slightly unhinged. And his nose was a bit hooked in that jagged Anglo-Saxon way and too long. Bright light didn't flatter it and cast a giant shadow. Beneath the skin of his face was an ensemble of expressions coiled and ready to spring. At any moment, Rhoads's face could contort itself into a firestorm of rage or could become the source of a stupid, inappropriate laugh.

On a bad day, like this day, after the bout with food poisoning and his search for relief in a bottle of rum, Rhoads could look like hell. The ensemble wouldn't show up, and his face would recede into dark gloomy pockets under his eyes, and that was all you could see.

This morning, he was too hungover to go to work, too embarrassed to go in and pretend not to see colleagues and subordinates avert their eyes while thinking *look what Rhoads did to himself again*. Anna Maria Trichina, his boss, had had enough of his so-called alcohol-abuse problem. He was certain that this time he would be fired. The best defense is a good offense. He'd quit.

Instead of showering and dressing, Rhoads paced slowly back and forth throughout the rooms of his small apartment in a high-rise in the heart of Asheville. Rhoads had hardly furnished the place. When he had moved to Asheville from Philadelphia years earlier, he installed expensive off-white wall-to-wall carpeting and bought a dozen large indoor trees. Fichus and avocado and Norfolk Island pine. When the flora didn't produce the dense woods effect he was after, he went out and bought eight or ten more. That had done it. He used a water bottle with a spray nozzle and misted the trees three or four times a week. Large windows flooded the apartment with sun for most of the day.

Eventually, Rhoads replaced his futon with a real bed, bought bar stools for the breakfast counter in his kitchen, and a big television, VCR, and audio system. He didn't own much more than his clothing and what he had in the apartment. He drove a company car, a Taurus SHO.

Tommy Rhoads sat himself down at the breakfast counter and dialed his secretary's voice-mail number, timing it for when he knew she'd be in the Monday morning staff meeting covering for him. He asked her to tell Trichina that, *sorry, but I'm history.*

After leaving the message, he called his brother Teddy in New Jersey. Rhoads was always prepared with a Plan B. Out of the blue, he asked his brother if he was ready.

"Ready for what?"

"Isn't tomorrow the first Tuesday of the month?"

"Yes."

"Isn't that the day they auction boats at the Atlantic Marina?"

Rhoads's brother's heart jumped. "You serious this time?"

"Yep."

"How serious? You sound bombed."

"Celebrating is all. This is how serious I am. As of today, I'm no longer an employee of TobacCo, Inc., the world's largest producer of fine smoking products."

"Whose idea was that? Theirs?"

"It was a You-can't-fire-me-I-quit kind of thing."

"What about the money? It costs to buy a charter fishing business."

"Already called the bank," he lied. He knew he'd have enough, but he'd have to wipe out his IRA and pay a big penalty for early withdrawal. "Sixty thousand dollars is waiting for me. I'm going to take it in blank money orders for the auction like you said. I'll give it to you to hold if you're so worried. And," he paused for effect, "I've got a ticket on USAir for a flight in less than an hour. Destination, Philadelphia."

"Shit, Tom, don't take money out like that. Leave it in the bank. The blank money orders were for a repossessed car auction we were going to go to a couple of years ago. If we make a deal, we'll get it wire-transferred."

"No, I'm bringing the money with me. That'll make this all seem real to me."

Teddy's wife was shouting something in the background. Rhoads couldn't hear what she was saying.

"Look," Teddy sighed into the telephone. "Just come. We

can't pick you up, though. Joyce's got the kids, and I'll be stuck at Dresson's all day."

"No problem. I planned to rent a car anyway."

"So you'll have dinner with us here tonight."

"Please. Not Joyce's meat loaf."

"I'll see what I can do about that. Anyway, Tommy, listen. Maybe this is a good sign. There's a big-assed fifty-two-foot Can Grande trawler they're going to auction tomorrow. It's already rigged for charter fishing. It'd be perfect."

"Here I come."

"Tommy. We've been talking about this for a long time, Brother." Teddy cupped his hand over the telephone and shouted to his wife. "Yes, *today*. Tommy's coming up today, we're going to try to buy Donleavey's big blue boat tomorrow."

Rhoads heard his brother take his hand away from the telephone. For a long moment, there was only the sound of his brother breathing.

"Tommy, look," Teddy said, "this is for real this time, right? The dream of a lifetime?"

"I got a plane to catch, baby."

5

Monday, October 4
Philadelphia

Surrounded by ceiling-high bookcases in his living room, Martin Muntor sat quietly in a worn, green-leather recliner and faced a blank, large-screen television. A sleek cat jumped up out of nowhere into his lap, formed itself into a ball, and closed its eyes. Muntor put his hand on the cat's back and felt the heat under the fur. Without warning, Muntor began coughing, deep rasping coughs that startled the cat who jumped up and off his lap. Instantly, Muntor felt the absence of the warmth.

So that's how it's going to be, he said to himself as he watched a tail disappear into the kitchen. He sipped some water, and the coughing subsided.

Twenty years earlier, Muntor had made the living-room bookcases himself. He had used boards of redwood and fastened shelves into the frames with brass screws. He owned more than fifteen hundred books on almost every imaginable subject and organized them by subject. Physics and chemistry, classic literature and cheap thrillers, political philosophy, biographies, music, the media, Westerns, popular psychology. Each volume cataloged in a spiral notebook that was kept in the basement in a fireproof safe. In the event of a fire, he could replace the books with the insurance money.

He had read every one of them. No book got onto the shelves unless he had read it entirely. That was one of his rules. Newly acquired books he hadn't yet read remained stacked in a small pile on the Oriental rug next to his recliner.

Muntor's house cat, Bozzie, a rare-breed Bengal, jumped up onto one of the shelves and rubbed its black-spotted, silvery fur against the clock that Muntor used to separate his collection of

Thomas Berger novels from his autographed set of *Mark Twain's Works*. When Bozzie finished and moved away, Muntor looked carefully at the clock.

Ten-forty.

It was happening now.

Wherever it was Eastern time, overnight deliveries had arrived, and the shipments to other time zones wouldn't be far behind. People were already beginning to die.

He couldn't deny feeling a dull throb of something like remorse. His hands perspired. *What I'm doing is for a greater good,* he told himself. *I have to complete this project. It is, without a doubt, justifiable homicide.*

Muntor dressed in black jeans and a black turtleneck. He made a big pot of coffee, and the aroma filled the small house. All along he had planned to keep himself busy on this day. He knew he'd need something to keep his mind from what he had done to 700 people.

During the past ten days, Muntor had used his video camcorder and a tripod to film himself at work on his tobacco project. He was making a documentary. *A great documentary,* he hoped. *Perhaps the greatest documentary ever made. And it will show the world that there was more to Martin Muntor than met the eye.*

This morning, in his living room, while waiting for the first news bulletin to interrupt the all-news radio station, he wanted to keep himself busy by editing his documentary.

Next to his chair, there were several videocassettes containing scenes of him preparing for the first series of attacks. Earlier, he had reviewed the tapes and decided which scenes to keep and which to discard. He found he could use almost all of them.

As he worked, he kept an ear on the functional antique radio on one of the shelves. It was only a matter of time before some news anchor broke in with the first bulletin. He could barely wait.

Muntor rose to get more coffee. On his way back from the kitchen, he stopped at the computer printer set up on the dining-room table. The printer had been there for a year. No loss. No one visited him at home anymore, even though everyone knew he was sick now. The kids hadn't been by for dinner or Sunday lunch in years. From the printer tray, Muntor collected a dozen pages of script he had written as narration for the documentary.

Before settling back into the worn green recliner, Muntor crouched by the VCR and picked up a cassette marked "Paradiso." He slid it into the slot and turned on the machine. Then he sat down and pressed the mute button on the television's remote control. He picked up the portable tape recorder, pressed the record button, held the microphone in his left hand, and the pages of the script in his right.

He planned to read the script aloud, keeping the words in sync with the images that were beginning to appear on the television across the room. Once he finished reading the entire script, and that might take days, Muntor intended to dub his tape-recorded voice onto the videotape's audio track. It would be worth the effort.

This was his documentary, this was his life's work, and he intended to produce the best record of it he could.

On the coffee table next to the recliner, Muntor's telephone rang, startling him. It was Lori, his daughter. She almost never called, and he did not want to be interrupted now. He told her he was drying off from a shower and asked politely for permission to call her back later. They both knew he wouldn't.

Muntor pressed another button on the remote, and an image jumped shakily onto the screen—a closeup shot of a computer monitor. Offscreen, someone typed. Bold, italicized capital letters appeared one at a time, spelling out the title *MUNTOR'S LAST STAND*. Under it, perfectly centered, a subtitle. *The Greatest Documentary Ever Made.* There were no production credits. Maybe, Muntor thought, he'd put them at the end.

Based on a story conceived and executed by Martin Muntor.

Script by Martin Muntor.
Produced by Martin Muntor.
Directed by Martin Muntor.

The title shot faded, the screen now pitch black. Muntor turned on the tape recorder and began to read into the microphone in a slow, almost mocking deep bass voice of an announcer.

"It's payback time . . . (pause). For hours, those words kept whispering themselves to Martin Muntor as he worked to set everything up exactly as planned . . . (pause). It's finally payback time . . ."

He pressed the stop button on the tape recorder.
Click.

Muntor watched the television as an image appeared, an over-the-shoulder shot of a man at a worktable facing away from the camera. Muntor had shot this sequence last Friday, the day he delivered the 700 envelopes to Federal Express. For most of the scenes, Muntor had mounted the camera on a tripod set up in the doorway of the room. He had kept a small remote control in his pocket and turned the camera on and off at will. If the script called for a panning shot, Muntor had done that manually. He couldn't be in those shots unless he passed by a mirror.

As he watched himself now, he realized his hair looked shaggy and almost reached his shoulders. *When had it grown so long?* He needed to get a haircut. And he had lost weight and was thin, too thin. He could clearly see his shoulder blades as they pressed through the white shirt that hung on him as it would a scarecrow. The figure leaned back against a bookcase and folded his arms.

That was Muntor's cue. He turned on the recorder and again began to read.

"Muntor stood back finally, arms folded, with the calm confidence of a Christian holding four aces. Sunlight and the low rumble of traffic penetrated the Philadelphia row house through open windows

*as he surveyed the assembly-line setup in his living room. Outside,
a few paces beyond a tiny rectangle of lawn, another rush hour
had begun to leave its yellow-gray haze on Roosevelt Boulevard."*

Click.

He kept a finger at his place on the page and observed the
images and waited for his next visual cue.

Last Friday, an hour before he shot the scene he was now
watching, Muntor had laid out everything he needed across the
surface of two side-by-side aluminum card tables. It had annoyed
him that the dented tables wobbled when he brushed against
them. *That won't look good on video*, he had thought. So he went
upstairs into one of the empty bedrooms and found some duct
tape in a dresser drawer.

He remembered now how musty the room had smelled.
While up there, a pang of homesickness yanked at him. He
walked out into the hallway of the house he had lived in since
birth—the home where he had grown up, fought with his parents and later, the home where he had totaled a marriage and
tried to raise two girls. This was the house where he now lived
and slept without human company for a decade.

During the divorce, Muntor's daughters, then seven and ten,
had clamored to live with their mother. That crushed him. He
had been the attentive one, the affectionate one. Muntor had
been willing to forgive his wife for moonlighting in a massage
parlor instead of as a manicurist—the lie she told him—but he
couldn't get over her refusal to quit. He thanked God for his cat,
his sole reason many nights for coming home at all.

He had brought the duct tape down and lashed together the
adjacent table legs. He had slapped the tabletop with his palm.
"There you go," he had said aloud to himself, satisfied the tables
were sturdier.

On the television, the camera began panning objects on the
worktables. Muntor glanced again at the clock on the shelf. Five

minutes past eleven and still no news bulletin. Muntor's eyes returned to the script.

> "Today was the day. Muntor knew exactly what to do. He had rehearsed the procedure in his head a thousand times. His first task was to organize all the pieces. He placed the Federal Express envelopes, the regular envelopes, and the shipping labels on the table to his left. His computer had printed out the cover letters on counterfeit stationery, and he stacked them neatly on his right next to the survey forms, pens, a box of paper clips. He didn't like being cramped. He left plenty of work space in the center."

Click.

Next to the boxes on a steel typewriter table, Muntor had placed a stoppered glass test tube upright in a wire rack. The tube contained a solution as clear as spring water. Next to the wire rack on a folded bath towel lay a syringe, a portable hair dryer, and a box of latex surgical gloves.

The closeup of the gloves was his cue. He turned the recorder on, found his place in the script, and picked up where he had left off.

> "No more putting it off. He had to get going. Thinking about what came next sent a shudder through him. Muntor felt the familiar clenched fist of pain behind his breastbone. Whenever he momentarily lost his confidence, that pain would return, reminding him, prompting him, spurring him."

Click.

Now the on-screen shot changed. Shooting from the living-room couch, Muntor aimed the camera at the worktables.

He could remember shooting this particular sequence as if he'd done it five minutes ago. Despairing thoughts had come to him while filming. He realized he had been stalling, delaying his project, not working as fast as he could have, finding distractions, exaggerating pain. This dawdling had rung a familiar bell. Muntor had a history of rarely finishing anything he started. The corpses of things he had begun and later abandoned cluttered his life the way trash blows down dead-end alleys and stays there.

When the images on screen panned away from the work-tables and moved unsteadily up the carpeted stairs and through rooms on the second floor of his old house, he picked up the microphone and began reading.

> *"Muntor had been a quitter, giving up easily and often. One of Muntor's specialties had been half-painted rooms. Another was his habit of launching into the newest how to quit smoking technique. But his greatest escapes involved people—and he had an ex-wife, two daughters, and countless employers to vouch for his unreliability . . . (pause). For Muntor, there had always been something else to do, somewhere else to go. There was always another distraction more worthy of that special vein of genius he knew he possessed but had never been able to apply. Until now. Now, finally, it was payback time."*

Click.

On the television appeared another closeup shot of a computer screen. Letters appeared again, one at a time.

7:15. A.M.

Friday, October 1.

On screen, Muntor walked into the shot, steam rising from the hot coffee he had poured himself in the kitchen. He had walked out into the living room and sat down, back to the camera, sliding his chair in, emaciated abdomen against the edge of the table.

His hand reaching up on screen to adjust the magnifying glass was the next cue.

> "Muntor began to treat the cigarettes, the most demanding step of the operation. A simple procedure really, but time consuming and painstaking. Hours passed while he used the fine narrow blade of an Exacto knife to slit open the cigarette packs. He made three slits along the bottom of each pack in order to expose the ends of a few cigarettes. He mangled a half-dozen packs—a casual glance and anyone would have known something wasn't right—before he found the trick was just to go slowly. Muntor had never bought the 'be patient' argument, regarding patience as nothing more than a lesser form of despair. Today, though, he was going to do it right."

Click.

At that point in the filming, Muntor had turned off the camera, disgusted with himself. Things were going slowly enough and stopping frequently to shoot scenes for the documentary wasn't helping.

After a few minutes of pacing, he went back to work. Being nearly finished gave Muntor a newfound energy. His production rate accelerated. With a gloved hand, he took pack after pack from the box on the floor. Then he would swing the adjustable arm of the illuminated magnifying glass into position. Using the knife, he cut through the cellophane wrapper, the cardboard, and finally the paper-backed foil inside the pack. Muntor's design was to lay bare the ends of the three cigarettes at the extreme right of each pack. He had used flip-top packs instead of soft packs. Flip-tops have a front and back, and therefore a right and a left. He had observed that when most smokers open packs, they take cigarettes from the far right.

Later, when his body needed to shift position, Muntor moved the tripod-mounted camcorder in and focused the lens on the close work. He filmed his hand using a syringe to inject the sodium cyanide solution carefully into the end of a cigarette, making sure none of the solution seeped out and stained the cig-arette paper. The chemistry stuff was easy. He learned all he needed through reading.

On screen, finishing one pack and reaching for another was his next cue to resume reading from the script.

> *"The latex gloves were difficult enough to use, but worse, Muntor's hands perspired profusely inside. The sensation made his skin crawl, and the trapped moisture impaired his sense of touch. After treating a pile of eight or ten packs, he would stack them, bottoms open and exposed, and dry them with a portable hair dryer. At first he had used the high setting to speed the process. The cigarettes dried in three minutes, but the heat caused the cellophane wrappers to crinkle. To avoid that, he used the low setting. That took six or seven minutes per batch."*

Click.

The last part of the procedure had been to reseal the packs. Muntor did that with meticulously placed droplets of quick-dry-ing clear glue. For quality control, he compared the bottoms of adulterated packs with those he hadn't touched. They looked good. His handiwork would not stand up to a close inspection, but it was more than adequate to fool the typical consumer. He'd done a great job.

Again, letters appeared on the screen.

11:20 A.M.
Friday, October 1.

The camera panned the living room where the worktables had been set up. This was not a tripod-mounted shot, this was shot live by Muntor. No one, except Muntor's cat, was in the scene. Muntor had zoomed in on the wall clock.

Again, he read from the script.

"Even though the Federal Express office on Market Street stayed open for drop-offs as late as 7:30 P.M., Muntor wanted to be downtown and parked sometime between 5:30 and 6. At that hour, the facility would be a madhouse, and he'd stand out less. It was early in the day, but he needed at least several more hours to finish all the cigarettes. If he'd work fast, he'd make it."

Click.

Last Friday, Muntor finally put down the last pack. His fingers ached, his neck seemed permanently cramped, and his back felt as if someone had taken a swing at it with a baseball bat. Hunching over the worktables had caused all of the muscles in his upper torso to knot.

During the assembly and packing procedure, he had risen and stretched frequently to relieve the strain. Very little could have stopped him, not even the pulsing throbs of pain behind each of his weary eyes. Every heartbeat sent spears there. Through all the discomfort, he had kept going. When he had finished treating the packs, he used a mantra to get him through to the end.

Stuff the envelopes, seal them up, take them into town. Stuff the envelopes, seal them up, take them into town.

A small pile of the paper strips from the adhesive on the back of the Federal Express envelopes lay curled like birthday-present ribbon on the floor. Then, all at once, there had been no more packs left to stuff.

Muntor had finished the assembly procedure.

He had not eaten all day.

Muntor then set up the camera to shoot from the living room through the dining room, into the kitchen.

The on-screen image showed Muntor standing in the kitchen, leaning against the massive refrigerator, drinking from a coffee mug. This was his book-jacket author's photo, the pretentious, brooding shot so many writers like to see of themselves.

Muntor read from the script.

"Standing in the kitchen, he gulped from a mug of cool coffee then went upstairs and showered."

Click.

The camera, now set up in a corner of Muntor's bedroom, showed the nearly emaciated man dressing.

Muntor read again from the script.

"After toweling off, Martin Muntor selected from his closet the prop he needed, a generic uniform purchased two days earlier at Sears. Perfect for a delivery man. He had washed it twice to give it a worn look. Khaki pants and shirt, and a brown cotton twill jacket, the name 'Arnie' stitched in red script on the pocket patch."

Click.

A closeup of a digital clock on a dusty nightstand.

5:25 P.M.

"On his way out, Muntor petted his cat Bozzie. He was less than an hour away from committing a crime, a federal offense, of unprecedented proportion. At any time after he left his house, in theory, he could be arrested. There was a slight chance, very, very slight, but real, that he'd never see this house or his Bozzie again. He left an envelope addressed to the twelve-year-old son of a neighbor. The envelope contained one hundred dollars in twenties, a letter describing

*how to care for Bozzie, and a dozen KatCrunch cat food coupons.
Just in case."*

Click.

Muntor carried the packages in heavy boxes to his car. It took several trips. Once inside the car and driving, Muntor propped the camcorder on the passenger seat, aiming the lens to shoot across him, past his face and out the driver's side window. It was the first time he allowed his face to be seen on camera. The camera also picked up passing images of Muntor's ride down the Roosevelt Boulevard, on the Expressway along the Schuylkill River and into Center City Philadelphia. The camera's microphone picked up the sounds of traffic and Muntor's troubled breathing.

Once in town, at a traffic signal, Muntor swung the camera around and pointed it at the clock in the car's dashboard.

6:11 P.M.

Next he edited in a shot of the computer monitor displaying three words.

Center City Philadelphia

There was a sloppy edit, some choppy white static, and shots of Muntor riding around Nineteenth Street, up Sansom Street, and right on Twenty-second, looking for a parking spot. He couldn't find one until he pulled onto a side street. Once parked, he turned off the camera.

All that had happened three days ago, and Muntor recalled it with vivid clarity. He remembered that while he had been in the car, he had to squirm out of the light blue windbreaker he had worn and into the brown jacket. He had looked into the vanity mirror on the sun visor, then outside. No one had seemed to be paying any attention. Muntor had opened the glove compartment and pressed a large gauze bandage on his chin. Earlier, he had dotted the underside of the bandage with iodine, and a little splotch of brownish-red seeped through. *Perfect.* The prop would draw the clerk's eye to the bandage, he hoped, not his features. He put on a cap and tugged at its bill, bringing it low on his forehead. He slid on a pair of sunglasses.

"Hey, is anyone alive under all that!" he had said out loud. Muntor climbed out and deposited two quarters into the meter. A slight tremor, a vague fear, had run through him. He noticed it in his shoulders and chest when he raised his arm to check his watch. Six-twenty.

He remembered thinking, just as he had locked the car door behind him, *It's not too late.*

Muntor had tried to take a deep breath but had to choke back a cough. He was learning that deep, satisfying breaths were a thing of the past. A light breeze caught his jacket and flapped it at his waist. He had bent near the rear of the car and wrestled in the open trunk with the hand truck he had thoughtlessly buried under the cardboard boxes.

People had walked by, the sidewalks busy with workers heading home. No reason for anyone to notice the colorless little man wheeling boxes down the street.

He had then rounded the corner onto Market Street, the hand truck rattling over the sidewalk. Low clouds gathered and blew easterly toward New Jersey, obscuring Muntor's view of the statue of William Penn atop City Hall.

The Federal Express office had been mobbed, but the line moved quickly. When he was next, he set the hand truck down, took a thick sheaf of shipping labels from atop the top box, and handed them to the woman behind the counter.

"I'll need a receipt for this please," Muntor had said, placing a cashier's check on the counter.

The woman glanced at the check and then up at Muntor. Her eyes fell on his bandage. She looked back at the check while another employee removed all the envelopes from the boxes on the counter and put them in a processing bin. The woman tapped her keyboard and looked at the check again.

"You got the exact amount," she had said as a receipt materialized at the printer. She tore it off and handed it to him.

"Do us a favor?" she had said, pointing to the six boxes that had held the envelopes. "Take those with you."

Muntor had nodded, not saying another word. He put the boxes back on the hand truck and strode out of the office and back onto rush hour Market Street. People moved by, traffic stalled.

He remembered having checked his watch. It had read 6:33. He had gotten into his car, switched on the camera, and pulled out into traffic.

Muntor now read from the script again.

"It was official. Six thirty-four P.M. and the war had begun. Martin Muntor had just fired the first, long overdue salvo. The missiles would fly all weekend long, taking serpentine paths to 700 targets with all the stealth of a cat on a moonless night, and the first ones would begin landing midmorning Monday."

Click.

6

Boston

"Unit three-four to dispatch."

"Dispatch to unit three-four."

"Unit three-four. Priority request for a supervisor to our location. Tunn's Tobacco, west side, Bay View Mall."

"Yes sir. Do you have multiple injuries there?

"Unit three-four. Negative."

"Do you need me to launch the LifeFlight?"

"Unit three-four. Negative."

A moment later, the fire department's West Division captain picked up the radio microphone in his car.

"Charlie One to unit three-four. What do you have there, Ray?"

"Unit three-four. You'll need to see this, Captain."

"Charlie One en route."

7

Philadelphia International Airport

The USAir flight from North Carolina had landed at Philadelphia International at 1:31 P.M.

Something about the airport bothered Rhoads. En route to the Avis counter with the pea-green duffel bag he used as carry-on luggage, he realized what it was. *I've been using this airport for thirty years, and every time I'm here,* he thought, *it's under major construction.*

Rhoads rented a car and headed east into New Jersey to his brother's home. He was sober now but still in high spirits. He and Teddy were about to make their teenage dream come true. *The Deep Blue* was being auctioned tomorrow. A big, creaky charter fishing boat hiding under a fresh coat of deep blue paint. Auctioned tomorrow at noon, and they were going to buy it and spend the rest of their days laughing their asses off, fishing, and overcharging tourists.

He hadn't planned it, but when Rhoads saw the green-and-white expressway signs for Atlantic City, he decided to go, have lunch, maybe try a little blackjack.

There was plenty of time to get to Teddy's.

He'd never been to a casino in his life, and now was as good a time as any to start doing all the things he hadn't done before. Since today was the first day of the rest of his life, and since there's no time like the present, and since Rhoads felt lucky, he was going to A.C.

8

Atlantic City, New Jersey

A little over an hour later, Rhoads found himself in the Boardwalk Hotel and Casino in A.C., listening to the loud clatter of coins dropping out of slot machines into the steel trays beneath them. People shouted and laughed and cursed at the craps and blackjack and baccarat tables.

Wisps of cigarette smoke rose and disappeared into efficient ventilation ducts. The manicured nails of blackjack dealers picked up the bright light and seemed to shoot sparks as they flipped cards to the gamblers. Long-legged, high-assed waitresses prowled the tables chanting, "Cocktails, soda."

By 3:25, Tommy Rhoads was well-situated, learning craps, drinking straight Bacardi 151, and gambling with green twenty-five-dollar chips.

He was ahead $600.

Damn! he thought, grinning like an ape, *I could get used to this.*

The green-felt craps table where slack-jawed Rhoads stood was jammed elbow-to-elbow with gamblers. A croupier's stick was held aloft, frozen in midair, while two other dealers, positioned opposite the croupier, paid winning wagers and collected chips from losers. The next roll of the dice was imminent. Some players stacked their chips high.

Rhoads, "T.R.," as he was known to friends and colleagues, was wearing a worn, brown leather bomber jacket that suited him well. He leaned against the wooden rail of the table, a bit unsteadily. A cigarette dangled from his lips. He managed to hang on to a scrap of the smile that slid from his face like snow off a roof when the dice shooter, a woman in her seventies, threw an ace-deuce on her come-out roll. Craps! An instant loser.

Pretending that he wasn't losing more money than he could afford, Rhoads glued an imbecilic grin back onto his drunken face. He took the croupier's chant, "Double-up to catch up," as wisdom from the Mount and stacked a fistful of twenty-five-dollar chips on the craps table's pass line. He didn't know *exactly* what he was betting on, nor how much. Maybe somewhere around 300 bucks.

The croupier slid five dice to Rhoads. He stared at them for a long moment. He tried to communicate with them. He picked them up and fired them down the table in an awkward overhand throw not often seen at a craps table. His arm suspended itself in midair. He focused his eyes on the far end of the table to see how the dice would land.

"Nine, nine, nine. A fine nine," the croupier shouted, announcing the new point. He turned to Rhoads who stood at his right elbow. "It's up to you, sir," the croupier said. "But you can make a nine in your sleep." To win, Rhoads needed to throw a nine again before he threw a seven.

The croupier slid Rhoads's two dice back to him with his stick.

"It's up to me, is it?" Rhoads heard himself yell, a little too loudly. "Well, watch this, my man."

Rhoads picked up the dice. "Nine! Come nine!" he said and threw the dice down the table. "Come on, baby!"

The dice bounced off the corrugated rubber at the far wall of the table and came to rest. Rhoads's eyes registered pain just as the croupier made it official.

"Ouch! Seven out! Line away," the croupier said, turning to Rhoads. "There was no nine," he shrugged.

The two dealers furiously collected the losers chips and paid off a few winning side bets. A pretty young blonde girl, maybe twenty-two or twenty-three, squeezed in along the rail between Rhoads and another man. Rhoads didn't notice. He was busy, frisking himself, looking for something. He reached into the pocket of his jacket and came up empty. He tried his shirt pocket and pants pockets. Nothing there either.

The girl observed his futile search. She was wearing a simple blouse and skirt and flat shoes. She might have been a secretary on vacation. Now Rhoads noticed her. She offered him a shy smile and looked away from him as she dropped a twenty-dollar bill onto the table.

"Sorry, miss," the croupier said, tapping his stick on the twenty. "This is a twenty-five-dollar minimum table."

She looked at Rhoads worried, not knowing what she'd done wrong.

Rhoads nudged her. "I think he's trying to tell you that you have to bet at least twenty-five dollars. I found out what that meant the hard way. Pick up your money. It tends to evaporate around here if you don't."

"Looks like you're disqualified, too," she said, eyeing the empty racks in front of him.

"Worse than that," he said, "I'm out of smokes." Rhoads turned away from her and waved to the pit boss. "Yo. Gimme another five thou, nah, wait, make it ten. And see if the waitress can find me a pack of Camels."

When Rhoads had to pay for cigarettes, out of spite he never bought TobacCo, Inc. products.

The girl's eyes widened. "Ten thousand! Wow! Back in Bloomington, Indiana, it takes me half a year to earn that much. And that's before withholding." She wasn't bad looking, Rhoads realized, and there was some kind of body under that Miss Hathaway clothing.

"Oh, *yeah*. I'm a real pro," he said. "Matter of fact, stick with me. I'll show you how to lose that pretty little shirt of yours."

The pit boss made a call to the cashier's office and determined that Rhoads still had twelve thousand dollars in credit in his line. Earlier, the casino credit manager had told him he was foolish to walk around with the blank money orders.

"Give him ten thousand," the supervisor said loudly as Rhoads signed a marker.

When Rhoads said, "All black," the dealer swiftly counted

out 100 black chips and stacked them in the rack in front of him. A cocktail waitress materialized with the Camels. The smokes were courtesy of the casino. He tipped her a red chip, five dollars, and set the pack in the rail. So far, the free cigarettes and free rum had cost Rhoads close to fifty thousand. Make that fifty thousand and five, including the tip.

He wasn't finished yet.

Rhoads opened the cigarette pack, fired up his lighter, took a deep drag, and exhaled a thick white cloud. The stickman, about to push the dice to the next player, caught a wink from the box man. It was a signal to wait for Rhoads to finish lighting up so he could place another bet. Rhoads looked up and sensed they were waiting for him.

"Oh, shit! I have to bet again?" He grinned. "Okay," he said, taking some of his black chips and putting them on the pass line in front of him. "Here goes shit! Let's go."

The shooter picked up the dice and blew on them before throwing. A two. Snake eyes. Another instant loser. The players at the table emitted a soft collective groan.

"Two! Crap! Line away," the croupier said. He looked to Rhoads, then eyed the spot on the felt where Rhoads's chips used to be and half whispered, "Time to reload."

"Well, there went shit." Rhoads shrugged.

"So what? You've lost a few bucks," the blonde said. "You're just backing up for a good start. That's what my Daddy, may he rest in peace, always used to say."

"Your daddy played craps?"

"No. He used to say that when things weren't starting out good."

"By the way, I'm T.R."

"I'm Wendy," she said.

"You've heard of two steps forward, one step backward, right?" Rhoads said to her. "Well, with me, it seems to be no steps forward, fifty thousand steps backward. Any farther, I'll be in the ocean."

Rhoads drained his drink in a single gulp and laughed.

"What's so funny?" the girl asked.

"You see a boat here?"

She looked at him. Her original suspicion was right. The guy was thoroughly smashed. "Not really," she said.

"You don't see a fishing boat?"

She shook her head "no."

"This table," he said, sweeping his arm in front of them, "was a boat. Belonged to me and my brother. We were going to buy it tomorrow at auction, but I seemed to have blown all the dough. Just quit my job, too. This morning, matter of fact. Damn good job, too, down in Asheville, and came up to Jersey to buy a charter fishing boat and go into biz with my brother. But I'm here instead. Practically in the ocean. And, like you, I don't see any boat either."

"Aw, you're just a little high. That's what's making you feel a little low," she said and dropped her eyes to the floor. Then she looked up and said so only he could hear, "I think you just need something to change your luck. Here, let me give it a try."

Now she was a different woman. She slipped into his arms and gave him a lingering kiss. As she pressed herself closely, she set her black patent-leather pocketbook, hooked by its strap around her shoulder, on the rail.

Rhoads, surprised and embarrassed, kissed her back. She was in no hurry to push herself away.

"Dang!" he gasped.

"Yeah, you can kiss, too," she said breathily. She touched her hair. She looked down again and took a deep breath. The kiss, it seemed, had made her day. "Excuse me for a sec," she beamed. "I think I all of a sudden want to say good-bye to my girlfriend. She's in the Briny Reef drinking. I'll go tell her—if you'll still be here in five minutes. I'll be back."

Rhoads looked down at his chips and back up at her. He nodded. As she turned to leave, his arm shot out and grabbed her, roughly, by the elbow. Yanked to a stop, she spun around startled.

"Hey! Let go!" Worry rushed over her face. *"What are you doing?"*

Rhoads tightened his grip and pulled her closer, quietly. He did not want to draw the attention of the security people. He burned his eyes into hers. With one hand, he took a cigarette from the pack on the rail and put it into his mouth. Through teeth clenching the cigarette, he said, "Listen, wiseguy. You need to loosen the spring. It snaps back too hard. You can hear it."

"What? What?" She appeared confused, then she turned ugly, her voice dropped an octave, all cigarette raspy and street smart. "Let go right now, fuck wad."

Rhoads noticed that she shifted her weight to her left leg. Rhoads moved, too, like a dance partner, and turned slightly into her, hip first, a defense against getting kneed in the nuts.

"Fuck wad!" Rhoads laughed. "That's pretty. And out of the same pretty little back-home Indiana mouth that just quoted poor ol' dead daddy."

The other gamblers, distracted by the dice, paid no attention to them.

Rhoads maintained his painful grip on the girl's elbow. With his free hand, he took hold of her pocketbook, turned it upside down, and smirked when he saw the false bottom. *The old Scranton Sweep trick.* The purse contained a bottom compartment covered by a latched sliding door. He looked at her. She turned her head away, something between a flinch and shame. Rhoads used his thumb to open the spring-tension sliding door. He slid it back until it clicked into place. Inside he found five black chips. His chips. Still holding her elbow, Rhoads took them out and put them back into his rack.

Again she tried to pull away. He held on.

Rhoads picked up his glass and emptied it into his mouth. He got ice cubes only. Rhoads sucked what rum was left and, holding the glass up to his mouth, spit the ice back into it.

"Know what gave you away?" He lightened his grip just enough to let her know he didn't want to hurt her unnecessarily while keeping it tight enough to remind her he didn't want her running away.

She answered obediently, "You just said. It snaps too loud."

"Well, yeah, that, too, but *before* that. What made me think you were going to go for my wallet?"

The girl shrugged.

"That rotten makeup job on your black eye," he said. "Really lame."

She started to reach up to touch the place that hurt but stopped and lowered her arm.

"What are you going to do?" she said, looking down at his hand on her elbow, then up at him. Firm, small breasts heaved under her blouse. She tried to make eye contact, but he looked away. "I'll apologize, real good. Anything you say. Please don't make any noise. The casino'll press charges."

"If I were you, I'd be more worried about your Kung-Fu John Travolta look-alike pimp over there." Rhoads pointed with his chin across the casino floor to a nasty-looking Asian kid, younger than she, who was watching. "Casino security probably won't hit you."

Rhoads picked up two black chips with his free hand and handed them to her, low. Reflexively, she took them.

She was completely baffled. Then he released his grip. She instantly took a step backward, out of range, but went no farther. She looked at the chips in her hand.

"Huh? Why? I don't get it." Now she looked at Rhoads. "I don't get it."

"Professional courtesy, whatever-your-name-is. Because, we're kin. I'm stupid. You're stupid. Anyway, won't 200 pacify Saturday Night Fever? Or will he bash you no matter what you fetch, just for good luck?"

She looked down for an instant, then back to Rhoads. "Probably, but thanks. Thank you."

She disappeared.

Rhoads turned back to the craps table. The waitress was

there, replacing his empty glass with a fresh drink. It was time for him to roll again. He dropped one black chip onto the pass line. The croupier slid the dice to him, he picked them up, held them high, and let them fly.

During the next ten minutes, Rhoads lost three more rolls, losing all his chips, and downed two more drinks.

"Hey, I have an idea," he said as he watched the dealer pick up the chips from the bet he'd made. "Let's see if these come up sevens, too." Rhoads then threw his drink—glass, ice cubes, everything, down the table, rolling and splashing and knocking over chips. Everyone froze while the pit boss bellowed for security. Before they got there, Rhoads shoved several gamblers aside, reached under the rail, and picked up their drinks and heaved them, splashing, onto the table.

"Come on, seven!" Rhoads shouted as he threw another glass onto the green felt. "Come on, seven!"

9

The Executive Suite
TobacCo, Inc. World Headquarters
Asheville, North Carolina

In the office of W. Nicholas Pratt's executive secretary, a large television peered out of a massive, elaborately carved teak credenza. Someone had turned the volume up too high. The CNN news anchorman's booming voice filled the room.

". . . deaths now reported in Cincinnati, Boston, Boca Raton, New Orleans, San Diego, and Tacoma. And as we've said, additional reports continue to come in. There is no way at present to know the full scope of this disaster. The FBI has issued a preliminary statement warning all consumers that cigarette packages may contain lethal poison. To this moment, however, we can confirm only that the 122 known deaths, and many, many injuries, are thus far all associated with the Easy Lights brand manufactured by TobacCo, Inc., of Asheville, North Carolina. An FBI press conference has been scheduled for . . ."

Executive secretary Genevieve DesCourt, a trim older woman in an expensive dark blue suit, stared flustered and aghast at the screen.

The intercom on her desk squawked, startling her.

"Have you located Rhoads yet!"

"No, Mr. Pratt, but I have gotten hold of one of our pilots, Jack Fallscroft. He and Rhoads are close friends. He said to tell you he has an idea about where Rhoads may be. He's checking. And Mr. Pratt? The men from the FBI, they're getting impatient. I told them . . ."

"All right, Genevieve. Send them in."

She rose and started around her desk to lead them to Pratt's office, but Deputy Director of the Federal Bureau of

Investigation Oakley Franklin stopped her with a wave.

"Additional FBI men will be arriving," he said to her. "Tell them I said to wait here."

He took a moment to check his watch, then crooked a finger at another FBI man. The two walked across the office to the massive redwood door that separated Pratt from the rest of the world.

The deputy director looked like a linebacker. Big, black, humorless, with a face full of scars. The other agent, no more than twenty-five, was forgettable, average in looks, weight, and height. His name was Brandon. His father was a congressman from northern California, and he was part of an experimental fast-track FBI training program. Franklin found him annoying but efficient.

Franklin motioned for Brandon to step in ahead of him. The two men strode toward the huge desk at the far end of the room. It was a considerable walk on the thick carpet.

Pratt stood staring out the floor-to-ceiling windows, silhouetted against the darkening skyline of Asheville and the Smoky Mountains. He looked as if he was born with the title of CEO. Tall, trim, with skin bronzed by many hours on the back nine of the most exclusive golf courses. His gray suit fit as if Pierre Cardin himself had been his tailor, and his shiny-as-steel silver-and-black hair looked good atop the dark face and dark suit.

Pratt shook the deputy director's hand perfunctorily and ignored the junior man.

"I'm Oakley Franklin, Mr. Pratt. Deputy director of the FBI. And this is Ben Brandon, a special agent to FBIHQ, FBI headquarters in Washington."

So that's what "HQ" means, Pratt thought, immediately and permanently dismissing Franklin as a lightweight, probably an affirmative action beneficiary.

"I'm not particularly pleased to meet either of you." Pratt swallowed as if pained by a severe sore throat. Then he looked behind him at the woman with the double-take legs seated on a couch. A stack of manila file folders weighted her down. "This is Anna Maria Trichina," he said, "one of our assistant vice-presidents."

"So, what do you have?" Pratt said as he sat down. The two FBI agents remained standing.

Franklin looked at the woman. Trichina, a voluptuous red-head with shoulder-length hair, had been out of sight on the couch until Pratt stepped aside and introduced her. She began to move the folders from her lap to get up and shake hands. Pratt preempted her by waving the FBI agents to the chairs on the other side of his desk.

Franklin spoke. "Well, Mr. Pratt, Ms. Trichina, what I have is a mess. Apparently someone has injected packs of your ciga-rettes, 700 of them, with a sodium cyanide solution and shipped them all over the country. It looks as if they've arrived at tobac-co shops as some kind of consumer opinion survey. The packages came with a cover letter. A cover letter that had been printed on your company's letterhead."

"Mother lover!" Pratt whistled as if he'd just seen an inter-ception against a team he had a big bet on.

Trichina rose. She seemed offended by Franklin's report. "TobacCo, Inc. letterhead? That's *impossible.*"

Brandon snapped open a soft-leather portfolio he had tucked under his arm and handed Franklin a flat sheet of paper enclosed in a clear plastic evidence bag.

"You tell me," Franklin said, handing it to Trichina. "An agent had to use a letter opener to pry this out from between the thumb and index finger of a cadaver in Annapolis about ninety minutes ago. Don't open the plastic."

Trichina held it up to the light.

"The logo looks good," she said, addressing Pratt. "But this isn't ours. The watermark is wrong. This paper is Philamy Linen. TobacCo, Inc. uses Strathmore Writing, 25 percent cotton." Then Trichina controlled a snarl and spoke to the FBI men. "Whoever did this didn't get the stationery here."

"Relax, Anna Maria." Pratt said to her. "He doesn't think *we* did it. He's simply trying to acquaint us with the situation."

"That's not entirely accurate, Mr. Pratt. At this moment, I have no idea who did it. The only thing I know for sure is that I didn't do it. That leaves five billion-minus-one potential suspects."

Ben Brandon's cellular telephone chirped in his pocket. He turned away when he answered it, spoke for a moment, closed his telephone, and turned back to the conversation without saying a word about the call.

"At this point, Ms. Trichina," Franklin said, "it is the policy of the FBI that we don't rule things out, we rule them in. We have nearly two hundred dead, seventy-two critically injured—and word is many if not most of them will die—and reports of new fatalities and injuries coming in every time I turn around. We're looking at a nationwide panic. And who knows if this is a single isolated attack by overnight mail or if poisoned cigarettes are right now sitting on retailers' shelves all over the country?"

Pratt looked as if he'd been rabbit-punched in the gut. He spoke quietly. "Who's on the top of your short list as of now?"

"Mr. Pratt, again, the list is five billion people long. This investigation is about three hours old. And all we know for sure is that whomever is behind this is an intelligent, crafty individual with at least some knowledge of how you test market your products."

"Oh for shit's sake, Nick," Trichina said, holding up the letter in the evidence bag. "Did you read this? Any community college Intro to Marketing student could think this up."

Pratt ignored her and spoke to Franklin. "You're saying it may be an inside job? An employee? A former employee? Someone like that?"

"As I've said, there's no reason to rule it out. What I want to do right now is talk to whomever heads up corporate security here. He may have someone in mind already."

Trichina said, "Tom Rhoads is . . ."

Pratt cut her off. ". . . expected to report at any moment. He will, of course, give you whatever it is you'll need. And, of course, so will Anna Maria and I."

10

Asheville

In the orderly master bedroom, a green oxygen tank on a roller sat beside a single bed by an open doorway to the hall. Vials and bottles crowded the nightstand.

A shower hissed as Mary Dallaness, thirty-four, entered from the hall and walked quietly toward the bathroom. She was barefoot and wearing jeans and a tank top. She stood just outside the bathroom looking in. Her husband, Anthony, was barely visible through a foggy shower door.

"Why didn't you call me before you got in there?"

"Probably because I don't need a nursemaid when I'm taking a shower."

But you do, she thought. "Why aren't you sitting on the folding chair, at least?"

A telephone rang in another part of the house. She looked in the direction of the ringing, then back at Anthony, torn over whether to answer or not.

"The telephone's ringing, Ant. Stay put. Don't try to get out until I come back. Do you hear me?"

"No," he rasped. She could hear the emphysema in his voice.

Mary jogged around the banister to another bedroom. Hers. A bright multicolored comforter, half thrown over a nearby rocking chair, lay in disarray on a double bed. Stacks of magazines and books, a compact stereo on the dresser cluttered the room. She hurried to pick up the telephone.

"Hello?" She listened. "Yes, this is Mary Dallaness. Mr. Pratt?" She listened again. "Goodness, no! I took a personal day, and I've been tied up with my husband and the doctors since this morning. *Oh, no.* No, the television isn't on. We just got in. Wait a moment, I'll put it on."

She crossed the room to a small television and pushed the

power button. She glanced at the clock on the dresser—8:52 P.M.
A news anchor was talking in front of a graphic luridly titled
"*CIGARETTE TERROR.*" The sound was low.

She picked up the receiver. "I have it on, Mr. Pratt, Channel 6.
I can't believe it." Mary watched the screen as she listened to the
CEO. "No. No, sir, no reporters have contacted me. Of course I
won't speak to them." She listened to Pratt. He spoke in urgent
bursts. "Yes, all the Level Three documents are totally secure. No,
sir. Nobody can access a Level Three file without my knowing
about it."

Pratt asked her if the computer database kept a record of
everyone who requested the top secret documents. She told him
yes, the system did that automatically and kept those names in
another Level Three document called "LTD-PULLS." He sounded
relieved. Immediately his voice tensed again. He asked if there
was a way that anyone, anyone, could access that document and
erase names of those who have seen Level Three files.

"Yes," Mary said, and then added, proudly, "only one person
not including you and Ms. Trichina are cleared to see LTD-
PULLS. Someone I know you can trust. Me."

Pratt said that was what he was hoping to hear. He thanked
her.

"Do you need me to come in, sir?" Mary asked, hoping he'd
say no. "All right. Yes, sir. First thing in the morning, then." She
paused, and Pratt said something else. "My, husband?" She lowered her voice. "As well as can be expected . . . but thank you for
asking, sir."

After hanging up, Mary Dallaness stood still, in the dark of
her bedroom, listening to herself breathe.

Something about Pratt's call left her unsettled, something
made her shudder.

11

Across town, Nick Pratt had just said good-bye to Mary Dallaness and hung up the telephone in the living room of Anna Maria Trichina's luxury condo in North Asheville.

A black leather couch stretched across two adjacent walls. Track lighting highlighted framed prints of several views of Monet's water lilies from his garden at Giverny.

Pratt and Trichina, both numb, both dressed in the business attire they wore earlier to World Headquarters, sat on separate sections of the long couch. Pratt looked at his watch, picked up the telephone, and checked his messages.

"Shit," Pratt said upon hearing the call from the company's investor relations manager. The manager had reported that huge blocks of sell orders on TobacCo, Inc. shares were already piling up for the opening bell tomorrow at the New York Stock Exchange. That on top of a point-and-a-half loss on high-volume trading earlier that day.

Trichina was still thinking about Pratt's call to Mary Dallaness.

"Did she sound suspicious?" Trichina asked.

"Not at all. In a crisis like this, it makes sense that the CEO would be on damage-control duty."

"I'm surprised you have any confidence that you can count on Mary Dallaness." Trichina flashed a bratty schoolgirl smirk when she mentioned her subordinate's name. "She's so . . . so *subordinate*. Anyone in authority can manipulate her. I wouldn't be surprised if a tough-talking meter maid could badger her into divulging top-level corporate data."

"That's what I like about you, Anna Maria, your tolerance when it comes to other people's frailties."

"And the other one you have to watch out for is Rhoads. He's a fuckup waiting to fuck something up. He's a drunk and a bum."

"Sometimes a drunk and a bum is exactly what the doctor ordered. You should know that." Pratt smiled at Trichina. She looked away.

He continued. "Every problem brings with it some benefit, even if it's hard to recognize. We should have more devastating crises around TobacCo, Anna Maria."

"What do you mean?"

"Ever since we learned of this product-tampering nightmare this afternoon, you've had the most adorable furrow in your forehead. It's quite . . ."

"Oh, Nick. Not now. Please."

Pratt tuned out her voice and looked at her. He wasn't smiling. His eyes narrowed on her like a predator spotting prey. Still seated at the other end of the couch, Pratt reached for one of the round white-leather throw pillows. He remembered paying the credit-card invoice for them. Trichina had bought six of the pillows for ninety dollars each on a business trip in Chicago and had them shipped to Asheville. He dropped the pillow on the floor between his shoes. He closed his eyes and indicated *come here* with a slight jerk of his head. Trichina pretended to miss the cue.

Pratt waited half a minute. He heard no sound of her rustling toward him. His eyes remained closed.

"All right, Anna Maria. I'll try it in English. Why don't you come on over here."

Pratt leaned back against the couch. He patted his knee three times. Trichina hesitated a moment too long before she forced herself to begin moving. Pratt heard her slide along the leather to him.

Fetch, he thought to himself as he interlaced his fingers behind his head and suppressed a grin. *Fetch, girl.*

12

In his limo, while riding home, Pratt picked up the secure cellular line and pressed a button to automatically dial Valzmann.

In a remote part of TobacCo, Inc.'s World Headquarters subbasement, a small room existed, lined with advanced electronic equipment, walled in cinder block and devoid of any natural light. The room did not appear on the floor plans on file with the Buncombe County's Emergency Management Services nor in the building's architectural blueprints. Officially, the room didn't exist.

In that room, a telephone's soft electronic tone hummed.

"Yes, Mr. Pratt," the voice said.

Pratt was on fire. "This tampering shit. Fucking Benedict's name is going to come up. I know it. The government never contacted us about his little telephone call to the Justice Department. You know why?"

Valzmann had been through this three million times. *Best to let Pratt vent.*

Pratt kept roaring. "Well, I'll tell you why. Because the Feds were just waiting for their chance. And, now they have it. I'll bet you money they start in with Benedict. *Where's Benedict? What happened to Benedict? Could Benedict be behind this?* And of course, we can't tell them why we know it's definitely *not* Benedict."

Pratt interrupted his tirade to say something to his chauffeur. Then, back to Valzmann. "We ought to make damned certain those documents are secure. I've already begun. And I want you thinking about the logistics of tying Rhoads to Benedict."

"I'm working on it," Valzmann said, making a note on a lined pad. "Mr. Pratt? Can I ask you something? Why do those documents still exist? Why do we even have them?"

"I wish they didn't, but they were logged in on the auditors' schedule long before they became a problem. Getting rid of them would be a red flag. It's better to keep them buried in the archive database."

"Then why are you nervous?"

"Because there's always the human element."

"As in . . ."

"As in Mary Dallaness."

"The name rings a bell."

"You don't know who she is?" Pratt seethed. *"Mary Dallaness, idiot. In the corporate documentation division. You keep an eye on her. She and her husband are buddies with you know who."*

"Rhoads?"

"Rhoads."

"How do they know each other?"

"Don't you bother reading the reports your own investigators write for me? Rhoads used to be a cop in Philadelphia. Mary's husband Anthony has a brother. He was a Philly cop with Rhoads."

"Small world."

"Yeah, and I think we're going to need to find a way to make it a little smaller, by two."

"But why are you worried about Mary Dallaness? What's the problem with her?"

"She's unstable. Her husband's dying. Chronic pulmonary emphysema, from smoking, of course. That makes her susceptible to pangs of conscience. You know, we had one like her not so long ago."

13

After Pratt left, Trichina poured herself a goblet of red wine, sipped it once, then took several larger swallows, and went to the filing cabinet in the home office set up in the spare bedroom. She set the wine down atop the cabinet and slid open a drawer. She leafed through the manila file folders, withdrawing her tax return and supporting documentation from last year.

Leaving the drawer open, she went to her bedroom with the folder and wine and lay down on the bed, propped up by several giant pillows and a thick bolster. Another few swallows and the glass was empty. Trichina turned the stapled photocopied pages until she came to one marked with a paper clip.

She read the entry line that itemized her voluntary charitable contributions for that tax year. National Center for Literacy. UNICEF. Cystic Fibrosis. EarthTrust Preservation Fund. Amnesty International. She read the list several times before flipping the folder closed. She did this periodically when she needed to reassure herself that she was a person of character. And she was even more than that. She recalled with self-satisfaction that once she even sought no tax advantage from the one-thousand-dollar check she had written to the American Cancer Society the same day she had her annual review and received notice of a fifty-five-hundred-dollar bonus.

She put the folder down, went to the kitchen and poured herself a goblet full of wine before returning to the bedroom. She stripped the rest of her garments off, did a slapdash job of removing her makeup, and reclined on the bed.

Closing her eyes, she exhaled deeply, almost a sigh. Images like film clips moved in slow motion through her mind, images of Rhoads and those many nights not so long ago when he lay there curled up next to her, so large in the bed she was used to sleeping in alone, and so strong, so dumb looking, asleep with his mouth open. The memories were a lullaby she sang to herself. Not sadly, though. Fondly.

Anna Maria Trichina knew the tampering chaos presented an opportunity to her, and her father had always insisted that she be on the lookout for opportunity, and when she saw it, she was to seize it. But he was gone now and it was up to her. She remembered his corny saying and the way he smiled when he said it. *You have to take responsibility for what you do in this world, Anna Maria. You have to know the ten magic words that make anything possible, that can make anything come true.* Then she remembered the little thrill she experienced every time he said those words. Because he wanted her to hear them, he said them very, very slowly, very, very carefully, each one in its own universe. He would take her tiny hand in his rough one and say, *If it is to be, it is up to me.* Then he asked her to repeat them with him, and they'd say the words together. *If it is to be, it is up to me.*

The wine had bathed every nerve in her body. She felt light and airy.

She knew she performed her job honorably, and she earned fair day's pay for a fair day's labor. Her father certainly would have understood that. No, there was nothing in the world wrong with that. At all. She didn't force people to smoke, she didn't even ask people to smoke. People smoked for thousands of years before she was born, and she knew, no matter what, that people would smoke for thousands of years after she was gone. So, if she could take advantage of this situation and rise within TobacCo, Inc., she was going to do it.

And once she got to the top, or near enough, she'd be able to influence company policy.

She could make a difference.

A positive difference.

Plus, she could buy herself one hell of a Jaguar.

14

Atlantic City

It was night, almost cold. Maybe forty, forty-five degrees.

The salty breeze that blew in from the Atlantic Ocean across the miles of south Jersey beachfront made it colder. Crisp and clear. Wave crests picked up the glitter of starlight.

Two beefy plainclothes Boardwalk Casino security men clattered across the planks of the boardwalk, struggling with a surly, drunker-than-ever Rhoads. They were walking him across the boardwalk, intending, against company policy, to dump him on the beach. It would save them and the Atlantic City Metropolitan Police a load of paperwork.

"Why don't you just shut up and keep walking?" one of the men said. "It'll hurt a lot less if I don't have to Mace you."

Then the other one chimed in. "Leave the stupid bastard alone, Leo. You'd be irritable too if you just blew fifty or sixty large."

"I'm goin back in and win it back," Rhoads assured them. Even he could hear that his speech was slurred.

Rhoads used an elbow to try to extricate himself from the security men's grip. He gave up after a few seconds of having both arms twisted painfully forward. When Rhoads had relaxed, Leo withdrew a canister of Mace from his belt and held it low, out of Rhoads's sight. Leo nudged his partner, showing him the canister.

"I don't want this can to expire without having used it once," Leo whispered, not really caring whether their prisoner heard or understood.

The men steered Rhoads to a sandy plank stairway that led from the Boardwalk down to the beach. They walked him down the handful of steps when, suddenly, without provocation, Leo pushed Rhoads. Rhoads went flying and fell hard, face down into the sand. From where he stood on the steps, the other security man threw up his hands in disgust. Rhoads lay there motionless.

"Jack off! What'd you do that for? You probably broke his neck. Now make sure you haven't freakin' killed him."

Leo lumbered down the planks and onto the beach, stepping carefully to avoid getting any sand into his shoes. He bent down next to Rhoads, grabbed a hank of his hair, and lifted his head. It was dark, and Leo had to lean in close to see Rhoads's face. Rhoads's eyes were closed, but he was alive, mumbling, his mouth bloody and full of sand.

"He ain't dead, Angelo, he's just hungry. He's eating the beach." Leo let go of Rhoads's hair, and his head dropped with a thud into the sand

"Leo?" Rhoads stammered, barely audible, his head rolling in a daze.

"Yeah?" Leo said, brimming with delight, as he looked back down at Rhoads. "What?"

Rhoads craned his neck toward Leo as if to speak his last words but instead blew a mouthful of bloody sand into the security man's eyes. Leo screamed. Angelo jumped off the steps towards Rhoads. Both he and Leo rolled onto the drunk, kicking and punching, pummeling, and cursing.

Rhoads sat spread-legged in the wet sand watching the surf, the hem of his bomber jacket wet, his face bloodier than before. The two security men had long before hurried back to the casino.

Rhoads held an unlit cigarette between his lips, the blood black in the faint light of the stars. He hurled a crumpled, empty cigarette pack into the surf. He watched it bob on the foam. In less than a minute, a tiny wave ran up between his legs returning the pack, depositing it in his lap. The water was cold and had thoroughly soaked his jeans. He stared at the cigarette pack that had come back to him.

His head hurt, his face hurt. He sighed and looked down into his right hand. At some point in the melee, he had gotten

Leo's canister of Mace. Rhoads flung himself backward onto the sand, looked up into the starlit sky. The foamy seawater smelled of fish and salt and felt good. Too cold, too gritty where the sand had washed up into his clothes and adhered to his skin, but he felt good.

He started to laugh out loud. He laughed at the two jerks with faces full of pepper spray. He laughed until tears rolled down out of the corners of his eyes and into his ears. He laughed until he remembered what else had happened that night. He had sunk the boat.

Oh, man.

And he couldn't face his brother.

The thought of another drink sounded good.

15

American News Syndicate
Washington, D.C. Bureau

```
AMERICAN NEWS SYNDICATE
SLUG: CIGARETTES TAMPERING—ART
ALL MEDIA: MAJOR STORY UPDATE: MONDAY, OCTOBER 4
11:42 P.M. EST WASHINGTON BUREAU

ART AVAILABLE: 8 COLOR CRIME SCENE PIX. NATIONAL.
```

1: Crime scene. Tobacco shop in mall. Seattle, WA.
2: Crime scene. Tobacco shop taped off by FBI. Memphis, TN.
3: Victim's distraught wife, children comforted by friends and police. Memphis, TN.
4: Antismoking protesters with signs at AmeriLeaf Tobacco, Co. distribution center. Long Island, NY.
5: Hospital spokesman, Fisher Memorial Hospital. San Bernardino, CA.
6: Closeup of Easy Lights package w/arrow indicating where tamperer opened pack. (Xmit FBI photo)
7: Crime scene. Victim under sheet in front of tobacco shop. Orlando, FL.
8: Massive media turnout at FBI press con. Wash/DC.

309 DEAD, 132 HOSPITALIZED AS OF 9:00 P.M.

By Fred Bird

American News Syndicate Staff Reporter

Monday, October 4—Washington, D.C. The estimated death toll in today's mass poisoning of Easy Light cigarettes has reached 309 as of 9 P.M. Eastern Standard Time, FBI spokesman Special Agent Walter Mitten said tonight. Mitten also told a packed press conference that 132 others have been hospitalized as a result of the poisoned cigarettes.

"The investigation is intense and we are pursuing several promising leads," Mitten said. "Hundreds of FBI agents, augmented by state and local police and officials from state, local and federal agencies have been mobilized. The operation is being managed by the FBI's Event Response Center here in Washington."

In Philadelphia, a Federal Express spokeswoman confirmed that the company delivered 697 of the suspect packages Monday. Exactly 700 packages were shipped from Philadelphia, but three had been inaccurately addressed or shipped to tobacco shops that had gone out of business.

Two Federal Express employees who handled the transaction say a Caucasian male, age fifty to sixty, weighing 150 to 160 pounds and dressed as a delivery man, dropped off the packages Friday evening. Investigators say that although that individual is the focus of their search, he may have been an employee of a legitimate courier service that unknowingly delivered the deadly packages. Other sources speculate the man may have been the perpetrator who intentionally poisoned the cigarettes contained in the packages.

16

Atlantic City en route to Poconos

Rhoads sat in clothes wet and smelling of the sea, cold against the seat leather. He drove the rental car—a too-expensive Lincoln—wildly along the dark, sixty miles of the arrow-straight Atlantic City Expressway, through Philly to the Pennsylvania Turnpike. He took the turnpike to the Northeast Extension and up into the Pocono Mountains.

Darkness veiled the colors of the early October foliage. When Rhoads opened his window part way to keep himself awake, the scent of the conifers in the cold air made him think about the field guide to North American trees he had in his duffel bag. If it hadn't been so dark, he told himself, he'd get out and look at the trees.

His mind reeled and wouldn't focus. Unpleasant images and negative ideas paraded themselves through his head.

Trees, he thought. *I need trees. Big, tall, windblown, swaying trees. I have to get myself into the woods and surrounded by high, tall trees.*

Ever since he was a young boy and had gone camping with his father and the YMCA Indian Guides, trees had helped Rhoads get perspective in times of trouble. He loved how they stood there and took it, whatever nature dished out. He wished he could be like them.

Later, in his teens, Rhoads had loved to drive up into the Poconos, search for the summits of mountain ridges, and climb the highest tree there, giving himself a wide view. Then, the winds had swayed the trees, and the mountain air had carried the scent of pine. He'd stay up high until his muscles cramped, and it began to get dark.

The route he took this night wound him around upstate dairy farms and stands of pine woods and ranch houses with huge picture windows set way back on two-acre front lawns. Bleary-eyed, he took sharp turns too fast, tires crunching gravel and shooting it out into ditches like bullets. On the winding roads, his headlights illuminated everything but the asphalt. In Rhoads's mind, the trip from A.C. to the redwood cabin was being made in one great careening sweep. He stopped only once to stand unsteadily and urinate into a trash barrel at a rest stop.

About twenty minutes after Rhoads exited the Northeast Extension in Carbon Country, around a bend in the road, he had to brake hard to avoid a car stopped in his lane.

There, next to the red Japanese compact, Rhoads saw a woman crouching by the rear of the car. The trunk was open. She had the car jacked up and was changing a flat. Rhoads pulled over behind her and put on his emergency flashers. He got out of his car slowly and made his way to her. She looked up, frightened, saying nothing.

"I don't blame you for being afraid, miss." Rhoads wobbled

a bit. The cold mountain air condensed his breath. Fatigue and alcohol slurred his speech. "I promise I just want to help. You stopped in a rotten place and . . ."

"You're drunk and you're driving," she said, looking worriedly to his car. Did he have a bunch of drunks with him? She regretted showing her fear and put a little feistiness in her voice. "I'm fine, I have it half-fixed already. I don't need your help."

Rhoads could hear a couple of kids talking in the jacked-up car.

"And it's not wise to have the kids in the car while it's on the jack," he said, even though he and his brother had loved it when once their father had changed a tire with them in the car.

Rhoads's eyes fell on the flat tire on the ground and the spare already in place on the axle.

"You blew out," Rhoads said, taking a closer look at the mangled tire. "At least let me tighten the tire for you and jack your car down. You can keep an eye on the kids."

The woman rose and looked at Rhoads, sizing him up. Then she burst into tears.

"What's wrong?" Rhoads figured she was terrified of him, a stranger in the dark, out in the middle of nowhere. Maybe she could smell that he was a man at the end of his rope, maybe she could sense he had just lost it all in Atlantic City. He stepped back several paces to reassure her. He put his hands up in surrender. "Okay, okay," he said. "I'll just sit in my car and keep my flashers on till you're okay. I don't mean to frighten you. I just want to help."

"No," she said, struggling to regain control. "I know you're all right. It's just . . ." She pointed to a hubcap on the road by the blown-out tire. ". . . that I had put the lug nuts in the hubcap to keep track of them, but then in the dark I kicked it over, and they all fell into the storm drain there. There's no service place open now within twenty miles of here, and I have the kids."

Rhoads didn't know what to do. He felt bad for her and knew she wouldn't let him, in his inebriation, drive her and her kids anywhere to get help. He almost offered to let her take his car while he stayed behind.

Now that she had explained the problem and said he was "all right," Rhoads felt he could move closer and examine the storm drain without upsetting her any more than she already was.

"I have a light," he said. He went back to his duffel bag and retrieved a small flashlight. He aimed the beam down the drain. He couldn't even see the bottom, he only heard water trickling somewhere below. He turned to the woman. "I guess they're gone."

Rhoads then stood up straight under a stand of tall trees. Balsam firs, he noticed. He shone his light into the trees to see them rustle in the light wind. He could see that one of the trees had long ago tried to fall but was caught and held almost upright by the high boughs of several others. Rhoads turned his flashlight off and paced slowly around the car, thinking. A moment later, a smile sprung onto his face.

"I've got it!" he said, excitedly, starting toward her, almost falling into the ditch that edged the roadway. "We'll take one lug nut from each of the other three wheels and use them to secure your spare. That will hold easily until you get to wherever you're going."

The woman stood and stared at her car for a moment. She sighed deeply and turned to him. "My God, that's brilliant. Absolutely brilliant! And you're . . . you're . . . so . . . *intoxicated*."

"Yes I am, ma'am," Rhoads said, proud of himself. "I am a drunk, but that doesn't mean I'm a half-wit."

After the woman and her kids thanked Rhoads, he got back into his car, watching for foggily remembered landmarks en route to the cabin. It had been a long time since he'd been there, and the last time, well, he was drunk then, too.

Switching to the black chips, each worth one hundred dollars, when he had started to lose had been a bad idea. So had the half-dozen Bacardi 151s.

As Rhoads sobered, his courage waned. Brave back on the

beach but too much a coward now to confess to his brother that he'd dropped their dream deep into a green felt ocean. *Fool of the Family*, Teddy had crowned him. And the title was periodically renewed by news of Rhoads's latest blunder.

Gerry Rhoads, Rhoads's uncle, owned a cabin in Deer Mountain and years ago had issued an open invitation to every-one in the family. Everyone knew where the key was, hidden behind a clay flowerpot at the foot of the mailbox post. *Uncle Gerry's is less than three hours from A.C.*, Rhoads had calculated. *That'd be a good place to regroup until I can figure out how to come up with sixty thousand dollars.*

All kinds of ideas flashed through his mind.

Some kind of quick loan from the credit union? Borrow it from someone at work? Appeal to Pratt? Scrounge up a couple of thousand, go back to A.C., and bet smart this time, make a comeback? Each idea more ludicrous and less likely than the one preceding it.

At least before he left A.C., he had called his brother, waking his sister-in-law, saying there had been a slight change of plans and that he'd show up the next morning, in plenty of time for the auction. That's when Teddy told him the auction wasn't at noon, it was at nine. Rhoads wouldn't have much time to sleep before getting up and driving back another three hours.

Rhoads made it to the cabin in one piece. He counted backwards by increments of twenty-seven and a half to stop him-self from thinking about the money. Once inside the cabin, too weary to find the linens and throw them onto the bed, he col-lapsed onto a crummy sleeping bag a previous guest had left on the floor.

In the middle of the night, he awoke, half the sleeping bag wrapped around him. He unzipped it, got in, and pulled it up around himself. The cabin door, ajar, inched back and forth, creaking in the cool, mountain wind. The last of the Lincoln's battery burned outside in the dying headlights. A few surviving summer moths flew in and out of the beam.

Rhoads rolled around, semiconscious, both sweating under

the thermo-lining of the sleeping bag and shivering where his skin was exposed to the cabin air.

He fell back asleep to half-dreams of warm sun and fishing boats and the thumping putt-putt-putt of a diesel engine.

17

Amherst, Massachusetts
City Room, *Amherst American*

"Carney!" Geoff Gavin, the night editor screamed. He chomped his cigar so tightly his teeth met. "Where in the hell is Carney?"

Carney came sprinting from the vending machine area, two minutes into her first break in six hours. "Yes sir?" she said. She was an intern from the University of Massachusetts working general assignment.

"Where'd you get these tobacco facts for the tampering story sidebar?"

The girl looked nervous. "From the current almanac and from a UPI story. Is that all right?"

"You didn't tell us that. ALWAYS USE ATTRIBUTIONS!"

She nodded.

"Let me see," he said, scanning the story on the computer

monitor. "Tobacco is a fifty-one-billion-dollar-a-year industry?"

"Yes, sir."

"Americans smoked 486 *billion* cigarettes last year? You sure that's not 486 *million?*"

"Yes, sir."

"Ninety-two percent of all lung cancer cases result from cigarette smoking?"

"Yes, sir."

The editor kept reading down the list she had prepared. "Now here's one I can't believe. 'The cigarette industry continues to zealously dispute any scientific evidence that links smoking to health problems.' That's preposterous. What's your source on that? *MAD* magazine?"

"UPI quoted that Pratt guy from TobacCo, Inc. who testified earlier this year before the House Subcommittee on Health and the Environment. And here's another one I found in the *New York Times.* Just as absurd. 'Seconds after being told that users of snuff were fifty times more likely to develop oral cancer than abstainers, U.S. Tobacco's Joseph Taddeo said, "Oral tobacco has not been established as a cause of mouth cancer." Asked if he knew that cigarettes caused cancer, Lorillard's Andrew Tisch replied, "I do not believe that."'"

"Okay," Gavin said, grinning. "Here's what we're going to do." Gavin screamed for the front-page man. "FISHER! Get in here!" Robert Fisher appeared. "Fisher, what do we have for the first edition headline?"

Fisher held up a banner that read, "300+ CIGARETTE DEATHS."

"Good," he said. "Now, make me up a nice big box with bold black mourning borders. Lead with the Tisch quote about cigarettes causing cancer. 'I do not believe that.' Then Carney's cigarette facts beneath it—with the attributions. At the *Amherst American,* we use attributions."

18

Tuesday, October 5. Early, A.M.
Deer Mountain, Pennsylvania

Somehow, around dawn, Rhoads had stumbled outside, probably to turn off what was left of the headlights. He fell asleep near the car.

From the ground, looking straight up, Rhoads could see the whirling helicopter rotors accompanied by the loud whump, whump, whump of the engine. He slammed his eyes closed. *The bad dream continues.*

From his bird's-eye vantage, helicopter pilot Jack Fallscroft could see Rhoads sprawled atop twigs and sticks and leaves. His feet rested inside the car, which was parked haphazardly off the gravel driveway of the small cabin.

The TobacCo, Inc. Bell Ranger landed two hundred feet from Rhoads.

Fallscroft shut down the helicopter, jumped out, and crouched to make his way beyond the still-whirling blades. He reached Rhoads, stood over him, and looked down.

"Well, well, well. What have we here? This is certainly not a fishing trawler. No, I think I recognize it though. Oh, yes. Now I have it. Thomas Rhoads, also known as T.R. the Grate. That's G-R-A-T-E. Living up to his title. Hi, Tommy! Where's your boat?"

Rhoads didn't move, he only opened his eyes. "Sunk."

"Sunk, huh? I think you're projecting. You're sunk, T.R. A moron who just quit the easiest, highest-paying job he'll ever have."

"Just go away, Jack," Rhoads groaned, shielding his eyes from what little light there was at that hour. "No, wait. Don't just go away. Just go away mad."

"I would, except that Pratt summons you. Can't go back

empty-handed to the boss. Besides, I flew all night long looking for you," Fallscroft said, reaching for a pack of cigarettes in one of his aviator jacket's zippered pockets. "Hey, T.R., I thought that was all a bunch of barroom baloney, you bailing out of TobacCo, Inc." He withdrew two cigarettes, lit them both, and held one out for Rhoads.

Rhoads, still lying on his back, shielding his eyes from the sun coming down through the fall leaves, put a hand up and waved away Fallscroft's offer. "Trying to quit. Now," he insisted, "will you tell me what's up? Why are you here? And how'd you remember where this place was?"

"You have a short memory, my friend," Fallscroft said. "We've been fishing here half a dozen times." He had figured Rhoads would retreat to the cabin after burning bridges.

He and Rhoads had been best friends since they met when Rhoads first came to work at TobacCo, Inc. They both have O-negative blood, and Rhoads was first in line to donate when the word went out that Fallscroft needed blood for surgery. "How could I forget those two girls in the lake? And how cold it was? The tall one's could've put somebody's eye out." Fallscroft's tone turned serious. "Something bad's happened, T.R. They wouldn't tell me exactly what. Just said to dig you up, wring you out, and bring you back. Right away."

"Huh? What could have happened so bad that they'd send you to find me?" Rhoads worried that Fallscroft was part of one of those family intervention things he'd read about. Your family gets together, makes a decision about you behind your back. It's like a surprise party, except the surprise is you're going to a rehab.

"They want to talk to you about it in Asheville, T.R. It's big. It's FBI."

"This isn't about me drinking, is it?"

"No. That's another subject."

Rhoads believed him. "You know that boner Pratt was going to fire me for being drunk on my own time?"

"Says who?"

"Anna Maria."

Fallscroft shrugged. "Well, I don't know if 10 A.M. on a workday is actually considered your own time. Besides, didn't he fire you once already for calling his wife a pig . . ."

"You know that's not what I said. I said the only difference between drug pushers and nicotine pushers is that the drug dealers get better girls. Not one personal insult directed to Lucille Pratt. That pig."

"Well, anyway, he rehired you, didn't he? He's used to firing you for being a jerk. Don't take it so seriously."

"I didn't show up for work yesterday. Or today. I don't even know what day it *is*."

"I know," Fallscroft said and dropped his half-smoked cigarette onto the ground. He carefully stubbed it out with the toe of his boot.

"He'd nuke me this time for good. I'm not in the mood to go in and stand there and wait for it. So I split. The prick, he's got brass balls, sending you."

"You were embarrassed is all. I told him you wouldn't budge."

"You're right. I'm not budging. You wasted fuel."

"TobacCo, Inc. can afford it," Fallscroft said, his breath condensing in the woods, every breath punctuated by a little puff. "This'll be a nice transition for you, Tommy. You come back to handle this. Then if you still want to quit, you quit from a position of strength, not as a wino."

Why does everyone think I'm an alkie just because I love recreational drinking? Who'd I hurt? Any time I miss work, I make it up. And then some.

A thought interrupted his rationalizing. *Go back to work for a while, just until I get that fifty-eight grand back.*

He tried to ignore the idea. Going back was a gruesome prospect.

"Listen, Jack," Rhoads said, trying to sit up. "I just got here a few hours ago. I'm not coming back for some silly crisis probably already under control. That corporate pack-mentality just doesn't register now. You salute anybody since you left the navy?"

Rhoads turned and a patch of sun shining through high branches above hit him. Fallscroft saw the near-black circles that almost enveloped his friend's face.

"Man, did someone beat you up last night?" He moved a step closer to get a better look. "What the fuck happened to you?"

Rhoads turned his head away and felt his face. The only damage Leo and his friend had done was to his lip. The rest was Bacardi.

Rhoads spoke. "It's called alcohol poisoning."

"You ought to do something about that. You don't wear it too well."

"Well, a week up here and I may shake the hangover," Rhoads said. Then he remembered the auction. He sat up. "Shit! What time is it?"

"Sneaking up on seven."

"Seven!"

It was getting lighter. More of the sun cleared a mountain ridge to the east and brightened the woods.

Fallscroft nodded toward the Bell, saying, "Let's get a cup of coffee."

That sounds so good I can taste it. "Where?"

"WHQ. TobacCo World Headquarters. You'll be there by lunch."

Rhoads couldn't see himself groveling at his brother's feet, begging for forgiveness, Joyce shooing the kids out of the house in case there was a scene. What could he say to him? He'd just not show up. Ted would figure it out. Ted would always forgive him. After a while. A few moments of awkwardness the next time they'd meet, and then it'll be back to normal. *Fool of the Family.*

"Forget it. I plan to live out the rest of my life without ever seeing Fifth Floor action again." At TobacCo, Inc., "Fifth Floor" meant something important. The Executive Suite was on the Fifth Floor. If the *Fifth Floor* made a decision, the *Fifth Floor* made a decision. End of story.

"Tommy, how's a thou a day and expenses sound? Nick wants you back on this one."

Rhoads figured that might be coming. He did a quick count. *Stretch this out for eight weeks and I'd have my money back.*

"I'm tempted, but," Rhoads said, "*nope!* Though I could use the money." He realized his words put him into a dangerous realm. He wasn't a good liar, and Fallscroft could easily get what happened in Atlantic City out of him if he caught the scent.

Fallscroft leaned in toward Rhoads and said, "Then do it for me."

Rhoads scoffed. "How's it 'for you'?"

"This doesn't get back to Nick?"

"He's my best friend. I tell him everything."

"Well, I told him I didn't want to come get you, that because we're friends, you'd find it easier to balk, right? That he ought to send someone else."

Rhoads nodded. "Keep talking."

"That you were a friend and I wasn't the one to pressure you. Then he antes up. He says, 'You get him back here today, and I'll cash-bonus you twenty-five hundred in your next paycheck.'"

Fallscroft opened his eyes wide, laughed, and let out a shrill war whoop that shot bolts of pain through Rhoads's aching head. "Come on, Tommy. I need that bread. Maybe you don't need the dough, big fishing magnate, but I'm trying to build a retirement fund, dude."

Rhoads's low spirits sunk another three notches.

If only Fallscroft knew. Rhoads closed his eyes hoping that he'd open them and find that his friend had flown away.

Fallscroft began to worry that Rhoads wouldn't fly back. He poked at Rhoads with his boot.

"All right, T.R., you want to know what happened?" he said, bending down to force Rhoads up and into a sitting position in the car. The pilot then pulled a newspaper out of his deep jump-suit pocket, unfolded it to the headline, and tossed it in for Rhoads to see.

A giant headline screamed.

CYANIDE CIGARETTES SLAY 341 ACROSS U.S. 200 MORE SERIOUSLY INJURED

Doctors Say Many Are On Life Support; Prognosis "Poor"

Rhoads squinted but couldn't make out the words. "I give up. What's it say?"

Fallscroft shook his head. "Get up. *Get up!*"

They were airborne.

Rhoads leaned against the glass door of the chopper. He had wrapped his jacket around his head like a turban. His eyes were closed. Below, the tall green and green-blue pine, spruce, and fir trees reached skyward out of the Pocono Mountains.

"So how'd you really know where to find me?" he mumbled through the material.

Fallscroft worked the chopper controls and banked the craft toward a huge red-brick building.

"I called your brother. He was pretty pissed when you didn't turn up last night. Jerk. Anyway, when he said he wasn't sure where you were or if you'd show this morning, I remembered you went up to the lake at Deer Mountain after you and Thalia busted up. . . and there were those two girls we met."

Rhoads paused for a minute, thinking about something. "What does Pratt want with me? They going to blame me for the tamperings?"

"Pratt didn't explain it to me, but I'd guess he just wants you around for general skeleton-control. Big companies always have a ton of embarrassing shit to hide. And what with the FBI rummaging through everything, you can bet Pratt is going to want one of his buddies running interference. Plus, the thousand-a-day fee he's offering you won't hurt."

"Buddies. Right. *Fucking viper.*"

19

The Bell Ranger bumpily avoided a bank of low clouds and climbed to ninety-five hundred feet.

"I have to drop you off in Harrisburg. They'll pick you up in the Learjet and fly you home." Fallscroft hadn't mentioned that he had been instructed to fly Rhoads to a rendezvous in Harrisburg where the TobacCo corporate jet would be waiting. The chopper's maximum cruising speed was 128 miles an hour. The eight-passenger Learjet could make better than 500 miles an hour and dodge rotten weather. Fallscroft had been trained and was approved to fly the jet, too, but Pratt had him tied up working another project. Two other pilots would deliver Rhoads to Asheville.

Rhoads seemed not to hear Fallscroft. He gazed out the window at nothing. "I've lived out half my life and I'm lost," Rhoads said as he removed the turban. "I know I drink too much, and now I've lost . . ." He caught himself. Instead of saying "all of my money," he said, ". . . too much money. I had my dream right in my hands, and I dropped it. Jack," Rhoads's eyes were welling, "I have no fucking idea how I got here. How do things like this happen?"

"I got a brother-in-law in jail," Fallscroft said as if Rhoads wanted an answer. "Regular working Joe, except that one night after a few beers, just a few really, he creamed a kid on a bike. Nobody knows how things happen. You just know they're going to happen, and you play the percentages."

Rhoads hadn't heard a word. "How did I get so stupid? I don't know where I'm supposed to be, I just know I'm not there. I'm not the man I was born to be, sure as shit not the man my parents wanted me to be, not the man I want to be. I've got a *déjà vu* going that feels like this time I was camping in Cub Scouts. Appalachian Trail. Eleven years old. Got lost in the woods. All the shit they teach you about not getting lost, and I get lost."

"You must have found your way back."

"I didn't," he said. "One of the scoutmasters found me." Rhoads's mind bumbled around, banging into old memories that cropped up like furniture in the dark.

"Well, you got out," Fallscroft said. "That's what counts at the end of the day."

"That's how my life always goes. I get lost. Then, one day a million years later, I hear TobacCo, Inc. is hiring for their security staff. Had to get away from Philadelphia. Took a shot and I thought I got lucky and got the job."

"You didn't get lucky, you played the percentages. Can't win if you don't bet."

Rhoads cringed at the word "bet." "Anyway, it seemed like a way out of my old life, a change of view, a career instead of a job, respect, more money, a different class of women, even a little house maybe. Then I moved to Asheville. But who do I meet? Sterling characters? Good people? No. Human garbage like Pratt. And Trichina. Those people make me vomit."

"Even while you were humping her?"

"You know I came to Asheville eight years ago? I was seven weeks sober then. Those people drove me back to it. Don't believe that twelve-step horseshit that drinking's all up to the individual. People can drive you to it."

Rhoads fell silent and peered out the window. They were approaching the airport in Harrisburg. Fallscroft radioed the tower. When he had finished making notes in the flight log, he turned back to Rhoads. Rhoads looked exhausted, he seemed to have shrunk.

"The whole thing," Rhoads continued, ". . . the whole move to Asheville, it was a mistake. I admit it. So I quit. I'm glad I quit. It's not worth it, working for people like that."

Fallscroft was about to say that's the way it was in corporate America, everywhere, really. He didn't bother.

20

Pensacola, Florida

It had taken Muntor two hours to find Oscar's, a coffee shop off on the west side of town.

Good. The last one on the list, Muntor thought when he saw it from his car. He was spelling out a five-letter word and had already taken care of the other four.

He circled around and parked a block away.

Before getting out of his car, he reached back behind the driver's seat and felt for the McDonald's bag, ostensibly filled with litter. He used it as camouflage for the various packs of cigarettes he brought with him. He grabbed a pack and looked at it. Winstons. He slipped the pack into his jacket pocket, locked the car, and headed for Oscar's.

The short walk caused pain in his feet. He couldn't wait to get out of the size twelve shoes he had purchased and padded with terrycloth to make him appear inches taller than his five-seven.

Inside the busy little shop, a half-dozen customers sat at the counter. Most of the booths were occupied. Only one waitress and a cashier were visible. The cashier smiled at him.

"Pay telephone?" Muntor asked in a deep voice.

"Sorry. Too many kids in here raising hell. We had to take it out." She pointed through the plate-glass window onto the street. "One right outside, though."

Muntor spun to see, as if he really cared whether a telephone was there. "Okay. Thanks," he nodded. He looked back and over her shoulder at a rack behind her. "How about a pack of Winstons then?" He pointed with his eyes.

"That I can help you with," she said and took down a white-and-red pack and set it on the counter for him. He paid her, said thanks, and picked up the pack with his right hand. As Muntor turned to leave, he made sure his left shoulder was blocking her view of his right jacket pocket. He dropped the pack into his pocket and, using only his Band-Aid-covered thumb and index finger, pulled out the other pack, the treated one he had brought in from the car.

"On second thought," he said, turning fully toward her, "mind if I get a pack of Carltons instead?" He put the Winstons on the counter. "They cost the same?"

"They're all the same except the generics," she said, handing him a pack of Carltons and returning the Winstons to the rack.

Muntor nodded again, pocketed the Carltons, walked outside, and faked a fast call at the pay telephone.

21

FBI Headquarters
Tenth and Pennsylvania
Washington, D.C.

Brandon waited until the others left Franklin's office.

"May I close the door, Oak?"

Franklin looked up from the stack of messages on his desk and nodded.

"I always thought Rhoads's personnel file from TobacCo, Inc. looked a little too clean," Brandon said.

"So you thought you'd dig up something negative."

"I did some research. There had been a problem when he was a Philly cop. Fourteen years ago and explains a lot about Rhoads. Somehow, the police department kept the story fairly quiet. Rhoads pleaded out to manslaughter and left the force."

Brandon put a newspaper clipping on Franklin's desk.

DA: "An Unbearable Tragedy For Everyone"

CRIME OF PASSION: COP SHOOTS HIS OWN WIFE

By Sara Jakeheart of *The News* Staff

A brutal beating and rape wasn't all fate had in store for Elizabeth Rhoads, 33, the day her life ended last Saturday afternoon. In the midst of the attack in the bedroom of her Center City apartment, her husband, Thomas R. Rhoads, 28, a Philadelphia policeman, returned early from an overtime assignment. Then things turned from ugly to monstrous.

A copy of confidential court papers obtained by *The News* reveals what really happened that day, despite an intense effort by the Philadelphia Police Department and Rhoads's attorneys to maintain total silence on the case.

Rhoads had returned home at 2:40 P.M. on April 6 after a stakeout assignment had been terminated early. When he entered the two-bedroom apartment at 2041 Walnut Street, a report said, Rhoads heard sounds coming from the bedroom he shared with his wife of five years. Rhoads paused at the door and interpreted the sounds as those "commonly associated with two people engaged in consenting sexual intercourse." Then, according to the statement prepared by Rhoads's attorney Maxwell Edison, Rhoads remembered becoming enraged. The next thing Rhoads says he recalls is waking up at Graduate Hospital where authorities informed him he had shot and killed both his wife and her attacker.

The dead man, Walter DiMannieri, 44, was a repeat sex crime offender on parole from a previous rape conviction.

Lane Duvall, a spokeswoman for the Philadelphia Police department did not return a reporter's calls but later released an official statement repeating . . .

Franklin stared down at the clipping long after he finished reading. He looked up slowly. "That's what the Bacardi 151 is all about."

"I would imagine so. I talked to some cops I know in Philadelphia. Rhoads was an exemplary cop before that day, they told me. Supposedly a decent man, but it's hard to imagine that knowing Rhoads today. They said before the shooting, Rhoads spent every weekend as a Big Brother."

"Volunteer work for fatherless kids. I had a Big Brother when I was growing up in Columbus." Franklin pointed to the clipping. "What do you want to do with this?"

"Bury it in the back of the file?"

Franklin nodded and handed the clipping back to Brandon with an inward smile. He had never before seen any evidence that his subordinate had a heart.

22

Fully dressed and reclining on a saggy king-sized bed in the Beachwood of Pensacola Motel, Muntor chain-smoked Camels and watched CNN. The news anchor announced that the network was preparing a special report to air in half an hour on developments in the cigarette-tampering story.

Courtesy of one Martin Muntor, Muntor added to the announcer's statement. He'd tune in then. He had seen all he needed to see for now.

Yet he kept watching.

Then a thought, a joyous, uplifting thought came out of nowhere. *Even if I drop dead here and now, they'll soon learn who did it and why. I'VE ALREADY SUCCEEDED! The rest of what I'm going to do? It's just icing.*

Exhilarated, he flipped through the channels until he found another network working the story.

The images and sounds that came from the screen, the newspaper articles, the conversations he'd be overhearing in restaurants and in line at the supermarkets were the world's acknowledgment of his might. He tried to control the agitated thrill that rushed through him, excited as a kid running home from school on the last day of classes.

While he daydreamed, the television image switched from the head-and-shoulders shot of a news reader to a recorded shot of a swarm of reporters in a residential neighborhood.

"He's gone. He was the one who cared about me," cried an elderly woman grieving over a lost grandson. "Of all my grand-children, he was the only one who visited." A crowd of reporters and cameramen stood around her on a lawn.

"*Oh, my!*" Muntor said in falsetto, putting his hands up to his face in mockery. But that woman's grief brought no satisfaction to him. Instead, he felt shame. His argument, after all, was not with the victims, and it certainly wasn't with their friends and rel-atives. His battle was with the cigarette manufacturers. He shouldn't have mocked that poor woman.

He resolved not to be so juvenile again.

This was, after all, deadly serious business.

The network cut to a reporter posing in the dusky light on the steps of the Lexington, Kentucky, Federal Courthouse. He summarized what was known thus far in the investigation, but

Muntor was too distracted by his own thoughts to hear it. The reporter then introduced a Kentucky State Police commander. Muntor listened attentively. The commander said tersely, "We can't say very much until our laboratory analysis identifies the substance we recovered from the crime scene."

"*Oh, go ahead, tell us anyway!*" Muntor said to the screen. "*We're dying to know.*" He caught himself again.

The reporter promised more information as soon as it was available. Muntor's heart rate picked up when he heard that a press conference was scheduled in Washington later that day at 3:00 P.M.

Then the report ended, and the network cut to commercials. Muntor's face fell.

He clicked off the television and turned one of the shabby armchairs toward the picture window. Beyond the glass, his room afforded a view of Pensacola Bay, obscured in part by a Texaco station and its revolving sign. He watched the sun reflect a prism of color on the water. A humid breeze blew in from the Gulf of Mexico and jangled the wind chimes someone, probably the Beachwood's resident manager, had installed not far from Muntor's room. He was tired. The chimes annoyed him.

He dozed off for a moment, but his slouching position caused his chest to compress, and that made it nearly impossible to breathe. He straightened up, his mind cleared. The events of the preceding twenty-four hours marched through his mind like troops returning on a soggy road.

Muntor had taken a red-eye just after midnight from Philadelphia to Mobile. There he rented a car and drove the hour to Pensacola. The fake ID he used had worked perfectly, and paying cash for the airline ticket, car rental, food, and fuel wouldn't leave much of a trail.

The flying and driving, and finally the running around once he arrived in Pensacola, exhausted him. He had spent the hours after daybreak walking in and out of convenience stores and restaurants, dive bars, and supermarkets. The "W" and "Y," contrary to what his research led him to expect, were easy enough to find. He knew from the Free Library of Philadelphia's telephone book collection that there'd be plenty of "H"s and "D"s. The stumper, at least for most of the morning, had turned out to be the "O." When he finally met with success at Oscar's, he knew his salutation would soon be heard around the world.

Muntor was enjoying the mental travelogue and regretted not taping some of it for the documentary. Then yammering from some talk show that had replaced the news on television intruded on his thoughts. He got up, found the remote, and tapped a key a few times to lower the volume. He dropped onto the bed, rolled onto his side, and reached down underneath. His hand found the McDonald's bag containing his cigarettes and other supplies. He patted it like he'd pet a cat. Reassured, he rolled over again onto his back.

Fatigue tugged at him like an undercurrent, but he fought sleep. He wanted to be awake when the CNN report came on at eleven. He closed his eyes hoping he'd just rest a bit, but even rest wasn't available. Muntor could not stop thinking about what had happened at the office a few weeks earlier.

It had been a Tuesday, he remembered. Tuesday was payday, and the New York brass of the American News Syndicate, Muntor's employer then, decided to close its Philadelphia operation. Laying off Muntor, who had served as bureau chief, and the rest of the five-person staff, had finally happened. Rumors had been circulating for months. Creditors pressured the company to close six of its thirty-six U.S. offices. New York assigned Philadelphia's responsibilities to the Harrisburg bureau.

The bad news came by telephone from the Information Services vice-president.

"Marty, I'm calling you unofficially," Cal Timonowski said. "I have some bad news. Although we hate like hell to do it, we have to close the Philadelphia bureau. You'll be getting formal notice sometime next week. We know you've done one hell of a job, but we're in big trouble. Just this morning the *Denver Post* nonrenewed us. I'm truly sorry, Marty."

Muntor listened and made no other comment than a deep rasping cough. He could picture runty Timonowski sitting in his office on Forty-seventh Street with a list of calls that he needed to make before he could go home. And this call, the one that savaged the only real accomplishment of Muntor's life, rising to the post of bureau chief, was just one minor item on that list, sandwiched, perhaps, between a detail the vice-president needed to address with the temporary employment agency and stopping to get French bread from the gourmet deli.

"You let the others know we'll be notifying them, too," Timonowski told him. Muntor remained silent. "You okay, Marty?"

Muntor sighed inaudibly. *At fifty-six they do this to me? Buggerers.* He clenched his teeth. A tiny ripple of pain radiated along his jaw line and up into his temples. He put his tongue between his teeth to force himself to relax the muscles in his face.

Timonowski kept talking. Muntor barely heard him. Muntor had been odd man out forever.

The best that Timonowski could offer was a take-it-or-leave-it early retirement package. In his case, with only seven years on the job, the deal amounted to monthly income of about $600 until age sixty-five. Then good luck and Social Security.

"Sure. Sure, Mr. T.," Muntor said, coughing again. "Whatever you say." Muntor had heard a rumor that ANS was in default of its health insurance premiums and that everyone was walking around without coverage. With what Timonowski was telling him now, maybe there was something to the gossip.

No longer obliged to be civilly subordinate, Muntor hung up. He cleared his throat and stared off into space.

"What's wrong?" the secretary asked.

"Nothing. Just some horseshit from Cal. You know what a pain in my ass that guy can be."

The secretary nodded. "Okay, Marty. I'm going home." Now Muntor nodded. After the door closed behind her, he glanced at his watch. It had been 4:45. He shrugged. Her hours were no longer his concern.

Muntor got up and walked to the window that overlooked Locust Street. He liked watching the tux- and gown-clad figures carry instrument cases in and out of the musician's entrance at the Academy of Music. He shoved the window open with a grunt. A small musical wheeze issued from his chest.

He took a pack of cigarettes from his pants pocket and lighted one, drawing deeply and then, leaning forward, blew a thick white cloud out into the gritty city air.

Muntor leaned out of the window thinking. *Two weeks notice! I'll see them in hell.* Then he had an idea. He spit his cigarette out and slammed the window down.

"Let me borrow your office keys, Danny boy," he said to the night reporter who had just arrived and was already busy transmitting a story from his terminal.

"Take 'em," Danny said, tossing a clattering bunch of keys to Muntor.

"Okay." Muntor wriggled the two office keys loose. He tossed Danny's keys back. Danny put them down on the desk without examination.

Muntor pocketed the keys and then sat down at his desk. A fury of ideas ran through his mind. He thought about how easily it would be to disrupt American News' communications network. He knew what he would do.

At his terminal, he tapped the keys required to begin a priority transmission, usually reserved for catastrophes with high fatalities, major developments in government or politics, or the sudden death of someone famous. When the system requested his user ID, he simply typed in the code indicating "Supervising national news editor, New York headquarters." Then he tapped a few simple commands and sent an "URGENT! STAND BY FOR FLASH" message to 100 ANS bureaus, newspapers, and radio and television stations worldwide.

Muntor had frozen the entire network, and it would stay

frozen until he transmitted his FLASH, which he did not intend to do. He toyed with the idea of announcing that the American News Syndicate had permanently halted operations and would be billing all customers through the end of the year even though the news and feature reports would cease immediately. He laughed at the idea but already didn't give a damn. Instead, he turned off his terminal and stretched in his chair and yawned loudly.

Stock market reports, weather, the Washington summary, sports, everything ceased moving over the wire, including the transmission of Danny's story. It would take the headquarters technicians half the night to trace the problem to Muntor's terminal in Philadelphia.

I wonder who'll nonrenew tomorrow! Muntor thought.

"Look at this shit," Danny said, turning to Muntor for sympathy. Danny extended an open hand at his screen. "A flash." The reporter had no way of knowing Muntor had crashed the system. "Bet you it's an Amtrak derailment."

"Who cares?" Muntor said. "As long as it didn't happen near here."

Muntor slid open a desk drawer and removed the only existing set of the office's critical computer backup disks. He put them into his jacket pocket. He opened another drawer and found the spare set of office keys.

"All right, partner," he said, as he did each night when he left, signaling that the bureau was now in Danny's hands. Danny, engrossed in trying to find a way to file his story, gave Muntor half a wave without looking up.

Muntor walked out of the office and pressed for the elevator, one of the world's slowest. He dropped all three sets of keys into a trash chute built into the space between the two elevator shafts. Straight into the dumpster. He pressed his ear against the chute to listen for the impact but heard only the laboring of the elevator cables.

The elevator arrived empty, and Muntor stepped on.

There goes Mr. T's plan for a smooth closing of the bureau, he smiled to himself as the cage descended. He could picture a disheveled Timonowski rushing down to Philadelphia the next day. "What happened here yesterday? Where the hell is Muntor?" he'd say. "No answer at home? Didn't any of you geniuses think to go there to see if he dropped dead or anything?" Muntor laughed out loud when he pictured little Timonowski fuming, sitting with his briefcase on his lap, reading the newspaper on the Metroliner. *Let him clean up his own mess,* Muntor thought. *Let him tell everyone about the health insurance. Let him tell everyone that they're looking for jobs.*

Muntor went straight home.

He had no idea where he would get a job or what he would do. He did a quick calculation. He owned the row house. It was worth $40,000 or $50,000, then again, actually *selling* it was a different matter. And, thanks to his lifelong, grandfather-instilled habit of putting a few bucks from every paycheck into one mutual fund or another, he had almost another $40,000. Getting a job wasn't something he had to worry about right away. Realizing that, he relaxed.

Before he went to bed, he made a telephone call. He reached an acquaintance who supposedly knew about layoffs and health insurance and employee's rights. The man told him that it wasn't possible for ANS to simply terminate his health insurance with only thirty days' notice. The COBRA rules protected employees. But, the man warned, if Muntor had been procrastinating seeing a doctor, even for something minor, he had better get an appointment pronto.

"Get it checked out and onto the books," the man said. "Then, no matter what happens, your current insurance company'll have to take care of it."

Muntor had been coughing with increasing frequency, and something ached in his chest. Why not run up a bit of a tab while he still could? Stick it to American News Syndicate while he still could.

The next day he made an appointment on an emergency basis and subjected himself to an examination, a battery of tests, and X-rays.

Pensacola rushed back in on Muntor like a wave crashing over his shoulders.

He had nodded off thinking about his unceremonious termination. He opened his eyes at the sound of the theme music that heralded the CNN Special Live Report.

He reached for the remote and turned up the volume.

23

En route to Asheville

At the Harrisburg airport, Fallscroft and Rhoads shook hands and separated.

In the Learjet, waiting to take off, Rhoads sat forward in the seat closest to the pilots. He was the only passenger. Rhoads guessed the pilots weren't told much about their mission, just that something big was going on and that Rhoads figured in somehow. Rhoads thought that made him a bigger man in their eyes.

"Wanna hear what my fucking brother did?" Rhoads asked

them. He thought they'd be interested in any kind of small talk from a guy so important that the CEO sent the Learjet for him. He had met both pilots before. They weren't Pratt's first-string team. They got the dog jobs. Then Rhoads realized that must have made *him* a dog job.

"As soon as we're finished with the preflight checklist, you can tell us all about it," the copilot said.

Ten minutes later, they were in the air.

"About my brother?"

"Sure," the copilot said. "Now what did he do?"

"The ass lives in Jersey near Sea Isle City. Got a beautiful wife, two great brats, and he works as regional marketing manager for Texaco. All our lives we've been talking about quitting the rat race—even if you win, you're still a rat, right?—and buying a charter-fishing boat business. He says we need a hundred and twenty grand to get it off the ground."

"Hang on, T.R." The pilot and copilot consulted each other about a starboard aileron light that kept blinking. Rhoads's head still hurt, and he didn't bother paying attention to what they were talking about. Whatever it was, it was their problem. A moment later, they were back. "Go ahead with your brother."

Dress rehearsal, Rhoads thought. "To make a long story short, he gets tanked and blows his life savings—$60,000—in Atlantic City in a matter of hours." The pilots looked at each other and whistled in unison.

There was more flight-related chatter between the pilot and copilot.

A minute later, the pilot turned back to Rhoads. "Sixty gees, just like that! What about stopping the checks? Can't he claim they got him drunk?"

"Nah. Dummy used blank money orders from his bank or something. He had them that way so when he bought the boat at the auction, he could pay and take possession right away. Dumb fuck. Signed the dough over to the casino. Plus, even though he's dumb, he's stand up. He wouldn't do something like weaseling out. He knows he lost it fair and square."

"For $60,000?" the pilot said. "I'd weasel Dixie."

"Not if they got him drunk, it wasn't fair and square," the copilot said.

Rhoads shrugged.

"Maybe I'll lay across the bench and try to get some sleep. How much time left before Asheville?"

"You have about an hour," the pilot said, checking his watch.

"Okay," Rhoads said and unbuckled his seat belt. "Shout back and wake me before we get there."

They gained on Asheville while Rhoads slept.

Fifty minutes later, the huge red-brick-and-glass edifice that was TobacCo, Inc.'s world headquarters squatted like an Aztec pyramid on a grassy hill in front of the Great Smoky Mountains. A minute before touchdown, they woke Rhoads and told him to buckle up. The Learjet landed on Pratt's private mile-long strip.

As the airplane taxied in toward the ground crew, the sun blinded Rhoads. He squinted and looked out at TobacCo, Inc. He wasn't quite able to believe that only a day after quitting, he was back already.

He rubbed his face with his palms. He shouted forward to the pilots. "My brother said it's not that he's lost so much money that bothers him, it's that he has to live with remembering he lost so much."

Neither of the pilots replied, or if they did, not loudly enough for Rhoads to hear. "With me," Rhoads added, "it'd be the money. Screw the memory."

A minute later, Rhoads heard the banging of the ground crew as they clamped the exit ladder in place. The copilot got out of his seat and unlatched the door. It swung open.

Rhoads stood up, rumpled. "Thanks you guys."

"Thank *you*, T.R.," the pilot said, turning to him over his shoulder. "And do yourself a favor. Try to keep away from those casinos. They're murder."

Both the pilot and copilot laughed heartily and a lot louder than Rhoads thought they should. After all, as far as they knew, he was the man with the solution to a huge crisis.

Rhoads exited and took the service elevator down to the Fitness Center in the basement of WHQ. He needed a shower. Because he had often worked undercover, he maintained a wardrobe of getups in three lockers he had commandeered.

Twenty-five minutes later, when he stepped onto the elevator in the basement en route to the Fifth Floor, Rhoads was dressed in a suit, but his tie was askew and his face bore two fresh razor nicks.

24

Asheville

The Fifth Floor lobby reeked of arrogance and power.

A full-sized marble replica of Blind Justice, the scales of which contained a display of TobacCo, Inc.'s various cigarette brands, towered in the lobby, greeting visitors. Forty feet of polished marble floor led to the reception desk. Two uniformed armed guards were stationed at either side, their posts manned twenty-four hours a day.

As Rhoads exited the elevator, three men brushed past him and entered. Rhoads then pushed through the huge plate-glass doors that led, on one side, to the board of directors conference room, and on the other to an expanse of computer work stations.

In the work station area were rows of file cabinets and a sign that read "Corporate Documentation Division." From an office beyond the computer work stations, Mary Dallaness entered, striding briskly, her wavy brunette hair cut short and bouncing as she approached. She moved with the quick grace of a dancer. Rhoads hailed her, and she waved back. They had never had any official business between them but knew each other through her brother-in-law and years of bumping into each other at WHQ. Once Mary and Anthony Dallaness had invited Rhoads and a date over for Fourth of July. It had rained like hell that day, he remembered.

"T.R.!" she said, speaking softly. She looked away. She thought he'd know she found him desirable if their eyes met. "You quit. Without saying good-bye."

Rhoads crossed the terminal area and greeted her with an affectionate one-armed hug. *If only she weren't married*, he fanta-sized. He didn't want to pursue that line of thinking. Her husband was dying.

"Okay. Good-bye," he said. And in a whisper added, "Spur of the moment thing, Mary D. And, I'm gone for one day, and you see what kind of a mess you all get into without me."

She didn't smile. "It's nothing to joke about. We just heard six more of the injured died from complications. TobacCo is a zoo, especially here in Documentation. I can't figure it out. Some lunatic starts killing people, and all of a sudden, everybody needs irrelevant documents that are years old."

Rhoads squinted. The cop in him reacted to something that didn't add up. "Archived documents? What kind?"

"What do you think? Level Three naturally. The kind nobody can authorize but me. At three o'clock in the morning, at eleven at night. Any old time. And there's a certain red-headed party who's about one irritating telephone call away from . . ." Dallaness stopped herself.

"Really? Who might that be?"

25

In Valzmann's room in the World Headquarters subbasement, an enormous array of color video monitors, green and amber lights, switches, reel-to-reel tape recorders, telephones, and other devices squatted on shelves and lined walls.

Valzmann, who wore a tiny ivory stud earring in his right lobe, stared without expression at Video Monitor #65. Without taking his eyes off the screen, he reached out and slid a glide switch forward, causing a camouflaged ceiling camera on the Fifth Floor to zoom in on Rhoads and Dallaness in conversation. He tapped a key that activated a directional microphone as he pulled a headset over his ears.

The sound quality was tinny but audible. He clearly heard Dallaness's response to Rhoads's question.

"Your ex-boss Trichina," she said.

"Don't worry about her," Rhoads could be heard saying. His back was to the camera. "She always likes to get her hands in everything. She's probably just trying to find an excuse to run to Pratt with some kind of brilliant idea. She may actually think she'll crack the case by reviewing the list of people who've been reprimanded for parking in the Executive Only lot."

26

Rhoads grinned good-bye to Dallaness and walked back, past the reception desk to the Executive Suite entrance. The two guards, formerly his subordinates, nodded.

The carpeting gave way to brilliant inlaid hardwood floors. Rhoads marched down the long hallway, his heels clicking as he passed portraits of past TobacCo, Inc. CEOs and deceased members of the board. He turned a corner and saw Pratt's executive secretary, Genevieve DesCourt. Her face lighted up as she rose to greet him.

"I thought you'd gotten safely away," she said quietly.

"I did, too, until some jackass highjacked me with a helicopter this morning. At your instructions, by the way." He paused and looked around. "Are they in Nick's office? Who's in there?"

"No. They're in the boardroom." She indicated the door on the other side of her. A burly man, presumably an FBI agent, stood in front of the door looking straight ahead. "Six or seven FBI men, including two high-level officials, and Anna Maria."

"And Anna Maria." Rhoads laughed.

"It's bad. You better get in there. I'll buzz you in. Mr. Pratt's been asking me every five minutes if I'd seen you." The secretary looked him over. "And, T.R., consistent with my long-held philosophy of never saying anything if I don't have something good to say? Your hair's still wet, and you look like absolute hell."

"Why thank you!" he said brightly. "Because that means I look a thousand times better than I feel."

As Rhoads moved toward the closed boardroom door, the FBI agent moved to block him. Rhoads attempted to squeeze by but was again blocked.

From inside the boardroom, Pratt, who had probably come to ask Genevieve again if she'd heard from Rhoads, opened the door and shouldered the agent aside.

"Rhoads," Pratt said. He ushered him in as if he were a VIP. The room was half the size of a football field and dominated by a giant walnut conference table with thirty matching chairs. Clustered around one section of the table were Trichina and two FBI men. From a wall paneled in burled cherry, another two FBI agents removed a gold bas-relief sculpture of a tobacco leaf. In its place, they tacked up a huge map of the United States upon which tampering death locations had been marked with bright red flags. Also on the wall was a giant enlargement of the counterfeit consumer-opinion survey letter the killer sent with the poisoned cigarettes.

"Good of you to join us, Thomas," Trichina said coolly. Rhoads nodded.

Pratt turned to the FBI agents. "I'd like to introduce our chief of security, Thomas Rhoads. He's broken off his vacation to be with us. The FBI recalls, I'm certain, the Harry Hill case two years ago. It was thanks to Thomas here, with an able assist from the FBI, that we shut down Hill, a small-minded man who had been siphoning a million and a half dollars a month of TobacCo, Inc. products to the Chicago mob. I believe he's currently a guest of the government at Elder Creek Federal Correctional."

"What I know of the Hill case," Brandon said, "is that the FBI worked long and hard baking a pie, and Mr. Rhoads butted in at the last minute and pulled it out of the oven. Then everyone applauded."

Pratt smirked. "And, Thomas, this is Deputy Director Oakley Franklin from FBI headquarters in Washington."

"Ah, ha. Now I know why I'd forgotten all about the Hill case," Franklin said half joking. "*The* Mr. Rhoads. You were willing to eat, sleep, and breathe in a dumpster for three days, Rhoads, and you deserved the collar. I only wish I'd had the same idea. I could have *ordered* someone to do that and taken the credit myself."

Franklin laughed deeply and shook Rhoads's hand.

"Have a seat, Thomas," Pratt continued. "We were just discussing a former employee. Loren Benedict, that scientist in marketing development out in Denver. He was a no-show one day. We never heard from, or about, him again. For some reason, the FBI has put him on their most-wanted-to-interview list. For one thing, they've discovered evidence that he received psychiatric treatment during the period that he was in our employ. It seems an improbable connection to me, but then I'm not an FBI agent."

Over Pratt's shoulder loomed the enlargement of the counterfeit letter. Rhoads glanced at it but did not understand why it was there.

Franklin spoke to Rhoads. "Perhaps you can help us. Information about Mr. Benedict seems to be in short supply. The fact is, there's no record of him anywhere after he left TobacCo, Inc. Does this ring any bells with you?"

"I remember the job. There was nothing suspicious about Benedict except the way he left. Suddenly and without notice. Which doesn't strike me as a crime. It happens."

"Yes. It does happen," Trichina said. "Sometimes people just drop out." She shot a quick glance at Rhoads. "Don't they?"

Franklin picked up the static between them and filed it away for further consideration. "I'm sure you're right," Franklin said. "But here's our problem. Employee files in your H.R. department list him as being the lead in a research project you all called 'Midas.' That's all there is in the file. No C.V., no address, no performance appraisals. Nothing. And there's no explanation of what Midas is."

Pratt knew he could tell Franklin that the Midas files were confidential, proprietary company property and none of his business. But he also knew not to do that.

"I've told you," Pratt said. "Midas never went anywhere. Midas has nothing to do with this tampering problem. It was some pie-in-the-sky new product effort. These marketing guys have a thing about secrecy. Whatever it was, it was a bust, believe me, or I'd remember it. We withdrew funding. That's probably why

Benedict quit. The documentation division manager is looking for the Midas files now. Last year we had a computer blowout. That cost us a lot of archived data. We still have the hard copies, but they're not at our fingertips. You'll get them as soon as I do."

Brandon turned to Rhoads. "Do you have any recollection of the Midas project?"

Pratt interrupted. "As I told you . . ." Rhoads got the signal, although he did not understand why Pratt didn't want to be candid with the FBI about something that clearly did not matter.

Genevieve DesCourt entered the room and placed a sheet of paper on Pratt's desk. Pratt casually walked over, glimpsed at the note, frowned, and turned the sheet face down. Genevieve had written,

TobacCo, Inc. Common
Last, $210^3/4$, - $3^1/4$, Volume 1,340,000.
Still most active stock

Franklin did not appreciate losing the CEO's attention even for a moment. "I'm sure," he said, "Special Agent Brandon is just looking for someone else's recollection, Mr. Pratt. You'd be surprised how many people can look at the same thing and still come away with wildly different observations."

Rhoads turned to Brandon. "Listen, I didn't have any contact with Benedict personally. At one point, after he split, we wanted to check his office. I went to Denver, bundled up his files, and shipped them to documentation for safekeeping. If anything had been missing, I'm sure I would have been notified to take follow-up action. But I never got any such call. That was the first and last of Midas, and Benedict, as far as I'm concerned."

"Then," Franklin said, "I guess we work on other ideas until your documentation people find the Midas files. Unless, Mr. Pratt, there's somebody here in Asheville or back in Denver who was involved with Midas."

Pratt masked a sour expression. "I won't know who was assigned until our archivists come up with the files. I assure you, I'll have information very shortly."

27

A cellular telephone chirped in Brandon's pocket. All turned to watch his reaction. He listened, his eyes opened wider. To Rhoads, it looked like bad news.

Brandon mumbled something into the telephone, hung up, and pulled Franklin aside.

He spoke so the others could not hear. "Chief, two things just came in to FBIHQ. One's bad news. Five new deaths reported, and not FedEx envelopes—cigarettes sold over-the-counter retail. All in Pensacola, Florida. The field team says it looks like our man, not a copycat. The other thing may be good news. A man claiming to be 'Cyanide Sam' called minutes ago. The call came from Pensacola. Caller says he wants to talk to. . ." and Brandon lowered his voice to a whisper, ". . . *Rhoads*. Says he's going to call HQ again at two o'clock."

Franklin nodded expressionlessly. He said something to Brandon who in turn issued instructions to the other FBI agents in the room. Then Brandon left.

Franklin addressed the TobacCo, Inc. officials. "I need to get going. There's a development I can't elaborate on. If you don't mind, I'll borrow Mr. Rhoads here so we can continue our interview in the air. He may know of some characters we should be talking to. And Mr. Pratt, Ms. Trichina, I'll trust you will call me as soon as you find any information about Mr. Benedict and the Midas project."

Pratt raised his eyebrows. "A development? TobacCo, Inc. related?"

Franklin did not reply.

Pratt said, "Of course. Of course. I understand. And, yes, take Rhoads if you think he'll be helpful. But might I have a word with Mr. Rhoads before you go?"

Franklin had Rhoads by the elbow and was already half a room away from Pratt. Rhoads, puzzled, looked back at Pratt and gave a small shrug.

Franklin turned back, too, still moving. "I'm sorry, Mr. Pratt. We're in quite a hurry."

"Yes," Pratt said. "I understand. Thomas?" He raised his voice to be heard by the departing men. "Give me a call when you get a moment."

Outside, the helicopter lifted off.

Inside the boardroom, only Pratt and Trichina remained. They stood in a hurried conference.

"How can you trust him?" Trichina asked. "He doesn't know what you don't want him to say."

"He doesn't need any *instructions*. He doesn't *know* anything. There's *nothing* to know. Now excuse me, I have calls to make." Pratt turned abruptly and reached for his telephone. Then he looked up. She was still there. *Damn, she was gorgeous.* Inside his mouth, his tongue jutted forward, an antecedent to licking his lips. He stopped himself, and a thin smile formed on his face.

"See you tonight," he said. It wasn't a question.

She turned abruptly and left. Once she had cleared the threshold of his office door, Pratt pressed a button on his desk and the heavy wooden doors swung closed in unison. Pratt, still standing, unlocked his desk drawer, picked up the telephone there, and pressed an autodial key.

28

Associated Press
Washington, D.C. Bureau

ASSOCIATED PRESS
ALL EDITORS
TUESDAY, OCTOBER 5, 12:13 P.M. EST.
WASHINGTON, D.C.
SLUG: **AMERICAN CANCER SOCIETY SPECIAL EVENT**

ART AVAILABLE: 1 COLOR PIX.
1: Elementary school students in Deerfield Massachusetts snuff out giant papier-mache cigarette in giant ashtray on school playground there.

AMERICAN CANCER SOCIETY RIDES TAMPERING WAVE

By Allan Jason

Associated Press Staff Reporter

Tuesday, October 5—Washington, D.C. The American Cancer Society today announced the launch of its national "There's Never Been A Better Time To Quit" antismoking campaign.

Spokeswoman Elaine Neyhorn said that "although the ACS absolutely condemns the activities of the cigarette terrorist, the organization intends to take advantage of whatever opportunities present themselves to trumpet the message that cigarettes kill and quitting now greatly reduces the risk of smoking-related cancer, heart disease and other serious health problems."

The Association of Tobacco Marketers in New York also released a statement that said "the American Cancer Society's irresponsible timing in the launch of their new campaign can have only one effect on the madman—it will encourage him to continue his rampage of death."

In thousands of public schools, private businesses, and government organizations all over the United States, people are rallying around the antismoking group's latest attempt at . . .

29

A low-tone hummed from the base of a telephone next to Valzmann as he sat in his subbasement office. His assistant looked up.

"Take a walk," Valzmann told the man. The man left the room immediately, and Valzmann answered.

"Yes, sir?"

"Were you watching the meeting?" Pratt asked.

"The whole thing."

"I don't like this. This could be Benedict-related."

"The tampering? Benedict is slightly dead, sir."

"I know that. What if we missed someone, what if one of the other Midas researchers has gone soft?"

"Not likely. Convincing them to be cool was some of my finest work. The video of what I did to Benedict was highly motivational."

"That even made me sick, that thing you did to his mouth with the tire jack."

"Well, you said to drive home the point that he had a big mouth."

Pratt paused, recalling the grotesque image, then changed the subject. "If everything is so under control, Valzmann, then why do I have a nagging feeling that Benedict's ghost is going to come back and bite me in the ass but good."

"No it won't, sir," Valzmann said.

"You're damned right it won't. Because your life is now dedicated anew to see that it doesn't. Unless you'd like to star in one of your own motivational videos."

"Very funny, sir."

"Put Plan B into place, set it up. Go back to the Poconos."

"Pin Benedict's disappearance on Rhoads."

"Right. Just put all the pieces into position. Don't do anything beyond that yet. Not until we absolutely *need to.*"

"What about this complication, him and Dallaness? Their friendship's on the verge of getting more intimate."

"Says who?"

"They're behaving like shy high-school kids. Twice, she dialed his number from home but hung up before he answered. And once he did the same. We've got all the dial-outs recorded. It's only a matter of time."

Pratt shook his head. "That could be a dangerous combination. She's all woman under that straight demeanor, and her husband is down for the count. I doubt he's providing much satisfaction."

"I thought of that. That's why I want to wait and see how things develop. We might have two problems that need taking care of." Then Pratt grinned. "That reminds me of a story . . ."

Oh, Lord, here comes another terrible joke. Valzmann braced himself.

". . . it seems there's this fellow who's convinced his wife's cheating on him. He hires a hit man, excuse the expression, Valzmann, and tells him, 'Look I want you to shoot my wife in the head and her boyfriend in the dick.'"

Valzmann laughed at the picture of that.

"So the husband goes with the hit man to watch the assassination. The hit man has a rifle with a scope, he's aiming and aiming, but not firing. The husband says, 'Come on, shoot already.' The hit man says, 'Hang on. In a minute I'm going to be able to hit both targets with one shot.'"

30

Anna Maria Trichina sat at her desk, mired in deep thought, her face set in stony silence.

In front of her was a yellow legal pad upon which she had been doodling. In large block letters, she had written B-E-N-E-D-I-C-T. She studied the pad. In crossword-puzzle fashion, she added to it the word M-I-D-A-S so that both words used the same "D." She stared at the page. To the "T" in Benedict, she added the letters P-R-A-T. Then, using the first "T" in Pratt she added the letter "R."

Trichina's face was hard. Her upper lip curled in a tiny snarl. She sought a place for herself. Amid the chaos descending upon TobacCo, Inc., she reminded herself, there would be pockets of opportunity, places to hide, chances to profit.

She had an idea, and at the same moment, using the "M" in Midas, she spelled out M-E! The tip of the pencil broke on the dot of the exclamation point.

Trichina leaned back in chair, her jaw set. She nodded once to herself, ripped the top sheet off the legal pad, crumpled it up, and put it in her purse which slammed shut with an angry snap.

After taking several deep breaths to calm herself down, she looked at her DayTimer. That night, at six, she was scheduled to tutor Sofia Vasquez, a seventeen-year-old with two babies, one more on the way, and no husband. The girl had taken the initiative to apply to the Asheville Center for Literacy, and Trichina liked her for that. She couldn't read the basic instructions on baby formula cans. Trichina took on the case and met with the girl once a week and tried to give her good counsel over the telephone whenever she could.

Trichina dialed Sofia's telephone number and got an answering machine.

"It's me, Sofia. Anna Maria. Got an emergency at work. We have to reschedule for tomorrow night instead of tonight. Sorry."

And she hung up.

She just wasn't in the mood to be patient.

31

From Asheville, en route to FBI Headquarters, Washington, D.C.

The pilot and Brandon sat up front, the Blue Ridge Mountains flashed by below. Franklin and Rhoads were strapped in two rear seats. Franklin glanced at Rhoads, who was sweating.

Franklin motioned to Brandon. "Hand me my briefcase."

Brandon handed it over. The deputy director opened it and found a packet of Pepto-Bismol tablets. He offered them to Rhoads.

"Go ahead. Not too many of us, except maybe Father Brandon here, are strangers to hangovers."

Rhoads forced a smile of thanks. He popped three tablets out of the foil and handed the pack back to Franklin.

He chewed them loudly. "I'd already gotten a pretty good start on my vacation."

"I know how that is." Franklin pretended to look out the

window at the landscape. "This thing's a real bitch, isn't it? Guy killing all those people. Makes me wonder."

"Doesn't make me wonder," Rhoads said, swallowing hard, getting the last pieces of the tablets down. "People are out of their fucking minds."

"Something I wonder about in particular though . . ."

"It's funny," Rhoads said, interrupting and looking around the interior of the helicopter like a kid. "Pratt's chopper is bigger, better, faster and has more range than yours. Costs two or three times as much. Now he has that, but he's not exactly running around trying to catch psycho serial killers and save lives. He uses his to pursue dollars."

Franklin went on. ". . . is why one of the world's preeminent CEOs, a guy who *Forbes* magazine says is worth a quarter *billion* dollars, would be so determined, I mean I'm talking about a smart guy who's facing the greatest crisis of his career—you with me on this, Rhoads?—would bend over backwards to press into service a total fuckup. Like you."

Rhoads recoiled as if slapped.

Franklin wasn't finished. "Can you explain that for me? I mean I can only think of about eighty thousand more qualified guys than you that Pratt can have with the snap of his fingers."

"First the Pepto-Bismol, then the anvil on the head. You're a regular good-cop bad-cop rolled into one, aren't you?" Rhoads said.

"You didn't answer me, Rhoads. Why you? Of all creatures? What's the matter? Pratt got your tongue? Oh, well, then maybe you can help me with this one. This same smart guy, Pratt, he suddenly develops a wicked case of total amnesia, about one of his company's own projects, at the very moment the FBI starts asking questions about it. Pratt strikes me as the kind of guy who never forgets anything. Unless he has a reason to."

Rhoads, his feelings hurt, raised his chin an inch and did not reply. *Some kind of setup*, he thought. *Didn't see it coming.*

Franklin was pleased he was able to shake up Rhoads. *His*

emotions surface easily, Franklin thought. *Those are the ones to go for first. That's what the Japanese taught their military interrogators. Find the emotional ones.*

Rhoads collected himself and then turned to Franklin. "Listen, Pratt already explained it to you. I heard it same as you, and it made sense to me. TobacCo, Inc. runs lots of projects, hundreds of 'em, probably *thousands.* This Midas thing, I guess, wasn't a very big one. Didn't work out, they cut off the dough, it just went away. Pratt's famous for cutting funding. His motto is 'lose early.'"

Franklin ignored Rhoads and addressed Brandon. "Funny, Ben, isn't it? Everybody keeps telling me how big Midas wasn't. A project roster of twelve scientists. Five of whom are Ph.Ds. And an annual budget of $4.1 million. Duh. To a civil servant like me that actually sounds kind of big."

Rhoads's head hurt. "Look, Schmanklin. I do *not* know anything about it. I never heard of the fucking thing until Pratt sent me out to Denver two years ago to clean out Benedict's desk and nose around and see if I could find out anything about why the guy split. I didn't find anything. I came home."

"Okay, *T.R.* Ben? Why don't you tell Mr. Rhoads here about the Midas project."

Brandon, turned toward the men, picked up a clipboard, and flipped through a couple of pages.

"Here it is," Brandon said and began reading. "Midas was a sixty-month-long scientific study designed to determine the optimum level of nicotine dosage needed to insure and maintain addiction to cigarettes. Project technically successful. Officially terminated when project leader Loren Benedict threatened to reveal analytical data to various federal agencies."

Rhoads's jaw dropped two inches. Brandon flipped forward a few more pages.

"Benedict disappeared January, two years ago," the FBI agent read, "three days after telephoning an official of the U.S. Department of Justice and agreeing to meet to discuss some sort of conspiracy-in-progress at TobacCo, Inc. Only problem was, the guy never kept his appointment. The DOJ official wrote a memo and forwarded it to us. To date, insufficient evidence to pursue prosecution of any party."

"Holy shit. Pratt must of shit!"

Franklin noted that Rhoads seemed to get a genuine thrill out of the news. He had to recalculate his impression of Rhoads. Based on Rhoads's reaction, Franklin now he thought he may have been telling the truth when he described the extent of his knowledge about Benedict.

"Pratt was cranking up the old nicotine count, was he? And Benedict ratted him out." Rhoads laughed. "Now there, *that's* my idea of something really funny." Franklin glared. Rhoads turned his mirth down a notch. "I'm not bullshitting," he said. "I'm telling you what I know."

"I don't believe you," Franklin lied. *Keep the pressure on.* "And anyway, what about my first question? Why is a loser like you Pratt's point man on the tampering thing? I'll tell you why. In Pratt's eyes, you're completely expendable. You think I don't know where you were. On vacation?"

How'd he know that? Rhoads wondered. Pratt sure as hell didn't tell him.

Franklin continued. "You can be blamed for *anything.* Yet you don't know enough to hurt *anybody.* I believe the word is patsy. Is that the nomenclature, Brandon?"

"Putzy, sir. The word is putzy."

"Rhoads," Franklin said. "I wouldn't be surprised if someday soon we receive a big fat envelope mailed anonymously containing all the evidence we need to tie you to Benedict's disappearance. Enough airtight evidence to put you in a very small room for a very long time."

Rhoads leaned forward and tapped Brandon on his shoulder. "If there are any cigarettes in that evidence envelope, feel free to smoke them, Benny." Rhoads turned to Franklin. "Now I *know* you're nuts," Rhoads said. "Evidence? Against me? Where would you get that? Someone would have to make it up out of thin air."

"From Pratt, you jackass. And maybe it would be made up. That doesn't mean we wouldn't believe it."

Rhoads exhaled deeply, not quite a sigh. He knew Pratt was capable of anything, and he'd heard the stories about things Pratt had supposedly done, frightening things. "What are you picking on me for, Franklin? You don't think I have anything to do with this tampering shit. And I told you I told you the truth about Benedict."

"We'll see about how much truth you've told me. But I know one thing. You need an ally, Rhoads, and I can be that ally. And here's how you're going to buy my friendship. As far as I'm concerned, starting now, I got me a new set of eyes and ears at TobacCo, Inc. You. You, now, work for me. And for starters, I want the project documentation on Midas, before Pratt sanitizes it. I'm sure you can figure out a way to get it. I'll let you know about other stuff I want as we go. You like this yet?"

Rhoads feigned a yawn. "Terrific. Just to humor you for minute, what if I can find the documentation, which I won't, because if it exists, Pratt's got it out of harm's way, how can you use it as evidence? You stole it."

Franklin grimaced and ignored Rhoads's question. "Now funny man, if you have any kind of an idea about going to Pratt and telling him about this conversation, I will charge you with obstruction of justice. And it will stick. We never approached him on the stuff Benedict sent to Justice. We had no corroboration, and there was nobody in Benedict's family to push a missing persons investigation. We don't want to go to Pratt too soon and tip our hand."

"We call that premature investigation," Brandon tossed in. Franklin flashed a snarl at his subordinate.

"We have no reason to believe Pratt knows Benedict ever sent anything to Uncle Sam," Franklin said. "Can you imagine the sentence they hand out for obstructing justice in a case with 300 counts of first degree murder?"

"Brandon?" Rhoads said. "Exactly what is it that you all

would like to think Pratt did?"

Franklin answered. "Buried Benedict, of course. That is, if *you* didn't do it for him. In other words, Rhoads, whatever actually did happen, I'm afraid, puts you somewhere between W. Nicholas Pratt and the Federal Bureau of Investigation."

Rhoads thought about that for a moment and burst out laughing.

"What's so funny?" Brandon turned to see Rhoads.

Rhoads looked at his watch. "Not too long ago I was drunk and sitting fully dressed, actually sitting, on my butt, like a smacked ass, in the ocean. Had just blown my life savings. Just quit a great job because I was too embarrassed to get into a program for alcoholics. Probably permanently lost my dear brother's respect. Now, there I was with a mouth full of bloody sand, thinking things really had nowhere to go but up."

"I see why that's funny to *us*," Brandon said. "But why are *you* laughing?"

"Well, while I was busy losing almost sixty grand, getting drunker and drunker, losing more and more cash, the craps pit boss looked at me and said, 'Don't worry, Mr. R., things are darkest . . . just before they get pitch black.' Well, I guess this is the pitch black part."

"Oh, come on Rhoads," Franklin said. "You haven't seen *nothing* yet."

32

Asheville

Valzmann let himself into Rhoads's tree-filled apartment.

With his gloved hand, he drew the curtains. Although the room became dark, there was enough sunlight seeping in through the translucent material that he did not need to turn on the lamps.

Although the Towers was an upscale address, Rhoads's unit didn't reflect that. The man entered Rhoads's bedroom as if it was his own, as if he'd been there many times before. The room was a mess, but the bed had been made and a sky-blue comforter covered it perfectly. He stood in the middle of the room and turned, slowly, 365 degrees, looking for the ideal place to hide the envelope. Leafy branches reached up toward the ceiling and hung over Rhoads's bed. Valzmann went to the spot he had thought about before he even entered the building.

He got onto his knees and removed the deep middle drawer of Rhoads's bureau. In it was a jumble of underpants and unpaired socks. He set it on the bed and put his arm into the void where the drawer had been. He reached down, measuring with his hand the clearance behind the drawer below. The clearance would be the same for all the drawers. He needed to know if the large, bulky envelope stuffed with $194,000 would fit. *It'll be close.*

He took from his pocket a roll of surgical adhesive tape. The tape crackled as he tore off two strips. He upended the drawer, spilling the garments on the bed, and taped the envelope to the slat at the back. He slid it back into place. Almost. Didn't quite fit. He removed the drawer and felt around.

Son of a bitch!

Valzmann found another envelope there, this one fastened to the inside of the bureau with brittle adhesive tape. He pulled out a bone-handled knife from his jacket pocket, depressed a small silver button, and a blade snapped out and clicked into place. Valzmann reached in, slit the tape, and removed the envelope. He used the knife again as a letter opener. The envelope contained several yellowed newspaper articles.

He read the first one and scanned the rest. Articles about when Rhoads was a cop and how he shot his wife and a rapist. *How could we have missed something like that!* Valzmann shuddered at how Pratt would react if he learned that Valzmann's background investigation on Rhoads had missed that. Valzmann put the articles back into the envelope and used fresh tape to secure it inside the bureau. From the brittleness of the old tape, it was obvious Rhoads hadn't touched the envelope in years. But Valzmann didn't want to risk Rhoads finding the money. He decided to tape his envelope behind the next drawer down.

He scooped up the underpants and socks from the bed and put them back into the middle drawer and then slid it into place. He removed the next drawer, taped the envelope with the money behind it, and replaced the drawer.

This time it fit.

He swiped his arm across the bed to remove the impression the drawer had made on the comforter. He stood up.

A loud bell pierced the silence and startled him. He shivered involuntarily then froze instinctively.

One second later, the sound again. The telephone. After three rings, he heard the answering machine click on and Rhoads's tape-recorded voice began to speak.

"Congratulations, you've reached . . . me. Well, not really. Don't hang up, just leave a message. Thanks."

Then the caller's voice.

"T.R.? This is Mary. Mary Dallaness. I know you're away, but I didn't know how else to reach you. I need to talk. I need to know . . . I think I may need your help. Please call as soon as you get this message."

The answering machine clicked off.

33

Seacrest, Florida

In Seacrest, a suburb of Pensacola, Muntor entered the Mr. Turkey restaurant lobby. On the street, it was warm and humid. Inside felt better. The air conditioning made it easier to breathe.

Two pay telephones were installed on the wall next to a rack of giveaway newspapers. Neither telephone was in use. Muntor went to one, dialed a long-distance number he had written on a three-by-five card, and when instructed by the digital voice, began dropping quarters into the slot.

He silently rehearsed his lines. He cleared his throat to warm up for the voice he planned to use. Muntor took note of the lightheadedness that accompanied the sudden rise in his blood pressure.

His chest ached, too, and he felt a swell, like indigestion, burning behind his rib cage. His hands and fingers quivered. Heat built up under his scalp, and a thin film of sweat emerged on his forehead.

Muntor had cause to be excited. For the first time in his life, he was about to claim the upper hand.

If only Mom could see me now.

34

FBI Headquarters
Event Response Center
Washington, D.C.

In the huge ERC—the Event Response Center on the second floor of FBI Headquarters—a dozen special agents and half as many support personnel sat at computer work stations. They moved about with files and faxes and photocopies. One woman monitored the FBI Telex terminal that agents called the hot line.

In another room nearby, Rhoads was being briefed and instructed by FBI forensic psychologists about what to say, and what not to say, to the subject if and when he called in. Agents and assistants answered telephones and made calls. Every few minutes one would dash from one end of the auditorium-sized room to the other with some urgent communication.

Two agents, their fingers working furiously at keyboards, were logged onto NCIC, the National Crime Information Center network. They were seeking matches on a series of known-violator variables that the Behavioral Sciences Section in Quantico and the Identification Section in Washington had prepared. Among the search targets were previous offenders in tampering cases, those who made threats of violence against corporations, and those who, by virtue of employment history, had access to dangerous chemicals.

That was just the start. As more field data became available, the search experts would be able to sharpen the focus of their queries by polling for matches on increasingly specific variables.

At a large conference table in the same room, Franklin and several other FBI officials sat talking. Telephones rang and support people answered them. When warranted, an assistant would tap the appropriate shoulder, fast whispers would be exchanged, and the call would be taken. For any call that was not urgent, pink callback slips were hastily filled out.

Product-tampering cases, the agents had learned in the FBI Academy in Virginia, are difficult. The perpetrators have all the advantages, and, unlike other classes of criminal, they usually have no history of other tampering offenses. The FBI hoped that the subject in this case was a previous offender. But that was not likely. The Tylenol-tampering case from 1979, for example, was still open.

In an Extra-Strength Exedrin tampering case two years later, the FBI worked hard but got lucky, too. Agents eventually arrested a woman who tried to conceal the murder of her husband in a thicket of seemingly random cyanide poisonings near Tacoma, Washington. The woman prepared the poisonous compound in the same chipped cereal bowl she used to store an algicide for her tropical-fish tanks. The FBI lab identified the cyanide as well as the algicide in a capsule they recovered from the crime scene.

When a field agent read the report, he recalled seeing an array of tropical-fish tanks during an interview with one victim's wife. The bureau worked exhaustively and traced the algicide to a nearby pet shop where a former assistant manager, who had recently quit and happened to be in the store to pick up his last paycheck when agents arrived, identified the woman from a photograph. Without the murderer's use of the cereal bowl, the excellent recall of the FBI agent, and the chance presence of the former employee, the Tacoma murders may have had the same fate as the Tylenol cases.

A telephone rang somewhere in the background. A moment later, an assistant rushed to Franklin's side and whispered to him.

Franklin stared down at the multiline telephone on the table like it was a water moccasin. He picked up the line the assistant indicated and listened for a moment to the FBI switchboard operator.

"Okay, everybody, headsets on," Franklin said to the agents, Behavioral Science Section experts, and Investigative Support Unit specialists who would be monitoring the call. "Here he is."

He waited several seconds for everyone to get the headsets in place. Then he spoke to the switchboard operator. "Put him through on line six."

A second later, a light began blinking at the sixth button on Franklin's telephone.

Franklin clenched his teeth. Then every discernible facial expression evaporated. He took a deep breath. Calls like this sometimes come only once in a career. He stood up, the telephone still pressed to his ear, and snapped his fingers hard, once, for silence. Everyone looked to him except the one he needed most, the communications tech busy at a terminal.

"Dan! Line six!" Franklin shouted. The tech spun around. Franklin gave him a sharp nod and pointed with his free hand to the telephone, signaling the tech to trap the incoming call. The tech's hands grew busy at the keyboard.

Franklin put his finger on the line-six button but did not depress it. He closed his eyes and slowly eased himself into a chair. Then he pressed the flashing light and was on the line with a man who, less than one minute earlier, had told the FBI switchboard that he was the person the papers were calling Cyanide Sam.

"Deputy Director Franklin," he said, measuring his tone.

"Howdy, Mr. Franklin!" a hoarse voice said, almost jovially. A rush of vehicles in the background suggested an outdoor pay telephone. *That could be faked,* was Franklin's immediate thought, *could be a sound effect.*

A few feet away, the technician assigned to trap the call reacted to something that appeared on his terminal. He picked up a telephone and, pressing his finger against the screen so as not to lose his place, he spoke excitedly in quiet tones.

Franklin, distracted by the tech's activity, turned away and closed his eyes. "To whom am I speaking?" Franklin asked. "And how may I help you?"

"Oh, yeah, my name? *Walter Winchell.* I didn't know you were a comedian, too. Anyway, you'll want to know it's really me.

Here's a hint. My salutation. Have you deciphered it?"

Franklin turned around to those monitoring the call. *What salutation?* he asked with his eyes and a hunch of his shoulders. Then to the caller, "I do not know with whom I'm speaking."

"I issued a greeting," the caller said, still speaking through a hoarse voice, "to demonstrate the lengths to which I am willing to go to accomplish my goal, which is, of all the damned things, to actually *save* lives."

The man, whether or not he intended to, succeeded in confusing Franklin. "What do you mean by salutation?"

"By salutation I mean *greeting.* What else would it mean? Check the names of the establishments in Pensacola where people recently went to quit smoking. First letters only. But you'll have to add the letter 'O.' If the news is reporting it accurately, the little trick-pack I planted at . . . at the mystery spot must have been a dud. Then you'll know I'm me."

He still didn't know what the caller meant. Franklin turned again to the people listening in. With his eyes, he asked them if they understood.

"Pratt got your tongue, Mr. Franklin?" Franklin had made the same bad joke.

The caller had scored one against him. "No. I'm here, sir."

"Then, if you want to resolve this . . . matter . . . as expeditiously as possible, I'll want to talk to that fellow who works as a security executive at TobacCo, Inc., down in Asheville. His name is Thomas Rhoads. You may even know him. He worked the Harry Hill case? The FBI was stuck, but Rhoads figured it out for you. That's the kind of challenge I'm looking forward to. Makes for much better press, I think. I'll tell him, Rhoads, what I'm up to. My advice is to get in touch with him right away and tell him I'll call back at this number at, oh, let me take a little ride now, say 4 P.M. sharp. Today."

"Sir, we have Mr. Rhoads here now, ready to . . ."

"How about if I stay on this telephone for another couple of hours, chatting with him? Would that be okay with you? Tick tock, four o'clock."

The subject hung up.

Franklin stood motionless.

"Let's have it," asked one of the agents who had not had the benefit of a headset.

Franklin looked to the tech.

"A public telephone in Seacrest. Number 11 Lightwood Street," the tech said.

The communications computer had locked the location of the subject's telephone into the system the instant the tech tapped the appropriate key, but the system took another thirty-one seconds to find and display the exact address. The caller didn't stay on the line much longer. The call had been clocked at seventy-two seconds.

"He didn't want to stay on the line. He said he will call back at four today to talk to Rhoads," Franklin said. "Specifically, he said 'tick-tock, four o'clock.'"

Franklin then turned to address everyone in the ERC. "Here's what the caller said." He paraphrased the conversation. "He said, '. . . you'll want to know it's really me. Did you decipher my salutation?' and then, '. . . check out the first letters of the places in Pensacola where people went to stop smoking, and add the letter "O" because that one must have been a dud.' Then he said he will call back here at 4 P.M. today."

Then, much louder, "Damn it!" Franklin slammed his beefy hand hard and flat onto the surface of the conference table. The director, who had entered the room during the call and stood behind Franklin, jumped back, startled at the outburst.

Franklin saw the movement, then realizing it was the director, quickly said, "Excuse me, sir."

People began scribbling on pads and scraps of paper, asking each other about the different names of the retailers who sold the Pensacola cigarettes.

"'W-H-Y' something?" a female agent proposed, working from her seat at the Serial Criminal Profiling Section terminal.

"'W,' Wilkens Pharmacy. 'H,' the Heart and Soul Bar, 'Y' for the vending machine at the YWCA. What was the other one?"

"Davidson's, the grocery," someone said.

Franklin, standing now, listened. He said, "And then add an 'O,' he must have planted one in somewhere that begins with the letter 'O,' only no one smoked it."

"Yet," the director said and turned to an agent. "Eddie, get on the phone. Let Pensacola PX know there may be a live pack out there in some establishment whose name begins with the letter 'O'! Then put a summary of what just transpired on the hot line. ASAP. I'm not happy about releasing the details, but we may save a life."

Everyone in the room doodled on pieces of paper for the next minute until the agent who suggested "W-H-Y something" sent a chill up the spines of everyone in the room.

"I think I have it," she said hesitantly. "At first I thought it could have been an interrogative— 'WHY DO?' But I'm afraid that's not it. I think it's in this order. Heart and Soul, then the 'O,' Wilken's, Davidson's, and then the YMCA. This guy, whoever he is, he's greeting us. He's saying 'HOWDY.'"

"Howdy?" Franklin asked almost inaudibly. His brow furrowed like he was trying to, remember something. Then he rose slowly out of his chair like a time-lapse film clip of a daffodil sprouting. "Howdy?" he repeated slowly. "Howdy? *Like in hello?*"

No one answered him.

To the deputy director with twenty-three years of experience, the one-word salutation sounded like a message from a madman indulging a freshly whetted appetite.

35

Association of Tobacco Marketers, New York

At Franklin's directive, a special agent in Washington called Nicholas Pratt and told him what the FBI had learned about the Florida incidents. At the end of the conversation, the agent was to lightly inquire about the status of the search for the Midas Project files.

From Pratt's perspective, the Pensacola incidents were good news. The FBI had reason to believe that none of the tainted cigarettes were TobacCo, Inc. products.

"We're almost there," Pratt said to the agent's question about the files. Then he hung up.

Pratt called Bill Marey in New York. Marey served, at Pratt's whim, as the executive director of the industry's effective trade and lobbying group, the ATM, the Association of Tobacco Marketers.

"We have a serious, serious problem, Billy," Pratt said. "You've got to call the others. The Federal Express thing was bad enough, but at least it was self-contained, people only had to avoid cigarettes that showed up in the mail. Now with the Pensacola deal, we're going to have the FDA or the ATF or some other agency pulling cigarettes off of shelves. In Pensacola, the guy used brands from four different manufacturers. I was left out this time. That is no accident. The guy's showing us he'll target whomever he wants. Plus, my common stock is off another two points."

Someone entered Marey's office, interrupting him. "Not now!" he said. Then, back to Pratt. "Okay, I'm sorry, Nick. Go on."

"Anyway, my damage control man here thinks we can get a recall restricted to Pensacola itself, maybe the county, or at worst, northwestern Florida. And possibly for just a few days. I want you to call the other CEOs. Organize an invisible meeting.

And I mean invisible. We can't have the public, and especially this lunatic, seeing us circling the wagons. If any of the others give you any friction about attending, tell them it's my idea. Tell them to fantasize about a nationwide product recall across all brand lines. They'll show."

"I imagine they will, Nick," Marey said.

36

Pensacola, Florida

Two senior FBI agents boarded a United commuter flight in Washington and landed a little after two-thirty in Pensacola. They were met at the airport by Special Agent Lewis from the FBI's Pensacola Resident Agency office. An unmarked Florida Highway Patrol car and trooper sat in the Authorized Vehicles Only lane waiting for them.

"The FBI doesn't have access to its own vehicles in Florida?" one of the men from FBI Headquarters asked.

"Yes sir, but my van is being used as surveillance on another job," Agent Lewis said. "The corporal here has kindly offered to escort us today."

Twenty minutes later, the four men pulled up to the prefab three-bedroom house on Avelina Court. Two unmarked cars blocked the entrance to the driveway. Just beyond them, flowers and framed photographs marked a spot on the asphalt. The news crews had been kept back half a block under some thin crime-scene pretext.

Earlier that morning, Jack Stein, fifty-five, a chain-link fence installer, had lived there with his family. By 11 A.M., he was dead.

Stein, the first known HOWDY victim, had purchased a pack of Kools after supervising a tricky fence installation at an under-construction residential development in Sunaville. Local police had learned Stein's wife and two daughters had been hounding him for years about smoking. He had ignored their pleas to quit. Instead he promised he would quit smoking inside the house.

For weeks, he had faithfully kept his word, smoking openly, standing with one hand in his pants pocket, in the driveway. Stein's wife thought the display had been designed to elicit some guilt from any family member who happened past the large kitchen and living-room windows that looked out onto the lawn and driveway. The first evening that Stein's own home had become one large no-smoking section, his family made him a dinner of steamed lobster and sautéed asparagus, his favorites, as a show of support.

The corporal stayed in his vehicle, and the three FBI agents walked up to the house, pausing briefly to look at the spot where Stein had died.

Lewis knocked on the front door of the residence. A young woman answered, dressed in shorts and a Grateful Dead T-shirt. The men identified themselves, and she immediately began talking.

"Daddy died right there where we set those flowers in the driveway," his daughter Donna said, tears building, pointing over the agents' shoulders. "If we hadn't a hassled him so bad, he might have taken sick right inside, where we could have called 911. I think me and Mom and Mary are as guilty as the man who did it to my dad."

"But you couldn't have helped your father, neither you nor

your mom nor sister was home at the time. That's what we understand," Agent Lewis said.

En route from the airport, Lewis had shown the other agents the crime-scene Polaroids and the initial incident reports. Stein's face and extremities had turned cobalt blue, and he died with his mouth open, gasping for air.

"Cyanide does that, you can breathe air in, but your lungs don't absorb any oxygen," the corporal had said on the way over. "Did you ever watch a fish flop around in the bottom of a boat trying to breathe?"

"Well, it might have turned out different if we would have left him alone," the teenager said. "Is smokin' really that much of a crime?"

Lewis asked Donna if she could think of any reason why someone would want to hurt her father.

"I don't know anything that I haven't already told about fifty other detectives."

"Donna, sometimes you can know something that doesn't pop up in your head right away," one of the men from Washington said. "Like when you have a dream and forget about it until something happens during the day that reminds you. That's why we want you to call us, anytime, even in the middle of the night, any day of the week, if something does remind you of something you think may help us. You just call my number here, collect." The agent took a card from his inside jacket pocket.

"Okay, I'll put this with my collection," she said, reading the card and running her finger over the gold-embossed FBI seal. "Can I tell you something about my daddy?"

Lewis nodded.

The wet in Donna's eyes ran as rivulets down her cheeks. "My daddy couldn't read anything harder than a stop sign. But when me and Mary were little, he wouldn't let one night pass that he didn't read us a storybook. He did it just by looking at the pi'tures and making up words to go with them."

Back in the car, the corporal asked the FBI agents if they

learned anything they didn't already know. His intent, most likely, was to determine if the two men from Washington succeeded in finding anything his own organization had missed.

"I think we are beginning to see that these murders are random. No pattern, just a lunatic with a chip on his shoulder."

The corporal said, "Yeah, if there was anything to get, we'd a got it first time around. In a case like this, everything gets quadruple-checked."

Most cops love to rub it in to the FBI when they get a chance.

37

FBI Headquarters

Franklin ordered a surveillance team to observe the pay telephone in Seacrest at the site where the first call originated. Getting lucky there would be a thousand-to-one shot on a good day. Chances were slight that the subject would use the same telephone for the second call, but missing him if he did, Franklin knew, would be unjustifiable.

If the caller was not the actual perpetrator, but instead a malicious prankster, then he could conceivably be naive enough to think that it would be safe to call from the same place. Or, if the man who called was in fact the subject but was deranged or delusional, he may arrive at the conclusion that the FBI did not know where the call originated, and he might use the same telephone again. Many psychopaths, however, are paranoid. Neither scenario was very likely.

"Still can't locate Sorken," an agent informed Franklin.

"Well that's nice," Franklin said, rubbing his eyes with the heels of his hands. "Try the locals."

Dr. Myron Sorken, a forensic psychologist widely published in the field of linguistics and dialects and on the staff of the psychiatric board at John Hopkins University in Baltimore, could not be reached at his office or home in Columbia, Maryland. Franklin had wanted him present for the first call. Now Franklin wanted him to hear the tape of the call and to hear the second call, if it came. Once, Sorken had successfully listened through a kidnapper's feigned southern accent and directed investigators to focus on suspects whose early language development had been in the Great Lakes region. One of a score of suspects in the case had attended elementary school in Benton Harbor, Michigan, and that suspect turned out to be Mr. Right.

The FBI asked the Columbia police to find Sorken. Two city detectives worked quickly and located him at the Rosewood Golf and Country Club not far from his residence. Sorken was sped by the detectives to a service station near the Beltway where he jumped into a waiting FBI sedan for the rest of the trip to FBIHQ.

Others, specialists in product tampering, serial murder, schizophrenia, and other disciplines, were being contacted and rushed to the ERC as rapidly as possible. Franklin wanted to have a big congregation on hand at four o'clock. He realized there wasn't much that could be done with such short notice. Invitees were briefed by various special agents as they arrived. Many experts had not yet been located, but Sorken was the one Franklin desperately wanted.

At 3:35 P.M., Franklin and the director entered the room to join the group of nearly fifty FBI agents, staffers, and consultants. They stood at the head of the room, stern-faced and greeting no one.

The director tapped the microphone. "Being called in like this without notice is a terrible inconvenience I know. We are grateful you could make it," the director said without introducing himself. "The FBI appreciates your presence, and so does the president of the United States with whom I just spoke. He asked me to thank you personally for interrupting your lives to help save others. That's a quote. But enough of the preamble. Let me get out of everyone's way. Most of you who have worked with us before know Deputy Director Oak Franklin."

The director moved back. Franklin stepped forward and cleared his throat. "Good afternoon. We are calling this investigation CYCIG, as in *cy*anide *cig*arettes. The individual we believe responsible for the hundreds of tampering deaths, our preliminary profile of him can be found on your information sheets, thought he would give us a call this afternoon. I spoke with him myself, by telephone, less than two hours ago."

A murmur rolled through the room.

"Ladies and gentlemen, this man, again *if it is him and we think it is,* is a cold, casual killer. He spoke to me as calmly as if he were ordering a pizza. This case presents numerous complications for us, and one of the most frustrating aspects is that the subject has a practically limitless window of opportunity. About fifty million packs of cigarettes are smoked every day, day in and day out, in this country. That's approximately one billion cigarettes daily.

"The problem is this, it would be almost impossible to apprehend a litterer who did not want to be caught. And by dropping a pack of sodium-cyanide-injected cigarettes here and there, this subject is not doing much more than littering. All he has to do is be patient and cautious. An apprehension during the actual commission of the crime, unless we get extremely fortunate, is remote. We're going to have to take this one by figuring out who he is. That's why you have been called here."

The director nodded in concurrence behind Franklin.

"What we hope to get from you are your subjective observations for the purpose of enhancing our SCRIPS profile of him.

For those of you haven't helped us before, SCRIPS is our new artificial intelligence Serial Criminal Profiling System. Anything you can contribute about age, mental status, educational background, regional clues from voice and language, all are incalculably valuable.

"Don't be bashful about wild guesses, intuitive feelings, gut reactions. We want, *we need*, them all. Candidly, we are all hoping his stated agenda, 'to save lives,' is the setup for an extortion attempt against the tobacco industry. At least then we could look forward to an eventual point of contact. Without that, we will have to rely on our Investigative Support Unit, the Behavioral Science Section, supported by the SCRIPS system, and what you, our consultants, can contribute."

A multiline telephone and headset sat in front of everyone present. Another dozen or so telephones were at the far end of the table.

Franklin glanced at his watch. "We have about twenty minutes until four o'clock, the time the subject said he would call. In the first call, he spoke in a gruff voice, probably contrived. Some of you have already heard the tape of that call. As far as we can determine, the subject didn't attempt any other voice modification. He called from a public coin telephone in a Mr. Turkey's at 11 Lightwood Street in Seacrest. The telephones are in an alcove between the street and the dining area. Restaurant employees pay little attention to people on public phones, and not surprisingly, none of the employees there specifically recalls seeing anyone use the phones. We have a team on the scene now, just in case.

"What we'd like you to do is this. You will all remain here in this room with headsets on. The subject told us he wants to speak to Mr. Thomas Rhoads, a security official for TobacCo, Inc. in Asheville, North Carolina." Franklin introduced Rhoads with a quick nod. "Mr. Rhoads had his fifteen minutes of fame when he was instrumental in helping us bust an organized-crime scam in Chicago a couple of years ago. He enjoyed extensive media coverage then and was profiled as, what was it Tom?, the Dirty Harry of the corporate security world. Ironically, it is that publicity that may have led the subject to target TobacCo, Inc. There's also the possibility that he and Mr. Rhoads may know each other.

"Rhoads will take the call in Lab C on this floor. That's down the hall. You can feel free to speak among yourselves. Any urgent ideas, notes, or questions you have during the call should be written down as quickly as possible. Staffers will be in the room with you. Hold your pad up in the air, and someone will bring your comment or question in to me immediately, though it's not likely the caller will stay on the line long enough for us to evaluate your ideas and use them. In the first call, he hung up after seventy-two seconds elapsed. We hope he planned on no more than sixty seconds but let himself get carried away. That tells us he may not be in complete control of himself. That's better than being up against someone with the precision of a Swiss watchmaker."

Franklin sipped from a cup and cleared his throat again.

"Any questions?"

38

Fifty yards away in Lab C, Behavioral Science Assistant Section Chief Juan Estevez advised Franklin and Rhoads on strategy for the expected call.

"The best thing to do is to go with your gut, Oak. These are just general guidelines," Estevez said. "Picking up the telephone the instant it is transferred to you demonstrates a posture of urgent attentiveness. I don't think we want to be that servile. Especially with a guy like this. Waiting for two or three rings communicates a concerned but casual interest. Answering in the four- or five-ring range suggests a nonplussed attitude about the caller's status. Not a good idea. I recommend you pick her up on the third ring."

Franklin, listening to Estevez and doodling on a notepad, wrote the numeral "3." He drew a series of concentric circles around it until no more could fit on the page.

Rhoads peered over at Franklin's pad. "Feeling a bit boxed in, Deputy Director?"

Franklin frowned, his brown face growing darker. He dropped the notepad on Estevez's desk.

"These are circles, Rhoads. Boxes are square."

"Same difference," Rhoads said. "Anyway, your caller's probably thrilled about what he's accomplished so far. But he's put a hook in his own mouth. Best not overexcite him until it's to our advantage. Let's let him run it out a bit."

39

Pensacola, Florida, and Washington, D.C.

At precisely one second after four o'clock, when the telephone did not ring, Franklin's mind began entertaining a menagerie of every imaginable negative CYCIG scenario. *The subject will never call again. The subject has launched another shipment of unstoppable death. The subject will turn out to be an FBI agent under my own command.* This parade of bad possibilities continued unabated for three and one-quarter minutes until, at 4:03:16 P.M., Muntor picked up an outdoor pay telephone and dialed the FBI Headquarters number he had now memorized.

When telephone company's digital simulated female voice requested $1.85, Muntor began dropping quarters into the slot with his white-gloved hand. Nervous, he lost count of the coins deposited.

"Thank you. You have forty cents credit toward your call," the voice said.

The call came into the switchboard, and a supervisor switched it to Franklin in Lab C. The telephone began ringing. Franklin picked it up midway through the fourth ring.

"Deputy Director Franklin." He thought he may have sounded a bit too authoritative.

"Hello!" The voice was gruff again, the tone familiar, but different this time. High-speed traffic could be heard in the background.

"To whom am I speaking?"

"Howdy, Deputy Director." The distinct whine of a tractor-trailer flying by. "Rhoads present and accounted for?"

"Yes. Would you like to speak to him now? I know he wants to speak to you."

"Time's a wasting. Eleven seconds down the drain."

Franklin nodded to Rhoads who pressed the button putting him on the line. Franklin tapped the receiver button to make an audible click but stayed on the line to listen.

"This is Tom Rhoads. They call me T.R. Hello." Warmer than Franklin but still clearly anxious.

"Mr. Rhoads. Thanks for coming."

"You're welcome. Do I get a name to go with the voice?"

"When I let you arrest me, I'll show you my driver's license, but until then, the name's *Virgil*. Now, listen up. I can't stay on this line gibber-jabbering with you all day." The caller's pace quickened. "We're going to launch a little public awareness campaign, you and me. You watch, it'll be quite educational. Now what I want to do is this. I want to make a trade. I'll cancel the next event I've planned if you can get your boss, W. Nicholas Pratt, to do me a little favor. I need him to make a personal appearance. Help kick off the campaign. Tomorrow night. He'll have to spend some of the company dollars, though . . ."

While the man who called himself Virgil continued his prepared speech, the communications tech spoke quietly to someone on the other end of his telephone.

"*The Denny's at service plaza 12-N, southbound on the Interstate, north of Pensacola,*" he said to a Florida Highway Patrol dispatcher.

Rhoads, still harboring some suspicion about the call's authenticity, calmly listened to Virgil.

". . . and he'll need to buy sixty-second spots on ABC, CNN, CBS, ESPN, MTV, and NBC." The caller was speaking so fast he was slurring words together, not sloppy, like a drunk, hurried. "At nine o'clock. P.M. It doesn't have to be precisely nine, but it should be within a few minutes. Don't keep me waiting long. I'm one guy you don't want to piss off. I'll be a big star burning bright while I'm waiting, and I don't wait patiently. I want to hear him, Pratt—no spokespeople, you understand?—read an excerpt from page 345 of *The Surgeon General's Smoking and Health Report to the Congress, Third Revised Edition*. He's to read the third full 'graph on that page. It enumerates how many lung cancer deaths there were in the U.S. last year and then goes on to state that 92 percent of all lung cancer cases result directly from smoking. This, this reading, constitutes Pratt's confession on behalf of the entire industry. And it must be delivered that way. Solemnly, contritely.

"I've timed it, it can be read easily in under a minute. Now, let's say Pratt balks. We got trouble, big trouble. I go to plan 'B'—something I like to call 'Back to School Night.' Whoa! I'm looking at the second hand on my watch." Virgil spoke even more rapidly now. "Let me tell you something, Mr. Rhoads, they say that in life, pain is mandatory, suffering is optional. I like that saying. Don't you? Here's how that concept applies to us. See, I have got a grand finale planned for all of this, something spectacular, a little ways down the road. It'll make the Kuwaiti oil fields infernos look like campfires. That's pain, the mandatory part. That *will* happen. But this 'Back to School Night' thing? Hell, we don't have to go through all that. That's an optional one. And it's Nick Pratt's choice. We'll see what he does. But I warn you, Mr. Rhoads, you won't like 'Back to School Night.' That much I guarantee. That is all."

An FBI agent handed Rhoads a note.

He paused half a beat to read it.

"Mr. Virgil, what do you mean by 'Back to . . .'"

"It's not *Mister* Virgil, jackass. Are you *Mister* Tom? It's just Virgil. Don't make that stupid mistake again, because I can spell 'RHOADS' as well as I spelled 'HOWDY,' except that one extra poor son of a bitch will die. R-H-O-A-D-S."

The sound of the subject's voice and the rush of background traffic ceased suddenly with a solid click. A dark silence, as thick as night fog, eased out of the telephone and into all the listeners' ears.

40

Dozens of state troopers' cars, lights flashing, sirens screaming, roared toward the Denny's. Emergency vehicles swerved passed motorists, careened across tree- and shrubbery-lined medians, accelerated up both exit and entrance ramps.

Troopers and rifle teams boiled from the vehicles, surrounding the plaza and closing in on a bank of telephone booths. A helicopter arrived, but the commander ordered it back. Its rotors chopped so loudly the men on the ground had difficulty hearing their radios.

Police took up tactical positions, terrifying confused civilians.

In one of the booths, the handset of a telephone dangled, swaying in the breeze. The handset cast a shadow that picked up the hue of the fading October light and threw a long purple line across the cement.

Florida Highway Patrol, Pensacola police, and FBI agents used dogs and helicopters to scour the service plaza and an adjacent gas station and surrounding woods. They immediately erected roadblocks on all highways within a fifteen-mile radius of the pay telephone.

Zero.

Inside the restaurant, Edward Constantine, a recently retired accountant from Dallas, and his wife Jean, traveling for the first time in their lives to Miami, comforted Agnes Wilson.

Edward's words couldn't stop the woman from her crying and shaking. Her hacking cough and her terrible color that showed through the heavy makeup made Edward uneasy.

Then Jean tried.

"Now Agnes, dear. You'll have to calm down. We said we're going to help you, and it's absolutely no bother. Right, Ed?"

"Right, honey. I'd want strangers to do the same for you if

you had trouble." Constantine winced inwardly at Agnes Wilson's excess of makeup, her terrible wig, and her appalling choice of perfume. He couldn't imagine driving far with that smell in the car. He held those thoughts. He was a good Christian, and this was a women in need.

Agnes spoke through her sobs. "But all those horrible guns and rifles while I was out on the pay phone. I could hardly hear the man from the auto club." She whispered, "Frankly, I nearly lost my water. Oh!" She stopped speaking to cry some more.

Jean patted the woman's gloved hand. "Now Agnes, you'll just have to relax."

The crying woman said, "And all that business and my car breaking down. Will it be expensive? What did you say it sounded like? The field pump?"

"The *fuel* pump," said Edward. "From the way you described it, it isn't the battery. It sounds like it's trying to turn over but can't get any fuel. Anyway, let the man from the AAA worry about that. They'll tow it in for you, no charge. And we'll have you at your son's in no time."

At the kindness of strangers, Agnes Wilson cried again. Mrs. Constantine, feeling so sorry for the lonely old woman, put one arm around her in an awkward hug.

41

FBI Headquarters

Franklin slammed down the telephone. "Damn it, we missed him! That son of a bitch! Someone get me a glass of cold water!"

"Oak," Brandon said. "Something here you ought to hear. This is Dr. Ertmann. Doc?"

A rail-thin, gray-haired man in a three-piece suit seated in a wheelchair rolled up and turned to face Franklin.

"You the top man?" the doctor asked in a nasal squeak.

"No, but in this investigation, I'm the next best thing," Franklin said, barely looking at the man. "The director of the FBI is the top man."

"Right. I don't want to be telling this story to eight different guys. I'll say it once, do with the information as you see fit. I've been a respiratory specialist for forty years. Let me speculate and make a diagnosis based on what I've just heard. This Virgil fellow? He is, in all probability, in a very late stage of malignant carcinoma of the upper respiratory system. You send a copy of the tape of that phone call to my office, and I'll have some fellows listen to it, see if they get the same thing I did."

"Take it from the top in English, Doctor. Are you telling me he's dying?"

The doctor nodded.

"How soon?"

"Can't say. Could be very soon, could hang on for a couple of years."

"Which team would you bet on?"

The doctor thought for a minute. Franklin waited, desperate to hear good news.

"Well," the doctor said. "I'll tell you. Wild guess only. His shallowness, the faint wheeze, the suppuration, the way he stridulates. Let's put it this way. I own stock in CIGNA, the insurance company. I wouldn't want them to take a $100,000 premium for a $101,000 payout, even if the policy term was two weeks."

Everyone within earshot in the ERC listened and absorbed the information. Tentative smiles became broader as the implication sank in.

"Could it happen inside of a week?"

"I said I can't say. Possibly, but that's a little too ambitious. But, in light of the strain he's under, it could happen quickly. But I couldn't say *how* long even if he were sitting here in my lap. If I'm right, and I usually am, it'll take him very fast from here."

A couple of agents at the periphery of the crowd around the wheelchair-bound physician erupted spontaneously in shouts and cheers. Franklin glowered at his subordinates, and they immediately calmed down and assumed straight faces.

Except for Rhoads.

The smile on his face had been the broadest of all. He was thinking about that fifty thousand dollars bonus he planned to get Pratt to promise him if the killer was brought down within thirty days.

"Yeah, baby! *Come to momma, baby!*" he shouted inexplicably, drawing all eyes toward him. He swung a chair around in front of him, making a grating scrape on the linoleum tiles, jumped up on it, and performed his interpretation of an Indian war dance, one hand and outstretched fingers behind his head for the head-dress, the other hand slapping at his open mouth in a loud war whoop. Rhoads didn't care what kind of ass he was making of himself. He was going to get his money and go to New Jersey and buy that trawler, *The Deep Blue.*

"*Come to momma!*"

42

Philadelphia

Muntor arrived home after his flight from Florida nearly incapacitated by fatigue.

In his second-floor bathroom, his video camera sat perched upon a tripod straddling the sink. A tiny red LED glowed next to the Power On button, and the videocassette inside rolled silently recording the scene.

The lens pointed at an ornate, claw-foot bathtub in the middle of the tiled room, bolted decades ago into the floor. Next to the bathtub, Muntor had placed a three-legged wooden stool. The bathtub was surrounded by a ring of candles in red globes. The candlelight drenched the room in the color of blood.

Later, Muntor would watch this tape.

Minutes earlier, before beginning to film, he had cradled the camera in his arms like a newborn. Then he turned it on and held it up to his eye and slowly panned the room, preserving every detail. He had recorded the images of an orange crate just outside the ring of candles, piled high with newspapers, newspaper clippings, *Time, Newsweek, U.S. News & World Report*, and others. The one visible page showed a screaming headline about the cigarette murders. The camera's microphone had picked up Muntor's labored breathing and the musical tone of his wheeze. In between breaths, the mike recorded the faint dripping of a leaky faucet at the sink.

Also in the shot, behind the bathtub, was the screen of a small black-and-white television sitting on a wooden board atop the radiator. The camera zoomed in. A CNN anchor sat reading a story against a backdrop labeled "Cyanide Killer."

Muntor stopped recording and screwed the camera into the mounting on the tripod. After adjusting the camera angle, he flipped the switch back to "On." With the camera rolling,

Muntor walked into the shot. It had been only five days, yet he appeared more emaciated than in the first scene he shot of himself preparing the 700 envelopes. His thin hair was even longer, and he was wearing nothing but baggy white jockey shorts. His features were twisted, his skin stained by the candlelight.

Later, Muntor would hold pages of script in a shaky hand and record the text over this scene.

> *"Act II. Scene Four. The Anointing . . . The One who has chosen himself has also chosen to wreak vengeance for the murdered millions. He must be initiated on his path. There can be no return. The commitment is final. The self-chosen one must be strong."*

Muntor needed something from another room. He clicked off the camera with the remote he had palmed in his hand.

The next shot, Muntor would later see, came from another angle and showed him walking into the bathroom carrying a large plastic bucket of ice. He dumped it into the water-filled tub. He reached back and pressed a button on a boombox. He got in the bathtub, showing no sign of reacting to the cold, and sat down. Strains of music rose from the boombox, and Muntor reached toward the wooden stool. Again using the remote, Muntor clicked off the camera.

The next camera angle was not perfect. Some of Muntor's figure was too far to the right and was out of the frame. What could be seen most of the time was Muntor's arm being tied off with rubber tubing. From a paper bag on the wooden stool, he took a syringe and held it up to the candlelight to see it better. The camera showed it filled with milky-white liquid. Muntor jabbed a bulging vein in the middle of his inner elbow. The plunger sank slowly.

A tentative serenity grew across Muntor's face as the drug rush caused synapses to fire riotously. At the same time, the music reached its crescendo. Muntor, filling with numbness and energy from the Biphetamine and Dilaudid combo, began to straighten up, giving the effect of levitation, as if drawn erect by the ecstatic surge of energy. He stretched his bony arms out. He raised them slowly and evenly until he held them straight up, fingertips stretching for the ceiling. Then he brought them back down, again, slowly, steadily. When they reached his sides, he repeated the motion. All the way up, all the way down. And again. And again. Each time, faster and faster and faster until it became clear what he was doing.

He was flapping. His *wings*.

The ice sloshed around in the bathtub and splashed over the side as Muntor maniacally flapped and flapped, trying to become airborne, paradoxically levitated by the effect of the drugs and weighted down by the cold of the ice and the water.

"Into the eternal darkness." Muntor cackled lines from a poem. *"Into fire,"* he screeched. *"Into ice!"*

Muntor opened his mouth wide. Several seconds elapsed before a long, shrill shriek rose from his gut and rattled the bathroom. Loud enough for the neighbors to hear, the sound twisted and turned like a snake in a sewer and finally gave in to what it was, a hideous, horrible, terrible laugh.

PART

2

43

Wednesday, October 6
FBI Field Office
Atlanta

```
FEDERAL BUREAU OF INVESTIGATION
SECURED TELEX TRANSMISSION
TX4555699233AX02
URGENT/CYCIG EVENT REPORTED
TO: WASHINGTON DUTY CHIEF.WX
     COPY ALL STATIONS.FX
FROM: WIREROOM SUPERVISOR.AX
T&D: 0719 HOURS, 06 OCTOBER
```

MESSAGE: URGENT URGENT URGENT
ATLANTA FIELD OFFICE JUST RECEIVED TELEPHONE
CALL FROM EDITOR-IN-CHARGE LES ALLISON AT
ATLANTA CONSTITUTION'S NATIONAL NEWS DESK.
MR. ALLISON REPORTED RECEIVING A ONE PAGE
FAX AS OF 0703 HOURS, 06 OCTOBER AND SIGNED,
"VIRGIL."

NOTE: MR. ALLISON IS KNOWN TO THIS OFFICE TO

BE RELIABLE. LEGITIMACY OF FAX HE RECEIVED
UNVERIFIED. AGENTS EN ROUTE TO INTERVIEW MR.
ALLISON AND RETRIEVE FAX. COPY OF FAX TO BE
XMITTED TO FBIHQ.

COVER PAGE THAT ACCOMPANIED FAX TO ATLANTA
CONSTITUTION CONTAINED MESSAGE FOR DEPUTY
DIRECTOR FRANKLIN: "IT'S REALLY ME, FRANKLIN.
IF YOU DOUBT IT, JUST SAY 'HOWDY' TO OUR
MUTUAL FRIEND HARRY HILL."

FULL TEXT OF MESSAGE FOLLOWS:

*"I AM WORKING IN TANDEM WITH OTHERS WHO
BELIEVE MY MISSION IS COMMENDABLE. MY CO-
CONSPIRATORS, HOWEVER, HAVE BECOME GREEDY
AND OVERZEALOUS AND THREATEN TO OVER SHADOW
MY ACTIVITIES BY CAUSING MORE DEATHS THAN I
CAN POSSIBLY ARRANGE (THUS OBSCURING THE
MEDIA ATTENTION THAT I'VE WORKED SO HARD TO
ATTAIN). THEREFORE, I HEREBY IDENTIFY THEM.
I CANNOT NOW PROVIDE YOU WITH THEIR EXACT
WHEREABOUTS, BUT KNOWING THEIR REAL NAMES
SHOULD BE A GOOD STARTING PLACE FOR THE CRACK
INVESTIGATORS WITHIN YOUR ORGANIZATION.*

CO-CONSPIRATORS

DONALD S. "LUCKY" JOHNSTON
THOMAS "TOMMY FATFACE" SANDEFUR, JR., A.K.A.
 "KOOL TOMMY"
EDWARD A. "LICK-IT" HORRIGAN
ANDREW H. "LOW BLOW" TISCH, A.K.A. KENT B. TRUE
JOSEPH "LOUIE THE LUNGER" TADDEO, A.K.A. THE
 COPENHAGEN SCOWL
JAMES W. "DICKNOSE" JOHNSTON
WILLIAM I. "SLIM" CAMPBELL

Virgil

CONFIRMATION PENDING.
SA/CARL O. OERTELL.
END OF URGENT

44

St. Ignatius Cemetery, Boston

A long line of black limousines, passenger cars, flower cars, and a hearse wound through the narrow paved pathways of the rolling burial grounds under a hazy blue sky. Television cameras and satellite trucks were set up on every patch of open grass or driveway. Throngs of spectators and uniformed police were visible outside an improvised rope fence around the gravesite.

A female television reporter stage-whispered a live broadcast no more than thirty yards away from the freshly dug grave.

"This morning the eyes of Boston and the world are witnessing the tragic end of a human life," she said in pretentious solemnity. "And one which marked the beginning of a tragedy that continues its death march as I speak. For grade schoolers Dolly and Brian Charlesdon though, this is not a symbolic or national event. It is the funeral of their mother, diabolically murdered forty-eight hours ago by a madman who flippantly calls himself Virgil. This funeral ceremony honors the first of the killer's victims. But the sorrow of everyone here is compounded by the knowledge that there will be at least 361 other funerals in cemeteries throughout the United States. How many more there may be, no one wants to guess. The mandate is clear. Somewhere out there is an indifferent killer who must be found and stopped, and soon, for the sake of all the Dollys and Brians in America . . . This is Evelyn Townes, On-The-Spot World News, live from Boston."

The reporter stared into the camera with an expression of barely controlled rage for several seconds. Then she drew an index finger across her throat.

"How was that?" she asked the cameraman as she pulled a cosmetic mirror from her pocket to see if her false eyelash had stayed put this time.

The cameraman responded by singing a line from a song. *"I'm all shook up"* and bent to pick up a coil of audio cable.

"Really, Bob, I'm asking you. Was it any good?"

"Yep, it works. Let's get something to eat, Evie."

"Not so fast, pudgy. I want to make sure to shoot all the bigs. The director of the FBI is here officially, and over there," she pointed to several blue vans, "I'll bet lunch, are the Feds doing surveillance in case Smokey's a funeral peeper. Shoot them as tight as you can. And I want you to get the kids looking down into their mom's grave, I want a sweep of all the tearful citizens, and get in tight when you see one with a hanky. And real important, the CEO of TobacCo, Inc. is here. I'll give you a hand job if you can get a shot of him by the casket with an arm around the dead lady's kids. His PR dork's already turned me down for an interview, so you get video no matter what."

"Which one's Pratt?"

Evelyn Townes pointed across the lawn to the tall thin man in the black suit, flanked by a group of raincoat-wearing security men. A few yards away stood Rhoads.

"I've had about as much of this as I can take," Pratt groused. "I'm going back to the airport."

"As your public relations advisor, Nick," Arnold Northrup said, "I have to tell you how important it is for you to stay. It's not going to look good at all for you to exit before the finale."

"So I pat the kids on the head, pay my respects, and do thirty seconds with CNN to say that it's a very private loss for the family and I don't wish to intrude? Oh, come on, Northrup. The media have made it enough of a circus already."

"You don't need the media antagonistic toward you, Nick."

Pratt exhaled deeply. "Yes, Northrup, you're right."

A few minutes later, Pratt stood with Danny Danielson, the CNN reporter who covered breaking stories in New England. Northrup promised Danielson the exclusive graveside interview if Danielson would promise not to bring the tobacco-cancer issue into it. Danielson agreed with a quick handshake.

". . . are you accusing the media of exploiting this event? Is that what you mean Mr. Pratt?" The interview had been under control until Pratt let his temper intrude. His upper-lip tic kicked in.

Pratt came to himself. Smoothly and with an air of great dignity, he replied softly, "Daniel, you know better. This is hardly a time for us to argue about things we've always argued about. In my opinion, we should all be thinking only of the two bereaved children who have been orphaned by this Virgil maniac."

Danielson did a quick calculation. *Probably never need Northrup again. Go for it, Danny.*

"And what of all the children who are orphaned by your products every day, Mr. Pratt? Do you feel for them, too?"

Northrup gasped and stepped in between Pratt and the camera and deftly pulled his client out of the interview with muttered apologies and a quick tap on his watch.

The boiling CEO ducked inside his waiting black limo and slid onto the leather seat. Northrup attempted to get in, but Pratt waved him away. Pratt signaled to an assistant outside.

"Get Rhoads." Then Pratt made a quick telephone call to

check on how the TobacCo, Inc. common stock opened.

A minute later, a piece of paper appeared in the fax machine on the seat next to the driver. He opened the window that separated him from the passengers and handed the page to Pratt.

TobacCo, Inc. Common
Last, 206-1$^1/_4$, Volume 880,000.
Third most active stock

Rhoads appeared a few seconds later and got into the limo, perching on the jump seat facing Pratt. He lit an Easy and took a drag. He liked Camels better, but he was with Pratt.

"Did you see that interview? That Northrup's incompetent." Pratt took a quick breath, a master at the quick change of mood. "Anyway, here we are alone at last. Fill me in, T.R."

The limo moved away from the curb near the gravesite, snaked through the rolling hills of the cemetery, and pulled out into traffic.

"Like I told you when I called from D.C., the FBI is playing it pretty close to the vest. They keep asking me about Midas, even though I've told them I don't know anything about it."

Pratt remained expressionless, but his eyes flashed interest. "Do they have any idea when they're going to apprehend this gentleman? Or are they thinking they'll just bumble about and wait for him to die?"

What's he want from me? Rhoads wondered. "I don't know, Nick."

"But that's what I'm paying you a thousand dollars a day for, T.R., and that fifty thousand dollar bonus you talked me into, *if* he's caught in thirty days. And that's a big if, the progress you're making. Nevertheless, I need to know what the FBI is thinking."

"My guess is they'll start to open up a little more once we satisfy them about the Midas-Benedict thing. Half of them think it's Benedict, and for all we know, it could be. When we give them the files, that will show them we're not holding anything back. Trichina's people find it yet?"

"Trichina's digging all the project-related information out of the archives. Okay? Now, tell me about your plan from here."

"I'm headed back to Asheville just for tonight, then back to D.C. to help Franklin's man Brandon analyze all of the tobacco companies' internal suspects. All the TCs have delivered everything we've requested, with the exception of us and the Midas stuff. The more I hang around FBI Headquarters, the more opportunity I have to slip into an occasional unattended file folder."

That was a great bullshit, Rhoads thought, proud of himself. *Nice and offhand.*

"That's my boy. That's why I like you so much, T.R., you always find some way to break the rules. I'd rather be going with you instead of explaining to the board why I'm probably going global tonight on television to meet this creep's ultimatum."

"Won't they be happy that you got the networks to give you the airtime for free?"

Pratt shrugged and while Rhoads sat there, he picked up the cellular telephone to check his voicemail messages, variously deleting the ones he didn't need and saving the others. In less than ten minutes, the limo pulled onto the tarmac at Logan airport where a jet and a helicopter waited and idled noisily side by side.

45

FBI Headquarters

```
FEDERAL BUREAU OF INVESTIGATION
SECURED TELEX TRANSMISSION
TX4555699406WX21
URGENT/ CYCIG EVENT REPORTED
TO: ATLANTA DUTY CHIEF.AX
COPY ALL STATIONS.FX
FROM: WIREROOM SUPERVISOR.AX
T&D: 0957 HOURS, 06 OCTOBER
```

MESSAGE: URGENT URGENT URGENT

DISREGARD FAX RECEIVED BY ATLANTA CONSTITUTION.
FAX IS HOAX.

ALL INDIVIDUALS NAMED IN FAX HAVE BEEN IDEN-
TIFIED AS FOLLOWS:

1. DONALD S. JOHNSTON, PRESIDENT AND CEO,
   AMERICAN TOBACCO COMPANY

2. THOMAS SANDEFUR, JR., CHAIRMAN AND CHIEF
   EXECUTIVE OFFICER, BROWN & WILLIAMSON
   TOBACCO CORPORATION

3. EDWARD A. HORRIGAN, CHAIRMAN AND CHIEF
   EXECUTIVE OFFICER, LIGGETT GROUP INC.

4. ANDREW H. TISCH, CHIEF EXECUTIVE OFFICER,
   LORILLARD TOBACCO COMPANY

5. JOSEPH TADDEO, PRESIDENT, UNITED STATES
   TOBACCO COMPANY

6. JAMES W. JOHNSTON, CHIEF EXECUTIVE OFFICER,
   R.J. REYNOLDS

7. WILLIAM I. CAMPBELL, CHIEF EXECUTIVE OFFICER,
   PHILIP MORRIS

REPEAT: DISREGARD FAX RECEIVED BY ATLANTA
CONSTITUTION. THOSE INDIVIDUALS SPECIFIED ARE
PRESIDENTS, CHAIRMEN, AND/OR CHIEF EXECUTIVE
OFFICERS OF DOMESTIC TOBACCO COMPANIES. PLEASE
DO NOT INTERVIEW THESE INDIVIDUALS. THEY ARE
OFFICERS IN CORPORATIONS OPERATING LEGALLY
IN THE UNITED STATES.

46

FBI Headquarters, Event Response Center, 8:50 P.M.

In the ERC auditorium, lined with tiers of classroom seating, more than 100 FBI agents, consultants, technicians, and representatives from a dozen federal, state, and local agencies sat expectantly. In front of them, a stage and a large projection screen. Rhoads was seated in the back row and looked bored.

On the screen, a huge projected image of a brown glass jar with a white label. The label read "SODIUM CYANIDE." That slide was replaced with an equally oversized shot of a syringe.

The briefer, a senior agent in the FBI's Investigative Support Unit, lapel mike clipped to the collar of his blue FBI windbreaker, described the projected images.

". . . and, just as in the case of the potassium and sodium cyanide we've seen, these syringes are readily available over the counter. Obviously we are pursuing all these avenues of physical evidence, but the odds are *not* on our side. Fortunately, however, we do have one individual we're anxious to talk to but cannot find. He's a former TobacCo, Inc. scientist named Loren . . ."

A hand reached out from behind and tapped Rhoads on the shoulder. Rhoads turned, rose, and walked a few steps to the doorway of the auditorium. It was Franklin.

As the deputy director spoke to Rhoads, a large photo appeared on the screen. It was that of a middle-aged man with a beard. The bold-faced caption read LOREN BENEDICT. Franklin drew Rhoads into the lobby.

"Rhoads, I've got an assignment for you."

"You bore me to death with all the routine physical evidence horseshit that isn't going to lead anywhere and just when you get to the part that concerns my company, you jerk me out of there."

"The appropriate verb, Rhoads."

"Okay, what's the goose chase?"

"Let me show you something, friend." Franklin cupped his hands below his waist. "What's this?"

"A guy about to take a leak on Allstate?"

"Wrong, funny man. It's the sum total of what you and TobacCo, Inc. have given us about Midas and Benedict. You haven't earned shit. Now that Virgil's given a tape of his demand to the press, everybody and his cousin is calling in with knuckle-head theories about who Virgil is. As usual, there are a few dubious ones we're politically obliged to look into. And this," Franklin said, handing Rhoads a pink message slip stapled to a photocopy of a fax, "is one of those. Since I can't spare any FBI personnel on it, you're elected."

"What is it?" Rhoads looked at the page.

"We got a call from a psychiatrist. Came through Senator Brackenham's office, so we have to respond. Claims to have some kind of special insight into Virgil. I want you to go see her."

"Her?" He seemed surprised. Then he shrugged. "Okay. Where?"

"Philadelphia."

"I'll call her to set it up."

"Embarrass us with her, Rhoads, and you'll be out of here." Franklin checked his watch. "Hey, it's almost nine bells. Time to catch your boss on the tube."

"I don't think you'll see him. He's trying every which way to get out of going on. He was going to ask the TobacCo's board of director's blessing to refuse."

"He'll be on," Franklin said. "He had dinner with the director and the president tonight, and the director left me with the strong impression he had explained to Mr. Pratt the advantage of doing as Virgil asked."

"In TobacCo's Investor Relations Department, they're betting the stock'll drop three points if Pratt makes the announcement, and one and one-half points if Virgil retaliates for Pratt not making it. Which outcome do you think Pratt's more concerned with?"

47

Philadelphia

Muntor glared at his television set from just before nine until the ten o'clock local news began, his fists clenched as tight as his jaw.

No announcement, that motherfucker.

At ten o'clock, Muntor enjoyed a minor consolation. A "university chemistry expert" had been brought into the studio of a local television station to play "what-if" someone wanted to poison cigarettes. The expert's identity was, for alleged university public relations purposes, obscured by backlighting.

"So," the interviewer began after introducing the guest as "Doctor B," "if you were a twisted individual, how easy would it be for you to pull it off, to do what the cigarette tamperer is doing today across America?"

"From what I could determine from news reports," Doctor B said, "this character must have obtained a container of any one of the widely distributed cyanide compounds available commercially. Then he, and I'm presuming it's a *he*, made up a solution, cyanide in most forms is water soluble, and injected it into ends of cigarettes. Then all he had to do was let them dry and repackage them. Frighteningly simple."

"He needs a lab and at least some technical expertise to do that, right?" the interviewer asked.

"Afraid not. It could be done in a lab, of course, but it just as easily could be done on grandma's kitchen counter. I'm sure anyone who can read is capable of finding out how to do it with no more reference literature than a standard Intro to Chemistry textbook."

"I had no idea . . ."

"Sure. Chocolate chip cookies from scratch would be more complicated and definitely more time consuming. The worse thing is, you don't need very much cyanide. My guess is that the cigarettes each absorbed maybe 300 or so milligrams of the cyanide. That's no more than ten or twelve grains of salt."

"How much do you think a victim has to inhale to be fatal?"

"The cyanide rides into the respiratory system at full potency in the particulate of the tobacco smoke. It's a direct hit."

"So . . . how many puffs?"

"How many!" the interviewee laughed, throwing his backlit

head back. "I'm sorry for laughing, but you'd never get halfway through the first drag. The smoke is, in effect, caustic. It'd burn like heck. And once it's done its job in the lungs, the cyanide makes it impossible for oxygen molecules to be used. You can inhale all you want, but it's useless. It's nothing you'd want to witness. They turn blue."

"How dreadful."

"Yes. So, to prepare for your interview, to see how Virgil might be doing it, we tried it ourselves. We did it two different ways. First, we got an Exacto blade and performed a simple operation at the bottom of the pack. Now I'm not saying this is how he did it."

"Right, you're just saying this is how he *may* have done it."

"Correct. What we did was slit the cellophane wrapping along three sides of the bottom to make a flap about an inch and a half. Then we used the blade again to open the foil on the bottom of the package. We withdrew the first cigarette on what would be, for most consumers, the top row—the likeliest to be withdrawn first from a flip-top pack. Pulled it right out with a slant-edged forceps. You can get forceps anywhere. Tweezers, really, would do it. Once we got it out, it got a little trickier.

"In the first of two methods we tried, we pulled a small clump of tobacco out of the center of the cigarette and set it down on a piece of paper. Then we seated the cigarette filter-side down between two telephone books we pushed together to stabilize it. But Virgil, of course, could use anything. Next he could carefully put in two or three measurefuls of the cyanide, let's say he's using sodium cyanide. It's a little granular when you first get it, so I wouldn't doubt he may pulverize it in a mortar and pestle to make more of it combust with the tobacco. He could have just spooned it into the space where the tobacco had been. That's what we did. Of course, you wouldn't want to dig in too deeply. You want the first drag to deliver the entire dose. Then we wedged back in the clump of tobacco we had removed."

"Weren't you talking about a solution of cyanide? That'd be

a liquid."

"Yes, that's the other way it could be done. Once you open the package and get a cigarette out, it's much easier to inject the solution. But as I said, we were just playing around in the lab, trying to find different ways he may be doing it."

Muntor felt a twinge of jealousy. There on television was Doctor B, a man who hadn't gone through what Muntor had, yet was basking in Muntor's glory. And he had gotten pretty close to the way Muntor had done it.

No problem though, Muntor thought. *Except that now, as tired as I am, I have to go to all the trouble of thanking Pratt for ignoring a reasonable request.*

48

Newark, New Jersey

Muntor knew from *Who's Who* that W. Nicholas Pratt grew up in Newark, New Jersey.

Between nine and ten, while glaring at the television screen, he had made up twelve trick-packs on the TV tray in his living room. He talked to himself the entire time.

That son of a bitch . . . If I didn't have to keep a low profile, I'd short TobacCo, Inc. stock first thing tomorrow . . . Mr. Limo . . . I'll say the magic word and—bingo!—it'll be a hearse.

Muntor put on his coat and made the trip in little more than an hour, hitting only normal traffic on the Jersey Turnpike. While driving, he used a flashlight and peered at the Newark street map on the seat next to him. He lost his way after exiting the turnpike and ended up driving around inner-city Newark for twenty minutes. He erred in assuming that the map's points of interest legend would include public schools. Finding a phone booth with a telephone book intact proved no easy matter. He finally did outside a supermarket. Hands trembling ever so slightly, he looked up the schools in the city government blue pages. He tore out the pages with the addresses and telephone numbers of the schools in the Newark Public School System.

He arrived at the first one, Jenkins Junior High School, on Sorrell Street just after midnight.

Under the map on the passenger seat, the twelve trick-packs sat in his open eel-skin briefcase. Should the police ever stop him and examine the briefcase, the jig would, doubtlessly, be up. *C'est la vie.* Muntor believed he would never be in that situation. He was prepared with his delivery service decoy props—clipboard with pencil tethered by a piece of dirty string, a receipt book, a counterfeit delivery request slip lifted from the inquiry desk of Fast and Faster, a Philadelphia courier service closed at night, and a suitable destination, Newark General Hospital. The maps scattered on the passenger seat added just the right insinuation. As such, the props were more than adequate. If drawn into interaction with police as a result of a minor accident, mechanical trouble, or other unforeseeable incidents, he would have a reason to be in Newark. A cop would think *here's some sorry old sap, confused, driving all the way from Philadelphia to make some stinking delivery for probably six bucks an hour under the table, plus gas and tolls.* Muntor realized with a grimace that he could cut a convincingly pathetic figure.

On Sorrell Street, on his left, a line of row houses sat in the dark upon raised tiers of lawn opposite the school's main entrance. On his right, the junior high school. Inadequate street lighting was his ally. He slowed to a halt at the stop sign in the block before the school. He picked up two trick-packs. He intended to make only one pass, hit or miss. He looked up the street and, in his rearview mirror, down it. A quick scan of the houses. Most were dark. No dog-walkers in sight. He lowered the passenger-side window and drove by the school slowly, but not too slowly.

When he reached the approximate halfway point between the corner and the wide cement steps that led up to the school's entrance, he winged the two packs at once through the open window, flicking his wrist in a Frisbee-like toss, aiming them to land at the base of the wrought-iron spiked fence that separated the sidewalk from the school's lawn. He drove past the center steps, and reached for another pack, and threw it out, too, before he got to the next stop sign. He had not attempted to see where any of the packs landed, but he heard the last pack hit the cement and skid. Probably an excellent shot.

By 1:45 A.M., Muntor had repeated the operation near or close to three more schools. Two high schools and, just for extra measure, the Wilson Primos Elementary School. He hoped that the elementary school trick-pack wouldn't be smoked. He threw only one pack there. Just having someone find it and calling it in was plenty good.

Out of ten packs, certainly two or three would be sampled before school. Teachers coming to school wouldn't be likely to find them. They usually entered from a rear or side door accessible to faculty parking. Of course, an alert crossing guard could find a pack, figure it out, and raise an alarm that went citywide. Police cars screaming toward every school in the city, screeching a warning over their roof-mounted loudspeakers.

No, it wasn't likely the operation would be discovered and an alert issued in time. And even if foiled, even if every pack found itself in the hands of authorities, still, excellent press. He'd see to that.

He couldn't fail.

Martin Muntor had never had such a win-win situation his whole life.

49

Thursday, October 7

Before he left Newark for Westport, Connecticut, Muntor took the package containing an audiocassette of a message to Rhoads and taped it to the underside of the shelf in a telephone booth. He wanted Rhoads to know in great detail why he was doing what he was doing, and the live pay telephone calls never allowed him the luxury of elaboration.

Then he made a call.

In an elderly woman's weak, mournful voice, he asked the night switchboard operator at the *Las Vegas Sun*, "Could you tell me, please, who is the person who writes the obituaries?"

"That's Jerry Fuller, but he's on vacation until the twelfth," the operator said considerately. "Ma'am, if this about a deceased party, let me connect you to the editorial assistant, and he'll help you."

"Thank you, dear."

A moment later, a male came on the line. "Gunthman."

"Mr. Gunthman," Muntor said in the high voice, "can you tell me who is covering for Jerry Fuller?"

"Me."

"Then I have some information for you."

"About who?" asked Gunthman suspiciously. The voice was definitely phony. Gunthman's regular assignments included covering high school sports and writing replies to queries addressed to the "Ask Dr. Houseplant" column, the horticultural insights for which he lifted sourly and without attribution from a shelf of gardening books. His wariness regarding the telephone call evolved from Fuller's warning of the occasional practical joke perpetrated by disgruntled subordinates, spurned mistresses, or failed students, listing otherwise hale bosses, ex-lovers, or American History teachers as recently deceased and about-to-be-interred.

Switching into a gruff version of his actual voice, Muntor answered Gunthman's question. "It's news about *me.* Now listen. Write this down, and don't fuck up. Write the words 'Pay phone, King Food Market. Newark, New Jersey.' Got it? 'Pay phone, King Food Market. Newark, New Jersey.' "

"Who in the hell is this?"

"You know me, Gunthman. Now. Write it down. 'Pay phone, King Food Market. Newark, New Jersey.' "

"Who is this, or I'm hanging up."

"Listen. I'm the cigarette guy. *Virgil.* Cyanide Sam. I think you're familiar with the story."

"Good-bye," Gunthman said. He continued to listen.

"Look, smacko. You think this is a phony phone call. I'm not asking you to do anything with it. The news I'm giving you hasn't broken yet, but when it does, you're the only one who knows where I placed an audiotape for the authorities. All I want you to do is check the time on the slug when the AP, or whoever has the story first, goes with the story later today. It's 1:47 A.M. Eastern time right now, 10:47 P.M. your time."

Even if he doesn't write it down, even an idiot couldn't forget it if I say it a fourth time, Muntor thought. "The pay phone. King Food.

Newark."

"All right, I'll bite. Why are you calling Jerry Fuller with this?"

"I'm calling you, smack. I asked to be connected to the obituary writer. Get it? *Obits?* I called somewhere where they won't be expecting me to call. No tracing, genius."

"I'm hanging up."

"*King Food. Newark.* You won't forget this day so soon, Gunthy. And I'll throw this in because I like you. You can tell your colleagues there on the national desk that Nick Pratt had advance knowledge of the Newark thing and chose to stonewall the public. *Nick Pratt at TobacCo, Inc.*"

Now, Muntor knew he had to say something so that the reporter would not alert the authorities just yet.

"Oh, and one last thing, there, newsboy. *April Fool, sucker!*"

Muntor hung up first, a grin lighting up his face halfway to Connecticut.

50

The man was surly, and the TobacCo, Inc. switchboard operator insisted that her instructions were to direct *all* media calls to the Corporate Communications department.

"Listen to me, dear," the man said. "I'm John Tranor. I am *USA Daily's* national news editor. I have a nine o'clock exclusive interview with Mr. Pratt, set up at Mr. Pratt's request, and you can see I'm ten minutes late as it is, and I'm calling from a cellular telephone, and you better not lose this connection while you're screwing around. I was told to ring Mr. Pratt's secretary Gennie DesCourt directly."

What a pain in the ass. "Yes, sir. I'll connect you to the Executive Suite as you wish. And thanks for calling TobacCo, Inc."

A black Swedish-designed telephone shaped like an amoeba rang on Genevieve DesCourt's desk.

"Good morning. You've reached the Executive Suite at TobacCo, Inc. This is Genevieve DesCourt. May I help you?" The display on her telephone indicated that call came from the main switchboard, a relatively rare occurrence.

She listened to the man speak. In an instant, her face flushed, and she involuntarily drew in air, almost gasping.

"Who? Yes? Yes, sir."

In his office fifty feet away, Pratt answered Genevieve's buzz.

"*What!*" He looked down at the blinking light on his telephone. "I'll take it. Call the FBI, then call Security." Pratt's faced hardened into iron. He shot his finger toward the blinking button, but stopped short, hesitated, then pressed it, almost delicately.

"Nicholas Pratt."

Although he had listened to the voice enough on the tapes, live it was softer, weaker than he had expected.

51

FBI Headquarters

A gaggle of special agents sat and stood, leaning over a table holding a bank of telephones, some wearing headsets. The revolving reels of audiotape decks spun. One agent furiously waved his arms in the air to get the attention of the on-duty communications technician across the room. Someone elbowed the tech who looked up and then sprinted toward the group.

The agents were monitoring Pratt's call 440 miles away in Asheville.

"The greatest stupidity of VIPs like you," Muntor said, "is that they are incapable of listening. They hear always what they expect to hear. They hear always what's most convenient for them. Usually they get away with it because they surround themselves with quivering white-bread Americans. People who would have been good little Nazis had they been born earlier and elsewhere. But you're not getting away with it Pratt. Not with me."

The Behavioral Science Section had anticipated such a call. Pratt knew what to say. "We haven't made our decision yet, we're working on it right now."

The caller laughed. "You see? So *stupid*. So *predictable*. So boring. I told your man your TV appearance wasn't optional. I gave a specific date and a specific time. And I know you heard it, too."

There was a pause, and Muntor's voice rose and raged.

"What did I say? I said 'confession,' not speech, not propaganda for your side! I said 'confession,' and I said it had to be delivered that way. Yet you delivered NOTHING! Well, here is the price you pay for your bluff."

Muntor paused for effect and began in a slow I-told-you-so tone.

"I am, right at this moment, standing across the street from a schoolyard in a city . . ."

"Shit! I knew it!" One of the agents tore off his headset and sprinted to a desk where another group of agents stood.

Back on the line, Muntor continued. ". . . and I can see children walking to school, and others playing before their first class. Any moment now, one of them is going to stoop and pick up one of the packs of cigarettes someone left there. I heard how concerned you are about orphans. And after I hang up with you, I'll be calling a journalist and letting him know that I targeted these schoolchildren on behalf of Nick Pratt. In Nick Pratt's hometown. Because *Nick Pratt* is so worried about orphans . . .

"Well, there will be no orphans from this encounter. The next time I tell you to do something, Pratt, you do it! All of it! Exactly the way I tell you. Good day. By the way, I see TobacCo's common stock is down almost sixteen points since Monday. Buy on the rumor, sell on the news, Nick. Now, what do you have, eight hundred and some-odd thousand shares? Times sixteen bucks? Ouch! What'd I cost you so far? Let me see. About thirteen million. You're going to have a big capital loss this year, jackass. So long."

Back in Asheville, Pratt sat, almost dwarfed by his high-backed chair, holding a dead receiver in his suntanned hand.

In Washington, a special agent observed a computer screen. "Lying son of a bitch. He's not standing across from any schoolyard. He's in a rural area, near Westport, Connecticut. *Bastard!* We're just going to sit here and wait for reports of schoolyard fatalities? Someone find out where Pratt's hometown is. Someone get on the hot line. Call the networks and wire services. Call the state police in all forty-eight. What else can we do? What else can we do?"

Special agents stood paralyzed, mouths open.

52

Every now and then during Muntor's travels, the wind would blow up, and fall leaves would swirl, and the sky would darken before a storm. These scenes filled him with a profound homesickness, such an ache to be with his daughters, to see them giggle and hear them argue. And that longing all the time counterbalanced with the dead weight of emptiness, the knowledge that he would probably never see them again. Scenes so emotionally overpowering that he'd have to pull off the road to cry, to watch the rain if it came.

Midday, en route home from Westport where he had gone to call Pratt, the sky grew gray-blue. He was too drained to continue driving and found a motel. He tried to sleep.

Four hours later, he arose. Coughing and working for breath, he hadn't been able to sleep.

He splashed cold water on his face and took a videocassette from his briefcase and slid it into the room's VCR.

Muntor lay down on the bed and watched.

After a flurry of video static, Muntor saw a moving shot of a deserted business office. When the sound of the voice-over came on, too loud, he rushed to find the remote to lower the volume. The camera panned a bleak room, lingering on objects as he mentioned them.

"Act I"

Muntor's voice came out of the television solemnly. He loved watching the parts of the documentary for which he'd already done the voice-over recording. It made it so real.

"Scene Nine. Crimes Against Martin Muntor. The End of a Career. His selfless good deeds always misinterpreted, slighted, undermined by the jealousy of others, Martin Muntor was held to the middling position of bureau chief for a failing news service in this pitiful, ugly office. All of his power and intellect was anchored to this battered desk . . . this backbreaking chair . . . and this file cabinet, the drawers of which refused to open . . . His only confidant, a Mr. Coffee that never quite could boil water . . . This bulb-eating light fixture . . . And finally, this telephone. The telephone on which eleven years of caring about the news stories he produced, eleven years of dedication, eleven years of unpaid overtime—all casually dismissed by a New York yuppie . . . And, told, by the way, 'start paying for your own health-care benefits.'"

Muntor had to slip a five to the weekend security man to get into the office for that scene, but it was worth it. Next came some jerky camera work and a staticky interval between shots. The next image to appear was a moving shot of a medical office building, photographed through a car window.

"Act One. Crimes Against Martin Muntor. Scene Ten. The End of a Life."

On the video, Muntor switched to a mincing, nasal voice.

"I have your X-rays here, Mr. Muntor. It's cancer, I'm afraid. Lung cancer, inoperable. Now, tell me again the name of your insurance carrier."

Another staticky interval.

The exterior of a suburban Philadelphia hospital complex. Also another moving shot through a car window. At the lower left-hand corner of frame, a cat's tail swept briefly against the window.

"Act One. Crimes Against Martin Muntor. Scene Eleven. Why?"

There was a genuinely pathetic puzzlement in his tone. This wasn't contrived emotion for the narration.

"A mother who shouldn't have been one. A father who never missed a chance to have something else, something more profitable to do. A child without a chance, you could say. Fifty-six years of misery that ends with the death of Martin Muntor. But out of his corpse is born his avenger. Out of his corpse rises . . . Virgil."

53

By the time Gunthman woke up and heard about the Newark schoolchildren and figured out that Virgil shouted "April Fool" to make him think the call was bogus, it was almost eight in the morning in Las Vegas.

He called his editor, who notified the FBI.

It took agents from the Newark field office less than twenty minutes to recover the tape from the pay telephone at the super-market. In it, Muntor addressed Rhoads, used the gruff voice again, and spoke much more slowly. The speech pathologists noted the voice seemed to be more relaxed than in any previous communication. Probably, they surmised, because he hadn't been anxious that a fleet of police sedans would materialize and interrupt him.

New Jersey State Police sped the tape to the FBI's New York office where it was played over a telephone line to agents at FBIHQ.

Rhoads sat closest to the audio speakers in Lab C and listened to the tape for the third time.

"I imagine you've noticed how busy I've been. It's wearying. Now, time for a change of pace. I think I'll do a little traveling around and about. Maybe Nick'll reconsider. So what happened there? Did you whisper to him that I wasn't serious? That I was bluffing? Big misread. Anyway, I'm a forgiving man. I'm willing to take it from the top.

"Now I understand that you boys don't like ultimata. Maybe I phrased my instructions too cavalierly, and, you know, you may have something there. It is discourteous to be so demanding. You know by now, I hope, that I am not an extortionist, at least not one from the traditional school. So here's my offer. Note that. IT'S AN OFFER, NOT A DEMAND. A fair trade. Mr. Pratt goes on the air sometime soon. No, let me be definite now. Next Wednesday, nine o'clock, prime time. That's October 13. With my travel plans so up in the air, I'm not exactly sure where I'll be watching from. Then, should he decide to read that material as I've asked, I'll call you and tell you where I've planted a bunch of my little trick-packs. It is only fair that you get something for something. No announcement by Pratt, no call from me. No announcement from Pratt, AND—I'M—GOING—TO—GET—REALLY— FURIOUS. No announcement from Pratt and Newark'll seem like a day at the beach. And in the meantime, my star will keep burning bright. So Nick can think about whether or not he wants to keep playing cute."

The recording ended and, once again, the room filled with the amplified hiss of blank audiotape.

54

Friday, October 8

From the front page of the *New York Post*.

Retribution For Failing to Make
Televised Announcement?
3 Newark Kids Dead; 3 Others 'Critical'
"Virgil" Targets Exec's Hometown

55

Anna Maria Trichina, twenty-nine, sat on the bed in the white-carpeted bedroom of her condo. She sat cross-legged, in jeans and a T-shirt, flipping through a stack of Midas Project files. Her reading glasses had slipped low on her nose. She pushed them back in place and focused intently on something she had just discovered.

Her hand trembled slightly as she held a document captioned, "Post-Allocation Budget Request." Her finger ran down a column of entries until it landed on *Amount: $200,000.* Then her finger slid across the page and stopped at the words, *Approved by: W. N. Pratt.*

Trichina pulled herself upright and looked in the mirror. She shook her head to tousle her hair. She knew she could look good even after a long, besieged day, and for the first time in a quite while, she smiled. She rose and padded into the kitchen, poured herself a full goblet of Amarone, and returned to her bed. She sipped the wine while thinking about what she would do with what she had discovered.

Trichina, alone and lonely, sat daydreaming as the wine went quickly to her head. She slipped out of her jeans and took another sip before going over to the stereo to drop a Sam Cooke disc into the CD. She sat back on the bed and dimmed the lamp without turning it completely off. Sliding open the second drawer in her night table, Trichina reached in and felt around. Her hand closed on a pliable rubber penis. She wriggled out of her panties and fell back onto a pile of pillows, adjusting one under her buttocks. She listened to Sam Cooke sing "Frankie and Johnny."

Her eyes closed.

Several minutes later, an involuntary yelp escaped from her throat. Then she sighed. Sam Cooke was still singing. Trichina kept her eyes closed a moment longer. An idea hit her. She sat up, gulped the rest of the wine, turned the light back up, and found her three-year-old edition of the Confidential Employee Directory in another drawer and dialed Mary Dallaness's home telephone number.

"We think—no, we know—there's a leak," Trichina said. "Mr. Pratt personally told me that you were the only one in all of TobacCo, Inc. who I could trust. Someone in the treasurer's office, we're not sure, may be working with a reporter from the *Los Angeles Times*. Corporate Security's looking into it, of course, but in the meantime, we . . ." Mary didn't try to mask her suspicion. "Who's 'we'?" *I need to get in touch with T.R. He'd help me sort this out.*

"Me and Mr. *Pratt*," Trichina said. *Pull right into her lane, she'll yield.* "What we need you to do is this. Under the strictest of security, with only me or Mr. Pratt present, you are to make one, single paper-copy of every Midas-related document. Then erase all the computer files. *All of them.*

"Then we're going to cause the computer system to crash, only for a few minutes. That way, if the *Los Angeles Times* or the ACLU or who knows somehow subpoenas the documents, there'll be a record the system crashed. We'll be able to say that the files were actually destroyed, lost forever, and no one can prove otherwise. Those are proprietary company records. No one else's business. TobacCo, Inc. has every right to protect them."

"Ms. Trichina, our system was designed by Metro Computer Consultants in Princeton. They're the best in the world. You were on the contract-award committee, you should know. The system's been designed to back up everything so something like what you're describing can't ever happen. Never."

"Don't worry. We'll take care of that part."

"Well, I . . ."

"Do you want to tell that to Mr. Pratt and his attorneys? This is the plan they devised, so if you . . ."

Mary shuddered at the thought of being in the same room

with Mr. Pratt.

"No, Ms. Trichina," she said in a small voice. "I'm sorry. It's just that we worked so damned hard to build a computer system that was fail-safe, that would never . . ."

"Mary. Relax. No problem. Tomorrow morning, even though it's Saturday, a courier's going to deliver to your home a copy of the memo to me from Mr. Pratt. Call him directly, if you really feel you need to disturb him at a time like this. That'd be okay with me, if you're uncomfortable with the . . . the *validity* of the memo. It spells out all the details. But time counts. We both have to drop everything and get this done first thing tomorrow. I have a meeting I can't get out of, but I'll be free by ten. Okay?"

"I understand," Mary said, barely audibly.

"Good," Trichina said, stabbing the word into her, *"good."*

56

The telephone rang late, and Rhoads answered it.

"T.R.?" the voice said.

"Mary?"

"Yes. Listen. I need to talk to you."

He sat up in bed and turned on the lamp. Light filled the room, and he noticed one of the ficus trees had dropped a lot of brown leaves. It needed more sun. "Go ahead, Mary."

"No. In person."

She can't mean now, he hoped. *Not a sex play.* He wanted her, but clean, legit. After Anthony's gone. "Okay," he said. "First thing in the morning? You usually go into work Saturday mornings. Meet you for coffee before. Name the place."

"No. Now."

"Now? Can't you tell me what this is about?" *Please don't invite yourself over here to tell me your troubles,* he thought.

"About halfway between your building and where I live is a little pizza joint called Slice O'Heaven. On Cadwalader near the movie theater. I don't care if you have a girl there in bed with you. It's important."

"Okay . . . okay," he said, relieved. "And I'm alone."

Thirty-five minutes later, Mary had told him half the story and started on the first of two slices of pizza and had a large Pepsi in front of her. Rhoads played with a plastic cup of lousy coffee. *God, she was perfect. Not beautiful, not even pretty. Just some primal attraction. Magnetic. That's what it was! It was like the force you feel when you hold two powerful magnets apart.* It reached out and seized him and it wouldn't let go, and he didn't know what to do with it.

"Sorry," she said, tucking her hair behind one ear and leaning forward to blow on the still-too hot slice. "But I get ravenous when I'm nervous." The mozzarella steamed, and she dropped the slice back onto the paper plate.

"Why are you so damned nervous? You're taking orders from the woman you report to. If she's forged a document, then no one is going to hold you responsible. You're just a cog in the wheel. Report it to Genevieve if you want to cover yourself."

"I know that. But I'm not at the top of my form. Anthony's dying, and taking care of him's killing me. I can't seem to control my mind, I worry and worry about everything. And what I'm worried about with Pratt is that he knows, or *thinks* he knows, that I know what's in those files. If it's something bad, something he doesn't want anyone to know . . . well, you've heard the rumors. Who knows *how* far he'd go?"

Mary, now upset, couldn't eat anymore. She looked through sad eyes at Rhoads and let him see her looking. "Okay, let's say I do what you said, make an extra set of disks before I erase everything. The disks won't protect me unless Pratt knows I made the copies, and if he knows, then he'll definitely do something about it. It's a Catch-22, and I'm the one who's caught. I'm frightened. Really frightened."

"At the police academy they taught us that any time you're in a situation and you have to draw your gun—you've already made about ten mistakes. But that was just smartass twenty-year guys spouting off. The truth is, there are plenty of times you're minding your own business and things just happen. Those are the times when you're glad as hell you remembered to bring your gun. So I recommend you make those disks. You may never need them."

"Then again . . ."

"Then again, you may be glad you have them."

"Let's say I do it. What do I do with them?"

"First, hide them. Hide them very carefully."

"What if I get caught making the copies?"

"Can't you fix it up so you don't? And if you do get caught, you can always say you weren't sure that Trichina was acting legally, and you kept a set to protect TobacCo, Inc. while you tried to figure out what to do. Which would not be a lie."

"But it's illegal to make those copies, no matter what bullshit I make up to explain it," she said.

"Let me tell you something. Have you ever heard the expression impersonating a police officer?"

"Of course."

"You think it's illegal to impersonate a police officer?"

"Of course."

"Wrong. It's only illegal if you get someone to do something they otherwise wouldn't do because you made them think you're a police officer."

She stared at him. "And your point?"

Rhoads rolled his eyes. "You make copies of computer disks and just lock them up somewhere, it's not too much of a crime. It's not like you're selling the information for personal gain. You're not damaging TobacCo, Inc. That's what law boils down to. Did one guy cause another guy to suffer somehow."

Mary nodded. That made sense.

"Or," Rhoads said, "if you want, give the disks to me." His mind started churning, and he had a second thought. "The thing is, you'll have to get in tomorrow and quick make a copy of the disks before Trichina comes to Documentation."

"Wrong. You can't copy Level Three documents that easily. It's a complicated, time-consuming process. I'll need hours and hours."

"How are you going to do it with Trichina standing right there making sure you don't make a second copy?"

"Already thought of that." Mary tried to conceal her pleased expression. "That'll be the easiest thing in the world."

"How?"

"Simple. First I have to print out a hard copy of everything."

"She'll be standing right there watching every keystroke."

"Then, after I've printed everything out, she's going to want me to delete every single Midas document from the computer."

"She'll be right there watching."

"So when the computer asks me which group of files to delete, I type in . . ." Mary took a pen from her bag and wrote on Rhoads's napkin. In all capital letters, she printed MID0CS. "That's the computer's shorthand for 'Midas Documents.'"

"That'll delete them, right?" Rhoads said.

"Wrong. Take a look at the 'O' in documents."

Rhoads did. "Yeah?"

"It's not the letter 'O.' It's a zero." She drew a narrower character, she drew "0." "As far as the computer's concerned, it's totally different."

"Won't the computer flash an error message or something to alert you there's no such set of documents to erase?"

"Not if I create a MIDOCS directory with a zero instead of a letter 'O.' Then it will have something to delete. That I *can* do quickly."

Rhoads studied the napkin. "All this is a little over my dinosaur head. You're sure it'll work?"

"If I don't have a heart attack or shake so hard that the computer tilts." She spoke lightly but was being brave. Rhoads could see her hands trembling.

Rhoads wanted to touch her. He wanted to reach across the table and take hold of her hand, squeeze it. Maybe kiss it.

Scratch that, he thought, *but she does have real spirit for such a timid thing. And a hot little ass, I bet. Rhoads, you prick, her husband's dying, and she's counting on you for help.*

Instead of taking her hand, he complained about his coffee and tried to flag down the restaurant's only waitress, who was busy laughing loudly and jumping back every time the guy making the pizzas grabbed at her behind the high counter.

"It'll be all right. You'll see, Mary."

She shrugged and picked up a slice of pizza, finally finding a place where she could take hold with her teeth, negotiated a bite, and struggled with a long string of cheese.

"I hope you're right. But something Pratt said is what's got me supernervous. Maybe I'm just paranoid."

"That's easy when you work at TobacCo. What'd he say?"

She leaned in a few inches and lowered her voice. "He asked me, when he called me at home Monday night, he asked me if someone could access the Midas files, then change the log that reports who's seen them."

"That's a good question. What's the answer?"

"Besides Mr. Pratt and Anna Maria? I'm the only one who can do that."

57

Saturday, October 9
Philadelphia

"Dr. Trice?"

She looked up from her desk.

"Mr. Rhoads."

Rhoads, wearing a suit, stood in the doorway to the cluttered office of Beatrice Trice, MD, Ph.D., professor at the Hospital of the University of Pennsylvania's Department of Psychiatry. He was there on Franklin's busy-work errand. In a letter transmitted to the FBI through U.S. Senator George Brackenham's office, Dr. Trice had suggested that she had possibly divined hidden meaning in the published accounts of Muntor's calls to FBI Headquarters.

Ceiling-high stacks of medical journals, files, reports, newspapers, and notebooks decorated the room. An overgrown wandering Jew hung in a plastic pot from the ceiling.

Dr. Trice was a small woman, exceedingly plump, as far as Rhoads could tell. She was seated. Maybe in her early seventies. She dyed her hair an attention-getting shade of red nature hadn't thought of. She sat, visible only from the shoulders up, behind her desk.

Dr. Trice used a spoon to scoop something out of a plastic container. Rhoads could not determine what. He walked in and sat down, opened a small soft-leather portfolio and removed a notebook. He turned to a blank page and took a pen from his breast pocket and clicked it open.

"Thank you for contacting the bureau, Dr. Trice. I understand you have a theory regarding the cyanide killer."

"Oh, I have a theory, all right. I also have a personal interest in this case. Anyway, you must be low man on the FBI's totem pole to get stuck interviewing me. Or is this assignment punishment for some infraction? The FBI, I know, mocks me."

"I laugh at the *FBI*, Dr. Trice. I'm not an FBI agent. I'm a corporate security consultant. I have expertise in tobacco company security, and I'm working *with* the FBI, not for them. I'm here because you probably have something of value to say. Besides, you said you have a personal interest in this case—as opposed to professional. Do you think you know the man responsible?"

"No. But I know people like him. That's why I can help. Now, back to you for a moment. You said *consultant?* But you looked away when you said that word."

She caught a white lie.

"I used to have a staff position at TobacCo, Inc., the company that makes Easy Lights," Rhoads said. "Manager of Corporate Security. But I quit. Wasn't fired, Dr. Trice, I quit. I'm looking right at you when I say that."

"Why did you quit?" she asked him.

"Okay. But then we're going have to stick to talking about Virgil, not me."

Dr. Trice raised her eyebrows.

Rhoads continued. "There're all kinds of people in the world, Doc. And believe me, I'm as bad as any of 'em, maybe worse. Maybe someday I'll tell you why I ought be in jail myself, but that's not a tale for today. Anyway, there's one breed of person I can't stomach. And they're crawling all over like cockroaches at TobacCo, Inc. Not only TobacCo, I guess, everywhere, but that's where I had to rub up against them. I call 'em *zeros*. They're people who treat everybody like shit in their pursuit of zeros, which, I'm sure you realize, Dr. Trice, is nothing."

"Zeros?"

"People work, save up a hundred bucks. I respect that. Then, they work harder, find another zero, stick it on the end of the hundred. Now they have a thousand. Then, usually after a lot more work, another zero. Now they have ten thousand, then a hundred thousand, then a million, then a billion. It never stops. Turns my stomach. Nothing matters except this insane compulsion to get more zeros. Meanwhile, they're kidding themselves, killing themselves, taking themselves so seriously, socking away those zeros, out buying a lot of . . . crap. Who said, 'We waste our lives buying and selling'?"

"I don't know, Mr. Rhoads. Who said it? I'd think you'd know who said that since it seems to embody an idea so important to you."

"Walt Whitman or Thoreau or Walden. One of those. Anyway, it never stops. They're hooked, and then they trap themselves forever with a set way of seeing the world just so they can have a reason why they have to keep collecting zeros." Rhoads paused. "So that's what was behind my quitting TobacCo, Inc."

"Yes, Mr. Rhoads, but what would it say in TobacCo, Inc.'s Human Resources termination summary?"

"That I'm irresponsible."

"Mr. Rhoads, I'm going to make a guess now, about you. I'd say that you have no significant love relationship, you have a drug- or alcohol-dependency problem, you act first and think later, and like taking big risks and often regret it. And, if you yourself have any 'zeros' at all, they'd be on the wrong side of the decimal point. But you are right that we can get back to you later. In the meantime, you've returned to TobacCo, Inc. and accepted this so-called consulting assignment. All in the heart of the land of zeros. Why are you back there?"

"The CEO wanted me, and I need a few zeros myself. I'm kind of a point man for the FBI's investigation. They need all kinds of things from TobacCo, Inc., as well as the other Big Eight cigarette manufacturers. I gather and coordinate information. For example, I'm here today."

"Until I complained to George Brackenham, no one at the FBI seemed very interested in hearing me out. Nevertheless," she sighed and took another scoopful of whatever she had in front of her, "what inspired my call is the published transcript of Virgil's communication with the FBI."

"What about it?" Now he could see. She was eating frozen yogurt, something pinkish, possibly strawberry. Dr. Trice took several man-sized spoonfuls in succession and seemed to be chewing the yogurt.

"One quick thought about your zeros, Mr. Rhoads," she said with her mouth half full. "Do yourself a favor. Don't waste your precious time hoping any of them will ever see it the way you want them to. That won't happen. You just work on yourself. There's plenty to do there. What are you, forty-one?"

"Forty-two," Rhoads said, shifting uneasily in the chair. "Now, what is it you'd like to contribute on Virgil?"

Dr. Trice scraped inside the container for the last of the yogurt. "Don't tell me the FBI actually thinks Virgil really revealed anything about himself in that call. Or do they?"

"I'm the one who's supposed to be asking the questions, Dr. Trice."

Dr. Trice smiled and made eye contact. "But I'm a psychiatrist. Even the FBI can't stop us from asking questions. And please call me Bea."

"Okay, Bea. Here're my answers to your next ten questions. 'Don't know.' 'Can't say.' 'That's classified.' 'Don't know.' 'Can't say.' 'That's classified.' 'Don't know.' 'Can't say.' 'That's classified.' Now, please go on."

Rhoads had nervous energy to burn. He reached into his pocket and pulled out Leo's canister of Mace. He turned it over and over in his hand, like a modern Captain Queeg. Dr. Trice half rose out of her chair to see what Rhoads was playing with. She frowned when she recognized what it was.

"Number one, you shouldn't carry that Mace around. An attacker could take it away and use it against you. Number two, your math is bad. That was nine answers. And number three, Virgil's message is disturbing. That's why I called. To make certain that the FBI understands, fully understands, the extent of the problem Virgil presents."

Rhoads put away the canister.

"*Disturbing*. You mean, apart from the fact that he's smart, sneaky, doesn't seem to mind killing hundreds of people, and probably has a legitimate reason to hate tobacco companies?"

"Yes," Dr. Trice said. "Normally, if you'll excuse the use of that term in this situation, people who behave as Virgil behaves are seeking attention, and therefore, whether they acknowledge it to themselves or not, they have a desire to be caught. For them, that's where the action is. Most extramarital affairs are motivated by the same desire. Not," she practically gushed, "that sex isn't the most wonderful thing, the most exciting thing. But in getting caught, cheaters are forced into a confrontation that creates a forum where none existed previously, forced to, or given the opportunity to, say the things they could not or would not say before."

Rhoads thought he ought to jot *something* down.

Dr. Trice continued. "Aside from the extramarital parallel, people who do the kinds of things Virgil does want their pictures in the newspaper. They want to be interviewed on television, even if it has to be from a prison cell. They want to be talked about. That attention-seeking child who brings home a pretty picture from kindergarten for all to praise. Such people rarely have the personal resources to endure the level of stress Virgil must be under for any extended period."

Rhoads shifted in the seat again. "And you think Virgil's an exception to this."

"No. I'm convinced he's an exception to this."

"So he's not looking for a forum?"

"Oh, no, he is, and he's already found it. The media. By the way, he seems to know a lot about the media. He's already impressed me with his skill at manipulating them. The exception part is that I'm afraid Virgil has no desire to be caught. It's even likely that the stress he is feeling is for him a positive experience, almost joyous. He has finally found the thing at which he excels.

"Mr. Rhoads, how will you feel when you finally find the

thing that feels right for you? And if my idea that Virgil's dying is correct—and I imagine it is—finally finding the thing he's good at in his last few days on Earth is a powerful discovery. It will spur him to heights of accomplishment he's probably never imagined."

"What makes you so sure?"

"For one thing, as far as I know, Virgil hasn't asked for money or anything which would benefit him personally. That means that his compensation derives from what he is already doing. And his behavior tells us exactly what that is."

"Which is . . ."

"Which is his control over the situation. He can make the CEO of a major corporation into his own marionette . . ."

There was something he could write down. *"Pratt's his puppet."*

". . . and no matter how advantageous you think it may be to humor him and obey his commands, don't. He will punish you anyway. That's what he meant when he called Pratt's reading of *The Surgeon General's Report* a 'confession' and said that it had to be delivered that way. Nothing will be contrite enough to satisfy him. First you confess, you've admitted guilt. Then he metes out justice. My guess is that Virgil's not a member of the Forgiveness-of-the-Month Club. Body bags will be used no matter what you do. Does the FBI understand this? No. Virgil is not a political terrorist. And if your apprehension strategy is based on the sup-position that he is a terrorist, you'll be in more trouble than you are now."

"Well, not to contradict you, Bea, personally, I *do* see him as a terrorist. He's getting something he wants through the use of terror. Now, what do you call that?"

"Virgil is, in his mind, an avenging angel. William Wordsworth, by the way."

"Huh?"

"Your mangled quotation. *The world is too much with us; late and soon. Getting and spending, we lay waste our powers.* It's by Wordsworth, the English poet. He was embittered, separated by the politics of his day from what he loved, a woman and a daughter."

Rhoads nodded and looked self-consciously down at his notebook. *Pratt's his puppet.* What a dumb thing to write. He sighed.

"Okay, Dr. Trice. Then who, in your opinion, should we be looking for?"

"I believe there are two different personalities to consider. There is the personality of the man Virgil was for most of his life. And there is a second, I will say, 'super' personality that has come into being through this crime. The original personality is that of a petty, resentful man, who has always felt that his abilities were slighted and unrecognized and . . ."

"He's getting recognition now."

"Your interruptions are juvenile, Rhoads. To look at him, you would think him an ordinary, perhaps rather unpleasant person, unworthy of much notice. The superpersonality is dangerous because the abilities he imagines he has, are, in some sense, real."

"You got all that from the transcript of a quick telephone conversation?"

"No, Rhoads, I got all that from forty-four years of sitting in offices like this, from working with thousands and thousands of patients, from observing my fellow man. I'm a natural when it comes to insight into the psyche. I was a prodigy. When I was four years old, I saw an article in *National Geographic* about horses. I remember then and there consciously plotting to manipulate my parents into moving out of the city and onto a horse farm. I succeeded. And then found out I was allergic to horse dander. Anyway, I'm scientist. And I can tell you that the test of any scientific theory lies in whether it can predict a specific outcome. I am prepared to predict a specific outcome that will enable the FBI to assess the value of my insights."

"You've got my attention."

"He gave you a hint about additional murders he'll commit before the next broadcast deadline, which is . . . when?"

"Wednesday night. He gave a hint? What is it?"

"I can tell you where it is in the transcript. He used it once in a call and once in the tape he left at the phone booth in Newark. Deciphering its specific meaning requires me knowing more than you are willing to share. But here it is anyway." Dr. Trice hesitated, possibly for effect. "It's his use of the word 'star.' He jimmied it into his speeches."

Dr. Trice picked a document that Rhoads recognized to be a copy of the transcript. Rhoads reached into his briefcase to get his own copy. She flipped through several pages.

"What page are you on?" Rhoads asked.

"Page four, beginning at line number fourteen. This comes in where he states what time he wants to hear the tobacco company CEO Pratt read the so-called confession. '. . . It doesn't have to be precisely nine, but it should be within a few minutes. Don't keep me waiting long. I'm one guy you don't want to piss off. I'll be a big star burning brightly while I'm waiting. And I don't wait patiently.'"

"'I'll be a big star burning brightly while I'm waiting,'" Rhoads repeated. "That means something to you?"

"If I'm right about who he is, it sure as hell does. Listen, read that line again."

Rhoads read it to himself, moving his lips to show her he was doing as asked.

She continued. "Now, doesn't that line sound a little forced, a little out of context? I think he had planned to work that line into the call. If only I could hear the tape. Then I might be able to say. Without more information, I can only guess. I think it's clear that until he gets what he's asked for from Pratt, he's going to keep burning. But the word 'star' is the tip-off. I had to think about it for a while. 'Star' has special significance.

"Listen to the tape again, and tell me if you don't agree. Probably 'star' has something to do with where he's going to strike. Too vague to help you now, but after he commits his next murders, we'll all see that he had already 'told' us about it, how clever he's been. Again, that attention-seeking child bringing home the pretty picture."

"Okay, Dr. Trice, you . . ."

"Bea, Rhoads. Bea."

"Okay, Bea. You've been honest with me, now my turn. I know you're a smart woman. Unfortunately, a lot of smart people turn out to be, no offense, crackpots. Well meaning, well intentioned, but crackpots just the same. You'll have to give me something a little more concrete to take back to the boys in Washington, They're a black-and-white bunch. Superpersonalities, burning stars, little kids showing pictures to their mommies. What can I do with that?"

"Rhoads, I can't give you anything concrete. I haven't enough information. The FBI probably doesn't either, or they wouldn't have sent you here, even as a practical joke in which you are the victim. But keep your eyes open for the 'star' hint."

Rhoads clicked his pen closed. Dr. Trice did not attempt to mask her disappointment that she hadn't wowed him.

"Okay then, Bea. Thank you for fighting the bureaucracy and trying to get through to us. I'll write my report and describe your . . . theory. I'm sure someone will get back to you soon."

Dr. Trice stood up and walked around her desk toward Rhoads. She wasn't much taller than when she was sitting. Rhoads saw her as a kind of Dr. Ruth, only heavier. She tossed the empty yogurt container into a wastebasket ten feet away. She didn't watch to see if it landed in the basket, she knew it would. A perfect shot. Then she pointedly took a long look at Rhoads's notebook. He had made only the one note. She studied his odd, childlike writing, big block letters. Then she looked up.

She pointed her finger at Rhoads. The friendly demeanor had disappeared along with the yogurt container.

Her lips curled in a snarl. "Listen, buster. We both know no one is going to do diddly with that report of yours, even if you do get around to writing it. You're overdue for a haircut, you think you'll take the time to sit down and write a thoughtful analysis of today? Doubt it. So let me warn you in no uncertain

terms. Virgil is a merry-go-round nightmare, and he's not planning to let anyone get any sleep.

"You know he's playing with you, right? What a sadistic,
powerful opponent does is give you hope. He wants you to keep
trying. It's entertainment. 'Star' is a valid hint. Virgil wants you to
realize he's given you the hint *after* the fact. He's not counting on
the FBI putting together some kind of 'star' angle now. This is
your opportunity. He may not give you another. And while you
and the FBI boys are trying to figure out whether or not I'm nuts,
Virgil will be proving what he is."

Rhoads nodded respectfully. They shook hands and he left.

He stood waiting for the elevator when she stuck her head
out into the hallway.

"Rhoads."

He turned.

"Yes?" He walked back to her, noticing her eyes measuring
him. "Yes?"

"Rhoads, you stick with me, and I will show you how Virgil
and you are quite similar."

"Okay, I'll think about that." Then Rhoads had a question.
"Dr. Trice, what will you get out of all this?"

"It's a petty thing, Rhoads."

"Go ahead."

She hesitated. "I don't like being laughed at, even if I don't
respect who's doing the laughing. It's a hang-up of mine."

"I understand that, Dr. Trice."

"Don't give up on me so fast, Rhoads. I can give you a leg up
on the FBI. Remember this. Murder starts in the mind. Virgil's life
traveled down a road that, at some point, diverged in a yellow
wood, and he made a choice. We see where that led him. You
made a choice, too, when you quit TobacCo, Inc. Only, for some
reason, you've circled back to that juncture. I think . . . I *know* . . .
it's to alter that choice, and I'm not talking about your decision
to have a career in the tobacco business."

"Then what are you talking about?"

"I'm telling you that Virgil's behavior is, at the end of the day, no different than the greedy, untrue, responsibility-shirking behavior that your so-called zeros indulge in. And if I'm correct that, emotionally, you are strikingly similar to Virgil, then you are strikingly similar to your zeros as well. I don't think you want to be there, do you? It boils down to accountability, Rhoads. So you come back someday and tell me about how quitting your job was a form of avarice. You think about it, we'll talk about it. I think then you'll be on the path to finding Virgil."

Rhoads looked at her the way a dog looks at a radio. "I don't . . ."

"Rhoads. Listen. Anybody can hit the lottery, right?"

"Theoretically."

"Exactly. Your chances of catching Virgil through some slip-up on his part? Won't happen. He can drop his, what does he call them—his trick-packs?—he can drop them anywhere, anytime, indefinitely. He knows it, you know it."

"So we just wait for him to die, whenever that happens to be."

"Your only chance, and I don't know how much of a chance it is, is to find him by using your intuition."

"That sounds like a Ouija-board thing to me, Bea."

"Underneath that dumb cop bit you like to believe in, there's four and half million years of mammalian experience, even wisdom, hard-wired into your brain. Respect it. Keep your mind open and alert for any ideas that seem to sneak up on you, tug at you. Maybe for no recognizable reason. Thoughts or ideas that have a different . . ." She searched for the right word, a word that would work for Rhoads. She found it and smiled. "Thoughts or ideas that have a different *texture* about them. They are usually gifts from the universe. Don't count on remembering them, write them down. If something keeps picking at you and you can't make sense of it, *write it down.* Then call me. Any time, day or night. I'll try to help."

"Okay, Bea. That kind of makes sense."

"Rhoads?"

"Yes?"

"You have a little more respect for me now than you did on your way up here?"

"Yes. I really do. And, if you have any respect at all for me, I'd like you to trust me on something."

"Such as?"

"Get yourself some Mace. Keep it at the ready in your hand, finger on the button when you're alone in the city here and any-place you could be attacked. Elevators, in the parking lot, anyplace dark where there aren't other people close by. Someone *could* take it away from you, but the odds are it'll do you more good than harm because just having it reminds you to be alert to your surroundings."

"I'll think about that, Rhoads. And now I'd like you to trust me when I tell you there are no coincidences in this universe. None at all. You're looking for Virgil because you are the best man for the job."

Rhoads wasn't so sure about that "no coincidences" thing, but something told him Dr. Trice was more trustworthy than most of the people he knew.

58

Asheville

In the subbasement of TobacCo, Inc., in Valzmann's office, amid the clutter of hanging wires and rows of monitors, electronic equipment, cameras and clipboards and disorderly shelves, Valzmann sat staring at a computer monitor. An obscene calendar hung on the wall and a mostly empty two-liter bottle of carbonated water sat on a desk.

His attention was absorbed in watching data scroll by on the screen.

TobacCo, Inc.

Corporate Security—Exception Reporting System

✦ ✦ ✦ SECURITY VIOLATION ✦ ✦ ✦

Unauthorized printouts completed 09:06:33 October 9:

Document #	Security Level	# Copies
MIDOCS-65391	3	2
MIDOCS-65392	3	2
MIDOCS-65393	3	2
MIDOCS-65398-A	3	2

Executed under User I.D. #03227

He stared at the screen watching the Security Violation line flashing and made notes in a little leather notebook. On another screen, he watched Mary Dallaness and Trichina at work in the Documentation Department.

Then he picked up the telephone and punched one button.

59

Martin Muntor sat watching television in the drab motel room in Scranton, Pennsylvania.

Bozzie curled in my lap would be nice right now, he thought. But it wasn't loneliness that bothered him. It was the loss of his spotlight.

For the second consecutive day, the ongoing FBI manhunt for Virgil had slipped from the top news spot. Last night, Muntor had noted, the major networks led with news about a secret Middle East peace summit in Geneva attended by leaders of Hamas. And now this evening, CNN led with a breaking story about a National League sports-betting scandal.

Muntor knew what he needed to do to regain the media's attention.

He had no appetite, and instead of eating, he made a quick stop at a local library. A reference librarian provided him with a tour guide to Europe. In it, Muntor found the name of Davidoff, a famous Swiss tobacconist at number 2 Rue de Rive in Geneva.

Back in the motel room, he packaged up six packs of Easy Lights. He left again and bought a *Congratulations!* card at a Hallmark shop. "Please consider adding this terrific American brand to your shop's inventory of first-class tobacco products." He signed the card "Nick Pratt," but presumed the store manager in Geneva would know who sent the package and notify the police there.

The U.S. Post Office provided Muntor with a padded envelope and airmail postage. He left the post office content that he'd soon be the primary focus once again of headlines and newscasts throughout the world. And as a bonus, he grinned, he'd probably be the subject of an Interpol investigation.

Why should Hamas guerrillas have all the fun? he thought on his way back to the motel. *Geneva's a big enough town for the both of us.*

60

FBI Headquarters

The telephone rang at the duty officer's desk, and the special-agent-in-charge from the Omaha field office reported that Omaha police had a tampering suspect in custody.

"I'm reporting the incident, but I don't want to shake everybody up and have this go out on the hot line," the SAC said. "Omaha police say this is guaranteed to turn out to be a copycat. The suspect is a Hispanic male in his midsixties and known to local police as a frequent crank caller."

"Keep us advised," the duty officer said, hanging up and making a note of the call in the day report.

The duty officer then called Franklin and told him what had happened.

"I should have warned you," the deputy director said. "We're not sure why, but Saturdays often present higher incidence of copycatting."

61

Asheville

Mary Dallaness parked two blocks from Rhoads's condo and walked nervously in jeans and sneakers and a peach silk blouse, fearful of the dark, fearful of strangers, into his lobby. She used the security code he had given her to open the locked doors, then she entered the elevator, rode up, and exited when it reached the twelfth floor.

She rang the bell at Rhoads's unit.

He opened the door, she stepped in, and they hugged as he kicked the door closed.

On a console in Valzmann's office in the subbasement, a light flashed under a piece of white tape upon which someone had written with a marker, "T. Rhoads Apt." The light flashed every time Rhoads's front door opened or closed, or any time his telephone rang or someone buzzed him from the lobby. A man with a stubbly three-day-old beard listened into headphones and heard the sounds of two people moaning, groaning, and crying out. He checked the counter on the reel-to-reel tape deck, looked at his watch, and penciled a note on the log.

In Rhoads's bedroom, a small boom box sat on a pillow on his bed. The sex sounds came from an audiotape player in the boom box. Rhoads had walked a bewildered Mary from the foyer, down the hallway, into his bedroom. She resisted and turned to him with wide eyes. Something in his expression told her not to worry. He pulled her by her elbow into the bedroom and pushed her gently toward the bathroom door.

He opened the door, ushered her in, and closed it behind them. The small white-tiled room was flooded with candlelight. Mary looked around, saw an ice bucket, liquor bottles, and beveled old-fashioned glasses on the radiator, plush cushions on the toilet and sink. She looked at Rhoads.

"Have a seat," he said quietly. Then, as if they were at the Big Tar Bar, with an open-palmed gesture toward the bottles, he offered her a drink.

"I could use one," she said, perching uneasily on a cushion atop the toilet seat. "Is this your m.o. for entertaining female guests? Or are you just being considerate because you've heard we all have weak bladders?"

"I'm always considerate. Besides, anatomically, women don't have weak bladders, they have smaller bladder *capacity*. There's a difference. You called this powwow, Mary. What's up?"

Mary didn't know how to start. She looked around, astonished at having a conversation in a candle-lit bathroom. Rhoads handed her a scotch on the rocks and sat down on the rug several feet away from her, his back up against the bathroom door. She took a tentative sip. She tried to compose her thoughts.

Rhoads spoke. "Let me help. How'd the Great Now You See It, Now You Don't trick go with the Midas documents this morning?"

Rhoads could see Mary was profoundly distressed. No making light of it.

"Okay, I'll be serious," he said. "We devised a plan that will protect you from Pratt and Anna Maria. You promise to call me by three o'clock. At the latest. You never call. I stayed here, worrying about how you are doing. And no call.

"Finally, I call your house, and you answer the phone. You sound upset. You say you can't talk, that you'll talk to me next week. You hang up. Now I'm really worried that something went wrong. I call you back. You tell me nothing went wrong, you tell me to just forget it. Then you call me back two hours later, more upset than ever, but you don't want to risk being overheard. So I invite you here. I *guarantee* this room is not bugged. *Now, what's up?*"

Mary looked up, wanting to watch Rhoads's reaction. "Do you know what the Midas Project was?"

The sex sounds penetrated the bathroom door.

"I give up," Rhoads said. "What?" He put a smile on. Candle-light flickered, making his expression difficult to discern.

A flash of apprehension fell across Mary's face. She exhaled slowly then shivered. She stood up and pointed accusingly at him. "Maybe you'd better tell me who you really are. Tommy Rhoads? Or Nick Pratt's bagman?"

Rhoads looked toward the ceiling. "Why is everybody always sneaking up on me and clubbing me with the Midas Project?"

"So you already know it was a top-secret research study on the most effective way to increase nicotine concentrations . . ."

". . . so that TobacCo, Inc. could build that customer loyalty, boost sales, maximize profits," he finished her sentence.

Mary breathed a little easier. At least he wasn't going to lie about everything. "Then why'd you pretend you didn't know what it was about? You have to be straight with me or you can't help me."

"Because I'm not supposed to know what it was about."

Mary drained her drink and handed the glass back to Rhoads for a refill. He stood up and poured another.

"T.R., this morning I spent three hours with Anna Maria answering the most incredibly detailed questions about the project documentation."

"How did the fake MIDOCS thing go?"

"Perfectly. I've got the disks put away, and very shortly, I'm going to give them to someone I *now* know I can trust." She smiled at Rhoads.

"Good girl!" Rhoads grinned proudly.

"And," Mary said, "Anna Maria wasn't even paying that close attention. I think she thought her mere presence was intimidating enough. Irritating is more like it. And her perfume absolutely reeks."

"The vanilla musk?"

"You know it? Ugh. It's nauseating. If I was a man, it'd turn me off permanently."

Rhoads shrugged. *Doesn't have that effect on everyone.*

"In any event," she said through her teeth, "it would have made ten times more sense to stay in my office to talk, but after I finished printing the documents and pretended to delete the files, she insisted we talk in her office."

"To tape the conversation."

"I'm positive, but I can't prove it. Once she even said Mary, speak up, I can't hear you when you mutter. "

"What was she asking you?"

"All about the security procedures that protect Midas files in the database. Not to mention having me prepare a written inventory of all hard copies of every Midas document."

"Everyone from Pratt on down is paranoid as hell right now," Rhoads said. He poured himself a healthy Bacardi 151, dropped in a few ice cubes, and squeezed a piece of lime in it. He sat back down against the door.

Mary looked at the glass in his hand.

"That your idea of a mixed drink? Looks like some kind of a toxic solvent."

"It is," he said, "but what's wrong with that?" He drank some. "Anyway, Pratt's convinced that Virgil's going to bring so much attention to TobacCo, Inc. that the Midas thing's going to blow up in his face. That's what's got him so upset. What is it that's got you so upset? There's something you haven't told me."

"I'm not upset, I'm scared. Damned scared. Trichina's demanded hard copies of certain Midas documents, and I made them. Off the log."

"Off the log?"

"Right. Off the log. That means without any record that she has a copy. I was supposed to make one set, period. Not one set and a bunch of extra copies for her. If she's using the documents for a private purpose, I guarantee I'll be fired the instant one of them turns up where it shouldn't. I'm even liable legally. And with Anthony so sick, I can't afford to get fired."

"Couldn't you just say no ?"

"She's got a memo signed by Pratt. It puts her in absolute charge of the Midas Project archives. First she hinted that it has something to do with some investigative reporter from the *L.A. Times*, then it's supposed to be about Virgil and that she can't discuss it with me. But I'm sure that's bullshit. It's something else. I feel it."

"Listen, Mary, I'm basically a dumb cop. I don't understand all of this high-tech database lingo. If she's got the memo, you're covered. Right?"

Mary, still sitting on the cushion, wrapped her arms around herself to stop from trembling. Then she burst into tears.

"T.R., I'm terrified," she said, then whispered, "I read those documents months ago during system maintenance. I shouldn't have, but, I thought, what the hell, they're there in the system that I'm in charge of. I wish I hadn't seen them. I don't exactly 100 percent understand them, but I have a good idea. Like you said. Seems illegal, sneaking higher doses of nicotine into cigarettes. But it's phrased very carefully. Lots of euphemisms and coy language. And, there's this letter from Pratt to Benedict making some kind of incredibly generous early-retirement offer. You know, kind of an offer he can't refuse. And then there's Benedict's reply. He wrote it by hand."

"Which was?"

Mary slid off the cushion and pressed herself against Rhoads's shoulder and her lips against his ear. The sensation and her warm breath sent a charge right through him. There was that magnetic field again.

She spoke, but barely audibly. "He said, Pratt, you are a dishonorable son of a bitch, and I'll accept your offer over my dead body. " She searched his eyes and bit her lower lip. Then she gasped.

It took Rhoads several seconds to register what he had just heard. Pratt was capable of it, all right. And Pratt was capable of sending Rhoads on a wild-goose chase to Denver. He looked at

Mary with an unflattering stupid expression, his jaw slack.

Now *he* was whispering. "The documents don't actually say Pratt killed Benedict?"

"Not in those exact words. It's complicated. I think . . ." An odd expression came over Mary's face. She didn't want to ask. She looked away. "T.R.? You used to . . . make love to her, Anna Maria, didn't you?"

Rhoads turned red in anger. "Shit, Mary! If it's any of your business. O.K. Sure. But you can't make love to that woman. I used to fuck her, that's all. I used to fuck her right in her office. During work."

Rhoads immediately regretted his tirade. It was mean. Why did he always react that way when embarrassed?

Mary winced at having her question answered, and how it was answered it, but she carried on. "I think she wants the documents to protect herself somehow, or she wants them to threaten, maybe even blackmail, Pratt. Think she could do something like that? She's like dry ice. That's why I asked if you . . . knew her well."

"That's not exactly how you phrased it, Mary. But I never could figure her out. I do know one thing, she seems to know what she wants, and what she wants is usually more, more, more."

They fell silent, and in a moment, the quiet was disturbed by a new round of tape-recorded grunting coming from the bedroom.

The mood and her scent, the candlelight and the rum and the erotic sounds from the other side of door melded into a rumbling shudder that climbed up Rhoads's back. He was either drunk or falling for this woman.

Probably both.

"Well," he said, swallowing hard and putting his arm around her waist. "The files are vague enough so that the police couldn't do anything with them."

She pressed herself closer and put her arm around his hard shoulder.

"And that's not all," Mary said.

"What else?"

"I don't know what to make of it. Something Trichina kept looking for. But we couldn't find it."

"What?"

"A line item from the budget. It's an accounting thing they call a postallocation budget request. It just means they have to redistribute funds from one project or department to another. They do it when one operation has a deficit and another has a surplus. Or when something unexpected comes up. Trichina is like a dog that knows the bone is buried somewhere in the backyard. She was digging everywhere."

Rhoads wanted to grab her, kiss her, hold her. But it wasn't time yet.

"Mary. This budget request thing. Is it in the amount of two hundred thousand dollars?"

She gasped again.

"How'd you know?"

62

Several hours later, Mary left.

Rhoads had walked her out to her car. Their breath steamed up between them as they kissed in the night air, the coldest it had been all fall. Rhoads took each of her shoulders in his hands, pulled her to him, and kissed her once more, hard, before she got into the car and drove off.

He hurried back home and dialed Jack Fallscroft, waking him.

"How 'bout a drink, Jackie?"

"Negatory, I'm sleeping."

Fifteen minutes later, Rhoads pounded on Fallscroft's apartment door. Fallscroft let his friend in, turning his head to avoid the light from the hallway. Fallscroft was exhausted and the only reason he let Rhoads in was he thought, maybe, he could restrain him from jumping into a drinking binge. Fallscroft loved Rhoads and couldn't bear to see another close person die in a bottle. Fallscroft's father and mother died early from alcohol. One from a failed liver, the other from a failure to recognize a red light.

Rhoads entered and tossed his bomber jacket toward a chair in the dark. It missed and landed on the floor.

"Remember two years ago when Benedict did his Houdini?"

Fallscroft wore briefs. The only light in the apartment filtered in from a distant streetlight, scattered through tree limbs beyond the windows. Fallscroft sat down on a sofa without turning on the lamp and rubbed his face. Rhoads stood there, lighting a cigarette.

"Jack, remember two years ago? I flew out to Denver to talk to Benedict?"

"Vaguely. Why'd you wake me up, man? I told you I was sleeping. This is the first freaking night in a week I get to bed early. What time is it?"

"It's let's-Bury-Benedict-So-He-Won't-Open-His-Mouth-About-the-Midas-Project time. That's what time it is."

Fallscroft reached out in the dark and turned on the lamp. Both men turned their heads away. "What are you saying?"

"Two years ago, Pratt sends me out to Denver."

"You mentioned."

"The story was supposed to be that I'm there to try to feel

Benedict out about some consulting contract and retirement bonus deal. Very lucrative. It would have set him and everybody in his zip code up for their next fifty lifetimes. All he has to do is be quiet."

"But you were there to rough him up?"

"Rough him up?" Rhoads laughed. "What do think this is, some kind of a made-for-cable movie? I don't rough people up. I'm out there with two hundred grand in green on me. I have Pratt's deal on paper for Benedict to sign, and I got the dough in an envelope. I'm supposed to get Benedict to sign on the dotted line. I'm supposed to wave the dough around if he appears . . . hesitant. Pratt wants me to explain to him for every beef he can make against TobacCo, Inc., Pratt's got 8,555,000 other researchers to say Benedict's incompetent and has it all backwards."

"Only Benedict balks."

"*Only Benedict ain't there.* I call Pratt. He's wringing his hands. 'Oh, shit, he's gone to the government,' Pratt says. 'Nose around and see if you can figure out where he went.' So, like an asshole, I'm breaking my ass working around the clock, tossing his office, his apartment, going nuts. can't find anything useful."

"What's his family saying?"

"What fucking family? Not married, has no girlfriend."

"Homo?"

"Don't think so. *Weirdo.* Three hundred IQ, workaholic. Supposedly went to bed at eight every night, got up at two, practiced his violin, no, not a violin—what's the one a little bigger?"

"Viola. Like a violin but they tune them a fifth lower. My dad played."

"Anyway, he fooled with that for an hour every morning and then goes into the lab. In the lab twenty-five hours a day. One sister out in, hell, I can't remember, and one of his parents still alive somewhere else. He didn't go see either of them. We checked but good."

"Meanwhile, what are you saying? Pratt goosed him? You think Pratt'd do that?"

"I think Pratt'd goose you if you hit an air pocket and somehow caused TobacCo, Inc. stock to drop an eighth of a point."

Fallscroft whistled in surprise.

"That ain't all. So after ten or twelve days of getting nowhere fast in Denver, it's looking like a dead end, so I come home and say to Pratt, Now what do you want me to do? And what do you think he says?"

Fallscroft shrugged.

"He says, 'Ah, fuck it, T.R. Fuck Benedict. Let him go.' And just like that, he puts me on some other assignment. Something bullshit."

"Maybe he thought there was nothing else he could do."

"Pratt? Nah. The only time Pratt quits is after he wins. And there was only one way he could win with Benedict."

Fallscroft walked barefoot on cold linoleum into the kitchen. The room filled with a soft blue light from the refrigerator.

"You want juice or anything?" Fallscroft said into the refrigerator.

Rhoads didn't hear the question. He was trying to think out loud. "So I hand over the two hundred thousand to Pratt. But he won't take it, tells me to hang on to it, that something would come up sooner or later and then I'd have it handy. I thought he was maybe testing me, to see if I'd do anything stupid with the cash. Which I might have, me being so broke all the time. That night I can't sleep, though I have the money hidden pretty damn good. But what if it gets ripped off somehow, or there's a fire. A million possibilities are going through my head."

"So where's the money now?"

"The next morning, I'm still really paranoid something's going to happen to that money. Bright and early, I get up and go to Pratt's office with it. And what do you think? Genevieve tells me Pratt's gone for a week to Chamonix in the Alps. So I give the envelope to Genevieve to lock it up in Pratt's safe. 'What's in it?' she says. I say, 'I don't know what to tell you. Mark it petty cash.' 'How much?' she says. 'I don't know,' I say. 'Just put down anything but make sure Pratt gets it personally.' She's giving me a strange look, but she's in love with me. She'll do anything for me. She's got this little book, she writes out a receipt and hands it to me. I give her a kiss on the cheek, and I split. That's the last time I think about it, until . . ."

"Until?"

"Until Mary Dallaness mentions a certain number that seems to have people in high places all upset."

"What number would that be?"

"That number would be two hundred thousand."

63

Monday, October 11
Oberlin, Ohio

"You've reached Oberlin 9-1-1. What is your emergency?" the dispatcher said.

"Look, I'm at Big Ray's Diner, right? I go to buy a pack of cigarettes from the vending machine. Now there's this guy ahead of me, crouched down. I didn't get a close look at him . . ."

"Slow down there."

"I don't get a good look at the guy, but when he leaves, I see there's a pack of Camels wedged in the thing, just sitting. So I pick them up and *damn* if the pack doesn't look like it's been opened and resealed. On the bottom."

"Big Ray's on Diamond Road?"

"Yeah."

"What's your name, sir."

"Lee Rome."

Rome could hear the dispatcher telling someone, "Tampered cigarettes in the vending machine at Big Ray's."

"Describe this male's clothes."

"Black leather jacket and kind of dark pants. Like I said, I wasn't really looking at him."

"Color of hair."

"Dark. I guess black."

"Age."

"Never saw his face, but he was white."

"About . . ."

"About . . . I don't know. Thirty? Forty?"

"How'd he leave."

"I can help you with that. A beat-up old Bug."

"A Volkswagen?"

"Yeah, light blue. Turned right out of the driveway. I don't know what direction that is."

"Toward the university?"

"No, toward the Interstate."

Several minutes later, a State Police cruiser caught up with the Volkswagen. The officer pulled behind the car, emergency lights flashing, high beams on to disorient the driver. The driver rolled down his window, held his arm high, and gave the police officer the finger.

Corporal Jannson made the snap decision to proceed as if the driver was Virgil and that he was armed and dangerous. Jannson knew that backup was at least four or five minutes away. This was a once in a lifetime opportunity, and he was going to take it. There was no other traffic. Jannson pulled his Crown

Victoria halfway alongside the Volkswagen, remaining back out of firing range, and turned his steering wheel with a single, controlled jerk, to the right. He prayed the impact would not trigger the air bags. The cruiser's front quarter panel caught the Bug broadside and smashed it off the road.

The Bug rolled down a slight embankment, overturned, and disappeared into a cloud of dust.

Jannson radioed in the accident, saying the Volkswagen slowed, rammed him, and lost control.

He approached the vehicle, its engine still running, with his weapon outstretched, held in both hands. He stayed back thirty feet. The occupant did not move when Jannson shouted orders. The officer stood frozen, weapon trained on the occupant's head for several minutes until a dozen police vehicles arrived all at once.

Two paramedics rolled Richard Allan Driscoll, twenty-nine, into the emergency room at Oberlin Memorial Hospital. He was on his back, bleeding from the face and scalp. His hands lay in his lap, fingers intertwined, wrists bound by stainless-steel handcuffs.

The lacerations were not serious.

Two nurses and a doctor cleaned him up and administered sutures. Driscoll raised his wrists and pushed the doctor away. A police officer rushed in close with a wooden truncheon, ready to crush Driscoll's skull if he got violent. Driscoll dropped his arms and made a face, saying he wanted to call his father, a lawyer, and rambled on about the cop who tried to kill him just for speeding.

"We have five witnesses who saw what you did at the diner," a State Police captain said.

Jannson elbowed his way into the throng around Driscoll and whispered something into his ear. Driscoll grew wide-eyed. He edged back on the examining table, away from Jannson, and shut up. A minute later, glancing nervously at Jannson, he told the captain that he was a Virgil fan, and there was nothing against the law about that. But that putting a cigarette load into a pack and planting it in the vending machine was a stupid joke.

"Really stupid," the captain said. "Especially when your daddy explains to you that product tampering is a federal offense, a felony, even if all you do is put in a marshmallow."

64

Washington, D.C.

Pratt's lobbyists worked overtime on Capitol Hill to prevent even a temporary recall of tobacco products. They called in favor after favor. Favors due from insiders at the Food and Drug Administration, favors from the Federal Trade Commission, favors from sympathetic legislators.

Pratt's key lobbyist, Joel Chankron, even dug in and made some headway at the Bureau of Alcohol, Tobacco, and Firearms.

Chankron was after pressure, he said to the ATF official who quietly agreed to meet with him.

"Oppose any cigarette recall ideas as soon as you hear them. The story should be that a recall is exactly what the terrorist wants, and that is exactly why there should be no recalls."

Chankron felt the insider would be cooperative. He paid for the meal and the drinks, and it paid off.

"Listen, Mark," he said. "The Patriot Booking Agency in Boston is always looking for articulate people like you who might like to make speeches every now and then about, hell, anything that interests you. You're a golfer, right? Why not call this number," and he presented the business card of a Patriot Booking Agency executive, "and set up a tee time with this fellow here in Washington? I understand they pay a twenty-five-thousand-dollar fee just for signing up, making yourself available in case anyone ever needs you to make a speech."

The way Chankron was going, the booking agency exec was going to be playing a lot of golf.

"Plenty to be optimistic about," Chankron reported to Pratt. "And I can guarantee we'll know about anything before it happens."

"What good is it to warn me about something I can't doing anything about?" Pratt bellowed.

Chankron didn't have an answer.

Pratt thought that for $400 an hour, he was owed one.

65

Deer Mountain, Pennsylvania

A light fog hovered in the woods around Rhoads's poconos retreat in Deer Mountain. There were no nearby neighbors, but had there been, and had they been watching, they would have seen little more than the red glow of Valzmann's brake lights when he slowed for the gravel driveway of the Rhoads family cabin.

He drove the car as far around to the rear of the property as the driveway allowed.

He got out and opened the trunk. With some effort, he lifted out an oversized canvas duffel bag. Something heavy and rigid inside clunked against the rear bumper as Valzmann struggled with the bulky bag. Leaves crunched loudly under foot as he hoisted it over his shoulder.

Rhoads's cabin sat nestled under a grove of blue-green spruce trees. The man carried the bag about fifty feet into the woods and dropped it, caught his breath, and tried to pick it up again. Getting the dead weight back over his shoulder was more difficult than expected. Valzmann half-carried, half-dragged the bag. He made a mental note to obliterate the tracks he and the bag made.

He spent nearly an hour digging a hole in rocky soil with an awkward folding Army surplus shovel. When satisfied with the depth of the pit, he used his feet to shove in the duffel bag. Refilling the hole took only a few minutes. He removed his work gloves, pocketed them, and returned to his car, removing traces of his footprints and the bag as he went. He drove away over the bumpy one-lane county road.

With a sense of completion, Valzmann turned on the car's CD player and twisted his neck back and forth, stretching to relieve the strain from the digging. He was glad to be rid of the body once and for all. It'd been a pain sitting on it for two years. Keeping a stiff in cold storage always carries with it some risk.

66

Tuesday, October 12
En route to Washington, D.C.

Rhoads, coming from a meeting in New York with other tobacco company security men, sat in an uncrowded Metroliner, his briefcase open and papers and documents scattered on him and the adjacent empty seat.

"Union Station, Washington D.C., next stop," the conductor shouted from a car length away.

Rhoads leafed through papers one last time, a U.S. map partially unfolded in his lap. Too close to the seat in front of him, Rhoads couldn't get a good look at the map, and so he positioned it against the seat back facing him. He was working, trying to make a star shape somehow fit the crime-scene sites. It wouldn't quite work. In frustration, he pounded the map.

The woman sitting in front of him leaned around and glared. "Do you mind?"

"Sorry."

He sloppily folded the map and jammed it into a folder. As he did so, a document fell out. It was the current TobacCo, Inc. annual report. He absently thumbed through its glossy pages. He got to the last page and was about to put it back in the file folder when an idea barked at him.

He opened the annual report again, looked at each page carefully, not knowing why. What had he missed? He remembered Dr. Trice's warning to pay attention to nagging feelings. He turned page after page, his mouth ajar. Suddenly, his head darted forward in recognition.

A color two-page spread described TobacCo, Inc.'s recent acquisition of StarCity Properties, Inc.'s upscale hotels. Two beautiful hotel complexes in Princeton and Atlanta. There, on the right side of the spread was a sky-blue map that marked both cities with the yellow stars of StarCity's logo. He had made a connection between Dr. Trice's insistence about Virgil's "star" remark and the map in front of him.

Although he did not quite understand how he could use the information, he felt a surge in mood. He felt somehow closer to Virgil. He pounded the seat back again, oblivious to the uneasy stares coming from everyone on the car.

"Yeah, baby. Yeah!" Rhoads shouted out in glee. "Come to momma. *Come to momma!*"

67

Wednesday, October 13

Prompted by Rhoads's brainstorm on the Metroliner and reinforced by the FBI's models of likely behavior patterns and the computer-generated Probable Vectors analysis, the Investigative Support Unit believed the StarCity Properties' Princeton and Atlanta locations were the two most probable targets for any attack Virgil may attempt. Both were immediately staked out.

One day into the surveillance, nothing had happened.

Rhoads and Franklin sat talking in Franklin's sedan in the parking lot of the StarCity Hotel on Route One in Princeton.

Franklin thought Rhoads's idea wasn't bad, but that, at best, crossing paths with Virgil was a long, long shot. And if the FBI had any decent leads to pursue, they wouldn't have used the more than 100 agents to stake out the two properties.

Bored, Franklin said he would stretch his legs by taking a walk around the hotel complex. He wore a maintenance man's uniform.

"I'm going in with you," Rhoads said.

"No thanks," Franklin said. "Look, Rhoads. Every bellhop, clerk, cashier, janitor, and half the guests in there are on my payroll. What do you think you can do in there besides get in the way?"

"I don't need your permission. For one thing, this is property owned by TobacCo, Inc., where I'm a security consultant. And for another, I'll be the only one in there who's not looking for Loren Benedict."

"Okay," Franklin said, taking an official tone. "I think you had better go back to Asheville. Because you're getting ready to stick your ass somewhere it doesn't belong. And if you do that . . ."

"I know, I know. Two hundred and sixty-seven thousand, eight-hundred and forty-four counts of obstruction of justice. You're so dull, Franklin."

Franklin clenched his teeth and began to get out of his car. Rhoads got out on his side, slammed the door, and sauntered toward the hotel lobby. He looked back and winked at Franklin who had stopped to take something from the trunk.

Outside the hotel, and at nearby intersections as far away as a mile and a half, scores of unmarked federal agents' vehicles in every conceivable configuration—taxicabs and ambulances, beat-up wrecks and a limousine, a plumber's truck and a tow truck—idled impatiently or circled blocks, ready for the unlikely signal that Virgil had been spotted.

Martin Muntor, wearing a safari jacket and white Panama hat, was in the car of a ReMax real estate agent, a young woman, heavyset. Muntor told her he needed to make a pit stop. The car was marked with the agency's placard affixed to both driver's and front passenger doors.

"Come in with me. I'll buy you an ice tea, and you can try to tell me again why condo maintenance fees are really to my advantage." Muntor coughed. "And I'll sit there with as straight a face as humanly possible."

The real estate agent laughed politely. "I'll come in and get a seat in the coffee shop while you're in the rest room." She eyed Muntor warily. The man looked ill, and she hoped he didn't have that coughy flu that had been wiping out everyone at the office.

She pulled into a parking spot, and they walked across the lot toward the lobby.

Inside, Muntor livened his step at great effort. He saw at once several people who could have been agents, but he ignored them. And they ignored the little dandy with his seemingly lively step, fancy briefcase, and chubby associate. They were looking for a haggard man, wild eyed, and wheezing.

He walked her to the coffee shop, making himself available for scrutiny. Therefore, no one would bother. The hostess seated the real estate agent, and he headed for the rest room. Near a bank of pay telephones, Martin Muntor entered a men's room, locked himself in a stall, and, still standing, removed his belt. He took off his jacket, snagged it on the hook, and, white hat still atop his head, rolled up his sleeve. He sat down on the toilet seat, reached up and from the inside pocket of his jacket, he removed an envelope containing a syringe partially filled with a milky-white substance, a Band-Aid, and wad of alcohol-soaked cotton in a folded square of plastic wrap. Muntor used the belt as a tourniquet around his left biceps. He made a fist of his left hand and slapped at his inner elbow with his right hand to anger the veins there. Two popped up right away. With cool clinical efficiency, he swiped the cotton across one, jabbed the needle into his flesh, and slowly, almost erotically, depressed the plunger.

Muntor's blood energized and coursed through him with a

hot fury. His diaphragm contracted involuntarily, and he drew in a sharp breath full and rich with the oxygen he'd been cheated out of. Within moments, he felt lighter, stronger, fiercer.

He stood up now and snapped the belt from his arm. He quickly threaded it through his trousers's belt loops, pulled on his jacket, and took another deep breath. He dropped the cotton and square of plastic wrap into the toilet and flushed. He put the syringe back into the envelope.

In a flash, Muntor was out of the men's room, exhilarated and striding briskly in the direction of the parking lot, away from the coffee shop and the waiting real estate agent.

Rhoads pushed through the doors and into the main lobby.

He was noticed but rejected as a possible Virgil by the numerous agents who didn't know who he was, and those who did rolled their eyes or shook their heads. In the preshift briefing, they had been told about Rhoads and told to keep an eye on him. The assistant team commander referred to him as a troublemaker pressed upon the bureau by tobacco industry lobbyists with Justice Department connections.

Dead ahead, Rhoads saw the StarLight Lounge. To the left, the StarDust coffee shop. And, to the right, the StarBright gift shop, through whose entrance he could see the salesclerk and behind her, shelves packed with cigarettes, junk food, and condoms. He headed straight for it. The carpet changed color inside the gift shop. He walked to the over-the-counter section and examined bottles of painkillers.

Standing a dozen feet away was a man who appeared to be in late middle age, wearing jeans and a bulky beige cable sweater. Rhoads observed him out of the corner of his eye. The man picked up a copy of *Scientific American*, leafed through it, put it back in the rack. A moment later, he pulled it out again, turned to a page at random, and appeared to be reading.

Rhoads wanted a closer look at the guy. As he took a step toward the man, he felt a tug at his jacket. He turned and looked behind him. No one was there. He spun around and looked the other way. No one there, either. He tensed. He looked down and saw a boy, perhaps eight or nine.

"Hey mister," the boy said. "The man said to give these to you." The boy held up a pack of Winstons. "He said to see if you say 'Thank you. '"

This took a second to sink in. Then Rhoads grabbed the boy's wrist and squeezed.

"Drop those cigarettes right now, son," Rhoads ordered. "Just drop them on the floor. Right now."

The frightened boy yelped in pain and tried to pull away. Then he did as instructed.

The man in the cable sweater spun toward Rhoads and the boy.

Rhoads crouched down to get a closer look at the pack without touching it. He turned the pack with the temple piece of his sunglasses and saw immediately that the pack had been tampered with.

Rhoads looked up at the child. "Where!" Rhoads shouted into the boy's face. "Where did you get these?"

The boy shivered then cried. His fingers quivered, and he tugged at his lips.

"The man," said the boy, pointing toward the lobby doors. "Out front. In the parking lot."

"What!" Rhoads stood up. "A man. What was he wearing? What did he look like?"

The boy seemed paralyzed.

"Look, son, I'm a policeman. I need to find him. What was he wearing?"

"He was old. Had a hat, a big white one. A kind of tan jacket with things here," boy said, indicating his shoulders.

Rhoads snarled. He began to rise but felt a powerful hand push down on his shoulder. He was startled to see how many undercover officers had materialized in the shop. Most of them were men, a few were women. One male agent, made up to look aged, complete with a walker next to him, put a large silver hand-gun in Rhoads's face.

"I think that's Rhoads," someone said.

"Get out of my way," Rhoads said, twisting away from the heavy hand and getting up. He figured the shortest distance between two points was straight up the middle. "It's Virgil, you assholes. He's here!"

And he charged.

He rushed the crowd of agents and burst through them. He ran furiously through the lobby, burst out the front door, and looked wildly to the right. He saw nothing, no one. He spun toward the left. Six or eight agents, guns drawn, shouting into hand-held radios and cell phones, hesitated for a moment near Rhoads, then, as if on cue, splintered off and sprinted in different directions. Cars screeched and peeled out, horns honked.

At the far end of the vast mall-like parking lot, Rhoads spotted a figure, possibly a man.

That shape could be right, that could be him.

Immobile for a split second, the shape—now Rhoads could see it was a man—seemed to gaze back at him. The two were separated by 100 yards, but to Rhoads, their eyes met and flashed at each other. The sun glare from all the windshields in the parking lot seemed dull in comparison.

Rhoads broke into a run but jumped back not an instant too soon. He had come inches from darting out in front of a Greyhound bus pulling up to the front of the StarCity main entrance. Rhoads lost his balance, fell backwards and to the ground at the bus's exhaust pipe. Coughing, he was up in an instant. The bus had stopped, blocking his way. He sprinted around behind it and headed toward the corner of the parking lot.

Nothing was there. Not a man, not a car. Just black asphalt and white lines.

Franklin stood in the parking lot under a bright noonday sun and screamed at Rhoads. "What in the hell do you mean you didn't notice what kind of car!"

"It happened in an eighth of a second, Franklin. It barely registered in my brain before the fucking bus tried to kill me."

Two agents hustled over with the real estate agent. Another had the boy.

"Deputy Franklin," one of the agents said. "This woman may have been with Virgil. She said he came into her office an hour ago and . . ."

Franklin listened to the story of how Virgil posed as a prospective condo buyer, said he needed to the use the rest room, and never returned. When the woman inquired about all the commotion, hotel security brought her to the FBI.

"Where's your car?" Rhoads asked.

She looked around, confused. "There it is. The white Mazda." She pointed.

"Her car's a crime scene," Franklin barked to a subordinate.

Rhoads elbowed in closer.

"Ma'am. Describe the kind of gloves the man was wearing."

"You're right. He was wearing gloves. I thought that was odd, but he said he had bad circulation and that his hands were always cold, even when he lived in Florida."

68

Wednesday afternoon the duty officer at the FBI's ERC received a faxed transcript of a portion of a conversation on *National Talk*, a call-in radio show that had been broadcast earlier that day on National Public Radio.

In a cover letter accompanying the transcript, the show's producer said he took a call from someone claiming to be Virgil on their 800 line.

"SOP to record it," the producer had written. "The caller's voice is so muffled it was a chore to get even this much. We have no idea whether this is real or a prank. In transcribing, we found two brief unintelligible segments (see the notes in the transcript), each less than a couple seconds long. We think one was just a laugh."

The partial transcript read:

1:40 P.M. *WEDNESDAY OCT.* 13 . . .
HOST TONY LOPEZ: And here's Walt in Fort Myers.
CALLER: Hello, Tony. My name's not actually Walt. I'm more popularly known as Virgil, which I can prove. But I do have an intriguing question even if it isn't exactly on the subject, Tony. How do you think they will ever catch me . . .[THIS IS WHERE WE TOOK HIM OFF THE AIR BUT KEPT RECORDING] . . . *unless I lead them to me? Which I will, as soon as I've made my number. That number is, by the way, 430. It represents one one-thousandth—that's one tenth of one percent—of the 430,000 people who'll croak this year from smoking-originated diseases. Just one year! And I may be one of them, for crying out loud!*

Anyway, practically half a million men, women, even children. I'm just starting a backfire is all, combating a huge fire with a few

*well-placed little ones. I'm a saint just about, a damned folk hero,
and they can't stand it! Ambitious, yes. Doable? I think so. Stealth
is my watchword. I'm smart. I have no criminal record. And not
that I'd let them have one, but I don't even think my prints are on
file anywhere. I'm relatively sane. I'm motivated. I feel, no, I
know, my small crimes combat larger ones. I'm fully justified.
Listen, I take responsibility for my smoking. But why don't the
tobacco companies take responsibility for spending* six million
dollars a day *advertising their poison? [Unintelligible]. My so-
called victims are already smoking, voluntarily destroying their
own lungs and themselves in slo-mo. I'm just expediting. Is that
such a crime? [Unintelligible].*

*And another thing, unlike most people, I'm going to accomplish
something of real value before I die. Can any of you say that? And
here's the only sick part—it's kind of fun. I mean the killing is
scary, but, hell, I'm not there to actually watch it. What is it the
vegetarians say? If we had to slaughter our own hamburgers, we
wouldn't eat them! I'm killing hundreds of people and feel hardly a
twinge of guilt. Why not? Because I'm am truly saving them from
slow death. Plus what I'm doing will absolutely raise people's
consciousness about smoking. Hundreds of thousands of others
may quit, or better yet, never start. Once I've hit my number, then
they can have their way with me. Don't worry, I don't plan on
killing myself and leave you hanging. Suicide is nature's severest
form of self-criticism, and Tony, no matter what they say, I'm not
down on myself. Okay, now, Tony, sayonara! And make sure this
tape gets to a fellow named Rhoads, care of the F-B-I. The tape's
evidence. Even if you think I'm not me, you have to report it."*

69

Tucson, Arizona

The anchor on WTCR-TV Tucson began the six o'clock newscast with a local angle.

"The impact of cigarette terrorist Virgil has struck near home for the second time. A long-haul trucker was shot and killed when hijackers commandeered his United Tobacco truck early this morning . . . near the I-17/I-10 on-ramp north of Phoenix. The body of Jacob Edmundson was discovered just after dawn by the Arizona Highway Patrol in the Interstate's eastbound lanes.

"An Arizona Highway Patrol commander in charge of the investigation said as the threat of a nationwide cigarette recall increases, he expects more cigarette-related violence."

The newscaster's image disappeared and was replaced by Commander Harold Lamphreys at the crime scene. "People are addicted to nicotine. If the recall goes into effect, cigarettes will be selling for ten, fifteen, twenty dollars a pack. We'll be seeing killing and robberies like this one every day."

70

Asheville

Nick Pratt had decided it was in his best personal interest to go on the air and read the statement Virgil requested. Every molecule of his being resisted, but his sense of survival, financial and political, prevailed.

A pool camera crew had been invited to WHQ and were set up and waiting in TobacCo, Inc.'s media room.

Anna Maria Trichina and public relations consultant Arnold Northrup sat with Pratt in the Executive Suite. Surrounding them, propped up on aluminum easels, were poster-sized excerpts of the specified passage from *The Surgeon General's report.*

Northrup cleared his throat. "You're on the air in fifty minutes, Nick. You'll be on for a max of five minutes, basically within the time frame of local newscasts on the West Coast and prime time elsewhere. I can guarantee that every network will wrap your presentation with reports summarizing other Virgil publicity, including experts who will be commenting on what you are about to say or what you've just said." Northrup shouted toward Pratt's open office door, "Where's the makeup girl!"

Pratt fumed. "You're trying to tell me it doesn't matter. The CEO of the biggest tobacco company in the world announces to two billion people in every country on the planet that cigarettes will, contrary to previous statements, give them cancer, heart disease, everything, and it doesn't matter?"

"No, Nick," Northrup said. "I'm not saying it doesn't matter. I'm saying you don't have any choice, and we're doing it this way to control the damage."

"Of course I have a choice. There's nothing that says I have to push the company I'm responsible for out the window."

Northrup chuckled nervously. "Get it out of your system, Nick. The hardest thing for men in high places is to get over the illusion that they can control events like this one. You can scream all you want at the flunkies you see everyday, including me, and we'll do anything you want. Let me put it in plain English for you. Everybody in the country knows what's in *The Surgeon General's report*. Everybody knows cigarettes kill you. That's not your exposure here. If you don't do what this guy demands, everyone he kills after this is going to be seen as your victim. Not his."

Pratt's upper lip quivered. "Anna Maria, get me coffee. Decaf."

She rose stiffly and left the room.

"I ought to play my voice mail for you. Every other CEO in the business has plenty of guts when it comes to me taking a brave stand and telling Virgil to go fuck himself."

"That's another reason to play along. Don't forget Pensacola. Virgil used cigs made by everyone but us. Do what he asks, maybe he'll move on to the next Big Eight company."

A makeup artist appeared and set her box full of cosmetics on Pratt's desk.

Pratt eyed her without amusement. "I just had an idea," he said. "Let's slip ads into the *New York Times* and *Los Angeles Times* and *Wall Street Journal*. The headline'll read, 'We will never negotiate with terrorists.' Then we sign the ad RJR and Philip Morris!"

"Not funny, Nick." Northrup sat down in a leather chair, crossed and uncrossed his legs, and got up. He paced, thinking. "Listen. We have to get all this into perspective. This is nothing but packaging. You put little warning labels on every package of cigarettes, but you use tiny type against a dark background and the words just fade away. We can do the same with this. We write a preamble expressing your personal grief and sorrow over these insane murders. Make it clear that you are bowing to extortion only to save lives. You read the damned thing, then you close with a reminder about victims, orphaned children, psychotic serial killers."

Pratt glared. "And what about Virgil's specific instruction about appearing contrite?"

"What will he care? He'll be in the spotlight again."

"And the other CEOs riding me?"

"Make them regret it. Take the lead. Publicly call them to an industry conference to establish standards for preventing product tampering and for response to future situations like this one. Let this never happen again. That kind of horseshit."

The makeup artist went to work, and Pratt stared at the easels, shaking his head.

71

Valzmann, dressed as a delivery man, wore a windbreaker and baseball cap. He sat casing the Dallaness house from the driver's seat of a pizza truck parked across the street and half a block away. After several minutes, he spoke into a radio then exited his truck with a pizza in a cardboard box, walked to the house, up the path, and rang the bell. Anthony Dallaness, out of breath, went to the door in a bathrobe, pajamas, and slippers. A sitcom theme song blared from a television in the background. "Hold on! Hold on!" Anthony said. He opened the door and saw the pizza delivery man. Valzmann stepped in and kicked door closed behind him.

"Hey! What the . . . nobody ordered anything here."

At that, Valzmann drew a switchblade from his windbreaker. It snapped open.

"Sit down, Anthony."

Anthony, hair stuck in sweaty clumps, hadn't shaved for days. It was difficult for him to breathe, but he gamely drew himself up.

"Oh, get real, Anthony. Look at yourself. You're a wreck. Sit down."

He stood still. Valzmann slapped him across the face. Anthony stepped back and sat down in slow motion on the sofa, already wheezing loudly in fear.

"All right. What do you want, sir?" Anthony's eyes fixed on the man's tiny white earring. He'd describe that to the police for sure. Some kind of junkie or something.

"I'm afraid your wife Mary has been a bad girl. She took something that didn't belong to her, and I have to get it back. I think you know what I need, Anthony. Tell me where the computer disks are, we'll have a slice of pepperoni, and I'll be on to my next delivery." Valzmann smiled. "Where are they?"

Anthony's increasingly heavy breathing made it seem he was about to cry.

"Look, I'll tell you, you got me scared. Maybe someone gave you some bad information. Mary wouldn't be involved in anything like stealing."

"Anthony?"

"I'd tell you. I swear it. And I don't know anything about any disks. Do you want money?" Anthony reached toward his wallet on the end table next to him.

"*Anthony.*" The tone was menacing. Valzmann relaxed and smiled. "I really don't have time to screw around with you."

Swiftly, Valzmann drew from an inside pocket a large clear plastic trash bag. With virtually no resistance, he yanked it down over Anthony's head. Anthony hardly moved, like a kid resigned to take the hypodermic in the arm from the school nurse. Valzmann held the bag closed with his gloved fist at the neck.

Anthony's eyes grew large and were distorted by the plastic. Valzmann slapped him through the bag. Anthony's face twisted in pain. His chest heaved, and his arms flailed.

Valzmann removed the bag from Anthony's head. Anthony hunched forward into a paroxysm of coughing.

"Raise your hand when you're ready to tell me." He wanted to let Anthony catch his breath. "I'm counting to three, and then we'll do it again. Where . . . are . . . the disks?"

Wild eyed, Anthony shrugged. "I don't know. *Please.* Can't you call back? Mary will know. There may be some confusion."

I told Pratt she'd never confide in this jerk.

"You're not making any sense, Anthony." Valzmann put the bag back on. This time Anthony resisted, reaching up and grabbing at the gloved hand that held the bag tight around his throat.

Valzmann laughed.

Anthony turned purple and after several moments, his girlish flailing and flapping quieted down, then ceased. Valzmann removed the bag and pushed Anthony backward to an upright sitting position. He put his head close to Anthony's and examined the fixed and dilated pupils. After returning the bag to his pocket, Valzmann pulled out a cellular telephone. He pressed a button.

It answered on the second ring.

"Sir. I know this isn't your private line, but may I report? . . . Thank you. I tried to get the tickets from the first scalper. But we got canceled for lack of participation. We expected as much. Are you sure you don't want me to try for the second? I know she'll be here shortly. I've been told she's just left the store."

He listened for a beat.

"Yes I know you're in a rush . . . . oh, it's that late already? Okay. No sir. I won't try for the second game until we know for sure we can get the tickets. I know. It would be stupid to. Yes sir. Good-bye."

He hung up and glanced at a wall clock. It was 8:59 P.M. Valzmann picked up the TV remote and changed the channel to CNN. He sat down next to Anthony, whose warm body had slumped to the side. Valzmann reached over and again adjusted Anthony into an upright position facing the television. Valzmann then picked up Anthony's wallet, flipped through it, found his driver's license, and removed it.

Light from the television flickered on Anthony Dallaness's dead, staring eyes. Valzmann looked toward the television just as Pratt's image appeared on the screen. At that moment, headlights played across the living-room window distracting him. A half-minute later, he heard the sound of a garage door grinding open. Then it began closing.

"That's my music," Valzmann said, raising his index finger. "Got to go, Anthony." He rose and casually left via the front door. He walked to the truck, got in, rolled down the window, fastened his seat belt, and started the engine.

He drove away at the posted rate of speed.

72

Mary Dallaness opened the door that connected the garage to the kitchen and walked in. She kicked off her shoes onto the mud mat and dropped her purse and briefcase on the Formica counter. She could hear the television. She walked into the hall-way and stood there. The television was flickering with Nick

Pratt's image.

"Anthony?"

No answer. She stepped forward into the living room. Her boss was on screen, delivering his prepared remarks.

". . . Eight days ago on October 5, the murderer who calls himself Virgil demanded that I read an excerpt from a document titled The Surgeon General's Report on Smoking and Health. *While it has always been contrary to the policy of my company and the tobacco industry to repeat rumor and inflammatory rhetoric of this kind, we at TobacCo, Inc. have decided to make an exception in this case in order to prevent any further deaths. Therefore, I will read the material specified by the killer, although I do so with no endorsement of the content."*

She took a few more steps into the living room and stood behind the couch, directly opposite the television screen.

"I'm so sorry I'm late again," she said to Anthony, fixing her attention on the television. "Wow. How long has he been on?"

Mary watched Pratt. He had begun to read the text from *The Surgeon General's Report.* After a moment, she circled around the right side of the sofa, still watching raptly, and settled down next to her husband.

She reached out with her hand and placed it affectionately on his knee. Something was terribly wrong. For an instant, all the muscles of her face twitched. Her head jerked from the television toward Anthony, and she uttered a shriek.

"Anthony! Anthony! Oh my dear Lord, help us!" She dove across him and grabbed for the telephone. The handset clattered on the end table. She punched the keys. "9-1-1? Please! My husband. He's dying . . ."

Mary sobbed and rocked on the floor, cradling her husband in her arms, her tears splashing down onto his face. In the distance, an ambulance siren wailed.

On the television screen, Pratt had finished reading the excerpt and concluded his announcement with additional remarks.

". . . only to do our part in preventing more senseless slaughter of innocents. The terrible tragedies of recent days are the work of a sick, perverted, animal, not the tobacco industry or the good people who work in it. Nothing should persuade us otherwise. Thank you, and good night."

73

Thursday, October 14

Rhoads loved to wake Jack Fallscroft whenever he had that chance. Fallscroft was one of those people who bragged about how early he rose.

"'Trouble with those who get up with the roosters is they tend to crow about it all day long," Rhoads' grandfather had told him.

Today was Fallscroft's turn. He banged hard on the door of room 1617 of the Crystal City Hyatt in Arlington.

No response.

Fallscroft banged again.

"T.R. Open up. It's me."

Behind a chained door, inside a dark room, Rhoads stirred in a tangle of sheets and blankets. On the night table was a near-dead fifth of Bacardi 151, an ashtray overflowing with cigarette butts, and the telephone off the hook.

Rhoads rolled out of bed in his shorts and opened the door. Fallscroft entered and looked around.

"This is what I call progress. He's out of the coma, he's up, he's moving, he may actually be conscious, and . . . I don't see any transvestite hookers holding enema bags and nipple clamps. Good work, T.R."

"I just slept through the alarm."

"Very much unlike you," Fallscroft said, recradling the telephone. Rhoads sat down on the bed.

"I know you flew here from Asheville to give me A.A. lecture number sixty-two."

Fallscroft grabbed a big towel from the bathroom and flung it at Rhoads. "Hit the showers. Bigus Nickus wants to see you."

A minute later, Fallscroft was leaning against the doorjamb outside the bathroom, listening to the sound of water running.

"You must have seen Pratt on the tube last night, right? You catch the look on his face? Looked like he just ate a turd sandwich. The first time in a long time anybody ever pushed his nose in it. And quite an audience. They say it drew the largest audience since the O.J. verdict."

"Yup," Rhoads said from the shower. He couldn't really hear Fallscroft over the rush of water.

"I heard about Princeton. Swing and a miss. Not your fault, T.R."

Rhoads turned off the shower. "Is that what Pratt wants to hassle me about? Princeton?

"I'm just the taxi driver," Fallscroft said, looking absently through Rhoads's duffel-bag suitcase. He found a postcard from

Dr. Trice with a quotation from a book or poem scrawled on it and Rhoads's copy of *Tefft's field Guide to North American Trees*. He flipped through the guide and noticed check marks next to some of the photos.

"What's with this tree book, T.R.? You carry it around with you everywhere like a bible."

"It is like a bible," Rhoads said as he emerged with a towel wrapped around him. He shouldered Fallscroft away from the duffel bag and rooted through it. He found clean socks and underwear.

"I don't know why you're always yammering about charter-fishing boats. You're more the 'Ernest Goes Camping' type."

"You mean the Dan'l Boone type. Anyway, my brother's always wanted to get into the fishing business, and he's always wanted me to do it with him."

"But I never hear you talking about the ocean. You talk about the woods. You run away to the woods."

Rhoads had dressed and was putting his toiletries into the duffel. "Do you know there's 981 kinds of trees in North America, Jackie? And I aim to see every one of them with my own eyes before I die. Already seen 116. Look through it, and you'll see dates and places where I've seen them."

"And you're only forty-two. Only 800 more to go." Fallscroft opened the book again and stopped at a color photo with an entry next to it. *Longleaf pine, Hemphill Texas.* Fallscroft couldn't read the date Rhoads had scrawled. "Hey! I see you finally caught up with the old longleaf pine. Did that make your day?"

"Yes it did, Ignorant One. *Pinus palustris*. That species has the longest needles of any pine in the country. And the particular example I saw was the national champion, at least back then. Twelve, thirteen stories high, man. She was a big son of a bitch."

Fallscroft shrugged, tossed the book back into the bag. "Anthony Dallaness died last night," he said.

Rhoads stopped, a sock half on. "What?"

"He was just sitting there in front of the TV set, and, bingo.

It was only a matter of time. Right?"

"Jeez. How's Mary?"

"I doubt it surprised her."

"I asked you a question, Jack. How's Mary?"

What's he so touchy about? "I don't know, T.R. Trichina told me this morning."

Rhoads tried to call Mary, but he got her answering machine. He left a message saying he'd try her back in a couple of hours.

Fallscroft picked up the remote and scanned the cable TV stations the hotel offered. He was looking for the Weather Channel. He glanced at his watch.

"You ready, Professor?" he said.

"Yeah, but we have a stop to make first, taxi driver."

"Pratt told me to bring you straight back."

"And that you will do," Rhoads said, zipping up the duffel bag. "Right after I'm finished in Philadelphia."

74

Asheville

Valzmann needed Pratt's help to distract Trichina long enough to get a moment alone with her pocketbook. Pratt called

232 ◆ *Frank Freudberg*

her to his office precisely as scheduled, and Valzmann slipped in
and out in about twenty seconds.

75

Philadelphia

Dr. Trice had a consulting conference with the director of
the Employee Assistance Program at a South Philadelphia Coca-
Cola bottling facility, and it would be no trouble, she said, to meet
Rhoads at Primo Pasta in Terminal C at Philadelphia International
Airport.

Dr. Trice hurried on short legs to the restaurant. She took a
seat at a booth with a window looking out onto the tarmac, told
a waitress she was waiting for someone, ordered a cup of coffee,
and went to work on the bag of hot roasted toffee-covered
peanuts she had bought at the airport. She watched a helicopter
land and wondered if that was the aircraft Rhoads was in.

En route to the restaurant, Rhoads found a telephone and
reached Mary. He told her how sorry he was and that he'd like
to be with her tomorrow. She said she'd like that very much.
Then Rhoads excused himself and jogged halfway across the airport to meet Dr. Trice.

Ten minutes later, Rhoads slid into the booth and shook Dr.
Trice's hand. The plate-glass window provided a view of the

north light-craft runways. He watched Dr. Trice as she put four heaping teaspoons of sugar into her coffee.

"I thought you doctors were supposed to know better than that."

"Why do I know what is right but do what is wrong? Who said that, Rhoads?"

He shrugged.

"Some saint. I can't remember, either. I love sugar." She took a sip of her coffee and reached into the crumpled white paper bag holding the peanuts. "You're back like a stray cat who once got milk at the alley door. I take it, therefore, that you've reason to believe there was validity to my prediction."

"Yes, ma'am. TobacCo, Inc. owns the StarCity hotels. Your star idea. The FBI set up surveillance at both StarCity properties. Virgil showed up at the gift shop in StarCity's Princeton hotel, but he was too slick—and too lucky. Somehow, the FBI kept it from getting into the news. You couldn't have been any more on the money. Needless to say, everyone was impressed as hell."

"Yes" was all Dr. Trice said. Then she added, "Why is Virgil still free?"

"The truth is simple. He gave us the slip, and he's not going to give us another chance like that again."

The waitress returned, set down two glasses of ice water, gave Dr. Trice a sour look for eating the candy, and took Rhoads's coffee order.

"Obviously," Rhoads continued, "I'm interested in any more predictions you have."

"Good. But first I have to go out to short-term parking. I left the Ouija board in my trunk." She laughed at the expression on Rhoads's face. "Well, that is what you thought, isn't it?"

"I'm past that now, Dr. Trice." The waitress brought the coffee, and he took a sip. "But you did have some trick up your sleeve. How'd you do it?"

"Now *I* play dumb."

"First of all, I don't *play* dumb. I *am* dumb. If I ever have an

expression on my face that makes you think I don't get something, I probably don't. There is one thing, though, that separates me from the mass of dumb men. I know I'm dumb. And
dumb as I am, I'm just smart enough to know you weren't completely straight with me. You didn't use a Ouija board, so how did
you figure out the star angle?"

Dr. Trice went into the white bag for more nuts. Her fingers
were sticky and stuck to the paper. She held the bag out toward
Rhoads who simply shook his head "no." She chewed a handful
of nuts and started speaking before they cleared her palate.

"Institutions like the FBI tend to be categorical in their
thinking," she said. "In the FBI's eyes, chemists know about chemistry. The Hair and Fiber Section experts know about the material tailors use. Pathologists know about cadavers. Psychiatrists
know about psychology. In such organizations, intelligence outside one's official area of expertise is distrusted mightily."

She took another nut and chewed it thoroughly. Rhoads's
theory about fat people was simply that they ate too fast, not too
much.

"My deduction," she said, "was not psychiatric. It was literary."

"Literary? As in a book?"

Dr. Trice resisted rolling her eyes. "Yes, handsome, from
classical literature. You see, our friend calls himself Virgil. Virgil
was a Roman poet who wrote . . ."

"Hold it right there, doctor!" Rhoads broke into a moronic
grin. It was now his turn to best the psychiatrist. "We already
thought of that. The FBI looked up everything that guy wrote!
Couldn't find anything that clicked."

"There's that categorical thinking again. Virgil, you see, was
more than a poet. He was also a *character* in a work written by
someone else. The greatest poem ever written, for my money.
Written 700 years ago by Dante Alighieri. Called *The Divine
Comedy*. In it, Virgil takes Dante on a grand tour of hell—the
inferno. Well, what do you know. Our Virgil is giving us the same
treatment."

"Oh, okay. I can see that," Rhoads said nodding, his lower lip protruding in admiration. "But what does that have to do with the StarBright gift shop?"

"*The Divine Comedy* is a poem divided into three parts, three canticles. 'The Inferno,' 'The Purgatorio,' and 'The Paradiso.' Each one ends with exactly the same word . . ."

"Which is?" he interrupted.

"You tell me."

He shrugged.

"It's an easy one, Rhoads. Take a guess."

Rhoads wouldn't even make a serious try. "Mayonnaise?"

"Close. The word is 'star.'"

Rhoads regretted the stupid joke. Then he thought about explaining to Franklin that the poem thing was the key to catching Virgil.

"I can see why you didn't tell me," he said. "Do you think we can get some literature professors to study the poem and help us figure out what he's going to do?"

"That I don't know. This is where I become a psychiatrist again. Your Virgil has a connection to Dante's Virgil, who, in *The Comedy* is already dead. He is merely the shadow of the man he once was, doomed to live in hell and guiding the education of Dante. Later, Dante will return to the world of the living and communicate what he's learned about the penalties for misbehaving, for forgetting God."

"That superpersonality thing?"

"Whatever our Virgil once was, he now sees himself as dead, as a transformed spirit beyond the reach of mere mortals. He feels wise and invulnerable. And condemned. That's why he is so incredibly dangerous. There's a very good chance he has passed beyond the conception that what he's doing is murder. In a sense, he no longer believes in death."

"No guilt for the three schoolchildren he killed in Newark? Or the sucker he's going to kill today?"

"About the same level of remorse you'd have for the

grasshopper your helicopter landed on out there on the tarmac. Remorse doesn't figure into it."

Rhoads nodded and whispered *shit!* under his breath. That fifty-grand bonus was looking a long ways off. "Would it be pressing my luck to ask you what you think he's going to do next?"

"This one isn't a prediction, Rhoads, just a probability. Actually, nothing more than an educated guess."

Rhoads reached into an inside pocket and took out his notepad.

"Our Virgil's working on his own epic," Dr. Trice said. "And in every good story, there is a continuous building of tension, drama, risk, and excitement. All that leads to some kind of a climax, the grand finale he's mentioned in the few, very few," she shot him a glance, "transcripts you've been willing to share with me. So, I don't know if the grand finale is what he's going to do next, I just have a strong feeling it's what all this is leading up to. The problem is, I have no idea what sort of surprise he has in mind."

Rhoads suspected Fallscroft would be getting impatient. He checked his watch.

"I think the deputy director might be prepared to relax his grip on those transcripts for you," Rhoads said, making a note. "I'll see what I can do."

76

DALLANESS

ANTHONY A., on October 13, of Asheville, formerly of Vineland, New Jersey, at age 46 after a lengthy illness. Beloved husband of Mary (nee Steelman), brother of Michael. Friends and family are invited to his funeral at . . .

77

Anna Maria Trichina unlocked the door of her red Alfa Romeo Spyder and got in. She pulled out of the main entrance of WHQ, drove half a mile, and entered the eastbound lanes of I-240.

She tuned in an oldies station and accelerated. Then, without warning, her rearview mirror began to pulse with red and blue lights from the police cruiser behind her.

"Merde," she whispered to herself when she realized the cop meant her. She pulled over on the shoulder, gravel crunching under

her tires. The cruiser pulled up close behind her. The officer exited his car and approached hers. She rolled down her window.

"Officer, I . . ."

"Please turn your ignition off, miss. Then let me see your license, registration, and insurance card."

Well, he's no fun. She reached into her glove compartment and removed the leather folder that held the registration and insurance card. She handed them out to the policeman, pulled her arm back in, and rummaged through her handbag for her driver's license.

"Hang on for my license. I know it's here," she said, flashing a thin smile. "Somewhere."

The policeman glanced at the documents. "I stopped you because you seem to have a couple of lights out in the rear. Your tag light and your driver's side taillight are out. Did you know that?"

"That's weird. Both lights? Yes, here it is." She had found the edge of the license in the card section of her wallet, plucked it out, and handed it to the policeman. "The car was just inspected a couple of weeks ago. Could be the electrical system blowing them out."

"Maybe you backed into something. they're smashed."

Or maybe someone hit me, pig.

He examined the documents more closely. When he got to the driver's license, he wrinkled his brow.

"Miss? Is your name Dallaness?"

Oh good, she thought. *He noticed the TobacCo, Inc. parking sticker, and he knows Mary Dallaness. I'll milk this and get away without getting a ticket.*

"Dallaness? No. It's Trichina. Anna Maria Trichina. Do you know Mary? She reports to me at TobacCo, Inc. I love having her work for me. If you know her, then you must know her husband Anthony passed away."

The cop took half a step back in order to see into the car better. He looked Trichina in the face. "Say that again."

"Oh, I'm sorry. You hadn't heard. Anthony succumbed to emphysema last night. It was sad."

"I don't know what you're talking about, Miss. But I think you need to tell me why you just handed me a driver's license in the name of . . . Anthony Dallaness."

Like a man who's been shot but isn't yet aware of the wound, Trichina didn't understand. "Anthony Dallaness? What? Can I see that?"

The policeman showed her the license but didn't let go of it. She squinted, trying to read it. The policeman switched on a flashlight and shone the beam onto the license.

Now she got it.

She gasped and heard her heartbeat in her ears.

"What I'd really like is to see *your* driver's license. Do you have it in the vehicle?"

She dived into her handbag and rooted feverishly with shaking hands. The purse slipped from her lap and its contents spilled between her legs and onto the floor. She sat back in her seat, panting, staring.

"Are you all right in there, Miss?"

Trichina didn't respond.

"Miss, I said are you all right in there?"

78

Friday, October 15
Bala Cynwyd, Pennsylvania

"Wow. Look at this place," one of the FBI agents said as their unmarked van pulled up in front of Dr. Trice's Main Line residence. Autumn leaves stood in several huge piles on the full acre front lawn. Ivy climbed up the stone face of the mansion and glass-framed greenhouse next to it. "It's like the Ponderosa."

Two FBI agents exited the van, each carrying a large cardboard box filled with copies of files and transcripts, interviews, audiotapes, and behavioral assessments.

Dr. Trice, still in her bathrobe, watched at the open front door. She showed the men in. They entered her home and put the boxes on the dining-room table. Neither of the agents had eaten yet, and they both sniffed the air. Something spicy and garlicky filled the house.

"Please sign the receipt right there, Dr. Trice," one of the agents said, pointing to the signature line with the pen he was handing her. "And the deputy director said that for your convenience, a duplicate set of this information will be delivered to your office at the Hospital of the University of Pennsylvania. Is someone there to accept the delivery?"

She looked at her watch. "No, not this early."

"When, then?"

"Usually by eight forty-five. Ask for Karen Frederick. She'll lock them up."

"Fine. Thank you. We'll deliver them then. Eight forty-five."

"Thank you."

"One last detail, Dr. Trice."

"Yes?"

"You ve been informed that these documents are confidential

and sensitive, and that by accepting them, you agree not to discuss them, now or at any time in the future, with anyone other than FBI personnel."

"This is the third time I've been advised."

"Okay," the agent said. "Thank you."

Dr. Trice watched the two men get back into the van. She shook her head and hummed. *Nobody loves you when you're down and out.*

79

Asheville

In the Dallaness kitchen, Rhoads and Mary sat at an oak table drinking coffee. Rain streamed down the windows and drummed on the glass.

Mary's head was tilted slightly up, like she was trying to remember something. "They said he could go at any moment, but I thought it would be so much more gradually."

"Emphysema's tricky. I had a grand uncle and great grandfather who both had it. They went fast."

"Smokers?"

"What do you think?"

She shook her head mournfully. "All those hateful, endless details of dying. Any minute, I keep thinking I'm going to have to run upstairs and make sure he's taken his medication. Like when our beagle ran away. I kept thinking he was curled up next to the couch."

"The phantom limb idea, Mary. That will pass." He reached across the table and put his hand on hers.

"I never should have married. It didn't work from the beginning."

"Don't do it to yourself, Sweetie," Rhoads said, his heart going out to her.

"You're not married. You're smart."

"The loneliness that stays with you like an old bathrobe. That's the fine print you don't bother to read when they tell you all about the exhilarating freedom of flying solo."

Mary turned to watch the raindrops splatter on the window above the sink. "Well, still, I'm not sorry he's gone. Though I did love him in some silly maternal way."

"You know once I was on business in Chicago and stopped into Dalesford's and bought a wallet. You know those stupid pictures of models they put in new wallets? I walked around for a month with a woman's picture in my wallet, the woman who came with the wallet. It wasn't to fool the guys, it was to fool me. I told myself that if I had someone I loved, that's where she'd be, right there in the wallet. I wanted to see what it felt like."

"What did it feel like?"

"It felt like my life was counterfeit."

Mary smiled the smile women use to hold back tears, the smile that crinkles their eyes.

Rhoads went on. "I thought about that wallet and that photo the other night when you were over at my apartment."

"Why?"

"You were the girl who came with the wallet. There you were, in my life, sitting in my bathroom, we're talking *to* each other, not *at* each other, about something important. Yet, you were the girl in the wallet. You weren't mine, you were going home, you had a husband you loved and had to care for. It gave me an idea for a business. You see, you start something like a prostitution ring, except instead of sending a woman to screw a guy, the woman calls you up and asks you over to her house for dinner. And after dinner, she'd fake affection, pretend she liked you, and not let you help wash the dishes."

"Oh, T.R.," she said, standing up and taking a step toward him. He remained seated. "I know the timing's terrible, but here it is anyway. I think about you all the time. I don't have to be the girl in the wallet. I want to be the girl."

Mary stepped closer still and took Rhoads by the hand. He got up and started to reach out to embrace her. She stopped him and led him out of the kitchen and into the den. The air was chilly and damp. Several big, old blankets were on the floor.

Logs sat piled over a thatch of kindling in the fireplace waiting for a match.

"Light a fire, T.R.," Mary said. "Make it warm in here."

Outside, the October rain drummed on the windows. The mist swirled in the wind and leaves fell from trees, fluttering down onto soaked lawns and slick, black asphalt driveways.

80

New Jersey

Muntor had been driving for hours, across the Pennsylvania Turnpike, over to the New Jersey Turnpike, and north toward New York. He intended to go home, but he couldn't yet, not until he was far enough away to make another telephone call.

First, though, he stopped at a turnpike service plaza. He thought he needed coffee, but once inside, he knew he needed more. Muntor shot up in a grimy bathroom stall. His energy level and mood skyrocketed as soon as the syringe left his arm. He forgot about the coffee.

Back in his car, seeing the road became difficult. The lights from oncoming cars were beginning to get bright, too bright, in contrast to the darkening sky. The Biphetamine had the effect of hypersensitivity to light. Muntor finally arrived at JFK Airport with a stunning headache and difficulty breathing. He found an outdoor pay telephone and double-parked there with his flashers on.

What if a cop drives by and makes a note of my license plate? Muntor surveyed the scene. He didn't think it was much of a possibility.

He dialed the telephone number on the scrap of paper he removed from his pants pocket and spoke fast as he left his message with the WWW-FM newsroom on Long Island. He told the person who answered that he would be calling FBI Headquarters at noon Saturday, the next day. He had a big announcement, he said, and he wanted Tom Rhoads to be available.

The news intern, who answered, was a Cigarette Maniac news addict, and after receiving the call from someone purporting to be the Maniac himself, he dialed the home number of the news director and let the telephone ring barely three times. Then he hung up, glad his boss didn't answer. He relished the idea of becoming involved in the case. The news director would have insisted on handling the matter himself or worse, snorting and assuring the intern that the call was a phony. And even if the call was a prank, the intern was still well within reason to sound the alarm to the FBI.

The intern took a piece of printer paper and wrote out, as best he could remember, the exact text of what the caller had told him. He called directory assistance in Washington and asked for the FBI's emergency number. He said "Wow" when informed that the Federal Bureau of Investigation has no public emergency number, just a main switchboard number. The operator gave him the number—202-324-3000—without comment. The intern really wondered about the kind of people the telephone company hires. Couldn't she appreciate the gravity of the matter which was clearly evident in his voice?

He called. He told the FBI switchboard operator he had information on the cigarette-tampering case "of the most urgent nature." He smiled at his legitimate use of such a phrase. The operator, flushed with panic, paused a full second before activating the Centrex circuit-seize key. Had the caller disconnected during her moment of hesitation, investigators would have lost an opportunity to record the call origin site. That thought coursed through her like cold pond water.

"Please remain on this line, sir," she said and connected him to the CYCIG Task Force in the ERC.

A special agent, monitoring a bank of eight television screens, each attached to a VCR, was watching SportsDay on CNN when the telephone rang.

His headset had been pushed back so he could hear the sportscast better. In one quick motion, he pulled the headphone ear tabs into place, tapped the mute key on the audio-system remote, and picked up the telephone. The switchboard operator announced the call on line 6260.

Without comment, he disconnected her and finger-punched the 6260 line.

The special agent asked the intern whether the radio station automatically records calls to its newsroom. The answer was no. The agent asked many more hurried questions, determined that nothing had been said that was ultra time-sensitive, made two pages of quick notes, thanked the intern, and told him to sit tight, that FBI investigators would be there shortly to interview him. They'd want to know, he said, among other information, if the intern had any idea whether Virgil called WWW-FM, or him, for any particular reason.

The special agent sat up straight and spun his chair around toward the three other special agents clustered in conversation half a room away.

"Call from Smokey!" he shouted, running his finger across the supervisors' schedule. He had prepared himself to awaken Franklin if anything significant happened, but the three-card schedule told him Brandon was to be called first. He thanked the Lord he didn't call Franklin in error.

The other agents looked over, wondering what had happened.

"He called a radio station on Long Island then hung up," the special agent told them. "Said he's going to call here noon tomorrow with some sort of important message. The station's news intern called us. Sounds real."

One of the other agents jogged out of the room in shirt-sleeves to the Telecommunications Section where they probably were already duping the recording of the intern's call onto cassettes. The director and deputy director would get one, and copies would go to the Behavioral Science Section, the Investigative Support Unit, the case agent serving as liaison with the consultants. Within the next few days, the FBI planned to release a montage of Virgil's various calls, hoping the public might be able identify the voice despite his various vocal disguises.

Within minutes, a transcriptionist would type out the text of the intern's call in script format. As soon as it rolled out of the printer, it would be brought to the ERC and placed in the huge brainsbook that served as the central reference work of the case.

Franklin entered the ERC and silence swept in with him.

"What do you say to keeping Virgil away from Rhoads?" Franklin asked Dr. Myron Sorken, the linguistics expert from John Hopkins who had arrived minutes earlier. Franklin ignored Rhoads who was there as well. "That's what I'm inclined to do."

Sorken objected, saying he agreed, in part, with Dr. Trice's idea about nurturing the relationship between them. Franklin countered with the lost-ground argument. The FBI, he said, was playing along, but the killings were continuing, maybe even escalating. In a losing battle, change tactics.

Sorken threw in a complicating assessment.

"Virgil's dying. You can hear it in his voice. Whatever his announcement's going to be, you can bet it will be consistent with someone who is well aware that he is getting weaker. That can be good news or bad. Virgil will in some way, maybe some very subtle way, give away something that confirms he's fading fast."

81

Saturday, October 16
FBI Headquarters

Virgil telephoned one minute after noon. Franklin instructed Rhoads to answer.

"Good morning Mr. Rhoads," the gruff voice began, speaking too quickly for Rhoads to respond. Excessive static crackled on the line. "I haven't seen anything on CNN about upstate Pennsylvania. didn't hear about it yet? Or is the FBI trying a strategy of a news blackout? If so, it's ill advised. Everything I do should be duly noted by the media."

The communications tech wearing the headset had the approximate call-origin location. He scribbled "cellular phone, Long Island" in large black-marker letters on the pad he had for that purpose and held it up.

"Did you visit somewhere in Pennsylvania?"

"Sure I did. Groundhog day, sort of. You'll find out. Anyway, I'm calling to make another fair trade agreement. I can't stay on the line too long. I borrowed someone's car phone without asking, and I don't want to run up too big a tab, so here's the deal. You get in touch with the Association of Tobacco Marketers and see to it that the Big Eight tobacco companies begin a promotion offering postage-paid money-back refunds for any customers who wish to quit smoking and mail in their remaining cigarettes. I'll let the tobacco companies figure out the logistics. And since I currently work in corporate America myself, in the entertainment industry, I know that it could take a few days to organize such a promo. I'm not unreasonable, I'll give them time, on the condition that they publicly announce no later than nine o'clock Monday night that they are preparing the offer."

It sounded as if Virgil was calling from a cell phone in a moving vehicle.

"You said 'fair trade.' What are you offering?" Rhoads asked, reading from the script prepared by the Behavioral Science Section. BBS had predicted some kind of deal would be offered. "Because what we need is to put a stop to the killings. Otherwise, we have no more room to negotiate. As a matter of fact, if you won't give me that, the FBI is taking me off this investigation altogether. Virgil, you don't want to make a fool out of an ally, do you? You make me look bad to the guys here. Can you agree to a cease-fire?"

Muntor did not want Rhoads and the FBI to see this refund deal as just one more in a relentless stream of demands. If they thought they were just digging deeper and deeper holes, they'd soon quit playing along. He needed to make them think his requests came from a very short list.

"Oh, come on, T.R. they're just bluffing you. They wouldn't take you away from me. You're the one who's most intimate with me. *They* need *you*. Don't put up with their silly threats. Nevertheless, you just made a deal. I'll take a break. I believe I have a well-deserved vacation coming to me. How's that!"

Sorken bit back a shout of glee.

"Great," Rhoads said.

Virgil continued. "I'll tell you what. Maybe I'll even bail out of this ugliness early. It's tempting, it's very tempting, the way I feel, completely beat. Maybe I'll just fade away."

The agents and consultants wanted the killings to end but only by apprehending Virgil. If he simply quit, they might never find him. For how many years did the letter-bombing UNABOM subject remain free?

While Rhoads spoke, Franklin listened in on a headset. He thought the refund arrangement would be no problem. Didn't the cigarette manufacturers offer automatic refunds anyway as part of their standard customer-satisfaction policy?

Virgil wasn't finished. "My vacation, however, won't begin until Monday night *after* the announcement. Then, no more action until further notice, provided I see the refund plan moving along. If it is a nicely conceived refund deal, I may throw in a bonus. But we'll see. Shall I commit myself to more mayhem in the event the ATM is not inspired to launch the refund deal?"

"That won't be necessary," Rhoads said. "We'll contact them immediately."

"All right, thank . . ."

Rhoads thought fast and diverged from the script. He needed more, and he sensed he had only seconds left before disconnection.

"Wait wait wait wait wait, Virgil. One more thing. You want to help me personally?"

"Such as?"

"Such as no more trick-packs, beginning right now. That will demonstrate you and me have a working relationship. Please."

"Nope. Sorry."

"Please?"

"Deal's a deal," Virgil said and disconnected, his voice sounded as natural as they had ever heard it.

Virgil exited from the highway at a rest stop, tossed the car phone into a litter basket, and resumed his drive to Philadelphia.

The collective mood in the ERC turned heavy and somber. Rhoads could picture the sick bastard Virgil grinning.

"You believe him?" Franklin asked, removing his headset.

"So far he's done what he's promised," Rhoads said.

"What about that corporate America line? I think we have a hit on the VoiceStressor."

"If that's his idea of a red herring, we'd have caught him by now. He's just throwing in an obvious phony lead."

They were interrupted by Sorken.

"Which means his mind is in the deception and misdirection realm," the professor said, "instead of the strategize and attack realm."

"What does that mean to you, Doctor?" Franklin asked.

"Like the rest of it. It may mean absolutely nothing. How innocuous a lead is 'working in corporate America'? Or on the other hand, should this be a precursor to a change in his behavior, I would say that it suggests a turn toward more risk taking and more violence. This man is not the emotional Rock of Gibraltar. In him, changes are like prequake tremors. In most cases, they foretell an imminent, more powerful change."

Franklin rubbed his beard stubble. He hadn't been home for thirty hours. "What do you make of his refusal to cease planting his trick-packs until Monday night?" Franklin asked.

While Sorken pondered the question, Rhoads spoke up. He narrowed his eyes as if he were focusing on something in the far distance. "You know," Rhoads said, "Virgil may be even smarter than we think. He has never asked for something that we could have had reason to deny him. He's playing public sentiment like an experienced PR guy. We ought to check the Big Eight's public relations departments for unhappy employees, past and present. Guys laid off, et cetera. He knows that if we refuse him, he can simply report us to the media as uncooperative, then he kills fifty kids and signs it, 'Your Friendly Tobacco Companies.' We already know the bastard's tape-recording his calls to us."

"Wouldn't that be cumbersome from a cell phone on a highway?"

The communications tech spoke, "With a suction-cup mike and the wire run up his sleeve into a compact recorder in his pocket, he could stick it on a receiver of a pay phone or cell phone without being seen and remove it just as easily. That'd be no problem."

"Can't our communications people do something with the modulation of the phone calls to make taping us more difficult for him?" asked one of the Behavioral Science psych team members.

"Veto!" Franklin said. "Get off that track. No games like that. I need ideas on what he may do next and where he may do it. If we can assume he's going to keep his promise and put the brakes on, at least temporarily after Monday night, wouldn't it be safe to assume that he will want at least one last fling?"

Rhoads shut his eyes and painfully recalled his own last fling in Atlantic City.

"It's impossible to put every cigarette retailer under surveillance," an agent said.

Rhoads was busy figuring something in his notebook. "Why don't we go to the media and trumpet that we expect an attack, or series of attacks, between now and Monday night," he said, looking at his notes. "That will serve the cause three ways. First, it will put smokers on alert. Two, it will make an assumption that the manufacturers will float the refund deal. That will squeeze them into a 'yes' position. And three, it may force Virgil to perform, to take a risk that he wouldn't normally take. Like in Princeton." Rhoads turned to the members of the psych team who sat alongside each other at the conference table.

"No matter how angry he gets," an FBI psychologist said, "he can't do much more than he is doing now."

"Don't count on that," Rhoads said. "Would you want to see him twice as pissed? I wouldn't."

"He can only place so many cigarette packs. Practically everyone on the planet is on the lookout for him. He's probably not quite ready for his grand finale," the psychologist said defensively. "We've got him mapped to a probable home base in the metro areas of New York, Philadelphia, Baltimore, or Washington."

"Not bad," Rhoads said. "Narrowed down to forty million people."

Franklin looked at Rhoads. He thoroughly disliked the man's presence in FBIHQ, now more than ever, now that Rhoads had become an essential component in the investigation. Rhoads saw the resentment in Franklin's face.

Franklin said, "Forty million is a lot of progress compared to the two hundred and sixty million we had twelve days ago."

Rhoads shrugged, putting both palms up in a submissive pose.

82

TobacCo, Inc. World Headquarters
Asheville

Rhoads flew to Asheville. In the Executive Suite, he sat down, lit an Easy, and watched while Pratt paced and cursed. Pratt agitatedly folded and unfolded a slip of paper he had been handed by an assistant Friday after the stock market closed.

TobacCo, Inc. Common
Last, 193 $^3/_8$-1$^1/_4$, Volume 1,220,000.
Most active stock

The CEO spoke. "Any news on the suspect from the Newark schoolyard thing?"

"Yeah, *bad* news. Another copycat. He didn't pan out. Just a five-time loser looking to get on TV."

Pratt took a seat in a guest chair next to Rhoads, crossed his legs, and steepled his fingers, lost in thought. Rhoads saw the high hose pulled up over Pratt's skinny leg.

"Damn it, Rhoads, what the hell is going on with the FBI investigation? You haven't given me anything. Why do you think I assigned you to this thing?"

"I can tell you what the FBI thinks about that."

Pratt stood up impatiently and began pacing again. "Go on."

"They're hung up on the Midas and Benedict thing," Rhoads said. "That's all they want to talk about with me. All they have from TobacCo, Inc. is that three-page executive summary you or Trichina wrote. They think you whipped it up off the top of your head to pacify them."

"Essentially, that's what I did."

"So, if you want them to give information to me, how about

helping me out with something I can give to Franklin. Give them the project files, what could be so bad in them? Otherwise all I can do is follow them around."

"Or work that shrink angle, the woman in Philadelphia."

"I'm on top of that. She's important."

Pratt sighed and sat down behind his desk.

"I know this is difficult for you, T.R. Don't think I don't appreciate it. And I've been remiss in telling you this, but whatever happens, you can write your own ticket here. Any kind of job you want, you name it. I've already instructed Anna Maria to see to it. But this is not a simple situation. You've been around long enough to know that there are always eight sides to every story. I'm convinced that wherever Benedict is, he has nothing to do with what's happening. He couldn't be involved in killing hundreds of innocent people. Benedict's not a problem. But Midas? Midas is a problem. It's an embarrassment that could kick the legs out of our stock. The stock's sliding deeper into the sewer every day. The whole industry is getting creamed. Rhoads, I'd give Virgil one hundred million dollars to surrender himself. But no matter what happens, we can't afford to let the public know about what Midas was."

Rhoads looked at Pratt quizzically. "Is it as embarrassing as having people puking blood onto the sidewalk while clutching a pack of Easy Lights every night on the six o'clock news?"

"I'm going to confide in you, Rhoads. I've never told you what Midas was because, candidly, I didn't know if I could trust you. Now I think I can. Midas was a rather ill-conceived project, Rhoads. We thought better of it, late perhaps, but we did think better of it. That's why I killed it. The idea was, broadly speaking, to study the relationship between nicotine doses in cigarettes and, uh, brand loyalty. You get the picture?"

"Yes."

"It was 1,000 percent illegal, we knew that. But we thought we'd develop the products and *then* figure out how to get them into the marketplace legally. But things went awry before we got to that stage."

"So you're talking legally embarrassing, as in Senate sub-committee investigation embarrassing."

Pratt sighed again. He looked weary, his bravado of minutes earlier dissipated. "Something like that."

"And that's why Benedict . . . quit?"

"Yeah. He got a major attack of Holier-Than-Thou-itis, which, if truth be told, had a lot to do with our decision to kill Benedict."

Rhoads eyes widened. *"To kill Benedict!"*

Pratt narrowed his eyes hatefully and burned them into Rhoads s. "To kill Midas. *Midas!* You know what I meant."

Man, it got cold in here fast, Rhoads thought. *Did somebody turn on the air conditioner?* "Okay, okay, Nick, slip of the tongue," Rhoads said. "So, then why did he disappear?"

"Who knows why these Ph.Ds. do what they do? But it wasn't to take a walk on the wild side as a freelance domestic terrorist. He didn't, doesn't, have the nerve for something like Virgil. He used to just about pee himself when he had to make a presentation to the Executive Committee."

"So what is it you want from me? The FBI's not sharing. They won't as long as they think we're holding out. I've been doing the only thing I can, which is try to get info from Franklin and take it a step further. But I haven't had a chance. This shrink in Philadelphia has been the only decent thing I've developed."

"Of course I know you're doing your best. I'm going to send Franklin an expanded file on Midas. Now you know why I can't give him everything, and I need you to stay in closer touch."

"Listen, Nick, all I know is that the FBI's treading water. They've got a huge army of agents working all the physical evidence. But that's useless. This guy is very smart. The cyanide is untraceable. When he calls, it's always from someplace he can get away from. He's obviously a master of disguise. And he's patient as a cat at a rathole."

Pratt brightened. "That's why they're so mesmerized by

Benedict. They have nothing else going."

"Right. So it would be a tremendous help if we could dig up Benedict, wherever he is, and show him to the Feds and say, 'Look, this guy's a harmless nerd.'"

"I know, I know. That's what's killing me. Let's say we do find him. The last thing I need is some born-again humanitarian spilling his guts about private company business at a mass-media feeding frenzy."

"But people are dying, Nick, and that'll make the feeding frenzy worse. Without Benedict, it'll only get worse."

"Yeah," Pratt said, grimacing. "That's a problem."

83

From the October 16 edition of the *Daily Spirit,* Punxsutawney, Pa.

"He Seemed Like a Nice Old Man"

VIRGIL STRIKES LOCALLY PUNX'Y WAITRESS DIES

Found a Pack of Camels on Table

84

Sunday, October 17

The rain had stopped.

Mary and Rhoads awoke while it was still dark and quiet.

They held each other and listened to the rain. A little after dawn, he kissed her good-bye and left.

The doorbell rang so soon afterward that Mary thought he had forgotten something.

She looked through the peephole anyway, and in the fish-eye lens, she saw Anna Maria Trichina. She opened the door.

"I know it's early, but we have to talk," Trichina said, stepping in. Mary tensed and blocked the way. She smelled wine and fear on Trichina.

"First," Trichina said, "my sincere sympathy. I didn't know Anthony, you know. But I know this. I've never lost anyone close to me. I don't know how I'd handle it."

Saying nothing, Mary stepped back and let Trichina come in.

Trichina continued. "So, for whatever it's worth, I imagine it must be like a limb torn away. Unbearable."

Mary didn't want to discuss her emotional state with Trichina but felt she had to say something. "The second-guessing myself is what I have to get over. Anyway, I know that's not why you came. Come on in, I have some coffee."

"I know this may seem inappropriate, considering . . . that you are in mourning, but . . ."

"But?"

Trichina dropped her voice to a whisper. "But we have to talk and it'd be safer in my car. I'll explain. I'm sorry, I know this is inconvenient. Plus, it's cold. Throw something on."

I'm not going out now. Not with her.

"Can't we talk here. I have something on the stove and . . ."

"Put something on and turn the stove off. We'll only be a

few minutes."

Mary did not know how to say "no." She just stood there and blinked defiantly.

"Please," Trichina begged.

A minute later, Mary found herself sitting in the passenger seat of Trichina's Alfa Romeo. Trichina started the car.

"Don't look so nervous, we're not going anywhere," Trichina said. "Just around the corner. It's just that your house may be bugged."

"My house?" Mary hesitated. "I think you better tell me what this is all about right now. We've never been friends exactly."

Trichina put the car in gear and drove a couple of blocks until she came to the playground adjacent to an elementary school. Mary glared the entire way. Trichina parked the car and lit a cigarette. Mary had to ask her to turn on the key so her window could be opened.

"Sorry," Trichina said, lowering the window. "I've been a bitch to you, Mary, I know. Don't take it personally. I am a bitch. But if we don't work together now, we may both wind up like, like your husband."

Mary had her head turned toward the window, avoiding the smoke. Her head snapped around to Trichina.

"What in the hell are you saying?"

Trichina looked Mary in the eye. "Mary. They murdered him. Whatever it looked like, it was a deliberate killing."

Mary shook her head and smiled, relieved. *What a paranoid little fool you are, Anna Maria. So smart, so beautiful, so stupid.*

Like a patient grade-school teacher with a kid who keeps making the same mistake, Mary said, "Sorry Charlie. Anthony had emphysema. He lived way past the time they predicted. He couldn't breathe, his heart worked too hard, it just stopped. What reason could anybody have had to kill him?"

"Because of the copies of the Midas documents you sneaked. They must have thought Anthony would know where you put them. When he didn't tell them . . . well . . ."

Mary squirmed. Dread coursed through her. Her eyes filled. "I don't know what you're talking about!"

"Sure you do. You made a fake directory when no one was watching you, then you erased it instead of the directory you were *supposed* to erase. Smart. You fooled me, but you don't know Nick Pratt. He's got everything covered."

Mary shook her head, refusing to believe. "Anthony died from complications of chronic pulmonary emphysema. That's the certified cause of death. You're trying to say that I'm responsible for Anthony's death. I won't listen to that. Take me home."

For a moment, Trichina didn't say a word. She was distracted by a car approaching in the rearview mirror. Instead of pulling around, it pulled up along side of the Alfa Romeo. A middle-aged man took a long look at Trichina and leered. Then he sped off. Trichina exhaled in relief.

"Mary, listen carefully. I'm being straight with you. You may not know it, but you've got a tiger by the tail." She paused. "You've got *two* tigers by their tails. If you want to get out of this . . ."

"Get out of what?"

". . . then you have to stop lying to me. You made your own copies of the Midas financials. They know that. How do you think I know all this? *Pratt* told me. He wants me to get them back from you. He told me I'm supposed to act like I'm in danger just like you. But the truth is, I am." Trichina's eyes opened wide. "You don't know these men, Mary."

Trichina took hold of Mary's wrist and unconsciously squeezed hard.

"You're hurting me."

Trichina saw what she had been doing and immediately let go.

"Mary, listen. Pratt and his gang, they're like bank robbers. The number one rule they teach bank teller trainees is, *if you are being robbed, don't look at the gunmen's faces, you avert your eyes. Don't let them know you've seen their faces. If you can identify them, you have to assume they're going to kill you because they can't risk leaving any witnesses.* Mary, we both have seen those documents. We've seen their faces. Now your husband is dead, and both our lives depend on what you do next. *Where are the documents?"*

Mary's mind reeled. *Was any of this true? Was all of it true? Where was T.R.? He'd tell her what to do.* It took her a full minute to be able to speak. She could barely get her words out louder than a whisper.

"My copies are safe," Mary said. "What happened to the copies you had me make for you?"

"I deposited mine with an attorney who had instructions to use them should anything happen to me. But, again, the bastard Pratt found out. I imagine his man waved enough money in the lawyer's face, and the lawyer sold me out."

This is getting unbelievable. She's an actress, and she's acting scared. She's not in danger from Pratt, she's working for him. "Pratt?"

Trichina grabbed Mary's wrist again.

She practically screamed into Mary's ear, "STOP IT! Damn you! Don't play the dumb broad with me now. You read between the lines of those documents! You're no fool. You must know that Pratt gave T.R. two hundred thousand dollars to pay Benedict to keep his mouth shut about Midas, but something went wrong. Maybe Benedict threatened T.R. with the police or something. So T.R. killed Benedict, kept the money, then told Pratt that Benedict was gone when he got there. Or something like that. Who knows? I'm piecing this together by myself. All I know is that if we can't figure out how to use those documents to protect ourselves from Pratt and his jackboots, we're both going to die."

Mary held up her hands in surrender. Her head was spinning. *T.R. up to his neck in it? How could that be?* This was too much for her, too fast. Her body shook mightily.

"All right," she said, sobbing. "All right. What do you propose we do?"

85

Headline in La Suisse of October 17.

U.S. Terrorist Targets Geneva

CYANIDE-LACED CIGARETTES SHIPPED TO DAVIDOFF

"I Knew What They Were Straight Off," Clerk Says

86

Trichina opened her door and admitted Pratt. He stepped across the threshold and swung the door closed behind him. His upper lip twitched. Trichina read fury, rage, resentment.

"What's the big idea, Anna Maria?" he said, working to control his voice. "You call my chauffeur and tell him that it's for my own good to come here immediately. The one weekend you know my son's back in the U.S. What's the matter with you?"

Trichina turned her back to him and walked into the dining

room. She wore a short skirt, a bulky blue sweater and was bare-foot. Yellowing flowers stood in a vase. "Then why are you here?"

Pratt started to sputter.

She cut him off. *I have Mary running scared. Now let's see if I can get Nick to blink.*

"Shut up, Nick. You sit down. You listen for a change."

He regarded her narrowly and sat down on the sofa. He knew her well enough to know this, whatever it was, wasn't a bluff. Trichina retrieved her briefcase from the dining-room table, returned to the living room, and sat in a chair opposite Pratt.

"From now on, Nick," she said, opening her briefcase, "things are going to be a little different for me. I'll be designing my own career path. We're going to do things my way."

"Silly rabbit. What do you think you have?" In one compartment of his mind, Pratt was fantasizing about what he'd tell Valzmann to do to her.

"Or I'll put you in prison."

Pratt looked at her, saying nothing, his face blank.

"I have all the evidence I need about Midas and the Benedict disappearance to convince a grand jury that you should be personally indicted for first degree murder. The evidence is safe. I don't have to do a thing. Anything happens to me and the evidence will be sent where it will do the most damage, and . . .well, enough. I know you got through to my lawyer Finch, but he wasn't the only man on base. Sloppy of you, Nick. But then again, you suspected I had a backup or else I'd probably be at the bottom of some landfill with Benedict right now."

"First degree murder, Anna Maria," Pratt said, controlling himself. "That's a pretty dramatic claim . . ."

He rose and turned his back to her. He didn't want her to see his face.

In a fury, his teeth clenched with such powerful opposing force they nearly cracked. A vicious twitch materialized and clambered across his face beneath his flesh like a lizard on hot sand. Images of the bamboo tiger's cage the Viet Cong kept him in flashed in his mind. The facial spasm moved from left to right. The skin above his right eye twitched uncontrollably as if someone had taken a pinch of the flesh and twisted it. His breath came like gasps.

What happened to his mouth was most terrifying of all. It snapped open wide and silent as if under the command of a dentist, held its pose, and then snapped back down again. Trichina heard the sound, but it didn't register as tooth on tooth. She looked up to see his head shake from side to side three or four times with such force, so fast and hard, that she feared it might tear itself off and fall forward into the picture window.

And as fast as it had begun, the massive twitch stopped, like a sudden cloudburst. Pratt gasped again, nostrils flaring. Trichina looked away. She did not want him to see her watching. His face now burned a brilliant crimson. He turned slowly and mechanically, as if a mannequin on a revolving display. Unable to speak just yet, Nicholas Pratt concentrated all of his rage and focused it on the invisible spot he drew on the back of the head of Anna Maria Trichina.

Frightened by the little scene out of *The Exorcist*, Trichina feigned composure by flipping through pages of a blue notebook she had taken from her briefcase. She wanted to take back control of this meeting.

"No small talk, Nick." She read from a page in the notebook. "Exactly one week before you terminated Midas, you pushed through a postallocation budget increase request for two hundred thousand dollars. Which you actually signed off on! Sloppy, sloppy, sloppy. Or would that be cocky, cocky, cocky? Didn't Richard Nixon make the same mistake thinking no one would ever get to listen to those Oval Office tapes?" She raised her eyebrows in mock surprise. "Anyway, your little budget increase was turned into cash through a variety of transactions. One way or another, all two hundred thousand wound up in the pocket of a fellow by the name of Thomas Rhoads. Rhoads went to Denver, officially to meet with an alarm system contractor to write up specs for the Denver facility. But he had something else he was going to do for you, didn't he? Right around that time, Benedict disappeared. That must be a coincidence."

Trichina closed the notebook as if was the last page in a bedtime story and turned to face Pratt.

"The End," she said.

Pratt glared and said nothing.

"Now, Nick," Trichina said softly, "if you're innocent, why don't you just walk out right now. Otherwise, we are going to go over the list of my new job *benefits*, the conditions for my silence." Trichina swallowed hard. "Don't look so sour, Nick," she said, her tone dripping like warm honey. "I'm a reasonable woman. I can be had."

"I'll admit no guilt, Anna Maria. What I admit to is being curious to hear about the rest of this . . . this delirium. So I'll remain seated."

Trichina smiled. "Call it what you will, Nick. Nevertheless," she said, holding up her hand and raising one finger as she ticked off each demand, "I am to be promoted to position of executive vice-president of marketing, named an officer of the corporation, and given the compensation that goes with that rank. All retro to the first of the year."

"Anna Maria? Have you any idea what an executive vice-presidency at a company like TobacCo, Inc. pays? In excess of a quarter-million dollars a year."

"As a matter of fact, I did know that, Nick."

"Even if this whole conversation weren't ludicrous, your requests are impossible, Anna Maria. I have a board of directors and shareholders to report to. Executive vice-presidencies aren't handed out on the basis of long legs and . . ." Pratt crudely put his thumb in his mouth.

"You can explain it to the board any lying way you want. And thanks for reminding me. That's another change. You will never lay your leathery hands on me again."

Pratt rose. "Anna Maria, I'm leaving now. By virtue of this very conversation, you've proven yourself to be reckless and irresponsible. Perhaps you're under too much pressure, I don't know. I had big plans for you. They're dead now. And although you may imagine in some girlish fantasy that you have me at some disadvantage, I assure you, you do not." Pratt got uncharacteristically loud. *"I promise you, you do not."* He brought his volume under control and spoke almost serenely. "I encourage you, for your own good, not to expose yourself to . . . to legal action, Anna Maria."

"Save the euphemisms, Nick. I don't need to tape-record you. I have you by the nuts already. You have a week to set it up and announce my promotion. After that, I go directly to the Justice Department. And if I wind up dead before then, I'll see your raggedy ass in hell."

"Why are you doing this, Anna Maria?"

"Lots of reasons, Nick. But I'll give you one for starters. Remember the marketing awards trip to Acapulco? Your lie about a vasectomy? How'd you phrase it? *Oh, yeah. Don't worry, beautiful, all the little swimmers have been cut off at the pass?* Nice, and I wind up pregnant. Then that other . . . incident, the . . ."

"Oh for crying out loud, Anna Maria. I paid for the fucking abortion. It didn't cost you a *dime.* I saw to it you had two weeks vacation to recover from a twenty-minute procedure. I . . ."

"You sad, pathetic sack of shit, Nick. Is that all you got from that episode? That you saved me a few bucks for the surgery? I didn't realize it at the time, Nick, but that child that I got rid of . . ." She broke off. She was not going to let herself get emotional, not now. She took a deep breath and a different tact. ". . . don't you underestimate the power of the maternal instinct, Nick. You'll be a lot better off."

At that, Pratt laughed and started for the door. Another idea was forming. Trichina, he realized, could be helpful in retrieving all the runaway Midas documents and computer disks. If she was properly motivated.

Pratt faked a slump of shoulders, as if he was beaten, resigning to see it her way. He walked back and sat down on the leather sofa.

"I don't mind helping you, Anna Maria" he said. "But why wouldn't you think to discuss this idea with me? Why this unreasonable attack out of left field?"

Pratt's conciliatory tone succeeded in leading Trichina think she had won. At least this battle. She moved toward him.

"I'm so glad we don't have to leave this on an unpleasant note," she said. She stepped closer and looked Pratt in the face. *Thirty years ago, he was probably damn good looking, kind of a Sean Connery type,* she thought.

She took one more step closer and sat slowly onto the sofa, separated from Pratt only by a white pillow. He inhaled her musky perfume. She looked straight ahead, not at the CEO. Her hand moved toward him and stopped, resting on the pillow. Her deep maroon fingernails dug into the soft leather. She picked up the pillow and put it carefully on the floor in front of her. Her knees parted ever so slightly.

"Mr. Pratt," she said softly, caressing her thigh through the skirt's material. "I've got a very sensitive situation here, and it's fairly crying out for the expertise of a man of experience."

She continued looking straight ahead but could feel Pratt watching her.

"You said you wouldn't mind helping me, Nick."

Trichina closed her eyes and leaned back. It was Pratt's turn.

87

Tuesday October 19

Chicago Sun-Times headline:

CIGARETTE REFUNDS COULD REACH $200 MILLION

ALL BIG 8 TOBACCO FIRMS IN NATIONWIDE MONEY-BACK REFUND PROGRAM

Execs Concede Move Is "Virgil-Inspired"

88

Wednesday, October 20
Bucks County, Pennsylvania

Muntor needed a remote place to stage a dress rehearsal for the grand finale, and he knew a realtor could help him find one. He loved hiding behind real estate agents. The way they prefer to control the relationship by insisting that they drive you in their cars while you sit back and enjoy the view, the way they lead you about like you had a ring through your nose. The whole routine served as a perfect cover.

Muntor dressed as a country gentleman in a good seersucker jacket he had found in the closet. He bought a wide-brimmed sky-blue hat and cordovan wing tips and cotton pants to imitate the wardrobe he had seen in an ancient copy of an *Esquire* Fall Fashion Review.

At the realtor's office in Doylestown, Pennsylvania, Muntor misrepresented himself as a serious prospect. He had told her he was interested in farmland, preferably with an old farmhouse and a barn or stable. Something he could convert into an office. A spring or pond would be a plus. They spent hours Wednesday afternoon looking at properties.

Working from a list she had compiled, the agent eventually drove by a property with an old school building on it. They went up and around the long driveway. Muntor said he didn't like the looks of it. As they drove away, the realtor told him how the county had tried to sell the school at auction, but none of the bidders offered the minimum, and the sale was canceled.

"Interesting" was all he remarked. He tried to seem bored.

At about 3:30 P.M., after driving to two other properties, Muntor announced that he had seen enough for the day. The realtor moved and turned her car around. On the ride to be dropped off at his car, he made careful mental note how to return to the school.

Now that he knew where he could practice for the big event, Muntor drove to a diner and killed time reading and drinking coffee until 4:30 P.M. That would give him an hour or so of light, and then he could drive away when it had gotten dark.

He returned to the school. The vacant building was more than secluded enough for Muntor's purposes.

He proceeded up the gravel driveway to the sprawling

1930s-era fieldstone schoolhouse. The wall on the north side had caved in winters ago, the realtor had said, and part of the roof had rotted through and was ready to collapse. Every pane of glass, thousands of them, had been broken.

Muntor, confident that no one was around, stood out in the driveway next to his car and changed from his prospect's costume, carefully putting the slacks and shirt and jacket onto the wooden hangers he had brought. He changed into jeans and a flannel shirt, yanked a heavy duffel bag from the floor behind the driver's seat, another from the trunk, and took two trips to half-drag, half-carry them into the school. In his constantly exhausted state, the effort required was extreme.

Muntor set the duffel bags down. He walked crumbling halls until he found the giant auditorium. Wrecked and mostly empty, the high-arched ceilings seemed more fitting for an airplane hangar than an assembly hall. It was exactly as he had imagined.

The pain in his chest ripped at him, sharp and steady. He did not have enough strength to get the equipment from the duffel bags. He leaned back, up against a dusty tile wall, reached into his shirt pocket, and withdrew a small brown envelope containing a syringe. He removed his jacket, took off his belt, and rolled up his sleeve.

Invigorated and recharged, in both mood and energy, Muntor walked briskly and retrieved the duffel bags. He brought them into the auditorium. From one bag, he removed bright yellow fire-department hazardous-materials protective clothing, boots, suspendered-trousers, a full, knee-length tent-style overcoat, and a special helmet with a hood that protected the entire face, the kind firemen use when responding to chemical fires or toxic-fume alarms. Muntor laid all these articles out on the dusty floor that was once gleaming tile and waxed hardwood.

Then, using both hands, he removed another article from the second bag. Out came an orchard-fogger, a green-and-white-striped steel cylinder, designed to generate thick clouds of insecticide, and an oversized fire extinguisher whose hose was attached to a long, curved, black, gunmetal trigger nozzle. Liquid sloshed around inside the cylinder.

Muntor put on the protective clothing, all but the hooded helmet, carefully and quickly. He had practiced this part. As usual, he struggled a bit, wriggling the tank and its cobweb of straps into position on his back, but finally positioned it snugly without too much delay. He was getting faster at getting it on. Then he took his video camera and tripod from the duffel bag. He attached the camera to the tripod's mount and set it up in a far corner of the huge room. He looked around at the hundreds of broken, splintered wooden auditorium seats that had been screwed into the floor. He imagined them filled with the movers and shakers of the tobacco industry.

There was still enough light left for what he needed to do, but he had to work fast.

He was nearly out of breath and had almost forgotten a critical part of the drill. Muntor set the orchard-fogger down and removed a folded piece of paper from his pants pocket. He looked at the diagram he had drawn. Referring to it, he measured off a large rectangular area, sixty paces up, forty-five to the right, sixty paces down, and forty-five more, back to the spot from which he had begun. At each corner, to show him the rectangle's perimeter, he had stopped and marked an X into the dusty floor with the tip of his yellow rubber boot.

Muntor noticed a dozen wrens perched high on a rotting beam above him. He stooped and picked up a broken wooden seat leg and threw it toward the birds. He aimed wide, not wanting to hit them. The splintered wood crashed into the wall behind the birds and sent them scattering in a wild flutter of wings. A few feathers spun lazily to the floor.

"No need to get you guys involved," he said to them as they flew out of the auditorium through the missing roof slats. He hadn't spoken in hours. His voice creaked.

Next, Muntor retrieved from the second duffel a bath towel wrapped around two small wire cages, each containing a young white laboratory rat. Muntor walked the rats to the two farthest corners and set them down. An old joke popped into his head. *Laboratory rats are the major cause of statistics.*

He walked back to the duffel bags and orchard-fogger. One wren had returned to the beam above. Muntor picked up another piece of wood and tossed it toward the bird.

"Last chance," he shouted to it. "Get out of town."

Muntor pulled on the hooded helmet.

Later, Muntor would watch the video.

The sequence would open with billows of white-gray, like threatening storm clouds. Then the image of a man. And for the end of the sequence, a long shot, from the driveway, encompassing the entire building, the white-gray fog rising from holes in the roof and through the broken window frames.

89

Saturday, October 23
Harrisburg, Pennsylvania

Outside it was cold enough to snow. Inside, Muntor sat at a booth in Bob Diner in Harrisburg.

Bob Diner? Muntor thought, sitting under fluorescent lighting that was too bright, amid the noisy people and the clatter of dishes, waiting for the waitress to bring the coffee he ordered. A previous customer had left a newspaper folded open to the stock quotes. He nudged the paper into a position so he could see the TobacCo, Inc. price.

STOCK	DIV.	YIELD	P/E	SALES	HIGH	LOW	LAST	CHANGE
TimMir	.24	.7		1196	$36^1/8$	$35^3/8$	$35^3/8$	$+^3/4$
TimM pfP	1.37	5.3		254	$25^3/4$	$25^1/2$	$25^3/4$	$+^1/8$
Timken f	1.20	2.7	13	1455	$45^7/8$	$44^7/8$	45	-1
Titan Cp			28	470	$6^1/4$	$5^7/8$	$6^1/4$	$+^1/4$
TitanW s	.06	.4	9	377	$16^1/4$	$15^1/3$	$15^7/8$	$-^1/2$
TobacCo	**18.25**	**9.7**	**8.2**	**1720**	**189**	**$186^7/8$**	**$188^1/8$**	**$-^7/8$**
ToddShp			13	164	$6^1/4$	6	$6^1/4$	$+^1/4$
Tokhem			50	400	$8^1/2$	$8^3/8$	$8^1/2$	$+^1/4$
TolE pfK	1.87	10		57	$20^3/8$	$18^3/4$	$18^3/4$	$-1^1/2$

Beautiful! he thought. Then the pain in his chest distracted him and killed his appetite, and nothing on the menu interested him except the restaurant's name. *Bob* Diner? *Didn't someone forget the apostrophe "s" somewhere along the line?* But no, that's what it said on the menu, that's what it said on the paper place mats, and that's what it said on the illuminated blue letters atop the brick-and-chrome restaurant.

He wanted to ask the waitress about the diner's name, but he could not afford to draw any attention to himself. He missed small talk with strangers. It was true he had no close friends, but he loved to engage people in conversation on topics in the news, upon which he could be impressively authoritative.

Now, though, he was cold and tired and wanted strong, hot coffee.

The waitress brought the cup. He sipped it. *Tepid, damn it.* He tried to get her attention, but she had disappeared into the back.

Muntor looked around, reluctantly sipped more from the cup while he stole glimpses of the patrons.

Muntor held a pack of Winstons in his hand. He was waiting for the all-clear moment when he could wedge the trick-pack between the seat cushion and booth back. He had looked in the crevice earlier and noticed the crust of a slice of rye bread and several small squares of the wax paper that comes on pats of butter. Muntor knew that even in good restaurants, not that this place was one, all you have to do to find something disgusting is to look.

In this planting, Muntor chose to remove most of the cigarettes from the pack and leave the ace inside with the remaining ones. This method, he reasoned, suggests a *bona-fide* pack left behind by chance by an inattentive customer. He'd used the ploy several times before.

Just after wedging the pack in behind him, Muntor looked up. A man and woman, the female facing Muntor, sat several booths away. Blue-collaresque features in business garb. They didn't seem to be husband and wife, brother and sister, or casual acquaintances. They looked more like colleagues.

But they could be the cops.

Muntor tried to make a slight furrow of worry creep across his brow. He was acting now, psyching himself for what he was going to do. *I have this damned briefcase full of cyanided cigarettes,* he said to himself, almost as if reading from a script.

The thin line between paranoia and faking paranoia blurred. To Muntor, it was possible that the man in the booth could be looking at him out of the corner of his eye.

I'm getting out of here, he said to himself, *and I have to get rid of this briefcase. But not too quickly, not too slowly. This has to be handled subtly. This has to look good. Take it easy.*

Muntor left two quarters on the table and took his check to the cashier. She was a bosomy woman about sixty, who wore the kind of sequin-decorated eyeglasses that opticians should be prohibited from selling. A copy of the *Harrisburg Patriot-News* lay spread out on the rubber counter-mat used by cashiers to drop change. A front-page headline described the latest activity of "The Tobacco Terrorist." An FBI composite sketch, vague enough to fit one hundred million men, was displayed in a black-bordered box. The cashier moved the paper in order to accept Muntor's check and money.

"Everything all right?" she asked. She did not await a substantive answer but instead squinted at the waitress's penmanship and began to make change for the crumpled five Muntor had handed her.

To stifle the urge to cough, Muntor took a deep breath. A musical wheeze issued from his chest. The woman looked up, aimed her squint at him, held it for a beat, and then returned to her change-making task.

He swallowed hard and looked around toward the couple whose demeanor could be that of undercover police. Was the male turning away from him at that instant or just engaged in animated conversation?

Muntor left Bob Diner, walked fast but paced himself and got into his car. A young couple walked past his car as he drove off. *They did not seem to notice me, though they may have.* Muntor didn't like that possibility. *And now, should a police cruiser come down the street or around the corner and ask them if a guy walked by in the past few minutes, theoretically, they could describe me and my car.*

Muntor drove for several blocks and then turned into an alley. He saw what he had been looking for. The dumpster, green-gray in the poor light, one of its two steel lids raised and beckoning. To make it easier to find at night, he had used reflective spray-paint earlier to draw a yellow smiley face. Muntor lowered his window as he inched his car close to the dumpster and, without stopping, tossed in the briefcase.

Then he drove out of the alley onto the street and accelerated steadily.

90

FBI Headquarters

```
FEDERAL BUREAU OF INVESTIGATION
SECURED TELEX TRANSMISSION
TX2156191095HB05
URGENT/ CYCIG EVENT REPORTED
TO: DUTY CHIEF.WX
     COPY PHILADELPHIA.FX
FROM: WIREROOM SUPERVISOR.WX
T&D: 2156 HOURS 23 OCTOBER
```

MESSAGE: THE ASSOCIATED PRESS BUREAU OUT OF HARRISBURG RELEASED A STORY AT 9:53 P.M. THIS DATE REPORTING LOCAL PX RADIO DISPATCH OF A POSSIBLE FIND OF ADULTERATED CIGARETTE PACK IN BOB DINER [ED. NOTE: CORRECT SPELLING OF ESTABLISHMENT IS BOB DINER], 4545 W. CAPITOL DRIVE, HARRISBURG. NO INITIAL SUSPECT DESCRIPTION, NO VEHICLE DESCRIPTION, NO DIRECTION TAKEN. CONFIRMATION PENDING.
SA/D. EDMONDSON.
END OF URGENT.

91

FBI Headquarters

The telephone rang at the duty officer's desk. The officer spoke quietly for several minutes before making a note in the daybook. Then he called Franklin.

"Another copycat, sir," the officer said. "Detained in West Hollywood. Tried a Virgil-type switch in a grocery store at the checkout counter. We have a team en route now to interrogate him."

92

Sunday, October 24
Harrisburg, Pennsylvania

Just after dawn, a Harrisburg Police Department patrol car responded to the anonymous 9-1-1 call complaining about a bum making noise rummaging through a dumpster. The car stopped in front of an alley several blocks from Bob Diner. Two policemen got out and walked into the alley behind the Blue Note Cafe and approached a dumpster.

A pair of spindly, baggy-panted legs stuck out of the dented metal container, waving and kicking in the air. The left foot wore a white Nike, the right foot some sort of dirty sky-blue deck shoe. The two policemen stood watching with crossed arms and bored grins.

"Looks like Jeeter legs," one of the cops said.

"Jeeter must have struck pay dirt this time."

"Looks like he's drowning in there."

"Yeah. I guess we ought to pull him out."

Each policeman grabbed a leg and pulled hard. The rest of Lester Jeeter was jerked into the dim morning light and deposited, standing, on the cement. He was black and filthy, rail thin, wild eyed. In his right hand, he held a briefcase which he swung blindly at his attackers.

"Whoa, Jeeter!" the first cop said, ducking.

Knocked off balance by the swing of the briefcase, Jeeter fell to the ground. When he looked up and saw that he had swung at the police, he cowered and clutched at the briefcase.

"Don't hit me, man! I thought you was that jitterbug again."

The policemen ignored him. They stared at his shoes.

"Jeeter, who in the fuck dressed you today? You dress like a sixty-year-old crackhead wino," the first cop said. "Wait a second, you *are* a sixty-year-old crackhead wino."

The other officer, a sergeant, straightened up. A no-nonsense expression lurched across his face. "Hey, Keith? Wasn't there a briefcase in the description of the cigarette guy last night?"

At that, Jeeter drew the briefcase tighter to his chest.

"Get away from that, Jeeter," the sergeant said, holding out a hand. "Hand it over. Now."

Jeeter ignored him. "Shit! This is my suitcase. I found it."

The cop stepped forward and yanked the case out of Jeeter's arms.

"*Dang, man!*"

"Cuff him," the sergeant said. And then, into a hand-held radio, "Sixteen-two to dispatch. I'm at Westgrove in the alley, behind the Blue Note. I need the Virgil team back here. Might have something."

"Now look what you've done, Jeeter," the first cop said. All the excitement bewildered Jeeter.

"Don't talk to him, jackweed, cuff him! I know you don't pay attention to Donnelly in the shift briefing, but don't you even watch the news? If this briefcase here has anything to with that Virgil guy, this place is going to be wall-to-wall whiteshirts, wall-to-wall Feds, and wall-to-wall reporters in about eight seconds. We fuck this up and they'll be laughing at us coast-to-coast on Dan Rather tonight."

"I was the one who spotted his legs, you know."

Jeeter looked like he was going to cry. "I don't give a rat ass about no damn Rather tonight. I want my $100 now! What about my $100?"

"What $100?" asked the first cop.

Jeeter paused, not knowing what to say. Then he thought of something. "Hey, it's a nice case, man. It's made out of eels. That's worth a Ben at least! Ain't there some kind of reward for the cigarette man?"

"Eels? You're full of shit, Jeeter."

"Damn, it, Keith. Will you cuff his ass and put him in the car! How many times do I have to tell you? And get the yellow tape out of the trunk."

93

Ben Brandon called Rhoads at 10 A.M. and thoroughly enjoyed knowing he woke him.

"The deputy director asked me to call you," he said when Rhoads turned surly. "But I don't know why you count."

Brandon, who had been up almost four hours already, summarized the facts surrounding the possible recovery of Virgil's briefcase in Harrisburg and what events the FBI and Pennsylvania State Police believe may have precipitated Virgil's abandonment of this briefcase.

When Rhoads's conversation with Brandon concluded, Rhoads called Dr. Trice and told her the story. While he spoke with her on his cordless telephone, he walked through the rooms of his apartment, water bottle in hand, misting his trees.

"Remember this, T.R.," she said. "If you have something, if you have *anything*, you have it because Virgil *gave* it to you. Don't ever think otherwise, or you'll be sending yourself headlong down a primrose path."

Rhoads nodded, then realized she couldn't see the nod.

"T.R.? You there?"

"Yes."

"You remember what Br'er Rabbit said to Br'er Fox, don't you?"

"Refresh my memory, ma'am."

"Well, ma'am, it's an old story by Joel Chandler Harris. You see, Br'er Rabbit finds himself being held by the scruff of his neck by the nasty Br'er Fox who is trying to think of something unpleasant to do to Br'er Rabbit. So what Br'er Rabbit does is say, 'Do anything you want, but please don't throw me in the brier patch, it's all stickers and thorns.' So, Br'er Fox, not a deep thinker but a very *categorical* thinker, throws Br'er Rabbit into the brier patch and laughs and laughs—until he gets the surprise of his life. Br'er Rabbit jumps up with nary a scratch and deftly makes his way out of the brier patch, dancing and singing. As he's tearing away, Br'er Rabbit looks over his shoulder and with his own laugh shouts, Bred and born in a brier patch, Br'er Fox. Bred and born!'"

Rhoads made a mental note to ask Mary if she knew what in the hell Dr. Trice was talking about and what the hell a Br'er Rabbit was.

94

The FBI's Evidence Response Team flew into Harrisburg on a Learjet from Washington. In practically all investigations, crime-scene-evidence collection is conducted by the forensic specialists from the nearest FBI field office. Evidence is then shipped directly to the lab in Washington for analysis and often in nothing more secure than Federal Express envelopes. In high-priority cases, a courier will hand-carry the material. Only in the rarest of cases would lab technicians come from FBIHQ to supervise evidence gathering. The Washington-based forensics team arrived two hours behind the one from the Philadelphia field office. Franklin instructed the Philadelphia team to do nothing more than protect the scenes at Bob Diner and the dumpster.

The parking lot entrance to the Harrisburg Central police station sat at the end of a peeling, gray corridor tiled with ancient gray linoleum.

With a loud slam, the iron double-doors of the parking lot entrance burst open. A half-dozen Harrisburg policemen strode in at a pace somewhere between marching and running. Two of them dragged a cuffed and frantic Jeeter.

From the station's street entrance, at the other end of a nearly identical corridor, another set of double doors burst open. Leaves blew in as a throng of trench-coated federal agents, led by Franklin, strode in. The lanky figure of Rhoads was among them.

The two columns of serious men met in the middle and stopped abruptly, face to face.

Franklin, produced his badge. "Deputy Director Oakley Franklin, FBI. I need Captain Mulcahy."

One of the Harrisburg officers said, "Follow me."

In an observation area adjacent to the interrogation room, Franklin, Mulcahy, and Rhoads stood together holding coffee cups. They looked through the one-way glass at Jeeter being questioned by a black plainclothes Harrisburg detective and Brandon.

"Don't get your hopes up, Director," Captain Mulcahy said as he leaned against the smudged glass. "I can tell you right now this Q and A is kind of pointless."

"I understand Jeeter Lester is well known to you," Franklin said.

"Yes. The sector guys roust him out of that dumpster every couple of days. His mind is shot. Crack. *And vino.* A nice combo. Do you want to hear them?"

"Please."

Mulcahy flicked a switch on a battered old speaker mounted on the wall.

Inside the interrogation room, Jeeter sat, now uncuffed, across a plain wooden table from the Harrisburg detective and Brandon.

Brandon was in the midst of speaking. "So, you admit you

are now, and have been for many years, an alcoholic, Mr. Lester. Is that right?"

Jeeter turned to the detective, incredulous. "What's he talking about? Can't I just sit back in the cage like always?"

"Sure you can, Jeeter." The detective offered him a cigarette, and he accepted, nodding thank you. "But the briefcase you found is very important. Can you just tell us what you did this morning, beginning when . . . and where . . . you woke up."

Brandon rolled his eyes, not approving of the detective's approach.

While Jeeter thought about the question, Brandon grew increasingly impatient. Unable to contain himself any longer, Brandon butted in and pointed at Jeeter. "Yes or no, did you see the perpetrator?"

"Perp-a-what?" Jeeter asked, again looking at the Harrisburg detective. The detective looked toward the one-way mirror hoping the captain would come in and yank the FBI jerk.

"He wants to know if you saw who put the briefcase in the dumpster," the detective explained.

"I didn't see nobody. Somebody just threw it away. You should see all the stuff you can get from a dumpster. Chairs, half a big bucket full of warm Colonel Sanders. Once I got a computer, and I took it to a guy who just plugged it in and it worked. *He gave me a hundred.* Now this case, I found it. I found it and if you want it, I want to get paid for it."

"Are you aware, Mr. Lester," Brandon said, "that if this is your briefcase, you could be charged with more than 370 counts of first degree murder?"

Jeeter's eyes rolled, terrified. "I didn't kill nobody, man. All I did is find a damn suitcase in the trash." He appealed to the detective. "Barney. Just put me in the cage. Please."

"It's okay, Jeeter. We know you didn't hurt anybody. We're just trying to find the man who put it in the dumpster. The man who put it there is a dangerous killer."

"I didn't kill nobody, man," Jeeter said and turned away.

From the other side of the one-way glass, Mulcahy, Franklin, and Rhoads watched. Mulcahy looked disgusted, Franklin wore a sour expression, and Rhoads smirked.

"Oh well. Every 'no' brings us closer to a 'yes,'" Franklin said. "Let's call an end to this. Let Mr. Jeeter go. Let him calm down. We can always talk to him later. Do you agree?"

"Yeah," Mulcahy said. He spoke into the intercom. "Wrap it up, Barn." He turned to Franklin. "I don't think it would have gone any differently even if your man hadn't interfered. We'll keep our eye on Jeeter for you. If you ever need him again, just let us know. He won't go far. He's a creature of habit."

"Well, thanks, Captain," Franklin said. "I'm going back to Washington. My lab boys are prepping the evidence for transport to the FBI lab in D.C. First they need to X-ray it. The Pennsylvania State Police Bomb Unit's doing that now. They'll probably need another hour or so. If you don't mind, an Investigative Support Unit crew will be working out of Bob Diner for another twenty-four hours or so. I've asked them to clear everything with you."

The captain nodded.

"And, please, thank your men for not giving in to the temptation to open that case," Franklin said. "We won't open it until we get it into a sterile room at the lab. The right speck of dust can speak volumes."

"Every now and then, we get it right."

"By the way," Franklin said. "What's with that name? *Bob Diner?*"

"Once owned by a man named Charles Avery Bob. It annoys everybody. Part of Harrisburg's charm, don't you think?"

"Not really," Franklin said and turned to Rhoads. "You want to fly back with me?"

"Actually, I thought I'd stick around to see what I can learn from Inspector Clouseau in there," he said, nodding to Brandon in the interrogation room.

"Suit yourself," the deputy director said.

95

Rhoads had no intention of hanging around to needle Brandon. He wanted to stay in Harrisburg and nose around without chaperons.

He was out of cigarettes and couldn't find a vending machine in the station house. He walked down the main corridor and approached several policemen engaged in conversation by the processing desk.

". . . by the dumpster behind the diner," one of the officers was saying. "So Louie says 'what do you want with all them cups of coleslaw you take out of the garbage, Jeeter?' And Jeeter says, 'What do you think? I'm having homeless folk over for a buffet, asswipe.'"

The police laughed.

"That don't beat what we saw this morning. You should of seen them legs kicking around in that dumpster," the sergeant said. "Looked like a cartoon."

Imitating Jeeter's voice, the junior officer said, "That's my case, man. It made out of eels, man, eels!"

They all laughed again.

Rhoads jumped in. "Any of you guys tell me where I can get a pack of smokes?"

"If you don't mind Easy Lights, try the diner," a red-faced middle-aged cop said. "They got a fresh batch in last night."

Another officer, embarrassed at his colleague's rudeness to a stranger, pointed down the hallway to the street entrance. "There's a Seven-Eleven half a block away. Make a left when you get out front. The machine in the cafeteria here's busted."

Rhoads said thanks and walked toward the exit. He nodded to two special agents. They carried an evidence bag containing the briefcase on their way to Washington.

Rhoads stopped in his tracks, turned back toward the FBI

men, and ran to catch up.

"Hey. Hold up."

The men stopped.

"Can I take a peek at the briefcase for a second?" Rhoads asked.

"Who's he?" one of the agents asked.

"Rhoads, the guy from TobacCo, Inc.," the other agent said. He turned to Rhoads. "Sorry, it's already sealed."

"Shit," he paused, thinking. Then, to the one who knew him, "You have an inventory sheet?"

"Rhoads, what do you want to know about it? We're late."

"Just a basic description."

The agent closed his eyes to remember what he had written on the sheet. "It's twenty-two inches by eighteen inches by four inches. Hardside. Leather handle and a three-reel brass combo lock. Worn, brown eel-skin covering."

"What kind of covering?"

"Worn. Brown. Eel skin."

"Okay, thank you."

Rhoads struggled to contain himself until he was out of sight of the FBI men and the Harrisburg cops.

Outside, he skipped down the stone steps and along the street toward the Seven-Eleven. He almost broke his neck when he tried one of those jubilant click-your-heels-in-midair kicks.

Come to momma, he shouted. *You come here to momma, all fifty thousand of you.*

Rhoads knew Jeeter wouldn't know eel skin from Sanskrit—unless someone told him first. And Rhoads knew who that had to have been.

Now Rhoads had something the FBI didn't. It felt like a million bucks. He didn't know how to make use of the information, but he was going to protect it with his life until he could figure out what it meant. The closer he got to Virgil, the closer he was getting to *The Deep Blue.* He could see the trawler drifting and bobbing gently out there on the Atlantic under a hot sun with a capacity crowd of rich New York lawyers fishing for yellowfin. *Yeah, baby, I'm getting seasick already.*

And he pictured Virgil in his mind's eye. *Come here, you sick son of a bitch.* Rhoads could picture himself finally cornering Virgil somewhere, tackling him by the throat, holding him victoriously by his hair, pulling it a little more painfully than necessary. But he wouldn't hit the old man unless the man tried to fight, and then, just one clean punch to quiet him down.

Come here, he fantasized, *you little son of a bitch. Come on home to momma.*

Rhoads walked into the Seven-Eleven and got in line behind a heavy, flustered mother whose three noisy kids were tugging at her jacket. The youngest, a boy of about four, held up a Popsicle.

"Ma! Can I have this?"

"Where'd you get that? I told you no candy. You put that back."

"This isn't candy."

"Put it back."

The boy pointed toward a deep freeze in the rear of the

store. "I can't. It's too high."

"Stop it!" she screeched. "You got it out, you put it back. Now."

The boy pouted and did not move.

"You got it out, you put it back," his mother repeated through clenched teeth.

Rhoads watched as the boy slouched tragically back to the deep freeze. After a backward look at his mother, now busy paying the cashier, the boy managed to slide open the glass lid. Unable to see in over the top, he stood on tiptoes and felt around in the cold.

Rhoads watched, fascinated by the boy's determination. It wasn't obedience that motivated him, Rhoads realized, but the challenge.

The boy clambered onto the edge of the deep freeze, he leaned forward, and his head and shoulders disappeared inside. He lost his balance momentarily, fell in another few inches, and flailed his legs wildly in the air to regain control. He found a place to drop the Popsicle and tumbled out of the freezer, quietly proud of his effort. He returned to his mother empty handed and breathing hard.

Something the boy's mother said stood out, hard and cool, the way smooth stones do in a rushing stream. The words repeated themselves to Rhoads like a chant.

"You got it out, you put it back."

Rhoads looked at the boy intently.

"You got it out, you put it back."

He didn't know why the words had such a pull. Another thought flew to him—Dr. Trice's caveat.

Thoughts or ideas that have a different texture about them, she had said. *They are usually gifts from the universe.*

Outside, he took out his notebook and wrote down the mother's words.

Then he went looking for a telephone booth in a quiet place.

Rhoads hung up from Dr. Trice fifteen minutes later with new respect for himself. He proudly took credit for figuring it out, but he knew he never would have even gotten close if it hadn't been for Dr. Trice's guidance.

She had steered him away from the mother's words, although, when the puzzle was solved, it was the words that had told the story. Dr. Trice had known somehow to focus on the boy. She had asked Rhoads to describe what stuck out in his mind's eye about him.

"How much I liked him," Rhoads had answered. "The boy forgot all about not being allowed to have the Popsicle, and all of a sudden, he had this huge determination to find a way to put it back."

"That was your emotional reaction to him," Dr. Trice had said. "You admire him. Tell me about your mind's eye image of him. What picture do you see?"

Rhoads had to think. Then he laughed. He came around to saying that when the kid slipped and fell further into the deep freeze, he just kicked and wriggled that much harder, fighting to regain his bal- . . .

The kicking legs!

That's how the police described finding Jeeter.

Then Rhoads saw it.

All he said was, "Yes!" That was enough to spark loud laughter from Dr. Trice on her end of the line.

Earlier, the eel-skin clue told Rhoads that Muntor had given the briefcase to Jeeter.

Now he knew why.

Son of a bitch!

97

After an hour's delay while detectives processed the paper-work, Jeeter left the police station. On his way home, he crossed the street to avoid walking past the dumpster and the two FBI agents who stood on the other side of the yellow tape that cor-doned off a section of the alley.

He walked furtively, glancing backward frequently as he hurried along. When he got to a vacant building at the end of a certain block, he crouched down, raised a cardboard flap over a basement window, and crawled through head first.

Inside, he lighted a candle he had placed there earlier. He made his way through a series of collapsing, debris-laden rooms, rounded a corner, and lighted a few more candles before sitting down on a bed made of wooden crates and plywood loading skids.

The only illumination Jeeter had in the dark rooms were wax candle stubs stuck into wine bottles. He regularly retrieved the stubs from the trash behind an Italian restaurant on State Street. Picture frames without pictures had been crudely nailed over photos carefully cut from *National Geographic* and glued with Elmer's to the water-stained walls. Jeeter collected pictures of tropical beaches.

What served as his bed was a disarranged bedspread atop a stack of several coarse wooden skids. In one corner, a battered television set with its broken antenna sat on the case of a mal-functioning VCR. The lone table featured a standing frame filled with a generic print of a blonde woman and toddler. They both beamed.

This makeshift residence, without heat, without running water, without electricity, was what, in his own mind, made Jeeter a class apart from the homeless.

Jeeter's ears pricked up at quiet footsteps outside. In the near dark, he froze, listening. Another scuffle and the sound of some-one lifting the cardboard flap. He held his breath, his eyes show-ing alarm.

He heard someone lower himself into the back room. Jeeter looked for a hiding place and stooped into a corner behind a cor-rugated box to pull the bedspread over him. He knew he could look like the rest of the junk. *There's nothing wrong with you 'cause God don't make no junk,* his big sister used to tell him a long time ago.

He heard a sound behind him, like a faint sigh. He was too frightened to stay hidden. He tore the bedspread off and whirled to look, his face contorted in fear.

There, leaning against the doorway was Rhoads, somberly observing the man with the dirty bedspread shawl.

Still fearful, but not quite so terrified, Jeeter stammered, "Who you?"

"Who did you think I was, Jeeter?"

"I didn't think you was nobody."

Rhoads just watched him, then he spoke. "You thought I was him. Didn't you?"

Jeeter wagged his head "no" with great force. "No. I don't know who you talking about."

Rhoads took half a step closer. Jeeter tried to move back but found himself against a wall. The candlelight flickered.

"I'm not here to hurt you," Rhoads said. "I'm an investigator. I was on the other side of the glass in the police station. I saw that jerk from the FBI treating you disrespectfully. I just want to talk to you some more about what happened this morning at the dumpster."

Rhoads calmly entered the room. Jeeter, still crouching with his skinny back pressed against the wall, remained still. Without approaching him, Rhoads moved around, looking at the few pos-sessions on the walls and floor.

"You're a cop. This is my home. You got a warrant?"

Rhoads did not answer.

Jeeter spoke up. "I said all I got to about it this morning.

I told it all already."

Rhoads picked up the picture of the blonde mother and child and ran his finger along the frame picking up dust. "I don't think so, Jeeter. You told them you found the case this morning. That isn't true."

"Is too. I was taking it out. They saw me taking it out."

"When the cops grabbed you, you weren't pulling it out, were you?"

"I sure was!" Jeeter shrugged off the silly bedspread, stood upright, and took a tentative half-step away from the wall. "They my witness! Go back and ask them. The sarge and that rookie Keith."

"Jeeter. Tell me the truth." Rhoads reached into his pocket and took out a rubber-banded clump of cash, driver's license, credit cards, ATM card, and the assorted business cards he'd collected but never discarded. "Jeeter, you're not in any trouble. But I have to find the man who . . ." Rhoads flipped through the clump and found what he was looking for, a $100 bill. He removed it and put the rest of the money and cards back into his pocket.

Jeeter's eyes fixed on the bill.

"I'd sure like that hundred dollars, but still, I'm not going to lie. Nobody told me where to look."

Strike one, Rhoads thought, but he kept himself from reacting to the slip.

He held up the bill by one corner and slowly crumpled it until it was a compressed wad completely concealed in Rhoads's fist. "Ben Franklin's in jail, Lester," he said, "and only the truth can set him free."

Jeeter shook his head. Whatever was frightening him was real.

"The truth, Jeeter. I need the truth." Rhoads kept the bill hidden in his fist and extended his arm tauntingly.

"Whoever he was, Jeeter, you're the last guy in the whole world he ever wants to see again. He won't be back to bother you."

"You know that minimum-wage black-assed security guard in Washington, D.C.? The one who found the adhesive tape on the door at the Watergate back in the Nixon days?"

"Sure. The one man who all the ex-CIA burglars didn't count on."

"Yeah, him. What'd he ever get out of it?"

Strike two, baby.

"I imagine he's a pretty proud man."

"Dirt poor, too, I bet." Jeeter took a pack of cigarettes out of his pocket and lit one.

"Still . . ." Rhoads began.

Jeeter cut him off.

"Look, I just found it, man. I just found the damned case." Jeeter sat down on the bed. Boards creaked. "Now, I told you the truth. Give me the money."

"Not until you tell me what you were really doing back at that dumpster, Jeeter."

"I just did."

"No."

"I just found it."

Rhoads whispered. "You were putting it back."

Jeeter shivered. "Oh, no. No sir! I was taking it out. They even saw me. You can ask them."

"You used that one already."

Rhoads uncrumpled the bill, then slowly crumpled it in his fist again. "Let me help you get old Ben out of the can," he said. "You just nod when I tell you how it really was."

Jeeter shook his head "no," but Rhoads continued.

"He approached you two or three days ago. Right?"

Jeeter wouldn't nod.

"He told you what to look for, a brown eel-skin briefcase."

Jeeter looked away.

That's as good as a nod, Rhoads thought.

"He told you where to look for it, or maybe you suggested the dumpster. I mean it's your dumpster, right?"

Jeeter gave a tentative nod coupled with a small shrug.

"And he told you when it would be there. And he gave you money, and he promised you more, didn't he?"

Another tiny nod.

"He also told you if you brought it to the cops, you could get a few bucks from them, too, didn't he? He was the one who told you they'd part with $100."

Jeeter averted his eyes and looked down at his two mismatched shoes.

Strike three. Holy shit!

"Then you heard all the excitement last night at Bob Diner, all the commotion. And you couldn't wait. Maybe somebody else, some bum, some homeless bum, was going to poach on your dumpster. So you went to the dumpster, and you got the briefcase out, sooner than the man wanted you to. Right?"

Jeeter looked up at the ceiling like a kid getting a lecture.

"You brought it back here. Right? But you didn't think it would matter, because you were going to put it back and then find it later when he wanted you to."

Jeeter lowered his eyes, looked over to Rhoads, and nodded again, even more slowly. Rhoads let a small smile play across his face as he moved about the room, casually examining things.

"Good, Jeeter. Thank you. Now, there are just three simple things I need from you," Rhoa said. He handed Jeeter the $100 bill. "One, a description of the guy, as detailed as you can. And two, as much as you can remember about what he said to you, word for word. And three, whatever it was that you took from the briefcase."

Rhoads had worked his way over to the fractured television and VCR near Jeeter's bed. He looked at them closely. Neither had worked in years, but next to them there was a stack of six or eight dusty, sun-warped videocassettes waiting to be played someday when things were better.

"I didn't take nothing, man," Jeeter said. "Just kept the suitcase here so nobody else'd get it. Just like you said."

Rhoads looked through the stack of cassettes.

Jeeter pointed a finger at Rhoads and shouted. "Hey!"

That startled Rhoads.

"Hey!" Jeeter said. "I got a idea. How 'bout a drink, man? Gooood stuff. Special stuff." He went toward a wooden cabinet. "Special stuff for a special occasion. And real clean glasses, too."

Jeeter moved a box and from behind it retrieved a dirty shopping bag, but inside the bag was a wooden gift box. When he opened it, Rhoads saw it was lined in red felt. Two spotless crystal long-stemmed goblets and a bottle of Wild Turkey sat nestled inside.

Nice try. Rhoads could spot a decoy maneuver a mile away.

Now where had I been when he scared me? Rhoads thought. He furrowed his brow. *I was at the stack of videos.* Rhoads must have been close to something. He went back, reached out, and took one cassette from the middle of the stack, the clean, new cassette. It had a label, hand lettered, that read, "Six minute scene from Paradiso, shot Bucks County, Oct. 20."

Jeeter's face twitched, he swallowed hard and moistened his chapped thick lips. He looked away.

"Okay," Rhoads said. "Let's have that drink, Mr. Jeeter. And you can tell me all about it."

98

Forty-five minutes later, Rhoads left Jeeter's, stuck a ciga-rette in his mouth, and walked unsteadily back toward the police station.

He stopped before he arrived there. He wanted to see the video before the FBI did. He turned and walked in another direc-tion. He had no idea where he was going. He walked past a liquor store, a pawnshop, a grocery store with a Korean name, a couple of abandoned storefronts. He stopped in front of a sign that read Beaverly Hills Video. A porno arcade.

"Do you have a booth here where you can watch full-length videos?" Rhoads half-hoped no such booths were available. He worried about sitting in something sticky.

The place reeked of disinfectant and smoke. The clerk nodded to a row of freshly painted booths at the far end of the store.

"Five bucks an hour for the booth, five ninety-five for a full-length adult film," the clerk said. "You can pick any one of those." He pointed toward a wall of shelves holding hundreds of porno films classified alphabetically by perversion.

"I brought my own tape."

"Nope. You can't do it."

"I'll give you the extra five ninety-five anyway."

"I said no." He stood up from the bar stool he had been on.

"What's the difference? I'm paying the same as if I rented one."

"Because last year some asshole comes in here with the same story and I say okay.' Next thing I know, I'm closed down for thirty days. Asshole's watching some imported kiddie porn, and that's the same day the state's got some undercover inspector in here. So that's why."

Rhoads put thirty dollars on the counter.

"Ten for the shop, twenty for you. This isn't even porno. I'm a cop."

Inside the musty booth, after some fancy footwork explaining why he didn't have his badge, Rhoads slid the videocassette into the VCR. Rhoads could hear the machine running, and he could see the counter on the VCR clicking away, but the screen remained blank.

Virgil's idea of a joke?

Then a sputter of white static and something not quite discernible.

Roiling clouds of gray. Thick, turbulent, opaque. Then, gradually, like an image appearing in a developer tray, Rhoads began to see the shape and features of a human figure becoming visible among the clouds. The ambient light increased steadily. At last Rhoads was able to make out the details of a fireman's helmet, a full-face gas mask, a fluorescent yellow tentlike parka, and the long curved snout of an orchard-fogger belching gas from the green-and-white-tank strapped onto a, man's back.

The scene was interrupted by a break and sputter of static.

Another shot.

From one hundred yards back, a dilapidated building, perhaps an old school or hospital building in the countryside. Broken windows and a partially caved-in roof. At the near end of the building, everywhere, between the shattered panes of glass and the broken slats of the roof, the gray fog escaped, bleeding heavily into the sky.

What was it? Some kind of smoke? Steam?

Oh Lord, no, Rhoads realized.

It was gas.

Rhoads found himself walking on the street, his mind reeling. He sighed when he realized he'd have to turn the video over to the FBI. He hated having to lose his advantage.

99

Monday, October 25
Associated Press
Washington, D.C. Bureau.

ASSOCIATED PRESS
ATTN.: ALL EDITORS, ALL MEDIA / BREAKING
        STORY UPDATE MONDAY,
OCTOBER 25, 2:15 P.M. EST. HARRISBURG, PA.
SLUG: VIRGIL BRIEFCASE RECOVERED?

ART AVAILABLE: 2 COLOR PIX.
 1: Crime scene. Dumpster in Harrisburg, PA,
    where briefcase was recovered.
 2: Closeup of briefcase that may have been
    abandoned by 'Virgil' in Harrisburg, PA.
    (Xmit of FBI photo)

FBI: "VIRGIL EVIDENCE FOUND
IN HARRISBURG, PA."

By Fred Bird
Associated Press Staff Reporter

Sunday, October 24—Harrisburg, PA. In what may be the most significant evidence recovered so far in the cigarette-tampering investigation, the FBI today announced that technicians are analyzing an eel-skin briefcase that may have been abandoned by a skittish "Virgil" who fled nervously from a diner here. A pack of tainted cigarettes was also recovered from the diner.

The Virgil investigation began 20 days ago when an unknown person or persons poisoned 700 packs of Easy Lights cigarettes and shipped them to tobacco shops all over the United States. More than 300 died. Since then, at least 30

298 ◆ *Frank Freudberg*

others have died in subsequent tampering incidents authorities believe were perpetrated by the original killer.

As of noon today, 376 people have died and 41 remain hospitalized from injuries received when they smoked cigarettes laced with the residue of a sodium cyanide solution. Five people across the U.S. have been arrested in separate copycatting incidents, none fatal.

"We have not yet had enough time to confirm whether or not the briefcase is indeed Virgil's," FBI spokesman Walter Mitten said. "The evidence has been transported to the FBI Lab in Washington where it is under intense scrutiny at this moment. The FBI has released an updated description and sketch of the man believed to be Virgil. If anyone wishes to provide the FBI with information regarding this investigation, they are urged to call 202 324-3000. Agents are standing by now. There is no question about it. We need the public's help in apprehending Virgil who has now reached the dubious status of the country's most heinous serial murderer."

1oo

FBI Headquarters

In Lab One on the third floor of FBI headquarters, an FBI agent who specialized in locks used a dental pick to roll the reels of the lock on the eel-skin briefcase, feeling for the tumblers to click. He did not need the stethoscope in his tool kit. He knew as soon as he saw it that the three-reel lock would be easy to open.

"Got it," he said as he found the number on the last reel. A latex-covered index finger tested the two side latches. He looked up at Franklin who loomed over his shoulder. "Want me to pop it?"

"Go ahead. *Slowly.*"

His gloved hands carefully released latches, thumbs in place to catch the tiny brass plates from springing back with the familiar snap. Franklin and various agents and technicians clustered around the table on which the briefcase sat.

"Gee. How creative," the lock-picking technician said. "The combo was one-zero-zero."

"At least it didn't explode," Franklin said.

The lead technician looked at him with surprise. "Sir. We X-rayed it thoroughly before picking it up off of the detective's desk in Harrisburg."

"Just a joke, Galton. Disregard it. What have we got?"

Galton rose and another technician slid into the seat. With the aid of a large magnifying glass, he began looking through the briefcase, comparing items to images on 8"x10" glossy photographs he had removed from a file folder.

"I'm ninety-nine point nine nine nine certain it's his," the other technician said after a moment. He counted under his breath. "Fourteen packs of cigarettes, various brands. Four Aimsco Ultra-Thin half-cc 28-gauge syringes, one plastic jar of 100 tablets of Vitamin C . . . but . . . wait," he said, gently shaking the jar, "there seems to be a loose powder inside. I imagine we'll be taking a close look at that." He leaned farther into the open briefcase. "Three disposable Bic lighters and . . . Damn, sir! I think he may have blown it this time. I can see latent prints all over the place. All over the place."

The men look at each other with tentative grins.

"Are you sure?" Franklin asked.

"Yes. I am. They're everywhere in here. I don't think he was expecting anyone to get a hold of the briefcase. You know how meticulous he's been."

Two agents high-fived each other.

One of the agents leaned in over the technician's shoulder to get a better look. Then he shrugged and said, "I got twenty bucks to anybody's ten that says those prints index to one Loren D. Benedict."

Galton spent the next four hours taking apart the briefcase, molecule by molecule. As soon as he noted his initial impressions, he called Franklin who had gone home for a few hours sleep. The deputy director was just stepping out of the shower when the telephone rang.

"Good news and bad," Galton said. "First, there's no question about it, the briefcase is a bonanza. It's definitely him, Oak, or someone using the identical batch of sodium cyanide, the stuff from Tellman Chemicals and Supplies in Baton Rouge. And in the briefcase, we found seven newspaper clippings clipped together. All but one of the articles were Virgil stories. But the bad news is the prints belong to Lester Jeeter."

An alarm went off in Franklin's brain. "Something's wrong, Galton. Jeeter never opened the case, the police made that clear."

"Unless he opened it before he got caught, somehow."

"No. The police were definite about that. They saw him inside the dumpster before he got it out. We have to pick him up! Damn it. We had a material witness, and I released him! Hold on Galton." Galton heard Franklin shout for his wife. "Lydia!" Louder. "*Lydia!*" A woman shouted back from somewhere far off. Then Franklin again. "Lydia! Call my office. Tell them it's urgent and to pick up Jeeter in Harrisburg." The far-off voice said something in reply. Franklin repeated himself. "Pick up Jeeter in Harrisburg. They'll know. I'll call them in five minutes."

"Okay, Galton. I had to get that rolling."

"Also, Oak, there's a slight chance we may learn something about the water he used in mixing the cyanide solution. If he used tap water from a major municipal utility, there may be some markers. But don't get your hopes up. Back to the sodium cyanide, it is not likely someone else is using the Tellman batch. And there's something else, I don't know if it helps or not. A hair fragment."

"A hair fragment!"

"Not human."

"Canine?"

"Feline. The question is, when did it get in there? Are our evidence experts still up there in Harrisburg?"

"Yes."

"I'll call them, tell them I'm looking for any hint that a cat or cats have been in Jeeter's residence or anywhere else he may have opened the case. Ask Jeeter if he has a cat or if cats come into his place."

"Where was the hair?"

"Behind the built-in fanfold compartment in the side of the case. The little belt buckle thing was buckled closed. We unbuckled it and looked around."

Franklin thought. "How flat is the fanfold compartment when it's empty and buckled closed?"

"Like a file folder with nothing in it. Pretty flat."

"Tight enough that a junkie would figure there's nothing in there worth taking the time to unbuckle a fastener for?"

"Unless he's a crack addict desperate for cash. He wouldn't have cared how flat it was."

"Okay. You've made a case for him opening it. You know many drug addicts jonesing for the glass pipe who would take the time to rebuckle?"

Galton thought about that then said, "Good point."

"I'd say then whatever you found behind there probably belongs to Virgil, not Jeeter. And I doubt anyone would think to plant anything that subtle. Too much of a long shot that we'd even find it."

"Okay, Oakley. The problem is, is I'm not sure what we could do with a garden-variety cat hair."

"I know. In the meantime, get some extreme closeup color photos of the hair made while we try to figure how if it can help us."

"That's already being done."

"Galton? What was the subject of that other newspaper article?"

"A sheet torn out of *Adweek* magazine listing a bunch of ad-industry events taking place in Las Vegas. We're working on that, too."

101

Harrisburg

Six FBI agents peeled out of the driveway from Bob Diner after getting word, relayed from Washington, about Jeeter. The message had been terse. *Priority. Get to Lester Jeeter's residence and take him into custody and seize the building.*

Harrisburg Homicide's day-work One-Squad got the call from the FBI. The Fire Department arrived simultaneously in response to a report of smoke in the building.

The officers discovered Lester Jeeter dead on his side, laying on the floor by the front door of what seemed to be his living room. A section of greasy rug under Jeeter's head had smoldered from a cigarette that had apparently fallen out of his mouth, sending acrid smoke throughout the rooms and out onto the street where someone had noticed and called it in.

The Fire Department started an electrical generator and

brought in a set of lights to illuminate the crime scene.

"What a fucking loser!" a Harrisburg homicide detective said to one of the FBI agents. The FBI agent gazed at Jeeter and shook his head. On the body of a black man, cyanotic skin is tougher to determine by sight than on a lighter-skinned person. But there wasn't much question. Virgil had struck again.

The homicide detective stooped close to Jeeter's body and continued his inspection. "Can I ask you something?" he said to the FBI agent. " I mean how fucking stupid do you have to be to steal cigarettes from the guy who's known all over the universe for poisoning them! You got to laugh. You really got to."

The FBI forensic experts who had taken the briefcase to the FBI Lab in Washington were ordered back to Harrisburg.

Within the minutes after landing, they would begin tearing the place apart.

The experts found mostly what they expected. A lot of filth, and, right there on the kitchen counter, a pack of Montgomerys, the lot number of which indicated it had been distributed by TobacCo, Inc. to a retailer in Atlanta. The lot number matched that of another pack recovered from a previous CYCIG crime scene. Residue on the cigarette paper showed a water line, as had other cigarettes recovered from earlier crime scenes. Occasionally, Virgil had gotten sloppy while injecting the cyanide solution, and the solution would leave a watermark.

"Ironic, ain't it," one of Harrisburg cops said, "that the man who may have given you your most significant lead would be the only really *accidental* victim in this whole mess."

At that, the Harrisburg cop shrugged.

The county coroner signed the custody form that officially turned the decedent's body over to the FBI. The FBI's experts were not ready yet to have Jeeter shipped to the morgue.

The coroner took a last glance at the body and raised his hand to the others in a silent good-bye as he left the crumbling building Lester Jeeter had called home.

102

Asheville

"Why go overboard, why take any additional risk?" Pratt said to Valzmann who sat across from him in the Executive Suite.

Pratt took a scrap of paper from his pocket and looked at it. Genevieve's handwriting. She had given it to him earlier when the market closed at four o'clock.

Closing price TobacCo, Inc. 184 , - 1¨,
Volume 940,000.
Third most active stock

He crumbled the paper and put it back in his pocket. He looked up at Valzmann.

"Look," Pratt said, raising his eyebrows to emphasize that it was all Easy Street from here on in. "You've already, in effect, buried him. There's no need to do anything else. First they'll find the cash in his apartment, with a nice chunk missing. Then with a little help, if necessary, they'll get the idea to search his uncle's mountain lodge. And the stink that will greet them when they open that canvas bag!"

Pratt stopped speaking. His mouth parted into a white-toothed grin that burst into an ugly, raucous laugh. It took him a full minute to regain control of himself. A tear rolled down his cheek. He dabbed the wet with the end of his tie.

Valzmann smiled and nodded in agreement. He had a sudden thought.

"Mr. Pratt? What about the security violation copies Dallaness made? They're live grenades."

"Dallaness!" Pratt said and laughed again. He rose and walked over to the telescope that stood trained on a particularly scenic crest of the Blue Ridge Mountains. "Mary Dallaness?" he said, squinting into the eyepiece. "That mouse. She's nothing to worry about."

"Then why'd she make them in the first place?"

"Who knows? Because Rhoads told her to."

Pratt walked over and slapped Valzmann on the back. Valzmann took his cue to leave and made it as far as Pratt's door before the CEO called to him.

"Hang on for a second," Pratt said. "Come back in here. And close the door."

Valzmann liked the sound of this.

Pratt took a seat on the gray leather sofa.

"You gave me an idea, Valzmann. If you were Mary Dallaness and if you were fucking Tommy Rhoads and if you had stolen some critically important documents from a bunch of ruthless bastards—who would you give them to for safekeeping?"

"Exactly," Valzmann said, closing his eyes, already considering how he'd handle it.

"Wait." Pratt worried about a possible complication. "If Rhoads had an accident now, instead of later as we've planned, how would that affect his role as fall guy for Benedict's . . . *disappearance?*"

"I believe it would enhance it. He wouldn't be available to complain to his newfound friends at Tenth and Pennsylvania."

Pratt's countenance darkened.

"Okay," the CEO said rising, the scenes from the movie he was directing played on the screen before his mind's eye. He turned and pointed his long tan finger in Valzmann's face. "Listen carefully. Here's what you do."

103

New York

At 9:45 P.M., in ample time for overnight editors to use the material in morning editions or early newscasts, the Dow Jones news service released two stories analyzing the financial impact of Virgil's "public awareness campaign" on the tobacco industry and related business sectors.

The market's gut reaction when the news broke twenty-one days earlier had been negative speculation and wild selling by skittish institutional investors. That backlash had over the following days been counterbalanced by investors who thought recent erosion of industry stock prices presented outstanding buying opportunities. Although prices continued to fall, rumors abounded that institutional investors were planning to buy huge blocks of stock in the near future.

The Dow Jones stories were based on what staff reporters were able to sniff out from contacts at Wall Street's brokerage firms.

Since the Virgil story broke, the brokerage house analysts who covered the tobacco industry had been pressed into overdrive. They worked anxiously at terminals to be the first to forecast the correct direction of tobacco stock prices and beat competing investment firms who would offer similar investment advice to their customers. The analysts dug into just-released tobacco industry retail sales data looking for Virgil's impact on company earnings, market trends, and insider transactions.

The internal auditors at the Big Eight cigarette manufacturers worked overtime to tabulate retail sales reports and other data as it became available. Projections were in demand in the executive suites. Demographic "experts" from the Association of Tobacco Marketers were placed conspicuously in 250 retail sales locations throughout the U.S. to observe buying behavior, conduct exit interviews with cigarette customers, and distribute cigarette safety tip sheets, advising smokers how to search for telltale signs of package tampering.

Publicly, Big Eight media spokespeople stated that not only had sales not decreased, they had *increased* as a result of knee-jerk hoarding, a typical consumer buying behavior. Some people feared that cigarettes would be temporarily de-shelved until the tampering incidents could be controlled. Big Eight management was only vaguely concerned about the quirky drop in ten-day sales trends in the east and southeast. Sales were down .6 percent, something that never had happened in the fall. Cooler weather brought higher sales. Meteorological reports showed that temperatures had been lower than average so far for the season. Typically, sales rose 2 to 3 percent in comparable ten-day periods.

The research division of the Gallup Organization, retained in confidence by the ATM, worked to analyze reports calculating how many smokers, if any, had been inspired by Virgil's behavior to try to quit smoking. The ATM found the early numbers unsettlingly high. Twenty-one percent of survey respondents said they intended to quit smoking within the next two weeks. Typically 18 percent of those responding said they intended to quit "now or in the near future," when asked the week before New Year's eve.

In confidential memorandums, the industry's own experts determined that 8.9 percent of "serious" quitters never resumed smoking and from that they computed a model of a permanent-loss-of-revenue. The numbers got a grim reception in Big Eight executive suites.

And there was more bad news for the industry. The so-called twelve-step programs, at the heart of support groups such as Alcoholics Anonymous, were reported to be exceptionally effective for motivated cigarette quitters.

Sponsored by the National Respiratory Health Foundation, Smokers Anonymous meetings were launched in 325 cities and towns across the United States.

104

New York

Clipping from Monday's *New York Post:*

SIX ARRESTED IN "VIRGIL" SIT-IN
AT R.J. REYNOLDS IN NEW YORK

Crowds Jeer, Throw Bottles As Police Arrest Demonstrators

105

From the *Pittsburgh Post-Gazette*

Man Described as Thin, Grey, Sickly
Scalper at Three Rivers Sounds Virgil Alarm

"The Guy's Coughing Made Me Suspicious"

106

Tuesday, October 26
Asheville

It was Rhoads's turn to wake Fallscroft.

The pilot answered groggily.

"Can I be at FBI Headquarters in D.C. by 6 A.M.?"

"I imagine this is serious," Fallscroft said.

"Can I be there?"

"If this is serious, sure."

"The FBI called. There's a big development," Rhoads said. "Virgil wants money. Meet you at the helipad in how long?"

"What time is it now?"

"Three."

"Three in the *morning?*"

"That's the one."

Rhoads heard Fallscroft release a long sigh. "We can take off at four o'clock straight up."

"I'll be there."

"T.R., you're not drunk, are you?"

"Not yet."

107

New York

A stock quotation from the *Wall Street Journal*.

TobacCo, Inc. Common
Close, 182-2 ⅛, Volume 2,162,000.
Second most active stock

108

From the *Cincinnati Star*

Terrorist Stole Vending Machine Keys From Delivery Van

VIRGIL FILLS BUS TERMINAL VENDING MACHINE WITH CYANIDE CIGARETTES

Four Cincinnati Fatalities Brings Death Toll To 385

109

The national news editors of *USA Daily* sat around the huge budget table and tried to figure out how to handle the wild reaction to Virgil's $1.5 billion demand.

The publisher, an obnoxious, self-absorbed country-clubber who forced his inane twice-weekly conservative column on the paper and its readers, came late and disrupted the meeting in progress.

"We want to be supercareful that how we handle this does not encourage Virgil to up the ante," he said.

"Any more than we already have," a senior reporter added.

The publisher ignored the remark. "Let's see the headline candidates," he said.

An assistant held up an oversized sheet.

Authorities Believe Surrender Offer Is Legit

VIRGIL TO GIVE UP IF CIG FIRMS DONATE $1.5 BILLION TO RESEARCH

Staggering Sum "Pocket Change" For $45 Billion Industry

The publisher read it and looked at the picture of the FBI press conference announcing the demand made in an interview with a *Washington Post* reporter.

The publisher nodded. The assistant held up another headline.

Killer Made $1.5 Billion Demand Through Washington Post

A DYING VIRGIL WANTS TO GIVE UP IF CIG FIRMS 'DONATE' TO RESEARCH

Experts say Virgil's cancer is weakening him

The publisher rolled his eyes. "You're plugging the *Washington Post?* Are we going to include one of their subscription forms, too?"

110

FBI Headquarters
Event Response Center

The room was filled with FBI agents, terrorism experts from the United States Army and Central Intelligence Agency, state police representatives, technicians, and other specialists.

Franklin, Brandon, Rhoads and a dozen others sat and stood around a conference table.

A huge map depicting all CYCIG crime scenes hung on the wall behind them.

Franklin, at the head of the table, held up a newspaper. "I take it everyone has seen this. The early edition of today's *Washington Post.*"

The Washington Post's exclusive Interview with "Virgil"

VIRGIL: "I WILL QUIT FOR $1.5 BILLION"

Money To Fund Medical Research

"We'll get to specifics of that situation later," Franklin said. "But first, let's get caught up on exactly where we are. It's been twenty-three days since Event Day One, we have 387 dead, including 3 schoolkids. And about 100 hospitalized, most with permanent respiratory injuries. Plenty of them will die. There have been victims in thirty-six states. But the concentration of fatality sites, not including the Federal Express barrage at the beginning, has been focused more heavily in the northeast corridor. We've had a total of two verified sightings. The man can walk into a crowded bus terminal in Cincinnati, refill a cigarette vending machine, and no one can say what he looks like. He's Mr. Average, Mr. Unremarkable, the Invisible Man. Not even a consistent physical description, as you can see from the sketches."

Franklin indicated a series of oversized wall-mounted posters. "You all have tapes and transcripts and reports of all of Virgil's telephone calls, both to us and to other individuals and organizations. As a bonus, we've now had a total of twenty-one copycat incidents, mostly pranks just to frighten people, and none lethal, not even any serious injuries. For most of this period, our primary suspect has been Loren Benedict, a former scientist at the TobacCo, Inc. facility in Denver. Benedict disappeared from TobacCo, Inc., on 17 January, two years ago. Five days before that, someone, presumably Benedict, called the Department of Justice and then mailed in three pounds of files claiming that they were proof of TobacCo, Inc.'s conspiracy to covertly increase the nicotine levels in three of its major cigarette brands.

"As a bonus, he included a copy of a secret internal report showing that TobacCo, Inc. has had incontestable scientific evidence linking cigarette smoke to a dozen types of cancer. No one has heard from him since. And Virgil uses a gruff articulation to disguise his voice, so no one who knows Benedict can say Virgil is or isn't Benedict. For what it's worth, we've played the tapes for his mother and sister, and they're convinced the caller is not Benedict."

Franklin took a sip of water from a coffee mug.

"Now," he continued, "it's time for reports on the most recent incidents and evidence. Assistant Section Chief Danny Maharis of the Forensics Unit will update us on the briefcase."

Franklin sat down, and Maharis, a sandy-haired man with wire-rimmed glasses, rose.

"The evidence," Maharis began, "was recovered from a dumpster in Harrisburg, Pennsylvania, following a sighting of Virgil on Saturday, four days ago. Initially we believed that he had been pressured into abandoning the briefcase because of fear of apprehension, but subsequent events," he said and shot Rhoads a dark glance, "lead us to believe that the briefcase was, in fact, a plant intended, apparently, as communication of some sort. But we are not certain about that. However, it is also our conviction that we recovered, thanks to the outstanding efforts of Frank Galton, two items of substantial forensic value that Virgil, we're all praying, did not know he let us have."

Maharis clicked a slide projector's remote. An enlargement of a partial fingerprint appeared.

"First of these items is a partial print, still unidentified, which all but eliminates Benedict as Virgil. Frank had the good sense to take apart the three-reel combination lock and scan partial prints from the unexposed surfaces of the reels. Virgil hadn't wiped those surfaces clean. Then Frank compared them with known Benedict prints. Not even close. The second item. . ."

He clicked the remote again, and an image of a domestic Bengal house cat appeared.

". . . was a single cat hair. We traced it to a rare and exotic breed of domestic cat, known as a Bengal. This turns out to be the most significant lead we have so far. There are fewer than thirty approved breeders of Bengals in the U.S., and maybe fifty or sixty who are unregistered. As we speak, we are talking to every Bengal breeder we can find. And an additional item that *had* been in the briefcase . . ." Maharis leveled a scowl at Rhoads, ". . . a videocassette, will be discussed by Dr. Myron Sorken, who is working in conjunction with the Behavior Science Section.

Based on analysis of the videotape and what the subject recorded, we are confident that the images were indeed recorded in Bucks County, Pennsylvania. We also think the date was accurate, based on our study of the angle of the sun and shadows and visible flora. We also think we know what make and model of camcorder he used. The camcorder and video may yield additional information in the next twenty-four to forty-eight hours."

Sorken rose slowly and walked to the podium, adjusted the microphone, and began.

"Due to the attention focused on the suspect Benedict, my involvement with BSS in this investigation had, unfortunately, been limited prior to the recovery of the briefcase. We had been developing a profile which has been further enhanced and revised in light of the videotape. We are prepared to state positively that the perpetrator is a white male, of mid to late middle-age, perhaps of genius level I.Q., almost certainly afflicted with a terminal lung ailment. His latent tendencies toward paranoid schizophrenia have been amplified considerably by his medical condition. He is, we believe, in a partially or wholly dissociated state and believes himself to be a kind of Messiah—or avenger—who is above human morality. To put it more simply, he believes he's doing the right thing."

A murmur and someone whispered something about a Spike Lee movie.

"And," Sorken continued, "his determination is fueled by that conviction. The content of the videotape is hopeless, forbidding, threatening. From the little we have to work with, Virgil appears to be planning a mass murder event modeled on the Nazi gas-chamber atrocities. The scope of which . . ." Sorken said with high drama in his voice, punching out each word with a finger jab to the table, ". . . we-do-not-know."

Franklin nodded to Sorken and raised the newspaper he had previously exhibited. "Dr. Sorken, how does the *Washington Post* demand fit into your profile? Is this consistent?"

"As a manifestation of the overall delusion, his seeing himself as divine, or nearly divine, he affirms it to himself, and to us, through acts of control and intimidation. It is not nearly so important *what* the demand is, as that we obey it, as the unfortunate follow-up to Mr. Pratt's failure to make the required broadcast on 6 October makes clear."

Franklin said, "If I can cut through some of your language here, you're telling us he's on a divine mission and he can't be reasoned with and he won't stop until he's had his holocaust."

Sorken was pleased. "That's right."

"But he's dying. Won't it catch up with him at some point?"

"It's always a possibility he'll just expire, but many schizophrenics are capable of extraordinary feats of physical endurance regardless of their actual state of health. And if, as may well be the case, he is resorting to artificial stimulants, these will have a concomitant effect, increasing the psychosis, and thereby further increasing both physical strength and stamina. At present, our judgment is that he is an exceedingly dangerous and formidable person and far from out of gas."

Franklin turned from Sorken and addressed the rest of the ERC. "The demand issued through his *Washington Post* interview was, of course, targeted at the tobacco companies, and Mr. Thomas Rhoads, chief security . . . *consultant* at TobacCo, Inc., will report on the steps being taken in those quarters."

Brandon raised his hand as if he were in a classroom. Realizing that, he dropped it and cleared his throat. "What I'd like to know is why Mr. Rhoads is here and not in a cell charged with obstruction of justice, destruction of evidence, and an accomplice to first degree murder."

Franklin's prodigious nostrils flared wider. He spoke through clenched teeth. "You're out of order, Brandon. Rhoads is here because I have made the decision to include him in this briefing." Franklin relaxed his facial features and turned to Rhoads. "Go ahead, Rhoads."

Rhoads grinned and winked at Brandon before rising to speak. "Nicholas Pratt and the CEOs of the other seven leading cigarette manufacturers will be holding a joint press conference later in the week to announce how best to meet the terms and conditions for the transfer of one point five billion bucks to the research organizations Virgil named. Their plans will be closely coordinated with you guys. I'm the go-between. Now, there is something that I'd like to say about the way you all have interpreted the evidence. Unlike most of you, I have spoken with Virgil on the telephone, and I have been active in this case from day one. So my opinion means something . . ."

Several agents elbowed each other in mockery of Rhoads.

". . . when I tell you I think, *I know*, you are still underestimating him."

"Oh come on!" Brandon said, slapping his palm to the table and looking toward the ceiling.

Rhoads enjoyed the outburst but didn't register it outwardly. "A.S.C. Danny Maharis said the cat hair is the most important lead we've come up with. No way. If we have a cat hair," he continued, "it's because Virgil gave us a cat hair. The worst mistake we can make is to kid ourselves that we have any advantage over this guy. He's made fools of all of us, every step of the way."

Rhoads sat down. No one said anything.

Franklin walked to the podium. "There are differences of opinion in every investigation. The hardest thing for all of us is to remain objective. It is understandable, though not desirable, if one or more of us has lost his objectivity and succumbed to the irrational fear that Virgil wants us to feel. Keep that in mind. One thing we can agree on, just by looking at the map, Virgil is heading west. Okay. That is all for this meeting. Starting tomorrow, we will convene each morning at oh-seven hundred hours until further notice."

The room cleared out with the exception of Franklin and Rhoads.

"Thanks for getting Deputy Fife off my ass."

"Brandon's right. I just wanted to avoid a scene that would reflect poorly on me."

"Oh come on, I got Jeeter's videocassette to you within five hours. And you wouldn't have gotten that tape at all without me. I'm sorry the Benedict angle didn't pan out. That's what you're really pissed about. Nobody wants to nail Virgil more than me."

"Duh!" Franklin said. "That's why you're not in jail right now. Now get out of here. And do your best to not commit any federal offenses today."

Rhoads started out the door.

Franklin spoke. "One more thing, Rhoads. Something for you to think about. If Benedict isn't Virgil, then I have to start thinking that Benedict is dead. That means, after we've stopped Virgil, a few folks at TobacCo, Inc. are going to have a lot of questions to answer about Midas and the missing scientist. Including your boss. And including you. Got it?"

Rhoads nodded. As he proceeded out the door, he stopped and looked up at the poster-sized enlargements of police artists' renderings of Virgil. There were three, from three separate witnesses.

Each picture seemed to be that of a completely different person.

111

Asheville

The jet-black limo eased up silently to the curb. Valzmann stepped out of a shadow and leaned his head in as the tinted window slid down.

"Nothing to worry about, sir," Valzmann said, patting an envelope inside his jacket. "Rhoads didn't disappoint us. He's still as big a fuckup as ever. It took me two minutes to find the disks. They were just sitting out on his kitchen table under a pile of unopened bills."

"You just took them?"

"There are four disks, none labeled. I had to leave, go to CompUSA next to the mall and buy the same brand of disks, same color, and come back and switch them."

"You sure the disks you took are the ones we want?"

"I'm going to go check right now, but I'm sure they're the ones."

"Good. Next step. Find out if they have other copies."

"That will require. . . personal interviews and, in all likelihood, application of pressure."

"Let's change the plans slightly. Instead of one at a time, you go get Rhoads and Dallaness. You go get them both as soon as you can set it up. Any minute one or the other will get the idea that there's no time like the present to let the media have the disks. It's important you get them together. Be careful, he's so damned stupid, he might get . . . *heroic*. But you get them and put them in the same room. Bind them in chairs, turn Rhoads so he can't see what you're doing to her. Then you go to work on her with the pliers. Pinch a bit of the flesh along the underside of her arm to the thickness of tissue paper, and she'll react. Mr. Rhoads will soon volunteer to answer your questions."

Valzmann nodded that he understood.

Pratt seemed satisfied with his plan and exhaled slowly through his nose. "Then he'll talk."

"You want me to video it?"

"Of course."

"And after they've had a chance to *express* themselves?"

"'*And days of mourning shall follow.*'"

Pratt expected Valzmann to applaud the plan. Instead, there was an awkward silence.

"You don't like that approach?" Pratt asked.

"No, I do like it. It's excellent."

"Well? There's something else?"

"Sir, on my own time, I've been following Mrs. Dallaness with the security cameras."

"Yes?"

The man kicked at the cement underfoot. "I find her lean little body very . . . very *inviting.*"

Pratt nodded. "Be my guest."

"Thank you. Just getting prior approval."

Pratt nodded again, then had a thought and reached out and touched the man's sleeve. "When it's time for dessert, make sure you turn Rhoads's chair around so he can see what you're doing."

"That's SOP, sir." The man sighed. "It's a shame, though, that we have to give Rhoads Retirement Plan 86."

"You're getting soft, old boy."

" I mean it's a shame that we'll never get to see the expression on his face when the police show up and tell him how they just spent six hours digging up a dead scientist named Benedict behind his uncle's cabin at Deer Mountain. I pulled a neck muscle planting him."

Pratt thought for a moment. "You re right, Valzmann. It is too bad. But remember, nothing's perfect."

Without saying another word, Pratt's finger pressed the button that raised the window between them.

Valzmann turned and began walking away when Pratt lowered the window.

"Valzmann, come here."

Valzmann returned, hands thrust into his coat pockets.

Pratt grinned. "This guy's feeling terrible for weeks and weeks and finally goes to see his doctor, right?"

Valzmann nodded, masking his irritation at another joke.

"So," Pratt continues, "the doctor runs a battery of tests and tells the patient to come back to get the results the next day. So the next day, the patient comes back. The doctor calls him into his office, closes the door, and says, 'Well, I have good news, and I have bad news.' The patient says, 'Give the bad news first.' The doctors says, 'Okay, you've got lung cancer from smoking three packs a day for thirty years. You have a month to live.' The patient turns white. 'Oh my God,' he says. 'What's the good news?' The doctor leans across the desk to the patient," and Pratt leans out the limo window, imitating the doctor, "and whispers, 'Did you get a load of the red-headed receptionist out there—the one with the great legs and big tits?' The patient says, 'Yes . . . yes, I saw her.' Now the doctor leans in even closer and grins proudly, 'I'm *fucking* her!'"

112

After the meeting in Washington, Rhoads flew to Cincinnati with Brandon to check out the crime scene at the Trailways terminal. After less than ninety minutes there, he left for Asheville. Why he needed to accompany Brandon was a mystery to him.

Probably Franklin's idea of a joke. But no, Franklin's devoid of humor.

He got to Mary's house at midnight.

She seemed strangely distant, worried about something she wouldn't discuss. But by one in the morning, they were in bed, under a flannel sheet, glistening with the sweat of exertion. The day had exhausted Rhoads, and what little energy he had left, Mary wanted. He tried, but soon she realized how tired he was.

She took over.

"Don't move a muscle," she whispered. "Let me drive."

Later, he lay on his back, eyes open, staring into nowhere, and she on her side, against him, tracing the words "Mary and Tommy" on his abdomen. She formed the letters in an inexact way so he wouldn't know what she was spelling.

She was about to say "light a fire again" when his breathing told her he had fallen asleep

An hour later, his beeper went off.

"Do you have to get it?" Mary asked, as he got out of bed.

He used the telephone downstairs in the kitchen for a long time, long enough to smoke three Camels. When he came back up and got into bed, he told Mary nothing.

She just sighed.

Rhoads rolled away to sleep.

"What's the matter?" she asked. "You tired of me already?

"No. Just tired."

"Thinking about Virgil?"

"No. Just tired."

"I am."

"Tired?"

"Thinking about Virgil."

"Virgil himself? Or the whole Virgil mess?"

"I can't believe Pratt's going to hand over a billion and a half dollars to a certified madman."

"Why are you talking like that? You know Virgil's not getting a dime. It's going to fund heart, lung, and cancer research grants. And secondly, Pratt's only coughing up seven hundred and fifty million. The other tobacco companies are kicking in the other half. And nothing's definite yet."

"It's still negotiating with a terrorist in my book."

"Mary, tell me you don't get a kick out of seeing Pratt's face rubbed in it."

"You can't know Pratt and not laugh at that."

"And tell me you don't think Virgil has a point. Maybe his etiquette needs a little tune-up, but the man's got a point. He's claimed the moral high ground, and plenty of the public's with him. That's something nobody counted on."

"High moral ground! *Virgil?* Are you crazy?"

"Yeah, *Virgil.* He's raised the equivalent of a million dollars *fifteen hundred times* to heal the diseases we sell by the pack. That's a lot of money."

She wanted to turn away but stopped herself. "Don't talk like that. Even to joke."

"Who's joking? You've seen the news. Bastard's got people quitting left and right. Clubs and seminars. Smokers Anonymous is the fastest growing self-help support group in the world. Free university-sponsored wholesale hypnosis sessions. Tobacco sales are down, especially in kids, the kids the tobacco business hopes are too stupid to see Virgil as their folk hero. If he doesn't want them to smoke, plenty of them are going to play along. He's made more converts than thirty years of surgeon general's warnings."

Mary sat up, wrapped the sheet around her, and glared at him. "You make it sound like we're the villains. Tobacco is a legal product, T.R."

"So is sodium cyanide."

For a few minutes, they were just there next to each other, breathing. Then Mary started in again.

"Hundreds of thousands of decent, hard-working men and women earn their daily bread working in our industry. Including me."

"Four hundred and thirty thousand decent, hard-working men and women drop dead annually from smoking-related diseases. Including a guy named Anthony Dallaness."

That did it. Mary got out of bed and stood over him pointing a trembling finger. "Maybe to you it's nothing more than a bad case of rudeness, but to me, your friend Virgil has caused twelve-year-olds to vomit their lungs up all over the playground."

"Get back in bed. Come on."

"You agree with Virgil!"

"Come on, forget it. I'm just playing devil's advocate."

"No, you're not. You agree with Virgil! Admit it! You think he's better than we are. You're sick to twist the situation that way. I've never killed anybody, but I'm not sure about. . ." She stopped herself.

"What about *what*," Rhoads glared. Was she bringing up the nightmare in Philadelphia?

"What about your trip to Den- . . ." Then she caught herself and stopped abruptly. "Shit, T.R.! I hate to fight."

She turned and marched into the bathroom, slamming the door behind her. Rhoads got out of the bed, followed her to the bathroom, and tried to go in. She had locked it. He could hear her sobbing.

"Let me in."

"Go away," she said through the door.

Rhoads shrugged, backed up a pace, and lunged forward with his shoulder. The door burst open.

"My trip to Denver?" he said, blocking the doorway. She

looked up at him, terrified. He stepped back.

"You think I had something to do with Benedict? You think Benedict's dead?" Rhoads laughed at the idea that he'd kill for Pratt. He stopped. He didn't want her to think he was laughing at her. "Where'd you get that idea?"

She felt a chill.

Rhoads lowered his voice. "Is that what Trichina told you? That whore. Or is that the way Pratt makes it look in the documents you stole?"

She took a step forward and straightened up. "I don't know you well enough to know what you're capable of, T.R. What about the $200,000 that Pratt signed for, in cash, the day before you went to Denver? Where's that money?"

"Dummy! That was to pay off Benedict, to shut him up. He was going to open his yap to the government about Midas. I was to offer him a fifty-thousand-dollar-a-year consulting contract for the rest of his life *plus* the two hundred grand in cash *plus* Pratt's promise that none of the data Benedict developed would ever be used to sell cigarettes. But by the time I got there, he was already gone."

Trichina had cautioned Mary about confronting Rhoads. He was a convincing liar, she said. She knew that, she said, from personal experience.

Mary looked at Rhoads and realized how much she really didn't know him. Who was this, this . . . thing . . . this man who, for all she knew a cold-blooded contract murderer, was standing there naked in her bathroom.

"I think you'd better go," she said, her voice colder and more distant than he had ever heard before. She took a step back, her warm skin shuddered against the cool tile of the bathroom wall. "This was all a mistake. You and me." She turned her back.

"You don't believe me? don't you know yet I would never, ever lie to you?"

She stared straight at the wall in front of her. "I don't know anything anymore."

He tried to turn her around, to look into her eyes. When he touched her, she jerked away, as if she was about to be attacked. He dropped his arms submissively.

"I'm sorry," she said, her voice uncertain. "You have to go."

"Fine with me," he said. He got into his clothes as fast as he could and tore down the stairs. Mary, winced when the door slammed.

PART

3

113

Wednesday, October 27
Asheville

"T.R.?"

Mary Dallaness's voice said hesitantly as it crackled over the speaker on Rhoads's answering machine.

"Listen, I know I was upset last night. And I know I shouldn't be talking to you on your answering machine. But I don't know what to do. I don't know who to turn to. I just got a call from Corporate Travel. They're having a courier deliver plane tickets and a memo that sends me and a few others from Documentation to some investor relations meeting in New York. They want me to leave right away, tomorrow. I think it's an excuse to get us out of here so they can—uh, you know, *adjust* the computers. I'd better talk to you in person, T.R. Call me as soon as you can. Please. I'm scared. Really scared."

114

The Royal Carland Hotel, New York

"I go to bed early, very early," Valzmann said to the registration clerk. He registered at the Royal Carland under the name of Joseph Conrad. "Eight P.M. And I get up early, very early. Four A.M. I don't want to be hearing elevators banging and clanging."

"No sir, that's why we gave you 2502, the room you asked for. Very, very quiet there, sir."

"And who did you put me next to? The percussion section of Herb Alpert and the Tijuana Brass?"

"No sir. On one side of your room, there's a linen closet. The housekeepers use it only during the day. The guest room on the other side has been reserved by a woman who won't be arriving until tomorrow. And once she does check in, I'm sure she'll be very quiet, sir. She's here on business."

"The kind of business where she'll be bringing customers in and out all night long, probably."

"No sir. She's here for a tobacco industry meeting. Serious people."

"Well, you just make sure. You won't like it if I have to call down here and speak to your superior."

"No sir. You'll see, sir. There'll be nothing to disturb you. You'll get quality sleep here at the Royal Carland, sir."

115

Baltimore

Without the knowledge of Franklin or Pratt, Rhoads met Dr. Trice at the Inner Harbor Aquarium in Baltimore. She had called and said she wanted to show him something. She took the Metroliner down from 30th Street Station in Philadelphia.

They walked through the exhibits, stopping twice at refreshment stands. Rhoads ordered nothing. At the first stand Dr. Trice bought soft pretzels that left splotches of yellow mustard at the corners of her mouth. The stain remained visible until the second stop where the doctor ordered a large cola, insisting that no ice be added to the cup, and an ice cream sandwich in the shape of a Mexican taco.

When they got to the crustacean tanks, Trice winked at Rhoads, stretching her arm in the direction of the large glass wall that separated them from the sea creatures.

"Observe, if you will, the primitive Cordozo," she said, cutting the air with a wide wave of her flabby arm, directing Rhoads's attention to something moving on the other side of a brilliant red coral—a glistening, silvery fish that appeared to him to be a large, bulky version of a minnow. Dr. Trice had the demeanor now, not of a respected academic but of a stage magician. "This species has few physical advantages to recommend it for natural selection. It is large, weak, and slow, though note its substantial set of incisor-like teeth and protruding lower jaw. What it does have going for it is its ability to apply stealth and deception to mislead predators. This fish, when under apprehension of attack, will rub itself against an abrasive object, a rock or piece of coral, leaving a trace of blood, even bits of its own flesh. It instinctively never abrades itself on small objects, only larger ones. Predators olfactory glands draw them to the blood and flesh while the Cordozo circles back around the object and from the rear assaults the distracted pursuer, restating the terms of engagement."

Rhoads tapped on the glass with his knuckle. None of the sea creatures seemed to notice.

Dr. Trice rolled her eyes. *Everyone knows not to disturb the fish by banging on the aquarium.*

"For the first time," she said, "you find yourselves able to predict Virgil's movement. Doesn't that strike you as odd? Or, has the bureau suddenly gotten a whole lot more clever? Because with men like Franklin near the top of the heap, I doubt it. Is that what they think, that they know this man? I think otherwise. You think you've gotten smarter, and he's gotten weaker. I don't think so. I think he's going to circle back on you."

Rhoads listened carefully and stared into the tank. The three or four Cordozo swam lazily over a bed of crawling black lobsters. "What's he done that makes you think that?" Rhoads asked.

"He is moving steadily west. And he's moving slowly. That may be because he is tiring. He is most likely out of breath. Literally. He knows he hasn't much time left, despite his stated ambition of 430 victims. I say he never intended to make that number, although he's gotten surprisingly close. If he is truly seeking glory, nothing more than the attention he sought but never received from his mother, then you can be assured he will stage his 'grand finale' before the cancer and emphysema take much more strength out of him."

Rhoads withdrew a folded piece of printer paper, a list of the FBI's likely Vectors analysis of Virgil's potential geographical targets and the most probable, most vulnerable upcoming events. Anything the FBI thought might interest Virgil. Rhoads took the list from Brandon's desk and made a copy. He scanned the sheet now.

"He seems to be heading toward a Specialty Retailers Symposium at the Rio Hotel and Casino in Las Vegas. Nick Pratt's going to speak there. That's superconfidential, doctor. They know that from a schedule of retail marketing events they found with newspaper articles in the briefcase recovered in Harrisburg. At least that's what they're all figuring. And, from what I know, it makes sense. If he is headed there, then it will be all over. That is where we will grab him. They've got the Mother of All Stakeouts planned for Las Vegas."

"What else is on that list?" Trice demanded as she snatched the confidential eyes-only memorandum from Rhoads's hand. She ran her eyes over it quickly before Rhoads pulled it back.

Then he read to her from the page. "The American Advertising Association meeting, that's today in Los Angeles. Either of the StarCity properties, even though he's been to one already. They're both under constant surveillance. The American Vending Service Association, San Francisco. Their members operate vending machines. And the PAM Technologies seminar in Seattle, whatever that is."

"PAM? I think They're involved in the development of smokeless tobacco products and cleaner-burning cigarette paper."

Rhoads looked as if he thought she made that up. "Now how would you know that, doctor?"

"I follow the stock market, buster. They've been losing money for five or six years, running around patenting everything their engineers dream up. Too much development, not enough marketing. Now it looks as if they're a bit more organized." She pointed to the paper in his hand. "What else do you have there?"

"Nothing else in the next few weeks."

"Your list mentions events in the east. Name them."

"They don't count, Dr. Trice. Virgil moving west now. That's documented."

"What's on the list out east, jerkimo?"

Rhoads shook his head. "Okay. An investor relations meeting set up by TobacCo, Inc. this Friday in New York. A nicotine patch medical seminar for family practice physicians in Boston on November 2. An EPA conference on office environment health issues in Washington on November 5 and 6 . . . but, given what is known about Virgil's whereabouts, put together with the retailer's meeting in Vegas, the events in the east have just about been ruled out."

Saying that, Rhoads crumpled up the list into a tight ball and put it into his pocket. Dr. Trice did not look convinced.

"Look," Rhoads said. "The man is westbound. We know that for a fact. I didn't read you the events that are scheduled back east because the man's not in the east, is he? Las Vegas is the place. We know approximately where he is, and now we know where he's going. He is calling us more and more frequently, and it's easier to know where he is."

Dr. Trice dropped her handbag to the floor and reached up to grab Rhoads by each lapel. She exhaled through her nose like a snorting bull. He smelled her too-sweet perfume and the mustard on her breath. She burned her eyes into his.

"Rhoads! Listen to me. *I'm telling you.* Whatever he's going to do, he's going to do it soon, and he's going to do it back east. He's going to do it soon because he's almost used up. He's going to do it back east because you always build your snowman on your own front lawn. No one wants to spend all day building a snowman at someone else's house, and if you do, you wish you were doing it at home. He lives in the east, so does the cat that was the source of the hair in the briefcase. He's emotionally attached to that animal. He doesn't leave it alone for long. Did the Behavioral Science guy write a report about that? I'll bet you he goes home regularly to hold his cat, talk to his cat, overfeed the cat out of guilt. No, there's no question in my mind. The grand finale will be in his hometown. If not his hometown, then the nearest big city."

Trice paused only long enough to catch her breath.

"Now, think, Rhoads. He's changed something. He let you find what appears to be a clue. He's never done that before. But anything new in this behavior model means something has changed, and that is when you have to tread very, very carefully. What do changes in any one element of the behavior model suggest?" Trice asked.

Rhoads shrugged.

"Mr. Rhoads!" the doctor shouted, glaring at him like he was a sleepy student. "I asked you, what do changes in any one element of the behavior model suggest? "

Rhoads thought for a moment, then half-answered and half-asked, "Cause-and-effect changes in other elements?"

"Right, laddy! The grand finale is near, forget about that 430 people nonsense. That's just a cod. If he is leading you to the west, I urge you to look to the east. I tell you, he is going to circle back on you. And he's not going to wait much longer. I think the time is now."

116

Asheville

Valzmann's assistant, feeling full of himself because Valzmann was in New York, strolled in hours late to work. He leisurely read the paper, then donned the headset to review the audiotapes of the night before.

Shit! he said aloud. There was something on one tape that he should have reported right away. He removed his headset and pressed a speed dial number on his telephone. Valzmann's voicemail system automatically routed the call to Valzmann's room at the Royal Carland.

"They've had a big fight, sir," the assistant said. Judging from the sounds of a television in the background, Valzmann had been watching a professional wrestling bout. Valzmann clicked off the sound. "She kicked him out, and he drove away pissed as hell. He burned rubber so loud I could pick it up off the bedroom bug."

Valzmann listened to his inarticulate assistant's interpretation of what he had heard. Then Valzmann called Pratt.

"With Dallaness being sent to New York," Valzmann said, "I came up ahead of her. I figured it was a good possibility Rhoads would join her. Now this fight."

"That will complicate getting at them when they're together," Pratt said. "You might have to do them separately."

Valzmann didn't like this. "Separate deaths will be more difficult to explain."

"Yes," Pratt said, "but much easier than facing a grand jury."

"Remember your story about the hit man getting two birds with one stone . . ."

"Yes, Valzmann, I remember the story. The problem is, you've told me that they've had a serious fight."

"People make up."

Pratt was silent then excited. "Why wait? I'll come up with some reason for sending Rhoads to New York. A strategy meeting with other tobacco security chiefs. Something."

Valzmann lit up. "Yeah! Then'll I'll stage it to look like they were in bed, and Rhoads fell asleep with a cigarette in his big mouth. A hotel room fire with two fatalities."

Pratt sighed. "No, Valzmann. Don't you think cigarettes have suffered enough bad publicity?"

Valzmann winced at the gaffe. "Okay. Then what?"

"This is the story you have to stage. Rhoads knows he's going down for killing Benedict. Rhoads knows Dallaness has the goods on him. He kills her then feels bad about it and . . ."

"Kills himself."

"Enjoy New York," Pratt said, hanging up.

117

Thursday, October 28
FBI Headquarters

Brandon took the call from Salem, New Jersey.

"My name is Roberta Rail, and I breed Bengals," said the woman on the other end of Brandon's telephone, "and the lady at the Philadelphia FBI office said I ought to talk with you."

"Thank you, Ms. Rail. You have something you want to tell us?"

"Do you know Special Agent Montgomery from the Philadelphia FBI office?"

"I know the name. There are eleven thousand special agents. What about him?"

"Oh. Okay," she nodded into her telephone. "Because he and another agent, I don't remember the other one's name, came and asked a lot of questions about people who bought Bengals from me. I wasn't able to help, but I did make copies of all the sales I've ever made and gave them to the agents. But when I watched *Nightline* last night, what they were talking about made me remember something."

Brandon sat up straight in his chair, alert. "Ms. Rail, just in case we get disconnected, what is your telephone number and address, and how do you spell your name?"

"It's Mrs. Roberta Rail. R-A-I-L, and I live at 1616 Youngford Road in Salem, New Jersey. Do you want the zip code?"

"Yes, please."

"It's 08079. That's where my cats are, too. I breed them right here. And the telephone number, area code 609-555-6646."

Brandon scratched the information on a lined pad. "Okay, now we're all set," he said, giving the high sign for a communications tech to record the call. It wasn't beyond reason for Brandon to suspect Virgil may have arranged this call or have been the caller himself.

"Okay, the agents who came here? They were interested in anyone who ever bought one of my little sweeties. I've been a breeder for five years. Anyway, there was a man who came to check out my cats about two summers ago. I wasn't going to sell to him. He had a breathing problem, and I didn't think he would be able to get around very well. You see, Bengals are extraordinarily active little guys. Can drive you crazy, and I don't like to sell my cats to people who won't provide good homes. And the man who came here to buy a cat, well, he had something they talked about on *Nightline*. A respiratory condition. When he came to see the cats, I could see he was almost out of breath just from the walk up our driveway. Now you don't walk a Bengal like you do a dog, of course, but you should try to chase him around and help him burn off his store of energy, otherwise, it's not fair. They'll go stir crazy and destroy the furniture, and people will say negative things about the breed. It's not worth it just for a sale."

"About this man . . ."

"You'll think I'm a dizz, but before I called, I looked all over for the notes I usually keep in a spiral-bound notebook. You know, which cat had which litter, how many, which sex, coat colors, markings. Everything. Only, I can't figure out which name is the man I have in mind. It was nearly two years ago. I'm sorry. I've sold over 600 cats in five years. I'm the largest Bengal breeder in the world. "

"Well," Brandon said, "there's nothing wrong with that."

"Yes. I guess it was that breathing problem that make him stick out in my mind. And his nasty call a few weeks ago."

"He called a few weeks ago?"

"To curse me out because he didn't like the way the cat's markings developed as it matured."

"That's not your fault, is it?"

"Not only isn't it my fault, I sold him a nonshowing kitten. That's a cat that for some reason you know will never be a show cat. A perfect cat in every way, except some silly imperfection in coat or color that eliminates it from ever seriously competing. Anyway, when he was here in person, I was leery about selling to him. He complained about my price right off. *Four hundred for a nonshow cat.*' That's a bad sign if they bring up price right away. He said something under his breath loud enough for me to hear. On purpose."

"What was it that he said?"

"He said, 'Why does everyone always try to rip me off? I must have a big sign on my back.' A little paranoid, I'd say."

"Sounds like it," Brandon said. "Then what happened?"

"Then I made it clear to him how demanding my little sweeties are, and then he told me the cat was a birthday gift for his grandson. So I didn't worry about the health thing."

"How did he pay you?"

"Why I'm not sure. By check, I imagine."

Brandon spoke in a less solicitous, more official tone. "Mrs. Rail, what you've just told me is extremely important to us. What I want . . ."

"But I can't remember very much!" Her voice cracked.

"You don't have to be distressed about that, Mrs. Rail. Perfectly normal. We can help you jog your memory. We help people do it every day. I'd like to come right up to see you, to talk in person. Can you stay home and wait for me? Can you help us?"

"Yes. Of course. That's why I called."

"How well can you remember what he looked like?"

"Well, like I said, not too well. Maybe fifty, fifty-five? Hair turning gray? No receding hairline, I think I'd remember that. Kind of thin. Average height? I'm just guessing at all this, really."

Brandon wrote furiously. "How about a car?"

"I probably never saw it. Can't see that part of the driveway from the house."

"Okay. Was he accompanied by anyone?"

"I think he was alone. I remember that much. People usually come to buy a cat with a spouse or a kid or a friend. They make an event out of buying a Bengal. I don't think he did. He was kind of an odd man."

"How so?"

"I can't really describe it, just kind of, I don't know, awkward or uncomfortable to be around," Mrs. Rail paused. "I don't know."

"He leave you with a business card?"

"I don't think so."

"Okay. No problem. This is fantastic. Don't push yourself too hard. As a matter of fact, I'd like you to stop trying to remember anything about him and what he looks like until we get there. We can help you relax. If you try too hard now, you could get everything jammed up, memory-wise. Know what I mean?"

"Okay, but it's hard not to think about him."

"I understand. Okay. Now, let's see," Brandon said, glancing at the same standard-issue wall clock with a red sweeping second hand he used to stare at in grade school. "Can you wait in Salem for me? It's a little after ten now. We can be there by one o'clock."

Clearly excited, Mrs. Rail said, "I do have people coming today to look at some kittens. But, of course. What could be more important?"

"I can't think of anything, Mrs. Rail. I can't think of anything else more important. Hundreds of lives are at risk in this situation."

"Well, my husband and I, we'll be here."

"Thank you. Before I say good-bye, Mrs. Rail, one more thing. How do you think this man got your number?"

"That's easy. I used to advertise in all the cat magazines and go to all the shows. A good way to go broke. But for the last three years, all I do is run a tiny ad in the Sunday *Philadelphia Inquirer.* That's all it takes to keep me busy."

Brandon's heart began to pound. "Do you think maybe he left you a message and you called him back somewhere?"

"No, I doubt that happened. My husband. Hits the roof over the telephone bill. He says I lose more money talking long distance to buyers than I make in sales. If someone leaves a number that's not in area code 609, Brian, my husband, says I have to wait for them to call back."

Damn it all! Brandon's heart slowed down and sank. *What a break that would have been, to have his home number on one of her old long-distance phone bills.*

"All right then, Mrs. Rail," he said, masking the disappointment. "We are on our way."

118

New York

Valzmann called Pratt.

"Dallaness checked in half an hour ago, sir," he reported to the CEO. "But it will be tough to get Rhoads up here. He's in Asheville, all excited about going to Las Vegas where the Feds are setting their trap. What do you want me to do?"

"Okay, then," Pratt said without a moment's hesitation. "Go get her. Forget about getting them simultaneously. Kill her now. I can't take any more chances she'll open her mouth to the Feds or the media. Trichina was right. Anyone could bully Dallaness into anything."

"Okay, I'll let you know when it's done." A rush of excitement shot through Valzmann. No matter how many times he'd done it, it remained the ultimate trip.

Valzmann hung up and moved to the bed. He sat down, removed his leather shoes, and placed them on the rug, side by side. He reached down and found his sneakers and stepped into them. He tied them quickly and snugly, his mind working out the logistics.

He relished the science of meticulous planning, reducing his personal risk to three places to the right of the decimal point. That was a luxury he didn't have today. On the other hand, pulling off a successful spontaneous job was a mark of the gifted professional.

Nevertheless, he shook his head in quiet disappointment. He'd have to use a method he detested, that of the lumbering brute, and he'd have to move fast. One quick motion, into the room, seize her from behind and get his hand, the one wearing the padded glove he stitched together himself, over her mouth. Instantly. He'd have to pick her up by turning and thrusting his hip into the small of her back so that she couldn't kick effectively and carry her into the bathroom. Then, boom, throw her as hard as he could, head first, like a ripe tomato against a tree trunk, onto the porcelain edge of the tub. He'd only have one shot. Multiple concussions would not appear consistent with an accidental fall in the bathroom. He'd have to make it hard enough, but not too hard.

Then, if he did it well, she'd be inactive but still alive, still breathing. That would be essential. Next, he'd strip her down, turn the shower on, and set her body in a position that made sense. The drain would have to be blocked with a washcloth under her so the water would rise in the tub high enough to drown her.

Not very artful, he thought, *but any port in a storm.*

He looked forward to removing her clothes, but that pleasure would be muted. She'd be unconscious, and there'd be no fear for him to inhale.

Valzmann walked to the wall with her room and pressed his ear against it. The wallpaper felt cool, the wall solid. He could hear nothing, but, he reasoned, she should still be in there. Maybe asleep. Napping would be perfect. He'd be on her before her brain could organize a scream.

He picked up the key to her door, dropped it into his pocket, and let himself out of his room. No one was in the hallway to see him.

Okay.

119

Mary Dallaness sat on the bed in her room wearing only panties and pink polish on her fingernails and toenails. Anthony had hated pink. She carefully poured saline solution onto her contact lenses in the tiny matched cups of the plastic case balanced on her knee.

She faced the window and, she mocked herself, *a monotonous view of a high-rise office building, Ms. Dallaness, that one should come to expect if one is so stupid as to fail to make it clear at the registration desk that such a panorama is unacceptable.*

Outside in the hallway, Valzmann listened at her door. Again, he heard nothing. He stepped back and checked the hallway in both directions. Still no one coming or going. He reached into his pocket and withdrew the key. He steadied himself and positioned the key to slide into the lock. Then, using only lateral pressure from his thumb, he slid the key forward as slowly and gently as he could.

He cringed at a tiny *clink.*

Mary heard it, too, or heard *something,* and turned reflexively toward the door. The movement of her torso was enough to disturb the balance of the contact lens case. It fell from her knee.

Shit! she exhaled and shot her arm out to catch it. Too late. The case had fallen to the carpet and under the bed. In an instant, she was down on her hands and knees in the narrow space between the bed and the wall, searching the carpet fibers with fingertips for the transparent lenses.

The door crashed open with a deafening boom.

The sound startled her so that she convulsed as if shocked by an electrical current. In an instant, Valzmann's trained eyes had taken in the entire room, including the open closet. The heavy entrance door bounced back and slammed closed. *Where the hell is she?* He took one long stride and was in the bathroom. In another instant, his hand found the light switch. He looked behind the shower curtain.

Not in there either.

His adrenaline pumped at high pressure.

If she's not here in her room, where'd she go?

That didn't matter, in a second he'd be out of there. She wouldn't have been alerted. A free peek, but he would have preferred to have accomplished the mission.

Valzmann reached for the doorknob.

He opened the door, stepped out into the hallway, and scanned for people.

All clear.

He began to pull the door closed behind him when he abruptly stopped. Valzmann closed his eyes for a second, smiled, and went back in.

He had almost left the bathroom light on.

120

Rhoads was not home to get Mary's hysterical message about the break-in, but the hotel security people swore to her that what she heard had to have been the slamming of a nearby room door.

"What about the bathroom light going on and then off?"

The security people looked at each other and shrugged, saying sometimes power surges could be the culprit.

121

Amtrak Station
Indianapolis, Indiana

Muntor, wearing a bushy mustache, looked out the lounge-car window as the train creaked to a whining halt at Track Five.

A moment later, the door hissed open, and Muntor disembarked wearily, carrying a doctor's bag.

A conductor offered him help.

Muntor shook his head "no."

The conductor saw that all day long in the elderly. Independent. don't want assistance unless they ask for it, and when they do, don't dawdle. The conductor watched the old doctor stop, light a cigarette, then make his way slowly to the escalator holding his bag until he heard shouts coming from several cars down track. The lounge car.

"Get an ambulance!" someone shouted. "Some guy's choking to death back here. Call 9-1-1!"

The conductor took a step in the direction of the escalator, but it was too late. The doctor had disappeared.

Muntor intended to find a decent hotel and get some much needed sleep. Maybe he'd even stay a day or two in Indianapolis. He didn't want to think about Bozzie. He'd never see the sleek, leopard-spotted cat again. What a beautiful cat, what a smart cat. How he used to wake Muntor by tap-tap-tapping one of its velvet paw pads on Muntor's nose.

Maybe they'd put Bozzie's picture on the news after they found the house, some kind of psychological ploy.

That'd be a dirty trick, he thought. *That'd be a damned dirty trick, taunting me with my own cat. But I'd love to see him.*

122

"Mary," Rhoads said into her voice mail. He didn't give a damn who was eavesdropping or what kind of laugh Pratt and his goons might have when they heard what he was about to say. "I got your message. Thank God you're all right. I don't know what I'd do if something happened to you. And I know this is a hell of thing to say over the phone, but I'm saying it now. I'm falling in love with you, Mary, and I didn't know it until I heard your message, heard how frightened you were. I want to be with you. The minute this Virgil mess is over, I'm going to disappear from

Asheville, and I'm going to take you with me. Now, be careful. And I mean what I said. I want you, Mary. Focus on that—and you be careful."

123

St. Louis, Missouri

Alvin DeSotis, a clean-cut young recruiter for the Army Reserve in Montgomery City, accompanied by his two young boys, stood in the shadow of the St. Louis Gateway to the West arch. Once each month he had custody of the kids during the week.

One of the kids held a half-eaten fluff of blue cotton candy, and the other had his two hands wrapped around a large soda cup.

DeSotis pulled a cigarette pack from his shirt pocket, looked inside, made a face. Empty. He dropped it in a nearby litter receptacle.

He looked around. There was no cigarette machine or newsstand in sight. What he did see, however, was a thin, well-dressed gentleman wearing sunglasses. It was Martin Muntor leaning against a fence. To DeSotis, he looked harmless enough, certainly not too hostile to try to ask for a cigarette. DeSotis approached him.

"I hate to bother you, sir, but could I bum a cigarette?"

The old man coughed, swallowed, and reached into his overcoat pocket.

"My pleasure," he said. He had an odd, strained voice. "They're generic. Do you mind?"

"Not at all," DeSotis said, taking one. "My favorite brand. Thanks."

The old man nodded, and DeSotis walked away. Muntor finished smoking and stubbed out his cigarette on the ground with his shoe. He looked up and tensed. DeSotis was coming back.

"I bummed the cigarette," the man said. "Mind if I bum a light, too?"

"Can't help you there. I had to stop someone to get that one lit," he said, pointing to the crushed butt on the ground.

"All right," DeSotis waved. "Thanks again."

Muntor walked away.

The father returned to his kids waiting at a wooden bench. One wanted to find a bathroom, the other sat glumly, swinging his legs back and forth.

"We're not going anywhere until I find someone with a lighter," the father said, "so just relax."

A middle-aged couple approached. The woman had a cigarette. "Stay here," the father said to his kids and got up, heading to intercept the couple.

The kids watched as the woman handed their father a matchbook and kept walking. Sitting back on the bench, DeSotis struck a match, brought the flame to the cigarette, and drew in deeply.

The youngest of the boys looked up at DeSotis and screamed.

"Daddy? Daddy? *Daddy!*"

The other child began to cry.

A passing bicyclist turned toward the screeching.

"What now?" the father said, exhaling.

"I'm going to pee right now if we don't get to a bathroom."

DeSotis turned to his other son "And what are you screaming about?"

"Billy's pinching me."

"No, I'm not."

Then DeSotis turned to the first child. "Well, you'll have to
wet yourself then. Because I'm going to finish this cigarette." He
closed his eyes and took in five or six deep drags.

When he finished, he rose, dropped the butt to the pave-
ment, and stepped on it.

"Let's go," he commanded. "I have to pee, too."

En route to the public restroom, the trio passed an open-air
snack stand. Several people were there, some sipping sodas, others standing in line. Muntor, his back to the passers-by, sat on
one of the snack-stand stools. He had seen the father and his
sons coming and did not want to make eye contact again. He
allowed time enough for them to pass then got up from the stool
and walked away.

A few minutes later, one of the snack-stand employees
noticed that the man had forgotten a pack of cigarettes, a lighter,
and a few dollar bills all bound together by a red rubber band.

124

Salem, New Jersey

Brandon's finger trembled slightly as he stood in Roberta Rail's kitchen and dialed Franklin on his cellular phone. His heart beat so fast he worried about the possibility of following in the footsteps of two maternal uncles, who died from sudden myocardial infarctions, both before the age of thirty-three. He had obscured that family history from FBI doctors during the preemployment physicals.

"Franklin," the deputy director said, simultaneously picking up the telephone in the kitchen and lowering the flame under his crepe pan. Mrs. Franklin sat in the dinette reading *Meeting Evil* for the third time. She kept rereading it just for the subtle glory in the last paragraph.

"Sir, it's brandon."

"Go, Ben."

"I found the name of the man who is probably Virgil."

Franklin snapped his fingers and pointed to the telephone he was on, signaling his wife that this could be the call they'd been waiting for. "Go on."

"Two summers ago, on August 1, a man from Philadelphia roughly fitting our physical profile of Virgil bought a male Bengal kitten. He paid Mrs. Rail with a check drawn on the Mellon Bank."

"You've alerted the Philadelphia FBI?"

"They just came back with the preliminary information. His name is Martin Muntor. He's fifty-six. He lives in Northeast Philadelphia on Roosevelt Boulevard. Used to be a reporter and editor for the ANS wire service, the American News Syndicate. Bureau chief, actually. Forced into early retirement. *Eight weeks ago, sir. Perfect timing.* No NCIC hit on him. We don't have much more than that right now, but we are scrambling."

"This is the guy Mrs. Rail thought had emphysema?"

"Yes, sir."

"Where's he now?"

"That's the question."

"You like him?"

"So far, I love him. Especially the news bureau experience. It fits. In late August, ANS laid him off and closed their Philadelphia operation a week later. Haskell's on the telephone right now with a reporter who used to work with him in Philly. We'll have more shortly. Another thing. The breeder said he was a strange guy with a stiff, peculiar gait. Paranoid. Talked to himself under his breath, accused her without rational basis of ripping him off."

"What have you told the breeder?"

"She and her husband know it's obstruction of justice if they discuss what they've told us with the media or anyone else."

Franklin picked up the remote and turned off his television.

"Kick a Code One, Brandon."

"Did it."

"Call VICAP."

"Did it."

"Put everything on the hot line?" Franklin heard a bell ringing upstairs in his home office. It was the telex coming in.

"Did it."

"Fire up the Tactical Assault Team?"

"They're rolling now."

Franklin turned to Mrs. Franklin and pointed. "Get my driver."

"Call me in my car in five minutes," he said to Brandon, and he hung up.

He found himself standing.

He turned to a worried-looking Mrs. Franklin. "Here we go."

125

Dawn, Friday, October 29
Philadelphia

The houses along the stretch of Roosevelt Boulevard where Martin Muntor lived had been built in the 1920s on poorly compacted soil. Three-quarters of a century later, they were aslant and collapsing. Many had been condemned by the city.

The bright orange *No Trespassing* signs were invitations to the crack dealers. They moved in and most residents moved out. Some residents stayed, mostly the older ones, die-hards, because they wanted to. The neighborhood was their home. Others, like Martin Muntor, stayed because they had no where else to go.

Neighbors near and on both sides of Muntor's house were quietly evacuated. All telephone service on the block was interrupted to preclude a neighbor from calling Muntor or the media.

The FBI's Tactical Assault Team assembled in predawn darkness on a side street just off Roosevelt Boulevard. The team commander told them entry should be safe and surgical. The plan was to use stun grenades to temporarily incapacitate Muntor and reduce the risk of him destroying evidence. Even if Muntor was not there, he said, fragile evidence needed to be protected.

"Preserve your own asses first, evidence second, subject third," he said and made each man repeat it to his face. Then his men got ready and checked their equipment. The VHF headsets, the night-vision goggles, the thirteen-pound Doordown sledge-hammer, the plastic rope, the ballistic armor, the rifles with nightscopes.

If Martin Muntor was home, he was theirs.

Franklin and Rhoads stood together next to an unmarked FBI van a quarter block away from the Tactical Assault Team staging area.

"Don't talk to me," Franklin growled. "I'm an inch from having you cuffed and put away for safekeeping. I don't want you interfering in this."

Rhoads laughed. "You're comical Franklin. He's not going to be sitting in his kitchen wearing his slippers eating Fruit Loops. Give me the word, and I'll go up and knock on his front door."

"Okay, thanks for the information. I'll order eighteen highly trained members of the T.A.T. to stand down because . . . T.R. . . . has X-ray vision."

"Here's another thing. Why are you going in with guns ablazing? You have a fifty-six-year-old guy who can hardly breathe and who's dying of lung cancer. You have a warrant. Just knock on the door. He's not exactly from the shoot-em-up school. He's a sneaky bastard, not a tough guy."

"Rhoads. Please. Evaporate. Will you?"

"You still don't get it," Rhoads said, lighting a cigarette in the darkness. "How many times do I have to tell you? He *gave* you the cat hair. What, are there four or five thousand of these Bengal kitties in the U.S.? How many breeders? Twenty, thirty? It's *inevitable* that somebody would remember a nasty, wheezing man. Especially a nasty, wheezing man who calls up the breeder, a breeder who knows who he is and where he lives, and reminds her that he's a nasty wheezing old man. Therefore," Rhoads said, flicking ashes into the street, "you can bet he isn't coming back here."

"Everything suggests that he keeps coming back home after each incident, probably to feed his cat. And we know he just hit St. Louis."

"Okay, Junior G-man, I'll make you a deal then. I'll stand out here quietly. You do your big SWAT number. If he isn't there, you let me see the place. Deal?"

"You're in some position to make me a deal, Rhoads."

At first light, the team commander gave the signal. A climber on the roof dropped three percussion grenades down the chimney and rocked the neighborhood. Besides scores of broken windows, there was no other damage. T.A.T. members ran through the house, first floor, second floor, basement, attic, adjacent garage, checking behind every door and in every room and closet, every possible place a human could hide. Every room was unoccupied. By the second hand on the team commander's diving watch, twenty-one seconds later the Two Squad leader radioed that no human was in the house, although they did find a trembling spotted silver cat.

In the kitchen, Franklin, Rhoads, and one other agent, an evidence technician, all wearing latex gloves, examined the room, touching as little as possible. Franklin lifted the lid off a pot on the stove.

An agent popped his head into the kitchen. "There's a small stack of newspapers on the floor in the dining room," he announced. "Don't step on it. It covers a hole that'll drop you ten feet onto the cement in the garage below. Might have part of some crazy escape plan. But it hasn't been disturbed. Be careful."

"Right," Franklin said. Rhoads went out into the dining room to see the newspaper-camouflaged hole, then he returned to the kitchen. Without looking up from where he stood at the stove, Franklin said, "Muntor's fussy."

Rhoads and the evidence tech turned to him.

"What?" Rhoads asked.

"Remember Virgil mailed a disposable syringe to the *Wall Street Journal* reporter? Disposables are good enough for the cigarettes. But not for whatever it is he's shooting up."

Rhoads walked over and looked into the pot.

A glass syringe and several needles sat in an inch of water. Rhoads shrugged, distracted by something he had noticed before Franklin called his attention to the pot. He went back to the telephone mounted on the wall near the door that lead into the dining room. Next to the telephone, also affixed to the wall, was a message board with an erasable marker. A coupon for a JiffyLube oil change was thumbtacked to it, as well as an 800 number for the local branch of the auto club.

"Franklin!" Rhoads half-shouted. "He's got this note board here. I think I've got a partially erased telephone number."

Franklin turned, still holding the lid of the pot.

126

TobacCo, Inc. World Headquarters

At TobacCo, Inc., the news that the FBI had found the residence of the man suspected to be Virgil roared from the Fifth Floor down like a boulder in a rock slide.

Anna Maria Trichina had been at her desk, getting last minute details out of the way before going to New York for the investor relations meeting.

A company electrician popped his head into her office and interrupted her train of thought by shouting, "Ms. Trichina. They found Virgil! The FBI found a guy up in Philadelphia! Just heard it on the radio."

It was not a wholly accurate report.

Trichina reached Arnold Northrup and learned that the FBI had raided a property believed to be the residence of Virgil.

She resisted the implication. It sunk in slowly and reached her consciousness with the same jolt that wakes you up when you've overslept an important event. Now that Virgil's house had been found, she assumed, his apprehension wouldn't be far behind. That meant Pratt's paranoia would crest as the FBI intensified its investigation into the whereabouts of Benedict.

There'd be nothing stopping Pratt from going berserk, sicking his mad dogs to search every possible person and place for copies of Midas documents. And, Trichina realized with a gasp, there'd be little to stop him from silencing forever anyone who knew what they contained.

Trichina chastised herself for not going all out earlier, when she had the chance, to find the Midas disks Mary took and bring them to Pratt.

She was going to do something about it.

Right now.

She screamed for her secretary. "Get me Mary Dallaness. She's in New York at the Royal Carland."

While she waited for the call to go through, Trichina fantasized about reaching through the phone and taking Mary by the throat and squeezing the truth out of her. This was, after all, a matter of life and death.

In New York, a steady undercurrent of fear distracted Mary. She fought it by busying herself in her room with the material for the investor relations meeting.

The telephone rang. It was Trichina.

"There you are. I've left you a thousand messages, Mary, but you haven't returned my calls." There was a pause, and the soft tone came off Trichina's voice like a sheath being pulled off a knife. "If you're too fucking stupid to protect yourself, why stop me from protecting myself? The disks you have can save us both. *Now tell me where they are!*"

"I'm hanging up," Mary said.

Trichina lowered her voice. "Mary, don't. Listen. With this Muntor lunatic about to be arrested, Pratt'll stop at nothing to protect himself. *At nothing!* He knows the FBI is going ballistic trying

out what happened to Benedict, and Pratt'll risk anything to protect himself."

"I told you. I don't have the disks."

"Who does?"

Mary didn't answer.

Trichina spoke. "It's T.R."

"No."

"Liar."

"He doesn't have them, and I won't tell you who does."

"Bitch!" Trichina shrieked. "How stupid can you get? Our
only chance is to give them back. And even that might not be
much of a chance."

"You can't even keep your story straight. One minute we
need them to protect ourselves, the next minute we need to
return them. What plan will you have for tomorrow? Sell them
to the *National Enquirer?*"

"You little fool, you'll get us both killed."

"Good!" Mary said. "What would you do with the disks?
Turn them over to Mr. Pratt? What about your bank robbers who
leave no witnesses? I think you're the little fool. I think you're the
one who'll get us killed."

Mary trembled.

"Okay, I'll tell you who has them, but listen carefully. I'm
only going to say this once. *I gave them to Margaret Thatcher.*"

Mary slammed down the telephone before Trichina could react.

127

FBI Headquarters

On one wall in the ERC, there was a huge print of a three-year-old Commonwealth of Pennsylvania driver's license photo of Martin Muntor. On another wall, an enlargement of the partial telephone number lifted from Muntor's kitchen message board, and next to it an equally large print of a thoroughly burned sheet of newsprint, developed in high enough contrast to be vaguely legible.

The conference table was more crowded than ever with agents, consultants, and representatives of other federal and state agencies. Franklin spoke from a podium at the head of the room.

"I want to be cautious about this," he said, "but I think things are starting to break our way. As you all know, we now have a name, a face, and a house. We're still working on it, of course, but the subject's house was remarkably clean. This is a very careful guy. His name is Martin Muntor. M-U-N-T-O-R. Here's what else we've learned. The Bengal cat hair recovered from the briefcase in Harrisburg is an exact match with that of a Bengal cat we took out of Muntor's house. By the way, some of you have been asking. The cat's hearing damage is permanent. The percussion grenades were unavoidable. Also, Muntor has an ex-wife, two daughters—we're talking to them now—and a senile mother in a nursing home in Long Island. The mother's dementia is profound, and she's no help to us whatsoever."

Several agents entered the room and found seats. Another agent approached the podium, a file folder in hand, waiting to be introduced.

"That's not bad, that's not bad at all," Franklin said, as near as he would ever get to being ecstatic. "And, I believe, that A.S.C. Maharis is going to show us that we have even more than that."

Maharis opened the folder.

"Until eight few weeks ago, Muntor was the Philadelphia bureau chief of the American News Syndicate. Then the roof fell in. In the course of a single week, he got laid off, found out his health insurance was in jeopardy, and received diagnoses of terminal lung cancer and emphysema. Obviously, this made him mad."

Dr. Sorken slammed his open palm down on the table.

"I'll handle the psych profile if you don't mind."

Most of the room laughed. Franklin saw the laughter as a sign the agents were, for the first time since CYCIG began, beginning to feel relieved and hopeful. Except for Rhoads. He sat stony faced.

Maharis ignored Sorken and went on. "We even have his cat in custody. Also a wild animal."

Maharis rolled back his shirt sleeve to show claw marks. "The neighbor's boy who had been feeding him was delighted to surrender custody. But the really good news is it is very likely that we now know the target of Muntor's so-called grand finale."

"Oh yeah. He's in big trouble," Rhoads smirked.

Franklin narrowed his eyes at Rhoads, who tried with a grin to show he was only joking. Everyone else glared.

With the click of a slide-projector remote control, Maharis presented an extreme closeup of the partially erased telephone number Rhoads had discovered in Muntor's kitchen.

"Our friend Mr. Rhoads found this on a message board in the kitchen next to the telephone. I know it doesn't look like much, but based on characters taken from samples of Muntor's handwriting, we've been able to reconstruct the telephone number. These first three digits are seven-oh-two, the area code for Nevada. The remaining digits are two-five-two, seven-seven-seven-seven. That's the number of the Rio Suite Hotel and Casino in Vegas."

He clicked the remote again. An enlargement of a piece of charred paper appeared. Maharis picked up a laser beam pointer.

"The telephone number alone tells us very little. However, we also found in the fireplace the remains of a sheaf of papers. And these papers *were* burned. If Muntor had even touched them once with a poker, we'd be out of luck. But our Identification Section, with the aid of high-contrast photography, was been able to read some of them. All but one of the pages contained newspaper or magazine stories about Virgil and the murders. The exception was a brochure that included a registration form for attendance at the Specialty Retailers Marketing Symposium tomorrow. We've heard about that event before. It's being sponsored by the Association of Tobacco Marketers. Retailers who attend will be trained in placing tobacco products in their stores to bring in more customer traffic. And guess what. It's taking place in Las Vegas. At the Rio Hotel and Casino."

The noise level in the room rose as those present commented to one another.

"Hang on, hang on," Maharis said, quieting them down. "As a final confirmation, it's clear he's working his way west right now. He may have been seen in Pittsburgh. He's hit Cincinnati, Indianapolis, and St. Louis in the last four days. He won't get many more before we get him."

"The guy's consistent, all right," Brandon said. "As consistent as some people are in how much they drink all night and stink up meetings the next day."

"Come on, Brandon," Rhoads urged him closer. "Go for it."

Franklin interrupted them. "Shut up, both of you. He's not going to get anybody. This time we'll be waiting for him."

128

From the *Boston Globe*, Friday, October 29

FBI: 'VIRGIL' IS PHILADELPHIA JOURNALIST MARTIN MUNTOR

Former News Bureau Chief Is Dying Of Lung Cancer

129

TobacCo, Inc. WHQ

The main auditorium had been crammed with all the apparatus of a major press conference—microphones, cameras, lights, and more than 200 reporters, cameramen, and audio technicians from news organizations all over the world.

On the stage, Nicholas Pratt stood flanked by four other TobacCo, Inc. executives sitting in chairs. He fumbled with a slip of paper an aide had handed him before he entered the auditorium. The TobacCo, Inc. common stock had been falling precipitously.

TobacCo, Inc. Common
Close, $169^1/_2-1^3/_8$, Volume 1,088,000.
Most active stock

Pratt calculated he had now personally lost thirty-six million dollars in common stock alone since Virgil's first attack, and that figure did not include the beating his bonus contract would sustain. Knowing that Muntor was probably making the same calculation intensified his wrath.

In front of him, at the podium, before a multitude of microphones, stood Anna Maria Trichina, looking somewhat drawn.

"I thank you all for coming," she said. "Allow me to introduce myself. I am Anna Maria Trichina, executive vice-president of marketing for TobacCo, Inc."

Pratt camouflaged his grimace with a small smile.

"As you know," she continued, "the terrible crimes of the past twenty-five days have rocked the tobacco industry. And the rest of the world. But our concern at this time is not for the business impact of recent events, but, like everyone else, to find a way to bring this nightmare to an end. That's why we are pleased to be able to announce today that the CEOs of the eight leading tobacco companies have agreed in principle to a bold plan for restoring the peace of mind and physical safety of people everywhere. To provide you with the specific details of the plan, I'd like to introduce W. Nicholas Pratt, president and chief executive officer of TobacCo, Incorporated."

Trichina stepped to one side. Pratt moved forward and centered himself in front of the podium.

"Thank you, Anna Maria," he said. "As the media has reported so widely and wildly, it is no secret that Martin Muntor, the man who calls himself Virgil, has offered to surrender to the authorities in exchange for a one-and-a-half-*billion*-dollar charitable contribution by tobacco companies to seven named university and private medical research organizations.

"This is not a time for rhetoric, political statement, or discussion of any kind. This is a time for clear, direct, and decisive action. Today, I am taking that action. For the past two days, I and the CEOs of seven other companies have been meeting to determine how best to satisfy Mr. Muntor's demands. We have agreed to make the transfer of funds to the research institutions no later than Monday, November 1, at 2 P.M.

"The agreement I will now describe would be normally subject to official approval by the shareholders of TobacCo, Inc., for reasons that will be obvious in a moment. Collectively, the other seven companies will contribute $750 million. TobacCo, Inc. will also contribute $750 million. This is a considerable amount of money for one company. The means of financing it are complex. Drastic times call for drastic deeds. The minimum time needed to get shareholder approval exceeds the amount of time available. Another, fiercer wave of fatal attacks has been threatened, and the FBI believes the threats are real and unstoppable. Neither TobacCo, Inc. nor other companies in the industry dares the risk of ignoring Muntor's demands. I am confident that TobacCo, Inc.'s shareholders will support my decision and ratify the course I have chosen. The only condition we require is that Muntor surrender himself to the authorities, on or before, midnight, Monday, November 1. He will have ten hours to satisfy himself that the funds had, in fact, been transferred as directed.

"The tobacco companies have been legally committed to the transfer, and no *ex post facto* reversal or cancellation of the transaction is possible. Mr. Muntor is invited to call his contact at the FBI for more information about that. The transfer cannot be voided if he surrenders and is in custody by the deadline. Now, are there any questions?"

Scores of reporters leaped to their feet, discharging a roar of shouted questions.

130

Rio Suite Hotel and Casino, Las Vegas

Muntor, wearing a bushy mustache and baseball cap, sat in the auditorium-sized Race and Sports betting area in the Rio Hotel and Casino. He had an hour to kill until he had to be at the airport. He was in town under the name B. Doyle and had told the front desk to page him when the van was ready. He had to remember to listen for that name. Planting the decoy device in the ballroom off the mezzanine had been easy. The whole contraption cost him less than $200, and most of that went to buying an electronic timer at a hobby shop on Maryland Parkway.

In front of him was a wall of giant televisions. Many of the screens showed horse races and football games. Many of the sets, however, were tuned to a local television station broadcasting the TobacCo, Inc. news conference. Muntor sat smoking and drinking hot coffee. The air conditioning was too cold for his thin blood. His hands and feet were like ice, and he coughed hard and painfully.

On the screen, an unseen reporter shouted a question. "Mr. Pratt, do you have any personal message you wish to convey to Virgil?"

"Yes I do." Pratt looked down at the podium as if he were collecting his thoughts. He remembered Northrup's suggested response in anticipation of that question. "We are acting in good faith solely in the interest of putting an end to this unprecedented number of product-tampering homicides . . ."

Pratt paused for a long moment and looked straight into the camera and continued.

". . . I implore you, sir, in the name of all that is holy, to abide by the terms you yourself established. A tremendous number of people, now and in the future, will be well served by the medical advances that will inevitably occur as a result of this transfer of funds. You have gotten what you wanted. You will be treated fairly by the authorities."

Muntor took the cigarette out of his mouth and tapped its end into an ashtray. He sipped the coffee, his face impassive.

131

Philadelphia

As darkness fell on West Philadelphia, Dr. Trice sat at her desk, just about to take the first bite out of a wedge of cheese-cake layered with dark chocolate fudge.

Rhoads poked his head in.

"Hello, Dr. Trice."

"T.R.! You're in Philadelphia? You caught me," she said, nodding at her cheesecake.

"I won't tell anybody." Rhoads entered almost sheepishly, took off his jacket, and sat down in the chair facing her desk.

"I've got a ticket in my pocket for Las Vegas . . . and I'll miss my flight if I don't leave for the airport in," he checked his watch, ". . . wow, ten minutes. There's a cab waiting for me outside."

"Las Vegas?"

"The FBI. They're setting the trap for Muntor. They're convinced he'll be there."

She frowned. "I've made *my* position clear. He's not going to Las Vegas. I thought I had gotten through to you at the aquarium."

"Yeah, so did I. But I've been thinking about it. On one hand, we have these guys, the FBI guys. They've been in this business a long, long time. They have dozens of experts, thousands of highly trained agents, computers, databases, behavioral experts."

"So?"

"And on the other hand, we have you and me. On the outside, looking in. Trying to see what we can see through a foggy window."

"Maybe what needs to be seen isn't on the inside. Maybe we have a better view from out here."

"Bea, I know Muntor is the bad guy, he's killed close to 400 people. He's obviously insane, and he has to be stopped. But the other night, I got into a fight with the woman I think I'm in love with because there I was, curled up with her in bed, defending Muntor."

"Go on."

"The thing is, more and more, I find myself agreeing with him. I understand his rage at the tobacco business, at all of us who work in it and don't think we're doing anything wrong because we're not pulling a trigger or killing people instantly. I mean, he's made me think about things I've done in the past, or things I should have done and didn't. If he's so evil, why do I feel like he's got more courage than me? Like *I'm* the guilty one?"

Dr. Trice put down her fork.

"Do you believe in God, T.R.?"

Rhoads paused for a long moment. "I don't know. Maybe. I suppose so."

"You don't sound very convinced."

Rhoads shrugged and looked into his lap at his hands. He had interlaced his fingers.

"No one can tell you what to believe," Dr. Trice said. "And I'm certainly not going to. But I can tell you what *I* believe. I believe *without doubt* that there's some kind of . . . *consciousness* . . . at work in the universe. It's nothing anyone can understand very well, nothing we *need* to understand very well. I believe there's a tiny spark of that consciousness in each one of us. I believe that it is the physical world itself that comes between all the sparks and separates them, breaks the connection. When the connection is lost, we spin out of control. Sometimes more or less subtly, like your zeros. Sometimes wildly, like Muntor. Being separated hurts. The horror some infants experience at separation from their mothers catapults them over the edge into the abyss labeled *schizophrenia*. But for most of us, it is through faith, hope, and charity that we can diminish the gap. If we work hard enough, we can reconnect with that consciousness. In some quarters, they call that *salvation*. I call it going home again."

Rhoads took a deep breath. He tried to listen. It was difficult for him. God-talk always had been. But Dr. Trice wasn't preaching. She was trying to make a point. He could see that.

"I know, T.R., that you believe, on one level or another, that you have a part to play in this matter, that you feel some bond with Muntor. Something beyond the fact that you are both lost and lonely men. And that gives you a special responsibility. And you hate that. It's work, and you'd rather play."

Rhoads swallowed and looked again at his hands. He couldn't recall arranging his fingers that way since he was child, instructed by his father to kneel beside the bed and say bedtime prayers.

He looked up. "So what am I supposed to do about it? I've got a lot riding on being there when Muntor goes down. All I have to do is be there, and Pratt gives me my fifty thousand dollars. You know what that means? That means I get my boat. I refloat *The Deep Blue* if I'm there. It might sound selfish and shallow to you, but it's important to me, Bea. Indescribably important. Maybe that's how *I* go home again."

"So you're saying you agree with the FBI about where Muntor will strike next, do you? You think I'm all wrong about back east."

"Look, I want to believe you, but you know what they say, The race isn't always to the swift nor the battle to the strong, but that's the way to bet. "

"Forget about what *they* say or what's *easy* to believe. The other day at the aquarium, I thought I saw a glimmer of realization in your eyes, I thought you finally saw why it is that I am right."

"I'm sorry," Rhoads said quietly. "I'm always wrong, I'm a lifelong loser. No matter how strong my hunch is, no matter how much respect I have for you, I have to go with the odds."

"Lifelong loser? As in the Harry Hill affair?"

"Even a broken watch is right twice a day."

"Now I know why you feel like you are such a putz, T.R. Because you are. And a nerveless one, too. You don't trust yourself to be right when everybody else is wrong."

"Right," he said. "You've finally got my number."

"Okay, let's try it this way . . ."

Rhoads looked at his watch. He stood up. He had to get going.

". . . I'm a practical woman. I think we can have many engaging philosophical conversations later on, but right now, before you get in that cab and commit yourself to a course of action, I'm going to do away with the psychiatric insight and try to apply some common sense."

"Shoot," he said, half-listening as he reached for his leather jacket.

"The FBI has prepared its own trap. I assume they have hundreds of robust, well-armed young men ready to assassinate Muntor should he appear."

"I assume that, too." Rhoads moved backwards toward the door, worried about the time it would take to get to the airport.

"Then common sense suggests that you should follow your gut, not the percentages."

"How's that?"

"If you're not in Las Vegas, and Muntor is, I agree, you lose," Dr. Trice admitted. "You lose the fifty thousand Pratt's agreed to pay you and that *will* hurt. However, if Muntor *does* show up in New York while you're standing around out in Las Vegas, you lose. And that will cost lives, plenty of innocent lives along with the few guilty ones Muntor's gunning for. That will cost you something else, something much more precious. If Muntor shows in Las Vegas and you're not there, you're no worse off than you are right now. But if he shows in New York and you lose because you were playing it safe, well, it could finish you. By trying to risk little, you find you are risking much. You'll never forgive yourself. In a way, T.R., this is your big chance to believe in yourself, and what do you do? You fly out to Las Vegas. Las Vegas, *Nevada*, where everyone knows the game is rigged against the player. T.R., trust your hunch."

Rhoads took another backwards step toward the door. "One of the most important decisions of my life, and I haven't the slightest clue which way to go. Isn't that pitiful?"

"T.R., look at yourself. You're moving like a robot toward that cab downstairs. You've spent your life thinking you have nothing intelligent to offer, and you've spent your life doing foolish things to prove it."

Rhoads nodded, almost ashamed of himself. "Why would I do that to myself?"

"Maybe because if you know something, you have a responsibility to act. If you know nothing, you have no responsibility. Responsibility's a burden most of us like to minimize. I remember once reading a book review by psychologist Bruno Bettelheim. The *New York Times* assigned him a book called *The Nazi Doctors.* In the review, Bettelheim wrote he didn't know if he could do the book justice because its author believed that to understand is to forgive, and Bettelheim said he didn't subscribe to that belief."

"I don't get it."

"I didn't believe Bettelheim. I think he *does* subscribe to that belief, but in his mind he didn't *want* to forgive the Nazi doctors. Through the book, he had acquired a greater understanding of them and then found himself accountable in God's eyes to forgive them. *And he resented having to do that.*"

"Now how does that relate to me?"

"If you know something, you have a responsibility to act. If you have a gut feeling, you have the responsibility to act on it. You may not like it, just as Bettelheim didn't like his conflicting feelings about forgiving Nazi doctors."

Rhoads stood still, looking down. He rubbed his weary face. In the theater of his mind, cold winds blew hard against a stand of tall trees. They swayed and bent and held their ground. He stepped forward and dropped back into the chair.

He mumbled something.

"I couldn't hear you, T.R."

"I said, 'You want a ticket to Las Vegas?'"

Dr. Trice's eyes sparkled as she dug in to her cheesecake with ferocity.

"No, thank you," she said, mouth full and beaming. "I have better things to do."

Rhoads stood in the hallway awaiting the elevator when Dr. Trice stepped out.

"I didn't want to make it part of our conversation in my office there, T.R., but now that you're leaving—how's it going with the drinking?"

Rhoads looked down at the mat in front of the elevator. "Not so hot, Doc. I got pretty thirsty last weekend."

"And since then? Today's Friday."

"Bone dry. And now I'm going to find an AA meeting here in Philly and take the first flight to New York tomorrow morning."

"Is that how you plan to celebrate finding Muntor's house? Going to a meeting?"

Rhoads hadn't thought of it that way. "Yeah, Doc. I guess so."

"That's my boy," Dr. Trice said. "That's my boy."

132

Asheville, North Carolina
8:40 P.M.

"Ms. Trichina," Larry the doorman said over the intercom. "Sorry to bother you, but there's a delivery man here from Really Good who insists Unit 1202 ordered a pizza. But I know you always tell me if you're expecting a delivery. Is it yours?"

"Not guilty, Larry."

Trichina could hear the delivery man arguing with Larry. Larry told the bearded man with the big insulated pizza carrier to hold on.

"Ms. Trichina," Larry said. "This guy says the pie's been out too long to take back, and he wants to know if you want it. Large, onion and green pepper. Half price."

She took her finger off the intercom button and thought about it. She hadn't eaten a thing since lunch.

"How much is half price?"

Larry consulted the man from Really Good.

"He says four-fifty."

"Tell him two bucks and a buck tip. Take it or leave it."

Larry repeated the offer.

"He says he'll take it," Larry said into the intercom.

"Okay," Trichina said. "Let him in."

On the way up to Trichina's, Valzmann's assistant pressed himself into the one corner of the elevator the security camera couldn't focus on. He snapped on the surgical gloves and felt like a million bucks.

133

Saturday, October 30, 7:30 A.M.

The TobacCo, Inc. Learjet had been at the airport in Asheville for landing gear service. Fallscroft idled the jet on the runway, awaiting an okay to take off. Against regulation, he was making this run without a copilot.

Pratt wanted Genevieve DesCourt in Las Vegas for the Specialty Retailers Symposium. Fallscroft was to fly her to meet a USAir flight in Raleigh.

Over a flurry of radio traffic coming from the speakers in the cockpit, Genevieve spoke. She was in a passenger seat behind him.

"You said it was safe to talk once we were aboard."

"We're aboard."

"Why couldn't you just call T.R.? Tell him what's on the tape. Why do you have to go see him in person?"

"Because the second I contact him by telephone, they'll know. I'm almost positive his every move is monitored. For all I know, they have bugs in the heels of all his shoes and sneakers. They won't take the risk that he'll call the FBI. Thirty seconds after I'd tell him by phone, he'd be dead of lead poisoning."

"Doesn't telling him in person present the same risks?"

"Not if I get him out of harm's way, isolate him somewhere, *then* tell him. Plus, I brought him this." Fallscroft pulled back his windbreaker to reveal a silver-gripped semiautomatic handgun in a leather shoulder holster. "Knowing T.R., he probably didn't remember to take his."

"Oh, my," Genevieve said and looked away as if it were a dirty photo. "Tell me again how you know this. I can't believe Mr. Pratt's security men don't check his office for bugs every day after I leave and every morning before I get in."

"You re probably right, but if they do, they're going to be

looking for sophisticated transmitters, electronic bugs with microchips, stuff like that. They're not looking for a thirty-nine dollar Radio Shack voice-activated tape recorder wedged under the cushion of the chair I always sit in when your boss barks flight-plan info at me."

"That's some risk you've been taking."

"Not really. T.R.'s not heavy, he's my brother."

The tower called Fallscroft. He pulled on his headset and checked a sheet attached to a clipboard. He responded to the air traffic controller. Genevieve didn't understand the aviation lingo he used.

"How do things like this get started?" Genevieve asked herself as much as Fallscroft.

Fallscroft put the clipboard aside and shrugged. "Pratt probably tried a last-ditch effort to talk sense into Benedict."

"You mean Mr. Pratt's brand of sense," Genevieve said.

"And when Benedict wouldn't play patty-cake . . ."

". . . Mr. Pratt played hardball," Genevieve said quietly, not wanting to believe the meaning of her own words. She sighed. "And how did T.R. get involved?"

"If Pratt's guys got rid of Benedict, then they planned it carefully. And that means all along they've had someone who they had set up as a convenient culprit. Someone who could be made to look like he had motive, means, and opportunity. Someone named Tommy Rhoads."

Fallscroft had been listening out of one ear to the radio communications between other aircraft and the controllers. He held up a finger to silence Genevieve.

"That's strange," he said.

"What's strange?"

"The pilot who just spoke to the tower, that was Hank Freeman. At the Flight Prep desk, I asked him where he was taking Pratt. He told me Pratt and a couple of his security men were making a couple of stops en route to Las Vegas. But I just heard him confirm his heading to the tower. If I caught the coordinates right, they're flying north then northeast. Reach me that top chart, will you?" He indicated a shelf above her.

Fallscroft pored over the chart, making pencil notes in the margin. He did some figuring, then handed Genevieve the chart to return to the shelf.

"They're not flying to Las Vegas. I think they're heading for New York. That could mean LaGuardia, JFK, or Newark. I don't like this. Pratt must have decided he didn't want to be live bait for the FBI's trap. We have to find T.R. fast, and I don't know where he is. He hasn't returned my calls, and I've paged his beeper, too."

"Mr. Pratt told him to go to Las Vegas to keep an eye on the FBI."

"If Pratt said Vegas, then he probably didn't go. We'll start looking for him in New York."

"What do you mean we'll'?" Genevieve never disobeyed Mr. Pratt. "I'm supposed to go to Las Vegas!"

"Sorry," Fallscroft shrugged, "but I think your flight's been canceled."

"Well, then," she said. "You'll have to let me off this plane."

"You don't want to help me find T.R.?"

"I do, yes," she said. "But really, Jack. I definitely have to be in Las Vegas. Please take me back to the ramp."

She couldn't cross Pratt.

Fallscroft shook his head and made no effort to hide his disgust. He picked up his radio handset and requested permission to taxi back, saying he had a nauseous passenger.

"Last chance," he said while waiting for the tower to reply. "You never know what you may be missing."

"No," Genevieve said. "I'm sorry."

134

Philadelphia's 30th Street Station

Dr. Trice entered 30th Street Station, bought a muffin, a cup of coffee, and a newspaper, and sat down. The terminal was mobbed with Northeast Corridor business travelers, students, and local passengers.

Several pigeons had gotten into the building and flew about high overhead. An indigent man walked up to Dr. Trice and held out an empty soda cup, begging for change. Dr. Trice shook her head "no," and the man moved on. She donated to the city's twenty-four-hour shelter instead of handing out money to bums who'd likely buy a bottle of cheap wine or a cap of crack.

The Amtrak information board updated itself electronically and now indicated Dr. Trice's train would be ten minutes late.

That meant time for another muffin.

135

The Royal Carland Hotel, New York

Getting dressed in the cab from the airport was inconvenient. Rhoads changed from his jeans and turtleneck to his most expensive business suit, an Italian-cut black wool job. He brought a light gray tie and an out-of-character thick link gold ID bracelet and polarized sunglasses. He had borrowed the bracelet from an attorney who lived in his apartment building. "Going undercover as a lounge singer," he told the man. The suit jacket fit snugly. He certainly was not packing a weapon on his hip or under his arm. Anyone could see that.

The cab pulled up at the Royal Carland. Rhoads gathered his wallet, carry-on, and the leather portfolio that contained a nine-millimeter semiautomatic, a pair of plastic handcuffs, and his mini-aerosol container of PinPoint Mace. He paid the cab fare and jumped out.

Outside the Grand Imperial Ballroom, at a quarter past ten, Rhoads tried to walk the way he imagined a successful big-portfolio investor would. Strides that were long and fast, supremely confident. At least in a bull market.

He had a little than an hour until the meeting was to begin. He glanced at the headlines in the *USA Daily* and other papers in the racks in the lobby newsstand. The bureau had successfully kept the Las Vegas angle out of the news.

As Rhoads turned away from the newsstand to make an informal perimeter observation of the property, he noticed the open cigarette display. How simple it must be for Muntor. Maybe that would all be coming to an end. Rhoads moved around the inside of the hotel in a methodical concentric circle. Working the two elements of luck—preparation and vigilance— Rhoads studied a brochure that provided a simplified floor plan of the Royal Carland.

Someone once told Rhoads that belief in luck was nothing more than lack of confidence. With that in mind, he walked faster to cover more ground.

136

7:20 A.M. Pacific Time
Rio Suite Hotel and Casino in Las Vegas

The attendees filed in, packing the Brasilia Room. A banner displayed near the head table announced the Specialty Retailers Marketing Symposium. Beyond the four or five uniformed hotel security officers, there was no sign of other precautions.

In a corner at the back of the room, Franklin, dressed in the uniform of the hotel's maintenance workers, first listened then spoke softly into a cellular telephone.

". . . Received. A no-show at the airport. He hasn't been spotted here, either. The situation here is Condition A-Andy. Nothing happening. Out," Franklin said and punched a button on the telephone, then snapped it closed and slid it into one of the deep pockets in his overalls. Almost immediately, the unit chirped again. He retrieved it.

"Black Jack here. Talk to me."

"This is Bandit. Urgent. Repeat. Urgent. We're on the third floor, directly above the ballroom along the west wall. We're showing a hit on the meter. We're showing a hit on the meter. Oakley!"

Franklin shouted in an urgent whisper. "Black Jack to all even-number units. GO! GO! GO!"

Simultaneously throughout the ballroom, from out of nowhere, fifteen or twenty figures, all undercover agents, began moving, then running, toward the exit. They headed for the third floor.

Franklin snapped his fingers and Brandon, wearing a business suit and sitting in the back row of folding chairs, looked up. A second later, he and Franklin were racing from the room as well.

Franklin and Brandon took a stairway to the third floor.

They burst into a nearly vacant ballroom, much smaller than the Brasilia. Agents in jumpsuits were huddled several feet back away from a tablecloth-covered banquet table they had upended. A large black cardboard box sat there, a humming, grinding sound coming from within.

"Where's the fucking bomb people!" Franklin bellowed.

"Any second, Oakley, they'll be here any second," an agent said.

Franklin stepped forward. Sweat formed and glistened on his massive black brow. He turned and looked around. "All you fuckers out of here. I'm opening it. Muntor probably put together a pretty primitive bomb. Maybe it'll be simple to disarm."

No one moved.

"I said out of here!"

His men stayed with him. Franklin took a step closer and reached out toward the flap that obscured the box's contents from view.

The sound of a gun cocking caused everyone to look up and freeze.

Except Franklin. He had taken another step closer to the box.

"Move another inch toward the box, and I'll blow your fucking arm off."

Franklin looked up. He didn't recognize the man with the gun, but he knew the uniform. The ATF Bomb Disposal Unit. The man did not lower the weapon when he realized he was pointing it at the FBI deputy director.

"I'm operating under the assumption that you're stone crazy, sir, and I can't let you near that box. Step back."

Franklin half raised his hands and did as he was told.

The bomb disposal personnel moved in, and the other FBI agents backed farther away. Franklin ordered his men to leave. This time they did.

"The countdown display reads seven minutes and twenty-two seconds and counting," the bomb team leader said, crouching next to the box."My guess is someone started the clock two minutes and thirty-eight seconds ago, giving himself a full ten minutes to get out. I don't see a receiver or a timer. That means either one or the other's hidden inside and therefore not visible, or . . ."

"Or what!" Franklin bellowed.

"Or two minutes and," the bomb team leader looked at the still-counting display, "now forty-four seconds ago, someone stood right here, right in this room, and started the countdown manually."

"Then he couldn't have gotten out of the hotel yet," Brandon shouted. "Oak, broadcast an evacuation order. Get everyone out of the building now."

"No," Franklin said, turning to a senior agent. "Seal the building first. I'm not letting Muntor get out of here. Once we're airtight, broadcast the evacuation. Every human being leaving this building gets eyeballed. Regardless of age, sex, race. Go!"

Franklin turned to another agent. "You. Call FBIHQ. Tell them we've found a device."

"And Brandon . . ." Franklin said waving for him to join him in a sprint toward the elevators.

"What, sir?"

"And, Brandon, you were right," Franklin said, already half winded. "That jackass Rhoads is a fucking jinx. He's not here, we get lucky."

The elevator arrived and Franklin slipped in as soon as the doors parted enough for him to fit. Brandon grinned and banged his shoulder painfully on the still-opening elevator door as he squeezed in after his boss.

137

The Royal Carland Hotel, New York
10:25 A.M.

In a fifteenth-floor hotel room, Martin Muntor awoke. He did not know how long he had slept. It could have been ten hours, it could have been forty-five minutes. The injections had that disorienting effect. All he knew for certain was that today was the day.

What woke him finally and got him out of bed was a splinter of daylight that fell across his closed eyes. The rays had seeped in through the space in the heavy opaque drapes where he had failed to draw them tightly together.

He moved weakly into the bathroom, smashing his knee into the door frame and then steadying himself at the bathroom sink. He chose not to look at himself in the mirror.

The cold water he splashed on his face ran down his neck and onto the perspiration-soaked crew neck T-shirt he had worn to bed. He ineffectually toweled himself off. He had barely enough energy to make it back to the suitcase rack in the bedroom. He searched frantically, tearing a sweatshirt, maps, socks, and underwear, out of his suitcase.

Then he found the leather kit bag and lovingly removed the contents, setting each object carefully on the dresser.

He prepared another injection. There was not time for his full ritual.

Muntor closed his eyes for several minutes while the drugs coursed through his veins and gave him new life, new, indomitable power.

Invigorated, Muntor took a shower, changed into clean clothes and sat down on the easy chair facing the television. He pulled a brochure out of a file folder and stared at the floor plan of the ballroom, studying it for the hundredth time.

"All ye who enter here," he said, jabbing a finger at the entrance of the Grand Imperial Ballroom, "abandon hope."

Muntor put the brochure on a table and slid open the closet door. He removed first one, then the other large duffel bag—the same ones he had at the dilapidated schoolhouse in Pennsylvania. He unzipped them both, removed the equipment and dressed in the fireman's gear, the bright yellow protective overcoat, the full-face helmet and hood.

Dizzy with excitement and fatigue and drug-induced energy, Muntor sat upon the unmade bed to pull on his protective leggings and high rubber boots, then rose to wrestle the orchard-fogger tank onto his back. He leaned over toward the telephone, pulled the face plate up, and dialed the hotel operator.

"Help! I just got off the elevator. I was upstairs at the observation deck with the kids," he said, not attempting to disguise his voice. "A policeman's been shot, and another one's just lying there on the floor. You need to help them. I'm going back up to see what I can do. Send help!"

The observation deck, Muntor thought as he hung up. A long, slow ride on the elevators, on the other side of the hotel from where the meeting is. And every available man will be sent, far away from me. While they're coming up, I'll be going down.

Muntor pulled the faceplate back into place and adjusted the oxygen supply to the mask. He took the orchard-fogger's long, black trigger nozzle into his hand. He wrapped his finger around its trigger and teased it. It felt good. He knew he'd be able to use it. The trigger and trigger-guard assembly reminded him of the big-bore hunting rifle he had used to shoot up junkyard cars as a kid. Funny he had not thought of that until now.

He walked quickly into the hallway to get an elevator down before the police and security people commandeered them all rushing to the aid of their fallen comrades. He reached the bank of elevators. He pressed the "Down" button and waited impatiently to descend.

138

The Royal Carland Hotel, New York.
11:08 A.M.

The Investor Relations meeting had begun precisely at eleven in the Grand Imperial Ballroom. Rhoads, holding his leather portfolio, entered the room and looked around.

Three entrance doors gave access to the small ballroom. Inside, under a dozen sparkling chandeliers, a field of elegant luncheon tables had been set. One of the tables, flanked by a podium, had been hurriedly reserved for Pratt when it was learned he would attend.

Rhoads took a seat at one of the tables near the swinging doors that led into the banquet kitchen. The position afforded a view of the entire room and all entrances.

Forty of the nation's most influential tobacco business leaders were present including the CEOs of three other Big Eight companies, heads of mutual funds, investment houses, a cadre of handpicked journalists, the president of the world's largest agricultural conglomerate, congressional supporters, and two tobacco state governors.

Pratt wasn't scheduled to speak for another fifteen minutes, and Rhoads knew he wouldn't arrive until a couple of minutes before then.

Rhoads scanned the room methodically. Either the FBI's covert surveillance teams were so good that Rhoads couldn't pick them out from nearly forty multimillionaires, or they simply weren't there. In any case, he felt incompetent.

He continued scanning and soon spotted two TobacCo, Inc. security people. He had provided them with explicit instructions, "No matter what happens, ignore me. I'm no one you know."

Several times Rhoads's heart leaped out of his chest when a

suited man—what Rhoads thought Muntor would surely be wearing—appeared and seemed to be about the same size as Muntor. One by one, Rhoads eliminated them. Whenever he rose to check someone out, he took his portfolio and the automatic inside.

When ear-splitting electronic fire-alarm bells began to clamor from recessed public address speakers in the ballroom ceiling, Rhoads's body switched into a fight-or-flight level of adrenaline and muscle tension. Heavily oxygenated blood rushed into his eyes and ears to make those organs acutely sensitive. His nostrils flared back imperceptibly, a biological hat-tip to a mammalian history when sense of scent weighed heavily in the survival formula.

Had Muntor set the building afire or tossed a bomb? Rhoads had not anticipated that. Muntor was a product tamperer, not a Hamas guerrilla. Rhoads's gut instinct was to race to one of the hotel security people to find out what was being broadcast on their radios. Instead, he decided to stay still, keep low and alert. He thought of the lesson learned too late by the quarry of the Cordozo fish in the crustacean tank in Baltimore. When you least expect it—expect it.

Three or four minutes more of the alarm's deafening noise was interrupted by a recorded electronic female voice instructing occupants to exit the building and avoid using the elevators. Some conference attendees rose slowly, wondering if the alarm was real. Then the firemen appeared wearing fluorescent yellow coats, "NYFD" marked in bold reflective letters across their backs. They trudged through the crowded room in high rubber boots, burdened under heavy white helmets, steel air tanks strapped behind them like scuba gear, and aerator hose mouthpieces strung as medallions around their necks.

"Just hang in here for a few moments, please," one of the TobacCo, Inc. employees announced from the head table. "We're getting information that this is probably a false alarm."

Something about the firemen nagged at Rhoads.

A battalion chief spoke into a radio, and a reply crackled back. The men waded across the floor and disappeared behind the swinging doors leading into the banquet kitchen. A few attendees rose to get coffee from an urn attended by a white-coated member of the kitchen staff. The firemen's casual demeanor encouraged everyone to pay little attention to the incident.

The firemen, Rhoads wondered. What was it about them?

He remembered Dr. Trice's alert. "Thoughts or ideas that have a different texture about them . . . they are usually gifts from the universe."

Something, just a snippet really, from the transcript of Muntor's call to the radio program *National Talk*. Something like, "I'm just starting a backfire, fighting a huge fire with well-placed little ones."

Bingo!

Rhoads knew. Muntor thought of himself as a fireman. He sent them here. His little game. A little foreshadowing. Of course! Muntor called in the alarm. If there is an attack and the fire alarm auto-dialed again, the signal could be dismissed by fire department dispatchers, considered another faulty alarm from the Royal Carland.

From his seat, Rhoads craned his neck, seeing little. Impatient investment advisors rose and milled.

Rhoads began to doubt himself. He used a pen to write "RESERVED" on the back of an envelope and left it on his seat.

Am I being an alarmist?

Am I imaging a Muntor who is not here?

Did a potato tin left on a kitchen stove trip the smoke alarm?

He took his portfolio in hand and headed toward the kitchen to find out.

A dozen kitchen workers stood outside the door talking and yawning. They waited for the firemen to leave.

Rhoads walked past them. He felt the weight of his gun in the portfolio. Inside, six or eight firemen were spread about examining various sections of the huge, gleaming stainless steel-filled kitchen. The area was lit brightly like an operating room. Wide tiled aisles dotted every few feet with small drainage grates lying between rows of steel food-prep tables and sinks. Banks of ovens lined one wall, hooded grills and scores of giant pots and pans and baking trays were stacked atop a forty-foot row of refrigerators and freezers. The aroma of brewing coffee and the strong odor of commercial disinfectant wafted together, confusing the olfactory senses.

Rhoads moved forward. One of the firemen turned to him at the sound of the swinging door.

"We need you back on the other side of those doors," he said, pointing a surly finger.

"Security," Rhoads answered and kept coming. The fireman shrugged and turned back to the others in his troop.

The fire department battalion chief was satisfied that the call, made from a house phone in the hotel, had been a hoax. One of seventy or eighty false alarms each day in New York. He was about to radio the dispatcher and report that the alarm was unfounded but waited on one of his men for the last report—results of a gas leak test.

One of the firemen took a metering device from his pocket and stood over a field of gas burners built into the top bank of ovens. He waved the device like a wand above the burners and with his thumb pressed a button on the meter. In a moment, he looked at the meter's display and then snapped it off, putting the device back into his pocket. He gave a thumbs-down to the captain who then spoke into the radio. Another fireman used a key to open a utility box on the wall. He reached in and flipped a switch. The clanging alarms turned silent. The swarm of firemen left, walking past Rhoads, saying nothing to him.

As the last fireman passed through the large doors, several kitchen staffers entered.

"We need you to stay outside for a couple more minutes," Rhoads said, raising his hand. The worker did not recognize him but assumed he had the authority to make the command.

"Okay, but the firemen said . . ."

"Just another couple of minutes." The workers left.

Everything seemed to be in order, but Rhoads wanted one quick look around.

He strode quickly across the floor, carefully stepping over a puddle of greasy liquid that had dripped from packages of defrosting ground meat, and inspected a door on one side of the kitchen.

Securely locked.

He turned back the other way, just as quickly, toward the conveyor belts rattling silverware and saucers and cups through the dish-washing steamers. He squatted down and peered under them.

Nothing here either.

He exhaled wearily as he rose.

Better possibles in the ballroom. Better get out there.

As he walked toward the swinging doors, in an alcove behind the wall of refrigeration units, Rhoads heard a sound, a heavy, labored breathing, someone trying to catch his breath. He stopped and froze, then, silently, tiptoed closer, pressing his back to the cold ceramic that lined the wall there. He steadied himself with a flat palm pressed against the wall in order to lean forward as far as possible, trying to cock his ear and hear around the corner.

He heard it again. Something like a wheeze, like a musical sound coming from an off-key human accordion.

At first, he thought maybe a fireman had been abandoned by his fellows.

No, he realized, they had all left together.

He moved forward another few inches. He heard the sound again, then someone grunted softly. Rhoads got down on his hands and knees, his portfolio under him, lowering his head almost to the floor. The tiles were clammy and ice cold. He moved his head another inch forward, just enough for one eye to see back into the semidarkness of the alcove. There it was, a figure squatting down, pushing or pulling a box. Rhoads couldn't see. He eased back, straining to keep his balance. He drew a deep breath, steadily, slowly. He edged slightly forward, to see a little more deeply into the alcove. In close quarters, an inch was a mile.

There it was again, he heard it quite clearly.

A wheeze.

He pulled his head back, feeling for the portfolio. He opened it, reached in, and got a grip on his nine-millimeter with his right hand. He crouched lower on his hands and knees. He couldn't, of course, be sure that it was Muntor. Err on the side of caution.

His earlier thought of disarming an elderly lung cancer patient with Mace now seemed preposterously naive. This man had killed close to 400 people and was prepared to kill hundreds more.

Too many thoughts rushed into Rhoads's head at once.

Get help?

Shout "freeze"?

Is it only a straggling fireman?

Is it really Martin Muntor, right here, right on the other side of this wall?

Was he armed?

Still on all fours, Rhoads hunched awkwardly over the portfolio wanting to slide it out of his way, but that made noise. He could move himself more quietly than he could slip a leather portfolio over a floor. He moved forward a bit.

With a surge of cold panic emptying itself into his gut, Rhoads asked himself the question he should have asked a full minute earlier.

What was in that box?

Rhoads wanted to get a lay of the kitchen. As he eased back to improve his view, the heavy steel-lipped rim of a fire extinguisher smashed into the side of his head and sent him flying forward, stunned. Bathed in blood, his right eye swelled shut instantly. Rhoads had held on to his gun, but he was acutely disoriented. In the next instant, he covered his head with his left arm and rolled away. His reaction was based not on police self-defense training but on those millions of years of mammalian instinct. Tiny sparkles of white light poured into his brain from the tear in his scalp. He felt blood drip behind his ear in a warm rivulet. Rhoads found himself half under the shelf of a food preparation table. He crawled out and stood up, eyes burning into that dark alcove, trying to ignore the clanging in his head.

He inched forward, gun pointed into the dark. He saw no figure there now. He could not cry out for help. He heard his own panicked breathing.

The fireman stepped forward, face mask awry, a fire extinguisher held between both hands.

Why did he hit me?

The form moved toward him. The sound of labored, wheezing gasps grew louder. Rhoads stood up now, coming back to himself. He looked ahead at the fireman. The uniform was bright yellow but different than those of the firemen who had just left.

Rhoads understood.

This was Martin Muntor.

Rhoads began to bring the automatic up but lost his balance as a wave of dizziness washed over him. He was fading out, knees unable to support the weight of his body. The warm wet dripped from his head. Without a word, the man in the fireman's uniform bolted back into the dark alcove. Rhoads heard a heavy door slam. He regained his balance and followed, stumbling over a large cardboard box. Glass jars filled with something rolled against each other.

Rhoads easily caught up with him. The man, almost unable to breathe, had braced himself against a storage shelf. The man turned to Rhoads, eyes wide and wild behind the protective faceplate, able only to concentrate on catching his breath. He had no capacity to resist Rhoads.

Rhoads raised his gun and started to speak when everything slowed down and grew dim like the settling of a sudden fog. Dizzy, dizzy. His knees weakened, and he felt himself slowly,

slowly sinking, fading, melting into the floor. Rhoads was passing out and he knew it, and there was nothing he could do.

139

11:20 A.M.
New York

Dr. Trice took a cab from Penn Station to the Royal Carland. She checked her coat and carried her handbag and followed the signs to the Grand Imperial Ballroom.

Although uninvited, she felt that as a stockholder in TobacCo, Inc. she had every right to be there.

At one of the ballroom doors, a greeter handed her a schedule and a large information packet emblazoned with the TobacCo, Inc. logo. No one questioned her presence. She entered the ballroom and, without realizing it, took the seat next to the one Rhoads had been sitting in.

When she looked at the word "RESERVED" on the TobacCo, Inc. envelope next to her and the peculiar childish block letters, she recognized them instantly as Rhoads's handwriting.

"Have you seen the person who was sitting here?" she asked a man seated nearby, pointing to the empty chair next to her.

"I think he went in there," the man said, indicating the banquet kitchen's swinging doors.

Dr. Trice nodded. "Thank you."

140

11:24 A.M.
The Royal Carland Hotel

The ice numbed Valzmann's hip. He kept reaching under his jacket to make certain nothing was leaking. What a mess that would be. Stuffed into one of the Royal Carland's huge industrial trash dumpsters out back by the service dock was the body of a hotel plumber, minus an appendage. They'd probably never find him. Valzmann had the man's severed right hand in his pocket, wrapped in plastic and enclosed in a bag filled with ice. The low temperature would minimize the edema so the fingers would leave convincing fingerprints on Dallaness's body. He hoped the plumber's prints were on record.

Valzmann made his way through the service corridors behind the banquet kitchen. His cellular telephone chirped, and he answered it before it rang a second time.

"What's the situation with Mrs. Dallaness?" Pratt asked quietly. "I'm pulling up to the hotel now. My presentation begins in a few minutes."

"I'm ready sir," he said. "At the next break, I imagine she'll need the john. If she uses the one in her room, I'll do it then."

"What about Rhoads?"

"He's here. In the audience. Playing undercover."

"He's here? Perfect." Pratt laughed softly. "Prick's supposed to be in Vegas. He walked into a buzz saw this time. Now you can work your magic on both of them and make sure we've got all the disks."

"I don't think that'll be necessary, sir. Late word from Asheville. Trichina had only one set, and we got those from her lawyer Finch. She had tried to bluff when she said she had a second set. I was able to verify that the disks I took from Rhoads's apartment were the actual ones Dallaness made."

"And is our executive vice-president moping today?"

Valzmann paused. "I'm sorry, sir. The operation was a success, but the patient died."

Pratt exhaled from his mouth like a kid blowing out candles on a cake.

"You sure?" Pratt asked.

"Sir? She's dead."

"No, Valzmann. You sure we learned the truth? I'd hate to think . . ."

"Billy took care of it, Mr. Pratt. He said she fought hard, much harder than he expected. But no one can bear the blowtorch."

141

11:29 A.M.

Out front, a long black limousine pulled up at the Royal Carland's main entrance. Pratt emerged in the company of Arnold Northrup and three security men. Two doormen opened glass doors, and they entered the lobby, taking took note of the greeting sign.

American Investor Relations Society
Welcomes
the Leaders of the Tobacco Industry

Second floor, Grand Imperial Ballroom.

Earlier, Pratt's attorneys had circumvented Franklin and went straight to the director of the FBI to complain, considering Virgil's unimpeded progress, about the inadequate security plans for the conference. The director personally assured the attorneys that there would be more than met the eye at both the Rio and the Royal Carland.

Pratt and North were led by hotel personnel to a private elevator that arrived instantly and took only a few seconds to deliver them to the second floor.

As they stepped off the elevator, Northrup pulled out a chirping cellular telephone and answered it.

"Hold on, please." Then, handing the telephone to Pratt, "Nick. The FBI."

Pratt took the telephone. "Yeah?"

He listened. He beamed and snapped the telephone closed and handed it back to Northrup. He leaned in toward him and spoke out of the corner of his mouth.

"Looks like we finally got someplace Virgil was headed before he got there. The FBI was waiting for him to show up at the Specialty Retailers show in Las Vegas. They've found some kind of a device they think he planted in the Rio, and they've got the building sealed off. Arnie!" Pratt said, thinking that there was suddenly an excellent chance he wasn't going to have to spend seven hundred and fifty million dollars at two o'clock on Monday. "They don't think he had time to get out. They think they have him cornered."

Pratt lit up like a kid on Christmas morning.

Like a dog and its master, Northrup walked behind Pratt. At a respectful distance, Northrup stopped and stood still. Pratt continued to the podium by the head table. A roar of energetic applause greeted him.

142

11:32 A.M.

In darkness and freezing cold, Rhoads came to.

His head pounded excruciating pain, his arms and hands tied with something to an icy pole behind him.

Shit! My head. It pounded and ached.

He had no way to reach up to stop the bleeding bruise, his

blood warm as it ran down the cold skin of his forehead. Somehow, he reasoned, Muntor had dragged him here and bound his arms behind him.

The scent of food. Frozen meat.

Shit and piss! Locked in a freezer, freezing to death.

An image of a warm fire came to him, big and popping in a stone fireplace. He thought of orange flames and the smell of wet wool clothing in front of a fire. He thought of logs and the trees they came from and realized he did not want a boat or to be at sea. He wanted woods and mountains. Trees, tall, towering glorious trees.

Instead, he thought, he'd die right here, in a frozen puddle of his own blood.

He shivered violently, wondering how to tell his brother he didn't want the sea, he wanted trees.

Locked in here, with the flesh of the dead.

Left to die.

143

11:35 A.M.

"Step aside," the uniformed Martin Muntor said to one of the models hired to greet the *American Investor Relations Society* conference attendees. "Building safety violation inspection."

Muntor's words made no sense, they were intended only to confuse.

His fire department hazardous materials outfit had authority. The young woman did as ordered.

Muntor stepped forward, pulled the doors to the ballroom closed, and laced heavy chains through the handles of the exit. He secured the chains with a heavy padlock he took from one of his pockets. Then he strode as fast as his Biphetamine and Dilaudid-fortified body would go to the second of the three ballroom exits. He chained those doors, too.

Only the main entrance remained accessible.

144

11:38 A.M.

"Thank you," Pratt said, nodding to a few individuals. "Thank you. Ladies and gentleman, I don't think anyone will mind if I depart from the scheduled agenda to make an important announcement." Pratt hadn't smiled like this in almost a month. The audience hummed and grew excited. "We have just learned that, at this very moment in Las Vegas, the FBI is closing in on Martin Muntor. And, we are all hoping that . . ."

Boom.

Boom.

Boom.

From the back of the room, something banged loudly three times, disturbing the euphoria.

Pratt looked up.

All heads turned. Martin Muntor announced himself by hammering on the door frame with the long black gunmetal trigger nozzle attached to the tank strapped on his back.

"Excuse me, ladies and gentlemen. And law enforcement officers," he said, his voice both strained and strong. The faceplate of his gas mask was flipped up, enabling him to be heard. Some could see the large green-and-white tank strapped to his back. He held the orchard-fogger's trigger nozzle in one hand by his side.

He raised his other hand high. He held a small object. "A deadman control," he said, "is a mechanical-engineering term for any device similar to the one I have here in my hand." His arm straightened and jutted forward in a kind of *Sieg Heil* salute. "It's designed to take care of business if its operator loses consciousness."

A frightened murmur rippled through the room.

The eight FBI agents seated at the tables tensed, ready for instructions from the command post through their earphones. They all slipped their weapons from their holsters and into their hands without any obvious movement of body or limb. From Muntor's vantage, he had no way of knowing they had done so.

Conference attendees seated near Muntor could see that the device he held was no larger than a deck of cards. Right arm high, Muntor took two steps forward into the ballroom.

"Should I be harmed or rendered unconscious before I complete my presentation . . ."

From somewhere behind him in the hallway, a uniformed New York City policeman had been watching. Instead of calling for backup, he charged in, gun drawn. He stood four feet from Muntor. Muntor turned toward him and snapped down the gas mask's faceplate with a brush of his right forearm and, with his left hand, casually raised the long black trigger nozzle and squeezed once. A small puff of white gas shot out into the policeman's face. He dropped his gun and crumpled to the floor in a spasm of muffled choking. In a moment, he was still.

No one dared rise.

Muntor trudged back two paces and pulled the doors behind him closed, slamming them in fury.

As if there had been no disturbance, he raised his faceplate, held out the deadman control, and continued.

"Should I be harmed or rendered unconscious before I complete my presentation, my thumb will come off the button I am depressing here, there will be a massive explosion, and I will perish. And so will everyone in this room and most of those in this hotel. In a moment, I'll give a harmless demonstration to prove my capability. In the meantime, remain seated. And you over there by the swinging doors," he pointed to the kitchen staff, "you all move over toward the head table, away from the kitchen."

The workers moved as one. A small shriek came from one of the workers. At the head table, Pratt's face had turned bone white.

Two FBI agents rose in defiance of the Muntor's instructions to remain seated. Another agent, apparently their superior, shouted out to them "All posts, do as the man says. Take your seats."

The agents sank back into their chairs.

"And no radio communication," Muntor warned. "A device has been activated, and radio transmission could trigger it."

Without turning away from the people in the ballroom, Muntor tucked the nozzle under his arm, took a third chain from one of his suit's oversized pockets, and secured it to the door behind him.

145

11:42 A.M.

Dr. Trice, out of breath and shivering, knelt beside him in the frozen-food locker and struggled with the nylon rope that bound Rhoads's hands to the pole. She couldn't get it loose.

While she worked, Rhoads spoke to her in a calm voice. "I realized something, Bea, while I sat here thinking I'm going to die. It dawned on me I don't want to be in the charter-fishing business after all. For one thing, there aren't any trees in the ocean, unless they're floating on the surface." He laughed. "What I want is to be up in the mountains. With the trees. Maybe work with the forest service, something like that. Or invest in a quiet little vacation retreat."

"Can we talk about this later, T.R.?" she said, jerking with little successes at the rope. "You're not dying so soon. But I can't get your wrists free."

"Leave me here and go find a knife. Over by the prep tables."

The seventy-two-year-old woman stood up uncertainly and stumbled out of the locker, her hands frozen after only a long minute. The prep tables were on the other side of the huge food service area. Rhoads listened forever to the clicks Dr. Trice's heels made on the kitchen tile until they faded.

Then he heard other steps approaching.

Whoever was out there stopped.

A moment later, from beyond the freezer door, a large man entered, holding a gun.

"Here you are, Rhoads." He grinned. "Looks like your day's had a poor start. And it's about to get worse."

A bright light streamed in from the kitchen behind the man. Rhoads squinted. "Valzmann?"

"Correct."

Rhoads had known him as a building maintenance manager at TobacCo, Inc.

"What are you . . ."

"Silence, Rhoads. You are about to die. There's a loose end down in Asheville that's put Mr. Pratt at risk. And I'm going to tie it up—with you."

Rhoads's head spun. "This is about Benedict . . ."

"Good boy, Rhoads. Now, before I ice you, I'm dying to ask you something." Valzmann grinned. "Exactly what was it that went through your mind the moment the cops in Philadelphia told you your wife was being raped when you shot her?"

Valzmann's grin grew broadly across his face as he looked around and sized up the ricochet risk of shooting Rhoads right then and there.

Rhoads tried to block the memory from flooding into his mind. "How do you know about that?" As he spoke, he noticed a shadow flit by behind Valzmann.

"Found the little collection of newspaper clippings you hid behind your dresser drawer in your apartment. I went there to hide the $190,000 cash the FBI will think you stole from TobacCo, Inc. Sad to say, since you're not leaving here alive, you won't be spending any of it any time soon."

It was all too much for him to comprehend.

Dear Lord, help me somehow, Rhoads thought. Many times he had imagined how he'd behave or what clever things he'd say if he ever found himself in a situation where his death was imminent. Now, instead of making brave wisecracks, he wondered if anyone would take care of all the trees in his apartment, if anyone would know they had to be misted every other day.

Then he saw the shadow move again behind Valzmann.

"Speak up, Rhoads," Valzmann said. "Make your last words a plea for forgiveness. Isn't that what you all talk about in your AA meetings?"

From beyond the freezer door, a woman spoke. "Excuse me, sir. Where do you want me to put these salmon hors d'oeuvres?"

Valzmann hadn't realized someone had been behind him. He spun toward the voice.

Dr. Trice, an arm extended forward, stepped boldly into the locker.

Valzmann screamed and dropped his gun. He turned, putting his shoulder between himself and the woman. His hands flew to his face and eyes. He coughed and spat.

Dr. Trice stood firm, emptying her canister of cayenne pepper spray at Valzmann, trying to hit his upper lip where he'd breathe the spray through mouth or nose. Getting the eyes wasn't as important as making him choke. A blinded attacker can still grab hold of you and break your neck, but one choking half to death is effectively incapacitated.

"You cunt!" he gurgled through the saliva and mucous flooding his eyes and nose and mouth. She gotten him square in the face. He couldn't see.

Dr. Trice advanced with a serrated kitchen knife and plunged it hard, high on Valzmann's leg. She aimed for the external iliac artery that ran from the groin down the front of the leg. She twisted the knife resolutely. The blade had hit bone, and it stuck. She pulled her hand away. He was a broad, solid man. If she hit the femoral artery, too, his blood pressure would drop like a rock in a pond. He'd go down fast. She had had big men, patients, go berserk on her and knew from training to keep her thinking under control. It gave her a vastly superior position.

"Ahhhh!" Valzmann screamed and clutched at the wound. He fell to the floor.

"Get over here with that knife," Rhoads yelled, jerking against the rope. His breath condensed in the cold air.

"I can't, it's in his leg."

Valzmann screamed in pain and tore the knife out. It fell from his hands.

Very accommodating, Dr. Trice thought. This is a man who wants to be punished.

She picked it up. "I have it now."

Valzmann shuddered and started to move.

"You keep pressure on that, or you'll be dead in three minutes," she told the coughing, choking man. Valzmann slumped over onto his back, doing as told. She walked around him, crouched by Rhoads, and felt behind him for the rope. She found a place with her fingers where it would be safe to cut. She freed Rhoads with a few quick flicks of the gory knife.

Rhoads was up in a second, one eye swollen shut and warm blood still dripping. In the dark, he stumbled on Valzmann's gun, stooped, and took it.

Dr. Trice found a cloth and handed it to him. "It's not sterile, but pressure, Rhoads, pressure. Head wounds bleed."

Rhoads looked at Valzmann. "You sure he's down?"

"He'll stay for a while," she said.

Valzmann made a fruitless effort to get up. "Get the paramedics, Rhoads." The man was crying. "Please. I'm bleeding to death."

"Yeah. It's tops on my To-Do list."

Rhoads and Dr. Trice hurried out of the locker, toward the ballroom. Rhoads looked through one of the round windows in the swinging doors.

"Go the other way, there's got to be an exit back there," Rhoads told Dr. Trice. "Find a phone. Get 9-1-1. Tell them Virgil's sealed the Grand Imperial Ballroom. Then hang up, call back, tell them again. They take multiple calls seriously."

"What are you going to do?"

"I don't know."

146

11:44 A.M.

"Are you rolling? I want you to roll tape," Muntor ordered the nervous cameraman who stood on a platform in the corner of the room, there to videotape the conference. The man was a freelancer who earned his living recording business events for free—and then selling an edited tape back to the company involved. "You make sure you get everything."

The man nodded and put his eye to the camera, training it on Muntor wearing his yellow hazardous materials garb. Out of Muntor's view, an FBI agent leaned over at his table and whispered urgent words into a hand-held radio.

Muntor moved away from the chained door and trudged forward several paces. He kept his arm raised, clutching the deadman control.

Panic was in the air.

Those nearest him cringed.

"Do not move!" he shouted at them. With his faceplate open, they could see his sallow, sweaty face, his agitated eyes. He moved toward the entrance to the banquet kitchen. Muntor knew he had secured Rhoads adequately but was worried that other security people may have gotten in through a rear entrance.

Keeping his back to the wall, Muntor reached the doors and regarded them with concern as he stood between them and a small plastic trash can.

"Now for that demonstration," he said. He eyed the people near him. One middle-aged man in particular stood out. Was it his build or the quiet way he watched? Muntor did not know, but he was certain the man was some kind of agent. Muntor looked right at him but spoke loudly enough for everyone to hear. "You are about to hear a small explosion. It is harmless. Keep your eyes on my thumb."

Muntor narrowed his eyes on the cameraman. "Are you getting this?"

The cameraman nodded several times too many.

"Good," Muntor said to him. "Because if you continue to obey, you'll keep on living. And you'll keep on living with a lot more money than you have now. Why? Because I, at this very moment, give you—what's your name?"

"Alex S. Taylor," the cameraman, said, barely audibly.

Muntor looked into the camera from across the room."I give Alex S. Taylor all rights to my video documentary, *Muntor's Last Stand.* You can find a copy of it in my house in Philadelphia in my basement in a fireproof steel safe. Make sure you get yourself a good, tough lawyer who will work on contingency and be able to fight the Feds, force them to at least make you a copy of the tape I'm sure they'll say they need for evidence against me. But they won't. The consideration is that you must agree to edit today's . . . event . . . into the film as its grand finale. Do you understand, Alex S. Taylor? Do you agree?"

The cameraman again nodded rapidly many times. "Yes, sir."

Muntor then stretched his arm high and faced the device out to the ballroom. He lifted his thumb and beside him the trash can exploded with a loud blast and fell over, smoking. Most people ducked and screamed, others merely flinched. This was happening so fast. No one quite believed it. Moans of fear and hysterical cries rose toward the ceiling along with the odor of sulfur and a column of blue-black smoke.

"Just a firecracker," Muntor said.

One woman murmured, "Please, God, please."

At once, Muntor's hand was again raised high. He had taken another device from his pocket.

"This one," Muntor said, looking toward the new deadman control he held, "makes a boom you don't want to hear."

Despite the powerful injection he administered a little more than an hour earlier, the weight of the protective clothing and the bulky steel tank began wearing on him.

Near Muntor, a woman stood up at her table. Her voice trembled as she said, "Mister, before you kill us all, I'm going to say something."

It was Mary Dallaness.

Muntor turned and shouted back, his voice breaking. "Sit down. You have nothing to say. This is my forum."

"I don't care. I'm saying it." She turned and faced the rest of the room. She shook. Terror flashed in her eyes. "I have to say it. I don't care if I die, as long as I get to say that Mr. W. Nicholas Pratt," she glared at him across the room, "the high and mighty CEO of TobacCo, Inc., is responsible for the death of my husband, Anthony Dallaness, and the death of Dr. Loren Benedict. And I have evidence that proves at least one of those killings." She turned to Muntor. "You give me that hose, and I'll kill him myself."

"Mary!" Pratt's voice boomed. He had shouted into the microphone at the podium and startled even himself. The sound echoed through the ballroom.

"Sit down I say!" Muntor screamed. He snapped the faceplate down and raised the trigger nozzle as high as the deadman switch in his other hand. A half-dozen people threw themselves to the floor.

"No, you've got to listen to me," Mary cried.

"Silence!" Muntor said.

Pratt's heart pounded furiously and fell into arrhythmia. He gripped the corners of the podium, determined to remain standing.

A man stood up and raised his empty hands to show Muntor he held no weapon. He turned to Mary and bellowed, "FBI, lady. You sit down. Right now. That's an order. You're endangering everyone in this hotel. This man doesn't want to harm us. Don't push him."

The agent quickly sat down.

In the kitchen, directly behind Muntor, Rhoads's head appeared, partially visible through one of the round windows in the swinging doors. Muntor couldn't see him, but he must have noticed the movement of someone's eyes to the window at his back.

By instinct, Muntor threw himself backward. The heavy door swung back violently and knocked Rhoads down, onto the kitchen floor.

Muntor, weighted by all the equipment, came through the doors and stood over Rhoads. "I let go of this," Muntor said, showing Rhoads the deadman switch, "and everyone's gone. Get out there."

Rhoads, stunned by the blow of the door, crawled out into the ballroom. Mary rushed to him and knelt by his side.

147

11:45 A.M.

Outside the main entrance of The Royal Carland

It couldn't have happened so fast, but outside the Royal Carland, it seemed to Fallscroft as if thousands of police and FBI vehicles had materialized, lights flashing, sirens shattering the air. Mostly unintelligible loudspeakers blared on the street, ordering pedestrians away from the area.

News crews arrived and government helicopters chopped at the sky overhead. An FAA supervisor had broadcast an emergency ban on all private aircraft, including news helicopters, from the airspace near the Royal Carland.

Authorities began methodically evacuating all buildings proximate to the hotel. The city halted all subway lines that ran below the hotel.

Fallscroft, blocked by police, could only stare at the hotel and the commotion. He touched the automatic weapon it was too late to get to Rhoads. He felt like a parent watching his house afire with his child trapped inside.

148

11:48 A.M.

Muntor performed a quick survey of the kitchen area and returned to the ballroom holding the deadman switch high. He had been gone only five or six seconds. Everyone was still seated. He stepped out and faced the people in the ballroom, moving along solid wall, keeping his back to it, moving away from the swinging doors. From his new position, as long as everyone remained seated, he could see all three exit doors, the kitchen doors, and the head table.

"Here's what's going to happen," he said. "There's an excellent chance all of you, with one small exception, will be out of here in a few minutes. Out of here, alive and unharmed," he added. "If . . . if Nick Pratt cooperates."

On the other side of the room, Northrup whispered to Pratt. "Do as he says, Nick. He's crazy. But I think he's about to surrender. He just wants maximum attention."

Muntor cleared his throat. "Nick Pratt will trade himself for the lives of every man and woman in this room. He's going to stand up there at that table and smoke one of these."

Muntor slipped the orchard-fogger's trigger nozzle into one of the fireman uniform's giant pockets and produced a pack of Easy Lights. He waved them around for a moment before putting them back in his pocket. Muntor's upright arm ached. He carefully transferred the device from one hand to other, keeping steady thumb pressure on the black button, and raised it, this time only for a moment, for all to see. Its function was now well known, and he no longer needed to keep it elevated.

Muntor, remembering the cameraman, turned to him and pointed. "Are you still getting all this?"

"Yes, sir."

"How soon until you run out of tape?"

The man looked at the back of the camera. "I've got five minutes and thirty-three seconds."

"More than enough," Muntor said. "More than enough."

The room was deadly silent save for Muntor's wheezing. He advanced slowly toward Pratt. "An eye for an eye, Pratt," Muntor said. He used his other hand to again show the pack of cigarettes. "I'm dying of cancer and emphysema from these. You killed me with these, I'm doing the same for you."

Pratt, a third of the room's span away, took a step back from the podium, shaking his head "no." A collective shudder rolled through the room.

"Come on, Pratt!" Muntor's voice creaked.

"No!" Pratt said. He took half a step behind Arnold Northrup.

"Come on, Pratt. You light up, and I'll surrender. I'll surrender over your dead body." There was no humor in the remark.

Pratt took another step backward. "No! No! No!"

"Come on, Pratt. You light up, and I let everyone go. Shall I ask the crowd what they want? Because before the tape runs out, we're settling this. One way or another."

"Martin Muntor, sir," the FBI agent said, standing again, hands raised. "Let me use the house phone to tell my people what's happening. They don't know about the deadman control, and . . . and it might be better if they did."

That made sense to Muntor. He dropped the cigarettes back into a pocket and took hold of the orchard-fogger's trigger nozzle.

"Good. Use that phone there," he said, using the trigger nozzle to point to a telephone on a wall by the coffee service area. "First take off your jacket. Do everything slowly, except when you get to that telephone. Then you've got thirty seconds. When you're finished, pull the phone out of the wall. Remember this. I'm already dead, so play it smart and these people here may live. Go now."

The FBI agent did as Muntor instructed. When he got to the telephone, Muntor glanced at a wall clock and shouted a reminder that he had thirty seconds. The agent dialed a number. No one except the agent moved or spoke until Muntor told him his time was up. The FBI agent disconnected. Then, with one swift punch with the heel of his hand, he knocked the telephone off of the wall and sent it crashing to the floor before returning to his seat.

"How much time, cameraman?" Muntor asked.

"Four minutes, ten seconds."

149

"Hey, Martin, I'm coming out through here," Dr. Trice's voice said.

Muntor jerked his body around toward the sound coming from the kitchen.

"I'm unarmed. I'm an old lady back here in food prep. I'm coming out. Don't hurt me."

Muntor looked toward the slowly opening doors and the short, heavy woman who came through. That she knew his name seemed natural to him. In his delusion of grandeur, he presumed everyone now knew of Martin Muntor. She stood no more than ten feet away, looking directly at him. Her calm demeanor confused him. He thrust the deadman switch toward her threateningly. She half-raised her hands and then dropped them to her side.

"Who are you?" Muntor asked. Without waiting for a reply, "Take a seat. Take any seat, now."

"Martin. I'm Dr. Trice." She looked at his eyes in the shadow of the faceplate. Dull and wet. His respiration was rapid and shallow.

Rhoads spoke from the floor. Mary cradled him in her arms, the bloody cloth pressed against his head. "Bea, please. Sit down like he says. That switch in his hand can blow the place up. Let the professionals handle this."

Dr. Trice looked away from Rhoads. She looked at Muntor.

"Look, Martin," she said. She hadn't moved an inch toward a seat. "I heard what you said to Pratt, and he deserves to die that way. But I've got something better for you . . ."

"Please take a seat, lady," Muntor said. "I'm too tired to tell you again."

She pointed a finger up at him. "Look, Martin," she said, eying the tank strapped on his back. "I imagine you have the equipment necessary to kill Pratt and anyone else in this room.

But if you want to make more of an impact on the world, you want to hear me out."

"Three minutes, thirty seconds!" the cameraman shouted. He edged toward hysteria. "Please shut up, lady."

Dr. Trice continued. "Martin, listen. Turn that switch off, surrender. Make sure the one and a half billion dollars gets to where it's supposed to go. You said you want a public-awareness campaign. This is the greatest one in history. You kill Pratt, and no money gets transferred. You kill Pratt and all of us, in six months, maybe a year, maybe even two, after they've made the movie and A&E or HBO does an hour-long biography on you and five or six jerks write instant books about you, it'll all fade into oblivion. The tobacco industry will still be here, people will still be dying of lung cancer and heart disease and having low birth-weight babies.

"But, you let Pratt live? Every time he shows his face, they'll remember today and what you did. Every time people see the TobacCo, Inc. logo or TobacCo, Inc. cigarettes, they'll think about Martin Muntor and Virgil and what you did and the money you squeezed out of them for medical research. You kill everyone, and you go down as just another pathetic lunatic seeking a moment of glory. You surrender now, even though you are dying, you'll have a story a thousand times better than if everyone perishes."

Muntor looked at a wall clock and then at the cameraman. "How much?"

The cameraman sobbed. "Two minutes, twenty seconds. Oh, God, please, God."

"I've already killed hundreds," Muntor said to Dr. Trice. "I'm already that dismissible pathetic lunatic."

"No! It's not so." Her face grew red in angry indignation. "You surrender now, and the money transfer changes everything. You've accomplished something. You've accomplished something positive. As you said in one of your calls to the FBI. I'm going to accomplish something of value before I die. Who among you can say that? Very few of us can say that, Martin. Distinguish yourself."

Muntor nodded, thinking. He bit at his lower lip.

He looked across the room at Pratt who had backed himself into a corner by the coffee service table and a towering dieffenbachia. His shoulders pressed against the white wall. He shivered.

Muntor took a step toward Pratt. A tiny squeak came out of Pratt's mouth. Muntor took several more steps in that direction and stopped just as he stood over Rhoads and Mary on the floor. He looked down.

"Nice try in Princeton, Mr. Rhoads," he said. Before Rhoads could speak, Muntor moved forward, advancing toward Pratt. The room was as quiet as heavy snow falling in the woods. He stopped three feet from the quaking CEO. He took the long nozzle from his pocket and wrapped his index finger around the trigger. He raised it and moved it up, very slowly, to Pratt's face.

"Oh, Lord," Pratt said, arms folded across his chest. He tried to step backward, but he was already as far as he could go. He shook visibly.

Muntor didn't turn his head from Pratt but shouted to the cameraman, "How much time?" He tightened his grip on the deadman switch.

"Fifty-five seconds," the voice said, barely audible to Muntor under the helmet. Muntor withdrew the pack of Easy Lights from a pocket. It was difficult to do with one hand, but he succeeded in removing a single cigarette from the pack. He put it between his lips and held it there. With his free hand, he removed his helmet and gas mask. Muntor dropped them to the floor. Pratt flinched at the sound.

Pratt's wild, animal-fear eyes noticed a stain on the cigarette—the watermark from the cyanide solution. That made all this real to him, and he shuddered more.

Muntor's hair had matted under the helmet, and a clump stuck straight up. Perspiration beaded his forehead and soaked the back of his neck.

"Fifty-five seconds, Pratt?" Muntor spoke softly. This was

just between them. "Not a lot of time to make such an important decision. You want this?" Muntor said, wiggling the cigarette tauntingly between his teeth. "Or this?" He moved the nozzle in closer, pressing its gunmetal lip painfully against Pratt's mouth. "Cancer really hurts, Pratt. Tumors are painful. Like a hand in there that knows how to grab a fistful of nerves. It squeezes and squeezes till you go out of your fucking mind."

Pratt's legs gave out from under him. He sank back against the wall and slid down, slowly, to the floor. He shook and wept loudly.

"Oh no, please. You've made your point, sir. Haven't you cost me enough already? Please. No."

Muntor made a half-turn and positioned himself so that no one else in the auditorium could see him drop the fake deadman switch into his pocket. He crouched down and took Pratt by his hair, forcing him to look up. Pratt squealed and threw his hands up to protect himself. They were close enough to feel the heat of each other's breath. The people seated at nearby tables screamed when Muntor leaned in. They thought he was killing Pratt.

"Pratt," Muntor said weakly, "if I ever find out that you've somehow stopped the funds transfer, I'm going to track you down in hell and serve you a plate of your own liver and a glass of cheap Chianti."

Pratt's sobs revealed to the others that he was still alive.

Muntor struggled to his feet and turned to face all those present. His hand that had held the deadman switch was thrust deep in his pocket.

"Rhoads, over here," Muntor tried to shout in the direction of Rhoads. His voice came out crackling and breaking. "And hurry up." He clutched the cigarette between his teeth. Pratt, on the floor behind Muntor, whimpered.

Mary fought to hold Rhoads down, but he threw her off, got up, and stumbled as fast as he could across the ballroom to where Muntor had cornered Pratt.

Muntor shouted to the cameraman over his shoulder. "How

much time!"

"Twenty-one seconds," the teary voice said.

When Rhoads got within two paces of Muntor, Muntor held out the trigger nozzle to stop him.

"Close enough, friend," Muntor said.

"Ladies and gentlemen and law enforcement authorities." Muntor struggled to speak loud enough for everyone to hear.

He moved a half-pace to his right, making sure Rhoads was not blocking him out of the camera's view of the scene. "In accordance with the terms of a binding agreement between me and TobacCo, Inc. of Asheville, North Carolina, I hereby surrender myself to Thomas Rhoads, a duly appointed company official."

Everyone gasped.

Muntor still held the cigarette clenched between his teeth.

He held up his hand for silence. "And may God see fit to have mercy upon my soul."

Rhoads did not move a muscle.

No one in the room said a word.

Without warning, Martin Muntor's right hand came swiftly out of his pocket. He held a disposable lighter. He flicked it and raised the flame in a swift arc toward the cigarette he held between his teeth.

The crowd shuddered. Rhoads heard the rustle of what had to be security people leaping out of their seats, launching themselves toward Muntor.

Rhoads lunged forward and grabbed the frail man's wrist with one hand and pressed the palm of his other hand against Muntor's forehead. Rhoads kept him from leaning forward and bringing the cigarette to the flame. It was no contest. Rhoads stopped the flame an inch from the cigarette.

Muntor invoked all his strength and pulled hard, bringing his wrist toward his face, the lighter's flame now half an inch from the cigarette. Rhoads tightened his grip and braced himself against Muntor's forehead. He held the position. Muntor kept his thumb on the lighter to keep the flame alive.

Muntor's and Rhoads's eyes met, and all the world fell away. In that moment, Rhoads knew Dr. Trice had been right. She had once mailed a postcard with a line scrawled from a book or poem: Unless a man knows he's lost, he can never begin to search for himself.

With the last of his physical strength, Muntor tried again to pull the lighter to the cigarette.

"Please," he whispered, so quietly only Rhoads heard him. "Let me go." He peered into Rhoads's eyes searching for charity.

Rhoads stared back. He needed a glimpse of the lost soul behind Muntor's drawn, wild face.

"It's all right, Rhoads," he pleaded.

Rhoads turned away for an instant, his hand firmly holding Muntor's frail wrist. Then he looked back, straight into Muntor's eyes, and swallowed.

Muntor knew this was it. He acknowledged Rhoads's gift with a tiny nod. He almost smiled. He had come a long way, and now it was over. Muntor exhaled thoroughly, preparing his ravaged lungs for what came next.

He closed his eyes.

Rhoads relaxed his grip imperceptibly, and the gap between the cigarette and the flame ceased to be.

With a sharp gasp, Muntor drew his last breath.

The four FBI agents who landed on Muntor a moment too late were to be taunted about their hapless timing for the rest of their careers.

Muntor's Last Stand became the best-selling video of all time.